ASK

The logics maintenance man turned away from the screen in bewilderment. Nobody had told him about the new service of the giant computer-communicator complex. And it didn't make sense . . .

"There's gonna be a lot of complaints," he called out to the rest of the work crew. "Suppose a fella asks how to get rid of his wife, and the censor circuits block the question?"

"Why not punch for it and see what happens?"

Just for the fun of it he did—and on the logic screen appeared all the details: the poison, how to administer it, why he would never be suspected.

The screen went blank—and the maintenance boss yelled, "Check your censor circuits—but quick!"

For there was a logic in every home—now ready and willing to give foolproof instructions for gratifying *any* wish anyone might have!

The Critically Acclaimed Series of Classic Science Fiction

NOW AVAILABLE:

*COMING SOON FROM DEL REY BOOKS

THE BEST OF
Murray Leinster

Edited and with an Introduction by

J. J. PIERCE

A Del Rey Book

BALLANTINE BOOKS • NEW YORK

A Del Rey Book
Published by Ballantine Books

Copyright © 1978 by Random House, Inc.

Introduction: *"The Dean of Science Fiction"* Copyright © 1978
by J. J. Pierce

Library of Congress Catalog Card Number: 78-52210

ISBN 0-345-25800-2

PRINTED IN CANADA

First Edition: April 1978

Cover art by H. R. Van Dongen

ACKNOWLEDGMENTS

"Sidewise in Time," copyright © 1934 by Street & Smith Publications, Inc., for *Astounding Stories,* June 1934.

"Proxima Centauri," copyright © 1935 by Street & Smith Publications, Inc., for *Astounding Stories,* March 1935.

"The Fourth-dimensional Demonstrator," copyright © 1935 by Street & Smith Publications, Inc., for *Astounding Stories,* December 1935.

"First Contact," copyright © 1945 by Street & Smith Publications, Inc., for *Astounding Science Fiction,* May 1945.

"The Ethical Equations," copyright © 1945 by Street & Smith Publications, Inc., for *Astounding Science Fiction,* June 1945.

"Pipeline to Pluto," copyright © 1945 by Street & Smith Publications, Inc., for *Astounding Science Fiction,* August 1945.

"The Power," copyright © 1945 by Street & Smith Publications, Inc., for *Astounding Science Fiction,* September 1945.

"A Logic Named Joe," copyright © 1946 by Street & Smith Publications, Inc., for *Astounding Science Fiction,* March 1946.

"Symbiosis," copyright © 1947 for *Collier's* Magazine, January 1947.

"The Strange Case of John Kingman," copyright © 1948 by Street & Smith Publications, Inc., for *Astounding Science Fiction,* May 1948.

"The Lonely Planet," copyright © 1949 by Standard Magazines, Inc., for *Thrilling Wonder Stories,* December 1949.

"Keyhole," copyright © 1951 by Standard Magazines, Inc., for *Thrilling Wonder Stories,* December 1951.

"Critical Difference," copyright © 1956 by Street & Smith Publications, Inc., for *Astounding Science Fiction,* July 1956.

Contents

The Dean of Science Fiction

*"There were giants in the earth in those days. . . .
mighty men which were of old, men of renown."*
—Genesis 6:4

SUBCULTURES, TOO, HAVE their lengendary figures, and
in the world of science fiction, Murray Leinster was
one.

In his later years, Leinster came to be known as the
Dean of Science Fiction. His career in the field spanned
nearly fifty years—remarkable enough in itself. More
remarkable is that he remained a top-ranked writer for
all of those years.

Leinster, in real life an unassuming Virginian named
William Fitzgerald Jenkins (1896–1975), would have
been amused at the Biblical parallel. But like that of the
patriarchs of old, his longevity seemed unbelievable.
Dozens of writers vanished into obscurity; entire schools
of writing rose, flourished, and died—but Leinster carried on.

That took rare ability, but it also took rare dedica-
tion. Nowadays, when science fiction is taught in col-
leges, and a single, good sf movie bids fair to gross
$100 million, it is hard to appreciate the dedication re-
quired of writers like Leinster to make of a marginal
and despised genre something in which they, and their
readers, could take legitimate pride.

A fellow pioneer of those early days once remarked
that writing science fiction took more work and paid
less, than bricklaying—he'd tried both and knew. Bricklaying pays a lot more these days, and so does science
fiction—but there were and are easier ways of making a
living than sf.

It is important to remember that. The pioneers of science fiction were, by and large, commercial writers.
They never talked of Art and Literature; rather of

"craftsmanship" and "professional" standards. But that didn't mean, as some of today's less-informed critics seem to think, that they didn't care about their work. Science fiction might be better off today if some of these critics, and their favorite authors, *loved* sf as much as Leinster and some of his colleagues did.

When Leinster began writing science fiction, it wasn't even *called* science fiction. There weren't any sf magazines—what were called "scientific romances" or "different stories" appeared mostly in adventure pulps, mixed in with Westerns, spy thrillers, detective stories, horror tales and the like. Science fiction had no distinct identity, or any generally recognized standards.

Leinster's own first story, "The Runaway Skyscraper" (1919), was typical of what was called for by a market that demanded exciting stories but as yet had no real appreciation of scientific logic or scientific imagination. A New York skyscraper suddenly plunges backward in time—never mind how or why—and its occupants have to rough it in the wilderness.

But even in his early works, Leinster brought a new kind of imagination to pulp literature. "The Mad Planet" (1920), too long to include here, was in the tradition of the "scientific romances" and pitted men reduced to savagery against a world of giant insects and fungi. Yet the story still somehow seems fresh today. Leinster was fascinated by the world of insects, and he makes the reader fascinated—not merely frightened.

When the market called for stories about mad scientists who threatened the world with their mad inventions, Leinster could supply them—but his always had a distinct logic behind them. In "The City of the Blind" (1929), a scientific criminal's invention darkens New York to cover a wave of robberies. Only to Leinster would it have occurred to consider what such a device would do to the *weather*.

But Murray Leinster did more than improve on existing models; he wrote new *kinds* of stories. "Sidewise in Time," which opens this collection, is a classic case in point. One of the most influential sf stories ever written, it developed a concept of "parallel worlds"—worlds that exist in the same *time* as ours, but in which natural or human history has taken a different course. That idea has since been drawn on by H. Beam Piper, Keith Laumer, and a host of other writers. Some physicists are even reported to be taking the idea seriously—not the specific details, of course, but the concept that *our* universe may not be the only one in this space–time continuum.

Leinster wasn't a dour theoretician, by any means—he was a man who could have fun with ideas and share that fun with his readers. "The Fourth-dimensional Demonstrator" takes on the old dream of making money easily, but it never occurred to others who wrote parables of greed that a device producing money out of thin air would do the same for other things, including girl friends . . .

Or take "A Logic Named Joe," one of his funniest stories and one of his most prophetic. Most people weren't aware of computers back then, and nobody realized there might one day be computer information terminals all over the place—with their attendant problems. It's still fun (and sobering, on reflection) to read about the people who order computer data on how to rob banks or cure their neighbors of concupiscence, but it's also fun because we know Leinster thought out ideas that hadn't even occurred to others.

The same kind of disciplined imagination could be turned to a really *nasty* story like "Pipeline to Pluto." It's an uncharacteristically gritty tale of some unpleasant people who meet their comeuppance. But Leinster could create a whole new kind of comeuppance to satisfy morality and scientific logic at once, and he did.

Leinster's type of imagination was not a mere literary affectation, but was a basic part of the man. When he wasn't writing, he was inventing. He had a laboratory in his home, and some of his inventions seem the very stuff of science fiction.

Jenkins Systems, widely used in television and the movies, is a device that allows background scenes to be projected on a special screen, without showing up on the actors standing in front of the screen. As described by its inventor (under the double byline of Will F.

Jenkins-Murray Leinster) in "Applied Science Fiction," the system depends on a precise knowledge of the different ways light can be reflected. But it also depends on a certain psychology—the psychology of a man who can *see how* to make use of such natural phenomena.

Invention is a matter of problem-solving, and one of Leinster's favorite forms, especially in his later years, was what is usually called the scientific problem story. "Critical Difference" is one of a series he wrote in the 1950s, and his own experience in solving scientific problems is reflected in the manner in which his hero comes to grips with a natural crisis that threatens the existence of human life in the planetary system of an unexpectedly variable star. The same kind of insight was, however, shown even early in his career with the story of Burl, the primitive who discovers how to use his mind to cope with a savage environment in "The Mad Planet."

Leinster was a rationalist, a term which often seems to be in disfavor—perhaps through association with the dismal utilitarianism of the Gradgrind School in Dickens' *Hard Times.* Anything but a Grandgrind, Leinster saw reason as a normal part of humanity, and his stories are always human dramas, not mere classroom exercises.

An admirer of Thomas Aquinas, Leinster believed that there is a natural order in the universe. In "The Ethical Equations," for instance, he even suggests the possibility of a natural moral order in the imagined "mathematical proof that certain patterns of conduct increase the probability of certain kinds of coincidences."

But he was never heavy-handed about presenting his philosophy in fiction. One of his Med Service stories, concerning a doctor who deals with medical emergencies on far planets, quoted witty aphorisms from an imaginary book called *The Practice of Thinking,* by Fitzgerald. Intrigued readers pestered him for years afterward with inquiries about where they could obtain the book.

Nor did he ever forget ordinary human touches. On his interstellar ships, there are recorded sounds: "the sound of rain, and of traffic, and of wind in treetops and voices too faint for the words to be distinguished, and almost inaudible music—and sometimes laughter. The background tape carried no information; only the assurance that there were still worlds with clouds and people and creatures moving about on them."

Leinster saw no necessary conflict between reason and human emotional needs, but he was fully aware of the irrational in man and the evil men do. "Keyhole" is an emotional story, in which it is very fortunate for Butch and his kind that they are able to offer men a "reason" for leaving them in peace. A convert to Catholicism, Leinster never mentioned religion in his sf, never sought to preach—but the idea of sin is certainly there.

"First Contact" is the most famous of Leinster's stories of encounters between men and aliens. Here he sees them sharing the same weaknesses—fear, greed, and mistrust—but also the same strength of intelligent life everywhere: the ability to use reason to overcome their own weaknesses as well as the problems of their environment. The story earned Leinster a place in *The Science Fiction Hall of Fame,* a volume of stories voted the classics of all time by the Science Fiction Writers of America.

"First Contact" also occasioned a minor ideological flap in 1959, when Soviet sf writer Ivan Yefremov published "The Heart of the Serpent," a story in which humans and aliens make friendly contact and don't have any problems because they're all good Communists. A character in Yefremov's story speaks disparagingly of "First Contact," and sees in its author "the heart of a poisonous snake." Characteristically modest and gentlemanly, Leinster refused to be drawn into a debate, and on one occasion expressed more disturbance over Yefremov's apparent prejudice against snakes than over any criticism of himself.

It would take a very casual reader to suspect Leinster of xenophobia. "Proxima Centauri" was as close as he came to the BEM (Bug-Eyed Monster) story in which innocent humans are threatened by the monsters. And even in this case, the aliens have a very specific—and logical—reason for being a threat to their human visitors. One might almost view the conflict as the unfortunate by-product of a local environmental crisis.

In "The Lonely Planet," by contrast, the grim moments are all caused by the ignorance, malice, greed, and downright stupidity of humans. Leinster's sympathy for the world-brain of Alyx is characteristic of him—and of science fiction generally for the last forty years. There are those, not too well informed, who imagine this attitude to have been developed only within the last decade, usually by themselves.

Perhaps the most unusual of Leinster's contact stories, "The Strange Case of John Kingman," never moves off the Earth at all. There is a subtle irony to the story: the being in the mental hospital who has been classed as a lunatic for nearly two hundred years really *is* insane—but not for the reasons human doctors have imagined.

In the 1930s, Leinster wrote several realistic stories of future warfare, like "Tanks" and "Politics." In "Symbiosis," he returned to the future-war theme, but in a much subtler manner. Kantolia seems defenseless: no planes, tanks, or heavy guns, no fanciful death rays. But it has a truly deadly weapon—invaders are helpless against it. The fact that a man with a troubled conscience must wield that weapon makes this, too, a very human story.

"The Power" is a science-fiction story set in a period when science fiction would have been impossible. Before you can have either science or science fiction, you have to have the kind of imagination that makes both possible. Poor Carolus—he sees, but cannot observe, still less understand!

One collection could not possibly include all the best stories of a man who was a regular contributor to science-fiction markets for five decades—there are even important *types* of fiction Leinster wrote which could not be represented here because of space limitations. And there are, of course, novels like *The Forgotten Planet,* based on "The Mad Planet" and its sequels.

Readers haven't always had a chance to see Leinster at his best. After quitting an insurance company at age twenty-one—his boss wanted him to do something unethical, so he told the boss what he could do with the job—Leinster made his living as a writer, in other fields as well as in science fiction. Unfortunately, it seems that some publishers would rather reprint his potboilers than his classics. Then too, some publishers couldn't tell the difference between them even when he was alive.

One of his novels, serialized in a magazine, dealt with space piracy. An old and hackneyed theme, but Leinster redeemed it with a climax in which the hero uses his knowledge of the hijacked ship's communications system to drive the pirates insane. When a paperback publisher picked up the novel, however, virtually all the good stuff was cut out, without the author even being informed.

In recent years, it has become fashionable to look down on the pioneers of science fiction. One contemporary author pretentiously dismissed Leinster with the comment that he wasn't a Dostoevski—a comment that means about as much as saying Scott Joplin wasn't a Beethoven.

Leinster himself, of course, never claimed to be a Dostoevski—or anyone else so exalted. He took pride in doing what he could do well, but was never pretentious. Yet it was he, and others like him, who created a new kind of fiction with its own themes and traditions. Without them, there would be nothing for today's science-fiction writers to turn into Literature—indeed, today's science-fiction writers wouldn't be. Period.

A pioneer of the scientific imagination in fiction—Leinster was that. But more than a pioneer; that would not be enough to make him worth reading today. The history of any literary genre is littered with pioneering works that are of interest only to scholars, and plenty of those can be found in the sf magazines of thirty or forty years ago. Leinster's classics have escaped that fate.

Oh, you can tell which ones were written in the 1930s as opposed to the 1950s; styles change, after all. But his stories hardly seem dated at all. "The Fourth-dimensional Demonstrator," for instance, could be made the basis for a television comedy tomorrow with only minor changes. Given human nature, the ethical problems of "First Contact" are as real today as in 1944—much as one might regret some ethnic references inspired by World War II.

Leinster was a man who was *interested* in the world—in people and ideas. Too many writers can't seem to get interested in anything but themselves. Just as the best teacher is one who can get excited about what he's teaching, the best writer is one who can get excited about what he's writing. Leinster could and did, and his stories still communicate that excitement.

From the adventures in parallel worlds of "Sidewise in Time" to the moral conflicts of "First Contact" to the grim struggle to save a seemingly doomed world in "Critical Difference," Murray Leinster is still a good read.

John J. Pierce
Berkeley Heights, N.J.
June 28, 1977

Sidewise in Time

LOOKING BACK, IT seems strange that no one but Professor Minott figured the thing out in advance. The indications were more than plain. In early December of 1934 Professor Michaelson announced his finding that the speed of light was not an absolute—could not be considered invariable. That, of course, was one of the first indications of what was to happen.

A second indication came on February 15th, when at 12:40 p.m., Greenwich mean time, the sun suddenly shone blue-white and the enormously increased rate of radiation raised the temperature of the earth's surface by twenty-two degrees Fahrenheit in five minutes. At the end of the five minutes, the sun went back to its normal rate of radiation without any other symptom of disturbance.

A great many bids for scientific fame followed, of course, but no plausible explanation of the phenomenon accounted for a total lack of after disturbances in the sun's photosphere.

For a third clear forerunner of the events of June, on March 10th the male giraffe in the Bronx Zoölogical Park, in New York, ceased to eat. In the nine days following, it changed its form, absorbing all its extremities, even its neck and head, into an extraordinary, egg-shaped mass of still-living flesh and bone which on the tenth day began to divide spontaneously and on the twelfth was two slightly pulsating fleshy masses.

A day later still, bumps appeared on the two masses. They grew, took form and design, and twenty days after the beginning of the phenomenon were legs, necks, and heads. Then two giraffes, both male, moved about the giraffe enclosure. Each was slightly less than half the weight of the original animal. They were identically marked. And they ate and moved and in every way seemed normal though immature animals.

An exactly similar occurrence was reported from the Argentine Republic, in which a steer from the pampas was going through the same extraordinary method of reproduction under the critical eyes of Argentine scientists.

Nowadays it seems incredible that the scientists of 1935 should not have understood the meaning of these oddities. We now know something of the type of strain which produced them, though they no longer occur. But between January and June of 1935 the news services of the nation were flooded with items of similar import.

For two days the Ohio River flowed upstream. For six hours the trees in Euclid Park, in Cleveland, lashed their branches madly as if in a terrific storm, though not a breath of wind was stirring. And in New Orleans, near the last of May, fishes swam up out of the Mississippi River through the air, proceeded to "drown" in the air which inexplicably upheld them, and then turned belly up and floated placidly at an imaginary water level some fifteen feet above the pavements of the city.

But it seems clear that Professor Minott was the only man in the world who even guessed the meaning of these—to us—clear-cut indications of the later events. Professor Minott was instructor in mathematics on the faculty of Robinson College in Fredericksburg, Va. We know that he anticipated very nearly every one of the things which later startled and frightened the world, and not only our world. But he kept his mouth shut.

Robinson College was small. It had even been termed a "jerkwater" college without offending anybody but the faculty and certain sensitive alumni. For a mere professor of mathematics to make public the theory Minott had formed would not even be news. It would be taken as stark insanity. Moreover, those who believed it would be scared. So he kept his mouth shut.

Professor Minott possessed courage, bitterness, and a certain cold-blooded daring, but neither wealth nor influence. He had more than a little knowledge of mathematical physics and his calculations show extraordinary knowledge of the laws of probability, but he had very little patience with problems in ethics. And he was possessed by a particularly fierce passion for Maida Hayns, daughter of the professor of Romance languages, and had practically no chance to win even her attention over the competition of most of the student body.

So much of explanation is necessary, because no one but just such a person as Professor Minott would have forecast what was to happen and then prepare for it in the fashion in which he did.

We know from his notes that he considered the probability of disaster as a shade better than four to one. It is a very great pity that we do not have his calculations. There is much that our scientists do not understand even yet. The notes Professor Minott left behind have been invaluable, but there are obvious gaps in them. He must have taken most of his notes—and those the most valuable—into that unguessed-at place where he conceivably now lives and very probably works.

He would be amused, no doubt, at the diligence with which his most unconsidered scribble is now examined and inspected and discussed by the greatest minds of our time and space. And perhaps—it is quite probable—he may have invented a word for the scope of the catastrophe we escaped. We have none as yet.

There is no word to describe a disaster in which not only the earth but our whole solar system might have been destroyed; not only our solar system but our galaxy; not only our galaxy but every other island universe in all of the space we know; more than that, the destruction of all space as we know it; and even beyond that the destruction of time, meaning not only the obliteration of present and future but even the annihilation of the past so that it would never have been. And then, besides, those other strange states of existence we learned of, those other universes, those other pasts and futures—all to be shattered into nothingness. There is no word for such a catastrophe.

It would be interesting to know what Professor Minott

termed it to himself, as he coolly prepared to take advantage of the one chance in four of survival, if that should be the one to eventuate. But it is easier to wonder how he felt on the evening before the fifth of June, in 1935. We do not know. We cannot know. All we can be certain of is how we felt—and what happened.

I

It was half past seven a.m. of June 5, 1935. The city of Joplin, Missouri, awaked from a comfortable, summer-night sleep. Dew glistened upon grass blades and leaves and the filmy webs of morning spiders glittered like diamond dust in the early sunshine. In the most easternly suburb a high-school boy, yawning, came somnolently out of his house to mow the lawn before schooltime. A rather rickety family car roared, a block away. It backfired, stopped, roared again, and throttled down to a steady, waiting hum. The voices of children sounded among the houses. A colored washerwoman appeared, striding beneath the trees which lined this strictly residential street.

From an upper window a radio blatted: "—*one, two, three, four! Higher, now!—three, four! Put your weight into it!—two, three, four!*" The radio suddenly squawked and began to emit an insistent, mechanical shriek which changed again to a squawk and then a terrific sound as of all the static of ten thousand thunderstorms on the air at once. Then it was silent.

The high-school boy leaned mournfully on the push bar of the lawn mower. At the instant the static ended, the boy sat down suddenly on the dew-wet grass. The colored woman reeled and grabbed frantically at the nearest tree trunk. The basket of wash toppled and spilled in a snowstorm of starched, varicolored clothing. Howls of terror from children. Sharp shrieks from women. *"Earthquake! Earthquake!"* Figures appeared running, pouring out of houses. Someone fled out to a sleeping porch, slid down a supporting column, and tripped over a rosebush in his pajamas. In seconds, it seemed, the entire population of the street was out-of-doors.

And then there was a queer, blank silence. There was no earthquake. No house had fallen. No chimney had cracked. Not so much as a dish or windowpane had made a sound in smashing. The sensation every human being had felt was not an actual shaking of the ground. There had been movement, yes, and of the earth, but no such movement as any human being had ever dreamed of before. These people were to learn of that movement much later. Now they stared blankly at each other.

And in the sudden, dead silence broken only by the hum of an idling car and the wail of a frightened baby, a new sound became audible. It was the tramp of marching feet. With it came a curious clanking and clattering noise. And then a marked command, which was definitely not in the English language.

Down the street of a suburb of Joplin, Missouri, on June 5, in the Year of Our Lord 1935, came a file of spear-armed, shield-bearing soldiers in the short, skirt-like togas of ancient Rome. They wore helmets upon their heads. They peered about as if they were as blankly amazed as the citizens of Joplin who regarded them. A long column of marching men came into view, every man with shield and spear and the indefinable air of being used to just such weapons.

They halted at another barked order. A wizened little man with a short sword snapped a question at the staring Americans. The high-school boy jumped. The wizened man roared his question again. The high-school boy stammered, and painfully formed syllables with his lips. The wizened man grunted in satisfaction. He talked, articulating clearly if impatiently. And the high-school boy turned dazedly to the other Americans.

"He wants to know the name of this town," he said, unbelieving his own ears. "He's talking Latin, like I learn in school. He says this town isn't on the road maps, and he doesn't know where he is. But all the same he takes possession of it in the name of the Emperor Valerius Fabricius, emperor of Rome and the far corners of the earth." And then the school-boy stuttered: "He—he says these are the first six cohorts of the Forty-second Legion, on garrison duty in Messalia. That—that's supposed to be two days' march up that way."

He pointed in the direction of St. Louis.

The idling motor car roared suddenly into life. Its gears whined and it came rolling out into the street. Its horn honked peremptorily for passage through the shield-clad soldiers. They gaped at it. It honked again and moved toward them.

A roared order, and they flung themselves upon it, spears thrusting, short swords stabbing. Up to this instant there was not one single inhabitant of Joplin who did not believe the spear-armed soldiers were motion-picture actors, or masqueraders, or something else equally insane but credible. But there was nothing make-believe about their attack on the car. They assaulted it as if it were a strange and probably deadly beast. They flung themselves into battle with it in a grotesquely reckless valor.

And there was nothing at all make-believe in the thoroughness and completeness with which they speared Mr. Horace B. Davis, who had only intended to drive down to the cotton-brokerage office of which he was chief clerk. They thought he was driving this strange beast to slaughter them, and they slaughtered him instead. The high-school boy saw them do it, growing whiter and whiter as he watched. When a swordsman approached the wizened man and displayed the severed head of Mr. Davis, with the spectacles dangling grotesquely from one ear, the high-school boy fainted dead away.

II

It was sunrise of June 5, 1935. Cyrus Harding gulped down his breakfast in the pale-gray dawn. He had felt very dizzy and sick for just a moment, some little while since, but he was himself again now. The smell of frying filled the kitchen. His wife cooked. Cyrus Harding ate.

He made noises as he emptied his plate. His hands were gnarled and work-worn, but his expression was of complacent satisfaction. He looked at a calendar hung on the wall, a Christmas sentiment from the Bryan Feed & Fertilizer Co., in Bryan, Ohio.

"Sheriff's goin' to sell out Amos today," he said comfortably. "I figger I'll get that north forty cheap."

His wife said tiredly: "He's been offerin' to sell it to you for a year."

"Yep," agreed Cyrus Harding more complacently still. "Comin' down on the price, too. But nobody'll bid against me at the sale. They know I want it bad, an' I ain't a good neighbor to have when somebuddy takes somethin' from under my nose. Folks know it. I'll git it a lot cheaper'n Amos offered it to me for. He wanted to sell it t'meet his int'rest an' hol' on another year. I'll git it for half that."

He stood up and wiped his mouth. He strode to the door.

"That hired man shoulda got a good start with his harrowin'," he said expansively. "I'll take a look an' go over to the sale."

He went to the kitchen door and opened it. Then his mouth dropped open. The view from this doorway was normally that of a not especially neat barnyard, with beyond it farmland flat as a floor and cultivated to the very fence rails, with a promising crop of corn as a border against the horizon.

Now the view was quite otherwise. All was normal as far as the barn. But beyond the barn was delirium. Huge, spreading tree ferns soared upward a hundred feet. Lacy, foliated branches formed a roof of incredible density above sheer jungle such as no man on earth had ever seen before. The jungles of the Amazon basin were parklike by comparison with its thickness. It was a riotous tangle of living vegetation in which growth was battle, and battle was life, and life was deadly, merciless conflict.

No man could have forced his way ten feet through such a wilderness. From it came a fetid exhalation which was part decay and part lush, rank, growing things, and part the overpowering perfumes of glaringly vivid flowers. It was jungle such as paleobotanists have described as existing in the Carboniferous period; as the source of our coal beds.

"It—it ain't so!" said Cyrus Harding weakly. "It—ain't so!"

His wife did not reply. She had not seen. Wearily, she began to clean up after her lord and master's meal.

He went down the kitchen steps, staring and shaken. He moved toward this impossible apparition which covered his crops. It did not disappear as he neared it. He went within twenty feet of it and stopped, still staring, still unbelieving, beginning to entertain the monstrous supposition that he had gone insane.

Then something moved in the jungle. A long, snaky neck, feet thick at its base and tapering to a mere sixteen inches behind a head the size of a barrel. The neck reached out the twenty feet to him. Cold eyes regarded him abstractedly. The mouth opened. Cyrus Harding screamed.

His wife raised her eyes. She looked through the open door and saw the jungle. She saw the jaws close upon her husband. She saw colossal, abstracted eyes half close as the something gulped, and partly choked, and swallowed—— She saw a lump in the monstrous neck move from the relatively slender portion just behind the head to the feet-thick section projecting from the jungle. She saw the head withdraw into the jungle and instantly be lost to sight.

Cyrus Harding's widow was very pale. She put on her hat and went out of the front door. She began to walk toward the house of the nearest neighbor. As she went, she said steadily to herself:

"It's come. I'm crazy. They'll have to put me in an asylum. But I won't have to stand him any more. I won't have to stand him any more!"

It was noon of June 5, 1935. The cell door opened and a very grave, whiskered man in a curious gray uniform came in. He tapped the prisoner gently on the shoulder.

"I'm Dr. Holloway," he said encouragingly. "Suppose you tell me, suh, just what happened t'you? I'm right sure it can all be straightened out."

The prisoner sputtered: "What—why—dammit," he protested, "I drove down from Louisville this morning. I had a dizzy spell and—well—I must have missed my road, because suddenly I noticed that everything around me was unfamiliar. And then a man in a gray uniform yelled at me, and a minute later he began to shoot, and the first thing I knew they'd arrested me for having the American flag painted on my car! I'm a traveling salesman for the Uncle Sam Candy Bar Co.! Dammit, it's funny when a man can't fly his own country's flag——"

"In your own country, of co'se," assented the doctor comfortingly. "But you must know, suh, that we don't allow any flag but ouah own to be displayed heah. You violated ouah laws, suh."

"Your laws!" The prisoner stared blankly. "What laws? Where in the United States is it illegal to fly the American flag?"

"Nowheah in the United States, suh." The doctor smiled. "You must have crossed ouah border unawares, suh. I will be frank, an' admit that it was suspected you were insane. I see now that it was just a mistake."

"Border—United——" The prisoner gasped. "I'm not in the United States? I'm not? Then where in hell am I?"

"Ten miles, suh, within the borders of the Confederacy," said the doctor, and laughed. "A queer mistake, suh, but theah was no intention of insult. You'll be released at once. Theah is enough tension between Washington an' Richmond without another border incident to upset ouah hot-heads."

"Confederacy?" The prisoner choked. "You can't—you don't mean the Confederate States——"

"Of co'se, suh. The Confederate States of North America. Why not?"

The prisoner gulped. "I—I've gone mad!" he stammered. "I must be mad! There was Gettysburg—there was——"

"Gettysburg? Oh, yes!" The doctor nodded indulgently. "We are very proud of ouah history, suh. You refer to the battle in the war of separation, when the fate of the Confederacy rested on ten minutes' time. I have often wondered what would have been the result if Pickett's charge had been driven back. It was Pickett's charge that gained the day for us, suh. England recognized the Confederacy two days later, France in another week, an' with unlimited credit abroad we won out. But it was a tight squeeze, suh!"

The prisoner gasped again. He stared out of the window. And opposite the jail stood an unquestionable courthouse. Upon the courthouse stood a flagpole. And spread gloriously in the breeze above a government building floated the Stars and Bars of the Confederacy!

It was night of June 5, 1935. The postmaster of North Centerville, Massachusetts, came out of his cubby-hole to listen to the narrative. The pot-bellied stove of the general store sent a comfortable if unnecessary glow about. The eyewitness chuckled.

"Yeah. They come around the cape, thirty or forty of 'em in a boat all o' sixty feet long with a crazy square sail drawin'. Round things on the gunnel like—like shields. An' rowin like hell! They stopped when they saw the town an' looked s'prised. Then they hailed us, talkin' some lingo that wa'n't American. Ole Peterson, he near dropped his line, with a fish on it, too. Then he tried to talk back. They hadda lotta trouble understandin' him, or made out to. Then they turned around an' rowed back. Actors or somethin', tryin' to play a joke. It fell flat, though. Maybe some of those rich folks up the coast pullin' it. Ho! Ho! Ole says they was talkin' a funny, old-fashioned Skowegian. They told him they was from Leifsholm, or somethin' like that, just up the coast. That they couldn't make out how our town got here. They'd never seen it before! Can y'imagine that? Ole says they were wikin's, an' they called this place Winland, an' says—— What's that?"

A sudden hubbub arose in the night. Screams. Cries. A shotgun boomed dully. The loafers in the general store crowded out on the porch. Flames rose from half a dozen places on the water front. In their light could be seen a full dozen serpent ships, speeding for the shore, propelled by oars. From four of their number, already beached, dark figures had poured. Firelight glinted on swords, on shields. A woman screamed as a huge, yellow-maned man seized her. His brazen helmet and shield glittered. He was laughing. Then a figure in over-alls hurtled toward the blond giant, an ax held threaten-ingly.

The giant cut him down with an already dripping blade and roared. Men rushed to him and they plunged on to loot and burn. More of the armored figures leaped to the sand from another beached ship. Another house roared flames skyward.

III

And at half past ten a.m. on the morning of June 5th, Professor Minott turned upon the party of students with a revolver in each hand. Gone was the appearance of an instructor whose most destructive possibility was a below-passing mark in mathematics. He had guns in his hands now, instead of chalk or pencil, and his eyes were glowing even as he smiled frostily. The four girls gasped. The young men, accustomed to seeing him only in a classroom, realized that he not only could use the weapons in his hands, but that he would. And suddenly they respected him as they would respect, say, a burglar or a prominent kidnaper or a gang leader. He was raised far above the level of a mere mathematics profes-sor. He became instantly a leader, and, by virtue of his weapons, even a ruler.

"As you see," said Professor Minott evenly, "I have anticipated the situation in which we find ourselves. I am prepared for it, to a certain extent. At any moment not only we, but the entire human race may be wiped out with a completeness of which you can form no idea. But there is also a chance of survival. And I intend to make the most of my survival—if we do live."

He looked steadily from one to another of the stu-dents who had followed him to explore the extraordi-

nary appearance of a sequoia forest north of Fredericksburg.

"I know what has happened," said Professor Minott.
"I know also what is likely to happen. And I know what
I intend to do about it. Any of you who are prepared to
follow me, say so. Any of you who object—well—I
can't have mutinies! I'll shoot him!"

"But—professor," said Blake nervously, "we ought
to get the girls home——"

"They will never go home," said Professor Minott
calmly. "Neither will you, nor any of us. As soon as
you're convinced that I'm quite ready to use these
weapons, I'll tell you what's happened and what it
means. I've been preparing for it for weeks."

Tall trees rose around the party. Giant trees. Magnificent trees. They towered two hundred and fifty feet
into the air, and their air of venerable calm was at once
the most convincing evidence of their actuality, and the
most improbable of all the things which had happened
in the neighborhood of Fredericksburg, Virginia. The
little group of people sat their horses affrightedly beneath the monsters of the forest. Minott regarded them
estimatingly—these three young men and four girls, all
students of Robinson College. Professor Minott was
now no longer the faculty member in charge of a party
of exploration, but a definitely ruthless leader.

At half past eight a.m. on June 5, 1935, the inhabitants of Fredericksburg had felt a curious, unanimous
dizziness. It passed. The sun shone brightly. There
seemed to be no noticeable change in any of the facts of
everyday existence. But within an hour the sleepy little
town was buzzing with excitement. The road to Washington—Route One on all road maps—ceased abruptly
some three miles north. A colossal, a gigantic forest had
appeared magically to block the way.

Telegraphic communication with Washington had
ceased. Even the Washington broadcasting stations were
no longer on the air. The trees of the extraordinary forest were tall beyond the experience of any human being
in town. They looked like the photographs of the giant

sequoias on the Pacific Coast, but—well, the thing was simply impossible.

In an hour and a half, Professor Minott had organized a party of sightseers among the students. He seemed to pick his party with a queer definiteness of decision. Three young men and four girls. They would have piled into a rickety car owned by one of the boys, but Professor Minott negatived the idea.

"The road ends at the forest," he said, smiling. "I'd rather like to explore a magic forest. Suppose we ride horseback? I'll arrange for horses."

In ten minutes the horses appeared. The girls had vanished to get into riding breeches or knickers. They noted appreciatively on their return that besides the saddles, the horses had saddlebags slung in place. Again Professor Minott smiled.

"We're exploring," he said humorously. "We must dress the part. Also, we'll probably want some lunch. And we can bring back specimens for the botanical lab to look over."

They rode forth; the girls thrilled, the young men pleased and excited, and all of them just a little bit disappointed at finding themselves passed by motor cars which whizzed by them as all Fredericksburg went to look at the improbable forest ahead.

There were cars by hundreds where the road abruptly ended. A crowd stared at the forest. Giant trees, their roots fixed firmly in the ground. Undergrowth here and there. Over it all, an aspect of peace and utter serenity—and permanence. The watching crowd hummed and buzzed with speculation, with talk. The thing they saw was impossible. It could not have happened. This forest could not possibly be real. They were regarding some sort of mirage.

But as the party of riders arrived, half a dozen men came out of the forest. They had dared to enter it. Now they returned, still incredulous of their own experience, bearing leaves and branches and one of them certain small berries unknown on the Atlantic coast.

A State police officer held up his hand as Professor Minott's party went toward the edge of the forest.

"Look here!" he said. "We' been hearin' funny noises in there. I'm stoppin' anybody else from goin' in until we know what's what."

Professor Minott nodded. "We'll be careful. I'm Professor Minott of Robinson College. We're going in after some botanical specimens. I have a revolver. We're all right."

He rode ahead. The State policeman, without definite orders for authority, shrugged his shoulders and bent his efforts to the prevention of other attempts to explore. In minutes, the eight horses and their riders were out of sight.

That was now three hours past. For three hours, Professor Minott had led his charges a little south of northeast. In that time they saw no dangerous animals. They saw some—many—familiar plants. They saw rabbits in quantity, and once a slinking gray form which Tom Hunter, who was majoring in zoölogy, declared was a wolf. There are no wolves in the vicinity of Fredericksburg, but neither are there sequoias. And the party had seen no signs of human life, though Fredericksburg lies in farming country which is thickly settled.

In three hours the horses must have covered between twelve and fifteen miles, even through the timber. It was just after sighting a shaggy beast which was unquestionably a woodland buffalo—extinct east of the Rockies as early as 1820—that young Blake protested uneasily against further travel.

"There's something awfully queer, sir," he said awkwardly. "I don't mind experimenting as much as you like, sir, but we've got the girls with us. If we don't start back pretty soon, we'll get in trouble with the dean."

And then Minott drew his two revolvers and very calmly announced that none of them would ever go back. That he knew what had happened and what could be expected. And he added that he would explain as soon as they were convinced he would use his revolvers in case of a mutiny.

"Call us convinced now, sir," said Blake.

He was a bit pale about the lips, but he hadn't

flinched. In fact, he'd moved to be between Maida Haynes and the gun muzzle.

"We'd like very much to know how all these trees and plants, which ought to be three thousand miles away, happen to be growing in Virginia without any warning. Especially, sir, we'd like to know how it is that the topography underneath all this brand-new forest is the same. The hills trend the same way they used to, but everything that ever was on them has vanished, and something else is in its place."

Minott nodded approvingly. "Splendid, Blake!" he said warmly. "Sound observation! I picked you because you're well spoken of in geology, even though there were—er —other reasons for leaving you behind. Let's go on over the next rise. Unless I'm mistaken, we should find the Potomac in view. Then I'll answer any questions you like. I'm afraid we've a good bit more of riding to do today."

Reluctantly, the eight horses breasted the slope. They scrambled among underbrush. It was queer that in three hours they had seen not a trace of a road leading anywhere. But up at the top of the hill there was a road. It was a narrow, wandering cart track. Without a word, every one of the eight riders turned their horses to follow it. It meandered onward for perhaps a quarter of a mile. It dipped suddenly. And the Potomac lay before and below them.

Then seven of the eight riders exclaimed. There was a settlement upon the banks of the river. There were boats in harbor. There were other boats in view beyond, two beating down from the long reaches upstream, and three others coming painfully up from the direction of Chesapeake Bay. But neither the village nor the boats should have been upon the Potomac River.

The village was small and mud-walled. Tiny, blue-clad figures moved about the fields outside. The buildings, the curving lines of the roofs, and more especially the unmistakable outline of a sort of temple near the center of the fortified hamlet—these were Chinese. The boats in sight were junks, save that their sails were cloth instead of slatted bamboo. The fields outside the squat mud walls were cultivated in a fashion altogether alien. Near the river, where marsh flats would be normal along the Potomac, rice fields intensely worked spread out instead.

Then a figure appeared near by. Wide hat, wadded cotton-padded jacket, cotton trousers, and clogs—it was Chinese peasant incarnate, and all the more so when it turned a slant-eyed, terror-stricken face upon them and fled squawking. It left a monstrously heavy wooden yoke behind, from which dangled two buckets filled with berries it had gathered in the forest.

The riders stared. There was the Potomac. But a Chinese village nestled beside it, Chinese junks plied its waters.

"I—I think," said Maida Haynes unsteadily, "I—think I've—gone insane. Haven't I?"

Professor Minott shrugged. He looked disappointed but queerly resolute.

"No," he said shortly. "You're not mad. It just happens that the Chinese happened to colonize America first. It's been known that Chinese junks touched the American shore—the Pacific coast, of course—long before Columbus. Evidently they colonized it. They may have come all the way overland to the Atlantic, or maybe around by Panama. In any case, this is a Chinese continent now. This isn't what we want. We'll ride some more."

The fleeing, squawking figure had been seen from the village. A huge, discordant gong began to sound. Figures fled toward the walls from the fields round about. The popping of firecrackers began, with a chorus of most intimidating yells.

"Come on!" said Minott sharply. "We'd better move!"

He wheeled his horse about and started off at a canter. By instinct, since he was the only one who seemed to have any definite idea what to do, the others flung after him.

And as they rode, suddenly the horses staggered. The humans on them felt a queer, queasy vertigo. It lasted only for a second, but Minott paled a little.

"Now we'll see what's happened," he said composedly. "The odds are still fair, but I'd rather have had things stay as they were until we'd tried a few more places."

IV

That same queasy vertigo affected the staring crowd at the end of the road leading north from Fredericksburg. For perhaps a second they felt an unearthly illness, which even blurred their vision. Then they saw clearly again. And in an instant they were babbling in panic, starting their motor cars in terror, some of them fleeing on foot.

The sequoia forest had vanished. In its place was a dreary waste of glittering white; stumpy trees buried under snow; rolling ground covered with a powdery, glittering stuff.

In minutes dense fog shut off the view, as the warm air of a Virginia June morning was chilled by that frigid coating. But in minutes, too, the heavy snow began to melt. The cars fled away along the concrete road, and behind them an expanding belt of fog spread out—and the little streams and runlets filled with a sudden surplus of water, and ran more swiftly, and rose.

The eight riders were every one very pale. Even Minott seemed shaken but no less resolute when he drew rein.

"I imagine you will all be satisfied now," he said composedly. "Blake, you're the geologist of the party. Doesn't the shore line there look familiar?"

Blake nodded. He was very white indeed. He pointed to the stream.

"Yes. The falls, too. This is the site of Fredericksburg, sir, where we were this morning. There is where the main bridge was—or will be. The main highway to Richmond should run"—he licked his lips—"it should run where that very big oak tree is standing. The Princess Anne Hotel should be on the side of that hill. I—I would say, sir, that somehow we've gone back in time or else forward into the future. It sounds insane, but I've been trying to figure it out——"

Minott nodded coolly. "Very good! This is the site of Fredericksburg, to be sure. But we have not traveled forward or back in time. I hope that you noticed where we came out of the sequoia forest. There seems to be a sort of fault along that line, which it may be useful to remember." He paused. "We're not in the past or the future, Blake. We've traveled sidewise, in a sort of oscillation from one time path to another. We happen to be in a—well, in a part of time where Fredericksburg has never been built, just as a little while since we were where the Chinese occupy the American continent. I think we better have lunch."

He dismounted. The four girls tended to huddle together. Lucy Blair's teeth chattered.

Blake moved to their horses' heads. "Don't get rattled," he said urgently. "We're here, wherever it is. Professor Minott is going to explain things in a minute. Since he knows what's what, we're in no danger. Climb off your horses and let's eat. I'm hungry as a bear. Come on, Maida!"

Maida Haynes dismounted. She managed a rather shaky smile. "I'm—afraid of—him," she said in a whisper. "More than—anything else. Stay close to me, please!"

Blake frowned.

Minott said dryly: "Look in your saddlebags and you'll find sandwiches. Also you'll find firearms. You young men had better arm yourselves. Since there's now no conceivable hope of getting back to the world we know, I think you can be trusted with weapons."

Blake stared at him, then silently investigated his own saddlebags. He found two revolvers, with what seemed an abnormally large supply of cartridges. He found a mass of paper, which turned out to be books with their cardboard backs torn off. He glanced professionally at the revolvers and slipped them in his pockets. He put back the books.

"I appoint you second in command, Blake," said Minott, more dryly than before. "You understand nothing, but you wait to understand. I made no mistake in choosing you despite my reasons for leaving you behind. Sit down and I'll tell you what happened."

With a grunt and a puffing noise, a small black bear broke cover and fled across a place where only that morning a highly elaborate filling station had stood. The party started, then relaxed. The girls suddenly started to giggle foolishly, almost hysterically. Minott bit calmly into a sandwich and said pleasantly:

"I shall have to talk mathematics to you, but I'll try to make it more palatable than my classroom lectures have been. You see, everything that has happened can only be explained in terms of mathematics, and more especially certain concepts in mathematical physics. You young ladies and gentlemen being college men and women, I shall have to phrase things very simply, as for ten-year-old children. Hunter, you're staring. If you actually see something, such as an Indian, shoot at him and he'll run away. The probabilities are that he never heard the report of a firearm. We're not on the Chinese continent now."

Hunter gasped, and fumbled at his saddlebags. While he got out the revolvers, Minott went on imperturbably:

"There has been an upheaval of nature, which still continues. But instead of a shaking and jumbling of earth and rocks, there has been a shaking and jumbling of space and time. I go back to first principles. Time is a dimension. The past is one extension of it, the future is the other, just as east is one extension of a more familiar dimension and west is its opposite.

"But we ordinarily think of time as a line, a sort of tunnel, perhaps. We do not make that error in the dimensions about which we think daily. For example, we know that Annapolis, King George courthouse, and—say—Norfolk are all to the eastward of us. But we know that in order to reach any of them, as a destination, we would have to go not only east but north or south in addition. In imaginative travels into the future, however, we never think in such a common-sense fashion. We assume that the future is a line instead of a coördinate, a path instead of a direction. We assume that if we travel to futureward there is but one possible destination. And that is as absurd as it would be to ignore the possibility of traveling to eastward in any other line than due east, forgetting that there is northeast and southeast and a large number of intermediate points."

Young Blake said slowly: "I follow you, sir, but it doesn't seem to bear——"

"On our problem? But it does!" Minott smiled, showing his teeth. He bit into his sandwich again. "Imagine that I come to a fork in a road. I flip a coin to determine which fork I shall take. Whichever route I follow, I shall encounter certain landmarks and certain adventures. But they will not be the same, whether landmarks or adventures.

"In choosing between the forks of the road I choose not only between two sets of landmarks I could encounter, but between two sets of events. I choose between paths, not only on the surface of the earth, but in time. And as those paths upon earth may lead to two different cities, so those paths in the future may lead to two entirely different fates. On one of them may lie opportunities for riches. On the other may lie the most prosaic of hit-and-run accidents which will leave me a mangled corpse, not only upon one fork of a highway in the State of Virginia, but upon one fork of a highway in time.

"In short, I am pointing out that there is more than one future we can encounter, and with more or less absence of deliberation we choose among them. But the futures we fail to encounter, upon the roads we do not take, are just as real as the landmarks upon those roads. We never see them, but we freely admit their existence."

Again it was Blake who protested: "All this is interesting enough, sir, but still I don't see how it applies to our present situation."

Minott said impatiently: "Don't you see that if such a state of things exists in the future, that it must also have existed in the past? We talk of three dimensions and one present and one future. There is a theoretic necessity—a mathematical necessity—for assuming more than one future. There are an indefinite number of possible futures, any one of which we would encounter if we took the proper 'forks' in time.

"There are any number of destinations to eastward. There are any number to futureward. Start a hundred miles west and come eastward, choosing your paths on earth at random, as you do in time. You may arrive here. You may arrive to the north or south of this spot, and still be east of your starting point. Now start a hundred years back instead of a hundred miles west."

Groping, Blake said fumblingly: "I think you're saying, sir, that—well, as there must be any number of futures, there must have been any number of pasts besides those written down in our histories. And—and it would follow that there are any number of what you might call 'presents.' "

Minott gulped down the last of his sandwich and nodded. "Precisely. And today's convulsion of nature has jumbled them and still upsets them from time to time. The Northmen once colonized America. In the sequence of events which mark the pathway of our own ancestors through time, that colony failed. But along another path through time that colony throve and flourished. The Chinese reached the shores of California. In the path our ancestors followed through time, nothing developed from the fact. But this morning we touched upon the pathway in which they colonized and conquered the continent, though from the fear that one peasant we saw displayed, they have not wiped out the Indians.

"Somewhere the Roman Empire still exists, and may not improbably rule America as it once ruled Britain. Somewhere, not impossibly, the conditions causing the glacial period still obtain and Virginia is buried under a mass of snow. Somewhere even the Carboniferous period may exist. Or to come more closely to the present we know, somewhere there is a path through time in which Pickett's charge at Gettysburg went desperately home, and the Confederate States of America is now an independent nation with a heavily fortified border and a chip-on-the-shoulder attitude toward the United States."

Blake alone had asked questions, but the entire party had been listening open-mouthed.

Now Maida Haynes said: "But—Professor Minott, where are we now?"

"We are probably," said Minott, smiling, "in a path of time in which America has never been discovered by white men. That isn't a very satisfactory state of things. We're going to look for something better. We wouldn't be comfortable in wigwams, with skins for clothing. So we shall hunt for a more congenial environment. We will have some weeks in which to do our searching, I think. Unless, of course, all space and time are wiped out by the cause of our predicament."

Tom Hunter stirred uncomfortably. "We haven't traveled backward or forward in time, then?"

"No," repeated Minott. He got to his feet. "That odd nausea we felt seems to be caused by travel sidewise in time. It's the symptom of a time oscillation. We'll ride on and see what other worlds await us. We're a rather well-qualified party for this sort of exploration. I chose you for your trainings. Hunter, zoölogy. Blake, engineering and geology. Harris"—he nodded to the rather undersized young man, who flushed at being noticed— "Harris is quite a competent chemist, I understand. Miss Ketterling is a capable botanist. Miss Blair——"

Maida Haynes rose slowly. "You anticipated all this, Professor Minott, and yet you brought us into it. You— you said we'll never get back home. Yet you deliberately arranged it. What—what was your motive? What did you do it for?"

Minott climbed into the saddle. He smiled, but there was bitterness in his smile. "In the world we know," he told her, "I was a professor of mathematics in a small and unconsidered college. I had absolutely no chance of ever being more than a professor of mathematics in a small and unconsidered college. In this world I am, at least, the leader of a group of reasonably intelligent young people. In our saddlebags are arms and ammunition and—more important—books of reference for our future activities. We shall hunt for and find a world in which our technical knowledge is at a premium. We shall live in that world—if all time and space is not destroyed—and use our knowledge."

Maida Haynes said: "But again—what for?"

"To conquer it!" said Minott in sudden fierceness. "To conquer it! We eight shall rule a world as no world has been ruled since time began! I promise you that when we find the environment I seek, you will have wealth by millions, slaves by thousands, every luxury, and all the power human beings could desire!"

Blake said evenly: "And you, sir? What will you have?"

"Most power of all," said Minott steadily. "I shall be the emperor of the world! And also"—his tone changed indescribably as he glanced at Maida—"also I shall have a certain other possession that I wish."

He turned his back to them and rode off to lead the way. Maida Haynes was deathly pale as she rode close to Blake. Her hand closed convulsively upon his arm.

"Jerry!" she whispered. "I'm—frightened!"

And Blake said steadily: "Don't worry! I'll kill him first!"

V

The ferryboat from Berkeley plowed valorously through the fog. Its whistle howled mournfully at the regulation intervals.

Up in the pilot house, the skipper said confidentially: "I tell you, I had the funniest feelin' of my life, just now. I was dizzy an' sick all over, like I was seasick an' drunk all at the same time."

The mate said abstractedly: "I had somethin' like that a little while ago. Somethin' we ate, prob'ly. Say, that's funny!"

"What?"

"Was a lot o' traffic in the harbor just now, whistlin'. I ain't heard a whistle for minutes. Listen!"

Both men strained their ears. There was the rhythmic shudder of the vessel, itself a sound produced by the engines. There were fragmentary voice noises from the passenger deck below. There was the wash of water by the ferryboat's bow. There was nothing else. Nothing at all.

"Funny!" said the skipper.

"Damn funny!" agreed the mate.

The ferryboat went on. The fog cut down all visibility to a radius of perhaps two hundred feet.

"Funniest thing I ever saw!" said the skipper worriedly. He reached for the whistle cord and the mournful bellow of the horn resounded. "We're near our slip, though. I wish——"

With a little chugging, swishing sound a steam launch came out of the mist. It sheered off, the men in it staring blankly at the huge bulk of the ferry. It made a complete circuit of the big, clumsy craft. Then someone stood up and bellowed unintelligibly in the launch. He bellowed again. He was giving an order. He pointed to the flag at the stern of the launch—it was an unfamiliar flag—and roared furiously.

"What the hell's the matter of that guy?" wondered the mate.

A little breeze blew suddenly. The fog began to thin. The faintly brighter spot which was the sun overhead grew bright indeed. Faint sunshine struggled through the fog bank. The wind drove the fog back before it, and the bellowing man in the steam launch grew purple with rage as his orders went unheeded.

Then, quite abruptly, the last wisps of vapor blew away. San Francisco stood revealed. But—San Francisco? This was not San Francisco! It was a wooden city, a small city, a dirty city with narrow streets and gas street lamps and four monstrous, barracklike edifices fronting the harbor. Nob hill stood, but it was barren of dwellings. And——

"Damn!" said the mate of the ferryboat.

He was staring at a colossal mass of masonry, foursquare and huge, which rose to a gigantic spiral fluted dome. A strange and alien flag fluttered in the breeze above certain buildings. Figures moved in the streets. There were motor cars, but they were clumsy and huge.

The mate's eyes rested upon a horse-drawn carriage. It was drawn by three horses abreast, and they were either so trained or so checkreined that the two outer horses' heads were arched outward in the fashion of Tsarist Russia.

But that was natural enough. When an interpreter could be found, the mate and skipper were savagely abused for entering the harbor of Novo Skevsky without paying due heed to the ordinances in force by the ukase of the Tsar Alexis of all the Russias. These rules, they learned, were enforced with special rigor in all the Russian territory in America, from Alaska on south.

The boy ran shouting up to the village. "Hey, grandpa! Hey, grandpa! Lookit the birds!" He pointed as he ran.

A man looked idly, and stood transfixed. A woman stopped, and stared. Lake superior glowed bluely off to westward, and the little village most often turned its eyes in that direction. Now, though, as the small boy ran shouting of what he had seen, men stared, women marveled, and children ran and shouted and whooped in the instinctive excitement of childhood at anything which entrances grown-ups.

Over the straggly pine forests birds were coming. They came in great dark masses. Not by dozens, or by hundreds, or even by thousands. They came in millions, in huge dark clouds which obscured the sky. There were two huge flights in sight at the boy's first shouting. There were six in view before he had reached his home and was panting a demand that his elders come and look. And there were others, incredible numbers of others, sweeping onward straight over the village.

Dusk fell abruptly as the first flock passed overhead. The whirring of wings was loud. It made people raise their voices as they asked each other what such birds could possibly be. Daylight again, and again darkness as the flocks poured on. The size of each flock was to be measured not in feet or yards, but in miles of front. Two, three miles of birds, flying steadily in a single enormous mass some four miles deep. Another such mass, and another, and another.

"What are they, grandpa? There must be millions of 'em!"

Somewhere, a shotgun went off. Small things dropped from the sky. Another gunshot, and another. A rain of bird shot went up from the village into the mass of whirring wings. And crazily careening small bodies fell down among the houses.

Grandpa examined one of them, smoothing its rumpled plumage. He exclaimed. He gasped in excitement. "It's a wild pigeon! What they used to call passenger pigeons! Back in '78 there was these birds by billions. Folks said a billion was killed in Michigan that one year! But they're gone now. They're gone like the buffalo. There ain't any more."

The sky was dark with birds above him. A flock four miles wide and three miles long made lights necessary in the village. The air was filled with the sound of wings. The passenger pigeon had returned to a continent from which it had been absent for almost fifty years.

Flocks of passenger pigeons flew overhead in thick, dark masses equaling those seen by Audubon in 1813, when he computed the pigeons in flight above Kentucky at hundreds of billions in number. In flocks that were innumerable they flew to westward. The sun set, and still the air was filled with the sound of their flying. For hours after darkness fell, the whirring of wings continued without ceasing.

VI

A great open fire licked at the rocks against which it had been built. The horses cropped uneasily at herbage near by. The smell of fat meat cooking was undeniably savory, but one of the girls blubbered gustily on a bed of leaves. Harris tended the cookery. Tom Hunter brought wood. Blake stood guard a little beyond the firelight, revolvers ready, staring off into the blackness. Professor Minott pored over a topographical map of Virginia. Maida Haynes tried to comfort the blubbering girl.

"Supper's ready," said Harris. He made even that announcement seem somehow shy and apologetic.

Minott put down his map. Tom Hunter began to cut great chunks of steaming meat from the haunch of venison. He put them on slabs of bark and began to pass them around. Minott reached out his hand and took one of them. He ate with obvious appetite. He seemed to have abandoned his preoccupation the instant he laid down his map. He was displaying the qualities of a capable leader.

"Hunter," he observed, "After you've eaten that stuff, you might relieve Blake. We'll arrange reliefs for the rest of the night. By the way, you men mustn't forget to wind your watches. We'll need to rate them, ultimately."

Hunter gulped down his food and moved out to Blake's hiding place. They exchanged low-toned words. Blake came back to the fire. He took the food Harris handed him and began to eat it. He looked at the blubbering girl on the bed of leaves.

"She's just scared," said Minott. "Barely slit the skin on her arm. But it is upsetting for a senior at Robinson College to be wounded by a flint arrowhead."

Blake nodded. "I heard some noises off in the darkness," he said curtly. "I'm not sure, but my impression was that I was being stalked. And I thought I heard a human voice."

"We may be watched," admitted Minott. "But we're out of the path of time in which those Indians tried to ambush us. If any of them follow, they're too bewildered to be very dangerous."

"I hope so," said Blake.

His manner was devoid of cordiality, yet there was no exception to be taken to it. Professor Minott had deliberately got the party into a predicament from which there seemed to be no possibility of escape. He had organized it to get it into just that predicament. He was unquestionably the leader of the party, despite his action. Blake made no attempt to undermine his leadership.

But Blake himself had some qualifications as a leader, young as he was. Perhaps the most promising of them was the fact that he made no attempt to exercise his talents until he knew as much as Minott of what was to be looked for, what was to be expected.

He listened sharply and then said: "I think we've digested your lesson of this morning, sir. But how long is this scrambling of space and time to continue? We left Fredericksburg and rode to the Potomac. It was Chinese territory. We rode back to Fredericksburg, and it wasn't there. Instead, we encountered Indians who let loose a flight of arrows at us and wounded Bertha Ketterling in the arm. We were nearly out of range at the time, though."

"They were scared," said Minott. "They'd never seen horses before. Our white skins probably upset them, too. And then our guns, and the fact that I killed one, should have chased them off."

"But—what happened to Fredericksburg? We rode away from it. Why couldn't we ride back?"

"The scrambling process has kept up," said Minott dryly. "You remember that queer vertigo? We've had it several times today, and every time, as I see it, there's been an oscillation of the earth we happened to be on. Hm! Look!"

He got up and secured the map over which he had been poring. He brought it back and pointed to a heavy penciled line. "Here's a map of Virginia in our time. The Chinese continent appeared just about three miles north of Fredericksburg. The line of demarcation was, I consider, the line along which the giant sequoias appeared. While in the Chinese time we felt that giddiness and rode back toward Fredericksburg. We came out of the sequoia forest at the same spot as before. I made sure of it. But the continent of our time was no longer there.

"We rode east and—whether you noticed it or not— before we reached the border of King George County there was another abrupt change in the vegetation— from a pine country to oaks and firs, which are not exactly characteristic of this part of the world in our time.

We saw no signs of any civilization. We turned south, and ran into that heavy fog and the snow beyond it. Evidently, there's a section of a time path in which Virginia is still subject to a glacial climate."

Blake nodded. He listened again. Then he said:

"You've three sides of an—an island of time marked there."

"Just so," agreed Minott. "Exactly! In the scrambling process, the oscillating process, there seem to be natural 'faults' in the surface of the earth. Relatively large areas seem to shift back and forth as units from one time path to another. In my own mind, I've likened them to elevators with many stories.

"We were on the Fredericksburg 'elevator,' or that section of our time path, when it shifted to another time. We rode off it onto the Chinese continent. While there, the section we started from shifted again, to another time altogether. When we rode back to where it had been—well, the town of Fredericksburg was in another time path altogether."

Blake said sharply: "Listen!"

A dull mutter sounded far to the north. It lasted for an instant and died away. There was a crashing of bushes near by and a monstrous animal stopped alertly into the firelight. It was an elk, but such an elk! It was a giant, a colossal creature. One of the girls cried out affrightedly, and it turned and crashed away into the underbrush.

"There are no elk in Virginia," said Minott dryly.

Blake said sharply again: "Listen!"

Again that dull muttering to the north. It grew louder, now. It was an airplane motor. It increased in volume from a dull mutter to a growl, from a growl to a roar. Then the plane shot overhead, the navigation lights on its wings glowing brightly. It banked steeply and returned. It circled overhead, with a queer effect of helplessness. And then suddenly it dived down.

"An aviator from our time," said Blake, staring toward the sound. "He saw our fire. He's going to try to make a crash landing in the dark."

The motor cut off. An instant in which there was

only the crackling of the fire and the whistling of wind around gliding surfaces off there in the night. Then a terrific thrashing of branches. A crash——

Then a flare of flame, a roaring noise, and the lurid yellow of gasoline flames spouting skyward.

"Stay here!" snapped Blake. He was on his feet in an instant. "Harris, Professor Minott! Somebody has to stay with the girls! I'll get Hunter and go help!"

He plunged off into the darkness, calling to Hunter. The two of them forced their way through the underbrush. Minott scowled and got out his revolvers. Still scowling, he slipped out of the firelight and took up the guard duty Hunter had abandoned.

A gasoline tank exploded, off there in the darkness. The glare of the fire grew intolerably vivid. The sound of the two young men racing through undergrowth became fainter and died away.

A long time passed—a very long time. Then, very far away, the sound of thrashing bushes could be heard again. The gasoline flare dulled and dimmed. Figures came slowly back. They moved as if they were carrying something very heavy. They stopped beyond the glow of light from the camp fire. Then Blake and Hunter reappeared, alone.

"He'd dead," said Blake curtly. "Luckily, he was flung clear of the crash before the gas tanks caught. He came back to consciousness for a couple of minutes before he—died. Our fire was the only sign of human life he'd seen in hours. We brought him over here. We'll bury him in the morning."

There was silence. Minott's scowl was deep and savage as he came back to the firelight.

"What—what did he say?" asked Maida Haynes.

"He left Washington at five this afternoon," said Blake shortly. "By our time, or something like it. All of Virginia across the Potomac vanished at four thirty, and virgin forest took its place. He went out to explore. At the end of an hour he came back, and Washington was gone. In its place was a fog bank, with snow underneath. He followed the Potomac down and saw palisaded homesteads with long, oared ships drawn up on shore."

"Vikings, Norsemen!" said Minott in satisfaction.

"He didn't land. He swept on down, following the edge of the bay. He looked for Baltimore. Gone! Once, he's sure, he saw a city, but he was taken sick at about that time and when he recovered, it had vanished. He was heading north again and his gasoline was getting low when he saw our fire. He tried for a crash landing. He'd no flares with him. He crashed—and died."

"Poor fellow!" said Maida shakenly.

"The point is," said Blake, "that Washington was in our present time at about four thirty today. We've got a chance, though a slim one, of getting back! We've got to get to the edge of one of these blocks that go swinging through time, the edge of what Professor Minott calls a 'time fault,' and watch it! When the shifts come, we explore as quickly as we can. We've no great likelihood, perhaps, of getting back exactly to our own period, but we can get nearer to it than we are now! Professor Minott said that somewhere the Confederacy exists. Even that, among people of our own race and speaking our own language, would be better than to be marooned forever among Indians, or among Chinese or Norsemen."

Minott said harshly: "Blake, we'd better have this out right now! I give the orders in this party! You jumped quickly when that plane crashed, and you gave orders to Harris and to me. I let you get away with it, but we can have but one leader. I am that leader! See you remember it!"

Blake swung about. Minott had a revolver bearing on his body.

"And you are making plans for a return to our time!" he went on savagely. "I won't have it! The odds are still that we'll all be killed. But if I do live, I mean to take advantage of it. And my plans do not include a return to a professorship of mathematics at Robinson College."

"Well?" said Blake coolly. "What of it, sir?"

"Just this! I'm going to take your revolvers. I'm going to make the plans and give the orders hereafter. We are going to look for the time path in which a viking civilization thrives in America. We'll find it, too, because these disturbances will last for weeks yet. And once we find it, we will settle down among those Norsemen, and when space and time are stable again I shall begin the formation of my empire! And you will obey orders or you'll be left afoot while the rest of us go on to my destiny!"

Blake said very quietly indeed: "Perhaps, sir, we'd all prefer to be left to our own destinies rather than be merely the tools by which you attain to yours."

Minott stared at him an instant. His lips tensed. "It is a pity," he said coldly. "I could have used your brains, Blake. But I can't have mutiny. I shall have to shoot you."

His revolver came up remorselessly.

VII

To determine the cause of various untoward events, the British Academy of Sciences was in extraordinary session. Its members were weary; bleary-eyed, but still conscious of their dignity and the importance of their task. A venerable, whiskered physicist spoke with fitting definiteness and solemnity.

"And so, gentleman, I see nothing more that remains to be said. The extraordinary events of the past hours seem to follow from certain facts about our own closed space. The gravitational fields of 10^{79} particles of matter will close space about such an aggregation. No cosmos can be larger. No cosmos can be smaller. And if we envision the creation of such a cosmos we will observe its galaxies vanish at the instant the 10^{79}th particle adds its own mass to those which were present before it.

"However, the fact that space has closed about such a cosmos does not imply its annihilation. It means merely its separation from its original space, the isolation of itself in space and time because of the curvature of space due to its gravitational field. And if we assume the existence of more than one area of closed space, we assume in some sense the existence of a hyper-space separating the closed spaces; hyper-spatial coördinates which mark their relative hyper-spatial positions; hyper-spatial——"

A gentleman with even longer and whiter whiskers than the speaker said in a loud and decided voice: "Fiddlesticks! Stuff and nonsense!"

The speaker paused. He glared. "Sir! Do you refer——"

"I do!" said the gentleman with the longer and whiter whiskers. "It is stuff and nonsense! Next you'd be saying that in this hyper-space of yours the closed spaces would be subject to hyper-laws, revolve about each other in hyper-orbits regulated by hyper-gravitation, and undoubtedly at times there would be hyper-earth tides or hyper-collisions, producing decidedly hyper-catastrophes."

"Such, sir," said the whiskered gentleman on the rostrum, quivering with indignation, "such is the fact, sir!"

"Then the fact," rejoined the scientist with the longer and whiter whiskers, "sir, makes me sick!"

And as if to prove it, he reeled. But he was not alone in reeling. The entire venerable assembly shuddered in abrupt, nauseating vertigo. And then the British Academy of Sciences adjourned without formality and in a panic. It ran away. Because abruptly there was no longer a rostrum nor an end to its assembly hall. Where their speaker had been was open air. In the open air was a fire. About the fire were certain brutish figures incredibly resembling the whiskered scientists who fled from them. They roared at the fleeing, venerable men. Snarling, wielding crude clubs, they plunged into the hall of the British Academy of Sciences. It is known that they caught one person—a biologist of highly eccentric views. It is believed that they ate him.

But it has long been surmised that some, at least, of the extinct species of humanity, such as the Piltdown and Neanderthal men, were cannibals. If in some pathway of time they happened to exterminate their more intelligent rivals—if somewhere *pithecanthropus erectus* survives and *homo sapiens* does not—well, in that pathway of time cannibalism is the custom of society.

VIII

With a gasp, Maida Haynes flung herself before Blake. But Harris was even quicker. Apologetic and shy, he had just finished cutting a smoking piece of meat from the venison haunch. He threw it swiftly, and the searing mass of stuff flung Minott's hand aside at the same instant that it burned it horribly.

Blake was on his feet, his gun out. "If you pick up that gun, sir," he said rather breathlessly but with unquestionable sincerity, "I'll put a bullet through your arm!"

Minott swore. He retrieved the weapon with his left hand and thrust it in his pocket. "You young fool!" he snapped. "I'd no intention of shooting you. I did intend to scare you thoroughly. Harris, you're an ass! Maida, I shall discuss your action later. The worst punishment I could give the lot of you would be to leave you to yourselves."

He stalked out of the firelight and off into the darkness. Something like consternation came upon the group. The glow of fire where the plane had crashed flickered fitfully. The base of the dull red light seemed to widen a little.

"That's the devil!" said Hunter uneasily. "He does know more about this stuff than we do. If he leaves us we're messed up!"

"We are," agreed Blake grimly. "And perhaps if he doesn't."

Lucy Blair said: "I—I'll go and talk to him. He—he used to be nice to me in class. And—and his hand must hurt terribly. It's burned."

She moved away from the fire, a long and angular shadow going on before her.

Minott's voice came sharply: "Go back! There's something moving out here!"

Instantly after, his revolver flashed. A howl arose, and the weapon flashed again and again. Then there were many crashings. Figures fled.

Minott came back to the firelight, scornfully. "Your leadership is at fault, Blake," he commented sardonically. "You forgot about a guard. And you were the man who thought he heard voices! They've run away now, though. Indians, of course."

Lucy Blair said hesitantly: "Could I—could I do something for your hand? It's burned——"

"What can you do?" he asked angrily.

"There's some fat," she told him. "Indians used to dress wounds with bear fat. I suppose deer fat would do as well."

He permitted her to dress the burn, though it was far from a serious one. She begged handkerchiefs from the others to complete the job. There was distinct uneasiness all about the camp fire. This was no party of adventurers, prepared for anything. It had started as an outing of undergraduates.

Minott scowled as Lucy Blair worked on his hand. Harris looked as apologetic as possible, because he had made the injury. Bertha Ketterling blubbered—less noisily, now, because nobody paid her any attention. Blake frowned meditatively at the fire. Maida Haynes tried uneasily not to seem conscious of the fact that she was in some sense—though no mention had been made of it—a bone of contention.

The horses moved uneasily. Bertha Ketterling sneezed. Maida felt her eyes smarting. She was the first one to see the spread of the blaze started by the gas tanks of the airplane. Her cry of alarm roused the others.

The plane had crashed a good mile from the camp fire. The blazing of its tanks had been fierce but brief. The burning of the wings and chassis fabric had been short, as well. The fire had died down to seeming dull embers. But there were more than embers ablaze out there now.

The fire had died down, to be sure, but only that it might spread among thick and tangled underbrush. It had spread widely on the ground before some climbing vine, blazing, carried flames up to resinous pine branches overhead. A small but steady wind was blowing. And as Maida looked off to see the source of the smoke which stung her eyes, one tall tree was blazing, a long line of angry red flames crept along the ground, and then at two more, three more, then at a dozen points bright fire roared upward toward the sky.

The horses snorted and reared.

Minott snapped: "Harris! Get the horses! Hunter, see that the girls get mounted, and quickly!"

He pointedly gave Blake no orders. He pored intently over his map as more trees and still more caught fire and blazed upward. He stuffed it in his pocket. Blake calmly rescued the haunch of venison, and when Minott sprang into the saddle among the snorting, scared horses, Blake was already by Maida Haynes' side, ready to go.

"We ride in pairs," said Minott curtly. "A man and a girl. You men, look after them. I've a flashlight. I'll go ahead. We'll hit the Rappahannock River sooner or later, if we don't get around the fire first—and if we can keep ahead of it."

They topped a little hillock and saw more of the extent of their danger. In a half mile of spreading, the fire had gained three times as much breadth. And to their right the fire even then roared in among the trees of a forest so thick as to be jungle. The blaze fairly raced through it as if the fire made its own wind; which in fact it did. To their left it crackled fiercely in underbrush which, as they fled, blazed higher.

And then, as if to add mockery to their very real danger, a genuinely brisk breeze sprang up suddenly. Sparks and blazing bits of leaves, fragments of ash and small, unsubstantial coals began to fall among them. Bertha Ketterling yelped suddenly as a tiny live coal touched the flesh of her cheek. Harris' horse squealed and kicked as something singed it. They galloped madly ahead. Trees rose about them. The white beam of Minott's flashlight seemed almost ludicrous in the fierce red glare from behind, but at least it showed the way.

IX

Something large and dark and clumsy lumbered cumbersomely into the space between Grady's statue and the post-office building. The arc lights showed it clearly, and it was not anything which should be wandering in the streets of Atlanta, Georgia, at any hour of the day or night. A taxicab chauffeur saw it and nearly tore off a wheel in turning around to get away. A policeman saw it, and turned very pale as he grabbed at his beat telephone to report it. But there had been too many queer things happening this day for him to suspect his own sanity, and the *Journal* had printed too much news from elsewhere for him to disbelieve his own eyes.

The thing was monstrous, reptilian, loathesome. It was eighty feet long, of which at least fifty was head and tail and the rest flabby-fleshed body. It may have weighed twenty-five or thirty tons, but its head was not much larger than that of a large horse. That tiny head swung about stupidly. The thing was bewildered. It put down a colossal foot, and water gushed up from a broken water main beneath the pavement. The thing did not notice. It moved vaguely, exhaling a dank and musty odor.

The clang of police-emergency cars and the scream of fire-engine sirens filled the air. An ambulance flashed into view—and was struck by a balancing sweep of the mighty tail. The ambulance careened and crashed.

The thing uttered a plaintive cry, ignoring the damage its tail had caused. The sound was like that of a bleat, a thousand times multiplied. It peered ceaselessly around, seeming to feel trapped by the tall buildings about it, but it was too stupid to retrace its steps for escape.

Somebody screamed in the distance as police cars and fire engines reached the spot where the first thing swayed and peered and moved in quest of escape. Two other things, smaller than the first, came lumbering

after it. Like it, they had monstrous bodies and dispro-
portionately tiny heads. One of them blundered stupidly
into a hook-and-ladder truck. Truck and beast went
down, and the beast bleated like the first.

Then some fool began to shoot. Other fools joined in.
Steel-jacketed bullets poured into the mountains of reptilian flesh. Police sub-machine guns raked the monsters.
Those guns were held by men of great daring, who could
not help noting the utter stupidity of the things out of the
great swamp which had appeared where Inman Park
used to be.

The bullets stung. They hurt. The three beasts
bleated and tried bewilderedly and very clumsily to escape. The largest tried to climb a five-story building,
and brought it down in sheer wreckage.

Before the last of them was dead—or rather, before
it ceased to move its great limbs, because the tail moved
jerkily for a long time and its heart was still beating
spasmodically when loaded on a city dump cart next
day—before the last of them was dead they had made
sheer chaos of three blocks of business buildings in the
heart of Atlanta, had killed seventeen men, and the best
testimony is that they made not one attempt to fight.
Their whole and only thought was to escape. The destruction they wrought and the deaths they caused were
due to their clumsiness and stupidity.

X

The leading horses floundered horribly. They sank to
their fetlocks in something soft and very spongy. Bertha
Ketterling squawked in terror as her mount's motion
changed.

Blake said crisply in the blackness: "It feels like
plowed ground. Better use the light again, Professor
Minott."

The sky behind them glowed redly. The forest fire
still trailed them. For miles of front, now, it shot up
sparks and flame and a harsh red glare which illumined
the clouds of its own smoke.

The flashlight stabbed at the earth. The ground was

plowed. It was softened by the hands of men. Minott kept the light on as little gasps of thankfulness arose.

Then he said sardonically: "Do you know what this crop is? It's lentils. Are lentils grown in Virginia? Perhaps! We'll see what sort of men these may happen to be."

He swung to follow the line of the furrows.

Tom Hunter said miserably: "If that's plowed ground, it's a damn shallow furrow. A one-horse plow'd throw up more dirt than that."

A light glowed palely in the distance. Every person in the party saw it at the same instant. As if by instinct, the head of every horse swerved for it.

"We'll want to be careful," said Blake quietly. "These may be Chinese, too."

The light was all of a mile distant. They moved over the plowed ground cautiously.

Suddenly the hoofs of Lucy Blair's horse rang on stone. The noise was startlingly loud. Other horses, following hers, clattered thunderously. Minott flashed down the light again. Dressed stone. Cut stone. A roadway built of dressed-stone blocks, some six or eight feet wide. Then one of the horses shivered and snorted. It pranced agitatedly, edging away from something on the road. Minott swept the flashlight beam along the narrow way.

"The only race," he said dryly, "that ever built roads like this was the Romans. They made their military roads like this. But they didn't discover America that we know of."

The beam touched something dark. It came back and steadied. One of the girls uttered a stifled exclamation. The beam showed dead men. One was a man with a shield and sword and a helmet such as the soldiers of ancient Rome are pictured as having worn. He was dead. Half his head had been blown off. Lying on top of him there was a man in a curious gray uniform. He had died of a sword wound.

The beam searched around. More bodies. Many Roman-accoutered figures. Four or five men in what looked remarkably like the uniform that might be worn by soldiers of the Confederate Army—if a Confederate Army could be supposed to exist.

"There's been fighting," said Blake composedly. "I guess somebody from the Confederacy—that time path, say—started to explore what must have seemed a damned strange happening. And these Romans—if they are Romans—jumped them."

Something came shambling through the darkness. Minott threw the flash beam upon it. It was human, yes. But it was three parts naked, and it was chained, and it had been beaten horribly, and there were great sores upon its body from other beatings. It was bony and emaciated. The insensate ferocity of sheer despair marked it. It was brutalized by its sufferings until it was just human, barely human, and nothing more.

It squinted at the light, too dull of comprehension to be afraid.

Then Minott spoke, and at his words it groveled in the dirt. Minott spoke harshly, in half-forgotten Latin, and the groveling figure mumbled words which had been barbarous Latin to begin with, and through its bruised lips were still further mutilated.

"It's a slave," said Minott coldly. "Strange men— Confederates, I suppose—came from the north today. They fought and killed some of the guards at this estate. This slave denies it, but I imagine he was heading north in hopes of escaping to them. When you think of it, I suppose we're not the only explorers to be caught out of our own time path by some shift or another."

He growled at the slave and rode on, still headed for the distant light. "What—what are you going to do?" asked Maida faintly.

"Go on to the villa yonder and ask questions," said Minott dryly. "If Confederates hold it, we'll be well received. If they don't, we'll still manage to earn a welcome. I intend to camp along a time fault and cross over whenever a time shift brings a Norse settlement in sight. Consequently, I want exact news of places where they've been seen, if such news is to be had."

Maida Haynes pressed close to Blake. He put a reassuring hand on her arm as the horses trudged on over the soft ground. The firelight behind them grew brighter. Occasional resinous, coniferous trees flared upward and threw fugitive red glows upon the riding figures. But gradually the glare grew steadier and stronger. The white walls of a rambling stucco house became visible—outbuildings—barns. A monstrous structure which looked startlingly like a barracks.

It was a farm, an estate, a Roman villa transplanted to the very edge of a wilderness. It was—Blake remembered vaguely—like a picture he had once seen of a Roman villa in England, restored to look as it had been before Rome withdrew her legions from Britain and left the island to savagery and darkness. There were small mounds of curing hay about them, through which the horses picked their way. Blake suddenly wrinkled his nostrils suspiciously. He sniffed.

Maida pressed close to him. Her lips formed words. Lucy Blair rode close to Minott, glancing up at him from time to time. Harris rode beside Bertha Ketterling, and Bertha sat her horse as if she were saddle sore. Tom Hunter clung close to Minott as if for protection, leaving Janet Thompson to look out for herself.

"Jerry," said Maida, "What—what do you think?"

"I don't like it," admitted Blake in a low tone. "But we've got to tag along. I think I smell——"

Then a sudden swarm of figures leaped at the horses—wild figures, naked figures, sweaty and reeking and almost maniacal figures, some of whom clanked chains as they leaped. A voice bellowed orders at them from a distance, and a whip cracked ominously.

Before the struggle ended, there were just two shots fired. Blake fired them both and wheeled about. Then a horse streaked away, and Bertha Ketterling was bawling plaintively, and Tom Hunter babbled hysterically, and Harris swore with a complete lack of his customary air of apology.

Minott seemed to be buried under a mass of foul bodies like the rest, but he rasped at his captors in an authoritative tone. They fell away from him, cringing as if by instinct. And then torches appeared suddenly and slaves appeared in their light—slaves of every possible degree of filth and degradation, of every possible racial mixture, but unanimous in a desperate abjectness before their master amid the torchbearers.

He was a short, fat man, in an only slightly modified toga. He drew it close about his body as the torchbearers held their flares close to the captives. The torchlight showed the captives, to be sure, but also it showed the puffy, self-indulgent, and invincibly cruel features of the man who owned these slaves and the villa. By his pose and the orders he gave in a curiously corrupt Latin, he showed that he considered he owned the captives, too.

XI

The deputy from Aisne-le-Sur decided that it had been very wise indeed for him to walk in the fresh air. Paris at night is stimulating. That curious attack of vertigo had come of too much champagne. The fresh air had dispelled the fumes. But it was odd that he did not know exactly where he was, though he knew his Paris well.

These streets were strange. The houses were unlike any that he remembered ever having seen before. In the light of the street lamps—and they were unusual, too—there was a certain unfamiliar quality about their architecture. He puzzled over it, trying to identify the peculiar *flair* these houses showed.

He became impatient. After all, it was necessary for him to return home sometime, even though his wife—— The deputy from Aisne-le-Sur shrugged. Then he saw bright lights ahead. He hastened his steps. A magnificent mansion, brilliantly illuminated.

The clattering of many hoofs. A cavalry escort, forming up before the house. A pale young man emerged, escorted by a tall, fat man who kissed his hand as if in an ecstasy of admiration. Dismounted cavalrymen formed a lane from the gateway to the car. Two young officers followed the pale young man, ablaze with decorations. The deputy from Aisne-le-Sur noted subconsciously that he did not recognize their uniforms. The car door was open and waiting. There was some oddity about the car, but the deputy could not see clearly just what it was.

There was much clicking of heels—steel blades at salute. The pale young man patiently allowed the fat man to kiss his hand again. He entered the car. The two bemedaled young officers climbed in after him. The car rolled away. Instantly, the cavalry escort clattered with it, before it, behind it, all around it.

The fat man stood on the sidewalk, beaming and rubbing his hands together. The dismounted cavalrymen swung to their saddles and trotted briskly after the others.

The deputy from Aisne-le-Sur stared blankly. He saw another pedestrian, halted like himself to regard the spectacle. He was disturbed by the fact that this pedestrian was clothed in a fashion as perturbingly unfamiliar as these houses and the spectacle he had witnessed.

"Pardon, m'sieu'," said the deputy from Aisne-le-Sur, "I do not recognize my surroundings. Would you tell me——"

"The house," said the other caustically, "is the hotel of Monsieur le Duc de Montigny. Is it possible that in 1935 one does not know of Monsieur le Duc? Or more especially of Madame la Duchesse, and what she is and where she lives?"

The deputy from Aisne-le-Sur blinked. "Montigny? Montigny? No," he admitted. "And the young man of the car, whose hand was kissed by——"

"Kissed by Monsieur le Duc?" The stranger stared frankly. *"Mon dieu!* Where have you come from that you do not recognize Louis the Twentieth? He has but departed from a visit to madame his mistress."

"Louis—Louis the Twentieth!" stammered the deputy from Aisne-le-Sur. "I—I do not understand!"

"Fool!" said the stranger impatiently. "That was the king of France, who succeeded his father as a child of ten and has been free of the regency for but six months—and already ruins France!"

The long-distance operator plugged in with a shaking hand. "Number please. . . . I am sorry, sir, but we are unable to connect you with Camden. . . . The lines are down. . . . Very sorry, sir." She plugged in another line. "Hello. . . . I am sorry, sir, but we are unable to connect you with Jenkintown. The lines are down. . . . Very sorry, sir."

Another call buzzed and lighted up.

"Hello. . . . I am sorry, sir. We are unable to connect you with Dover. The lines are down. . . ." Her hands worked automatically. "Hello. . . . I am sorry, but we are unable to connect you with New York. The lines are down. . . .No, sir. We cannot route it by Atlantic City. The lines are down. . . . Yes, sir, I know the telegraph companies cannot guarantee delivery. . . . No, sir, we cannot reach Pittsburgh, either, to get a message through. . . ." Her voice quivered. "No, sir, the lines are down to Scranton. . . . And Harrisburg, too. Yes, sir. . . . I am sorry, but we cannot get a message of any sort out of Philadelphia in any direction. . . . We have tried to arrange communication by radio, but no calls are answered. . . ."

She covered her face with her hands for an instant. Then she plugged in and made a call herself:

"Minnie! Haven't they heard anything? . . . Not anything? . . . What? They phoned for more police? . . . The—the operator out there says there's fighting? She hears a lot of shooting? . . . What is it, Minnie? Don't they even know? . . . They—they're using the armored cars from the banks to fight with, too? . . . But what are they fighting? What? . . . My folks are out there, Minnie! My folks are out there!"

The doorway of the slave barracks closed and great bars slammed against its outer side. Reeking, foul, unbreathable air closed about them like a wave. Then a babbling of voices all about. The clanking of chains. The rustling of straw, as if animals moved. Some one screeched; howled above the others. He began to gain the ascendancy. There was almost some attention paid to him, though a minor babbling continued all about.

Maida said in a strained voice: "I—I can catch a word

here and there. He's—telling these other slaves how we were captured. It's—Latin, of sorts."

Bertha Ketterling squalled suddenly, in the absolute dark. "Somebody touched me!" she bawled. "A man!"

A voice spoke humorously, somewhere near. There was laughter. It was the howled laughter of animals. Slaves were animals, according to the Roman notion. A rustling noise, as if in the noisome freedom of their barracks the utterly brutalized slaves drew nearer to the newcomers. There could be sport with new-captured folk, not yet degraded to their final status.

Lucy Blair cried out in a stifled fashion. There was a sharp, incisive *crack*. Somebody fell. More laughter.

"I knocked him out!" snapped Minott. "Harris! Hunter! Feel around for something we can use as clubs! These slaves intend to haze us, and in their own den there's no attempt to control them. Even if they kill us they'll only be whipped for it. And the women will——"

Something, snarling, leaped for him in the darkness. The authoritative tone of Minott's voice was hateful. A yapping sound arose. Other figures closed in. Reduced to the status of animals, the slaves of the Romans behaved as beasts when locked in their monster kennel. The newcomers were hateful if only because they had been freemen, not slaves. The women were clean and they were frightened—and they were prey. Chains clanked ominously. Foul breaths tainted the air. The reek of utter depravity, of human beings brought lower than beasts, filled the air. It was utterly dark.

Bertha Ketterling began to blubber noisily. There was the sudden savage sound of a blow meeting flesh. Then pandemonium and battle, and the sudden terrified screams of Lucy Blair. The panting of men who fought. The sound of blows. A man howled. Another shrieked curses. A woman screamed shrilly.

Bang! Bang! Bang-bang! Shots outside, a veritable fusillade of them. Running feet. Shouts. The bars at the doorway fell. The great doors opened, and men stood in the opening with whips and torches, bellowing for the slaves to come out and attack something yet unknown. They were being called from their kennel like dogs. Four of the whip men came inside, flogging the slaves out, while the sound of shots continued. The slaves shrank away, or bounded howling for the open air. But there were three of them who would never shrink or cringe again.

Minott and Harris stood embattled in a corner of the slave shed. Lucy Blair, her hair disheveled, crouched behind Minott, who held a heavy beam in desperate readiness for further battle. Harris, likewise, held a clumsy club. With torchlight upon him, his air of savage defiance turned to one of quaint apology for the dead slave at his feet. And Hunter and two of the girls competed in stark panic for a position behind him. Maida Haynes, dead white, stood backed against a wall, a jagged fragment of gnawed bone held dagger-wise.

The whips lashed out at them. Voices snarled at them. The whips again. Minott struck out furiously, a huge welt across his face.

And revolvers cracked at the great door. Blake stood there, a revolver in each hand, his eyes blazing. A torchbearer dropped, and the torches flared smokily in the foul mud of the flooring.

"All right," said Blake fiercely. "Come on out!"

Hunter was the first to reach him, babbling and gasping. There was sheer uproar all about. A huge grain shed roared upward in flames. Figures rushed crazily all about it. From the flames came another explosion, then two, then three more.

"Horses over here by the stables," said Blake, his face white and very deadly indeed. "They haven't unsaddled them. The stable slaves haven't figured out the cinches yet. I put some revolver bullets in the straw when I set fire to that grain shed. They're going off from time to time."

A figure with whip and dagger raced around an outbuilding and confronted them. Blake shot him down.

Minott said hoarsely: "Give me a revolver, Blake! I want to——"

"Horses first!" snapped Blake.

They raced into a courtyard. Two shots. The slaves fled, howling. Out of the courtyard, bent low in the saddle. They swept close to the villa itself. On a little raised terrace before it, a stout man in an only slightly modified toga raged. A slave groveled before him. He kicked the abject figure and strode out, shouting commands in a voice that cracked with fury. The horses loomed up and he shook his fists at the riders, purple with wrath, incapable of fear because of his beastly rage.

Blake shot him dead, swung off his horse, and stripped the toga from him. He flung it to Maida.

"Take this!" he said savagely. "I could kill——"

There was now no question of his leadership. He led the retreat from the villa. The eight horses headed north again, straight for the luridly flaming forest.

They stopped once more. Behind them, another building of the estate had caught from the first. Sheer confusion ruled. The slaughter of the master disrupted all organization. The roof of the slave barracks caught: Screams and howls of pure panic reached even the fugitives. Then there were racing, maddened figures rushing here and there in the glare of the fires. Suddenly there was fighting. A howling ululation arose.

Minott worked savagely, stripping clothing from the bodies slain in that incredible, unrecorded conflict of Confederate soldiers and Roman troops, in some unguessable pathway of space and time. Blake watched behind, but he curtly commanded the salvaging of rifles and ammunition from the dead Confederates—if they were Confederates.

And as Hunter, still gasping hysterically, took the load of yet unfamiliar weapons upon his horse, the eight felt a certain incredible, intolerable vertigo and nausea. The burning forest ahead vanished from their sight. Instead, there was darkness. A noisome smell came down wind; dampness and strange, overpowering perfumes of strange, colored flowers. Something huge and deadly bellowed in the space before them which smelled like a monstrous swamp.

The liner *City of Baltimore* plowed through the open sea in the first pale light of dawn. The skipper, up on the bridge, wore a worried frown. The radio operator came up. He carried a sheaf of radiogram forms. His eyes were blurry with loss of sleep.

"Maybe it was me, sir," he reported heavily. "I felt awful funny for a while last night, and then all night long I couldn't raise a station. I checked everything and couldn't find anything wrong. But just now I felt awful sick and funny for a minute, and when I come out of it the air was full of code. Here's some of it. I don't understand how I could have been sick so I couldn't hear code, sir, but——"

The skipper said abruptly: "I had that sick feeling, too—dizzy. So did the man at the wheel. So did everybody. Give me the messages."

His eyes ran swiftly over the yellow forms.

"News flash: Half of London disappeared at 2:00 a.m. this morning. . . . S.S. *Manzanillo* reporting. Sea serpent which attacked this ship during the night and seized four sailors returned and was rammed five minutes ago. It seems to be dying. Our bow badly smashed. Two forward compartments flooded. . . . Warning to all mariners. Pack ice seen floating fifty miles off New York harbor. . . . News flash: Madrid, Spain, has undergone inexplicable change. All buildings formerly known now unrecognizable from the air. Air fields have vanished. Mosques seem to have taken the place of churches and cathedrals. A flag bearing the crescent floats. . . . European population of Calcutta seems to have been massacred. S.S. *Carib* reports harbor empty, all signs of European domination vanished, and hostile mobs lining shore. . . ."

The skipper of the *City of Baltimore* passed his hand over his forehead. He looked uneasily at the radio operator. "Sparks," he said gently, "you'd better go see the ship's doctor. Here! I'll detail a man to go with you."

"I know," said Sparks bitterly. "I guess I'm nuts, all right. But that's what come through."

He marched away with his head hanging, escorted by a sailor. A little speck of smoke appeared dead ahead.

It became swiftly larger. With the combined speed of the two vessels, in a quarter of an hour the other ship was visible. In half an hour it could be made out clearly. It was long and low and painted black, but the first incredible thing was that it was a paddle steamer, with two sets of paddles instead of one, and the after set revolving more swiftly than the forward.

The skipper of the *City of Baltimore* looked more closely through his glasses and nearly dropped them in stark amazement. The flag flying on the other ship was black and white only. A beam wind blew it out swiftly. A white death's-head, with two crossed bones below it—the traditional flag of piracy!

Signal flags fluttered up in the rigging of the other ship. The skipper of the *City of Baltimore* gazed at them, stunned.

"Gibberish!" he muttered. "It don't make sense! They aren't international code. Not the same flags at all!"

Then a gun spoke. A monstrous puff of black powder smoke billowed over the other ship's bow. A heavy shot crashed into the forepart of the *City of Baltimore:* An instant later it exploded.

"I'm crazy, too!" said the skipper dazedly.

A second shot. A third and fourth. The black steamer sheered off and started to pound the *City of Baltimore* in a businesslike fashion. Half the bridge went overside. The forward cargo hatch blew up with a cloud of smoke from an explosion underneath.

Then the skipper came to. He roared orders. The big ship heeled as it came around. It plunged forward at vastly more than its normal cruising speed. The guns on the other ship doubled and redoubled their rate of fire. Then the black ship tried to dodge. But it had not time.

The *City of Baltimore* rammed it. But at the very last moment the skipper felt certain of his own insanity. It was too late to save the other ship then. The *City of Baltimore* cut it in two.

XII

The pale gray light of dawn filtered down through an incredible thickness of foliage. It was a subdued, a feeble twilight when it reached the earth where a tiny camp fire burned. That fire gave off thick smoke from water-soaked wood. Hunter tended it, clad in ill-assorted remnants of a gray uniform.

Harris worked patiently at a rifle, trying to understand exactly how it worked. It was unlike any rifle with which he was familiar. The bolt action was not really a bolt action at all, and he'd noticed that there was no rifling in the barrel. He was trying to understand how the long bullet was made to revolve. Harris, too, had substituted Confederate gray for the loin cloth flung him for sole covering when with the others he was thrust into the slave pen of the Roman villa. Minott sat with his head in his hands, staring at the opposite side of the stream. On his face was all bitterness.

Blake listened. Maida Haynes sat and looked at him. Lucy Blair darted furtive, somehow wistful, glances at Minott. Presently she moved to sit beside him. She asked him an anxious question. The other two girls sat by the fire. Bertha Ketterling was slouched back against a tree-fern trunk. Her head had fallen back. She snored. With the exception of Blake, all of them were barefoot.

Blake came back to the fire. He nodded across the little stream. "We seem to have come to the edge of a time fault," he observed. "This side of the stream is definitely Carboniferous-period vegetation. The other side isn't as primitive, but it isn't of our time, anyhow. Professor Minott!"

Minott lifted his head. "Well?" he demanded bitterly.

"We need some information," said Blake. "We've been here for hours, and there's been no further change in time paths that we've noticed. Is it likely that the scrambling of time and space is ended, sir? If it has, and the time paths stay jumbled, we'll never find our world intact, of course, but we can hunt for colonies, perhaps even cities, of our own kind of people."

"If we do," said Minott bitterly, "how far will we get? We're practically unarmed. We can't——"

Blake pointed to the salvaged rifles. "Harris is working on the arms problem now," he said dryly. "Besides, the girls didn't take the revolvers from their saddlebags. We've still two revolvers for each man and an extra pair. Those Romans thought the saddlebags were decorations, perhaps, or they intended to examine the saddles as a whole. We'll make out. What I want to know is, has the time-scrambling process stopped?"

Lucy Blair said something in a low tone. But Minott glanced at Maida Haynes. She was regarding Blake worshipfully.

Minott's eyes burned. He scowled in surpassing bitterness. "It probably hasn't," he said harshly. "I expect it to keep up for probably two weeks or more of—of duration. I use that term to mean time elapsed in all the time paths simultaneously. We can't help thinking of time as passing on our particular time path only. Yes. I expect disturbances to continue for two weeks or more, if everything in time and space is not annihilated."

Blake sat down.

Insensibly Maida Haynes moved closer to him. "Could you explain, sir? We can only wait here. As nearly as I can tell from the topography, there's a village across this litle stream in our time. It ought to be in sight if our time path ever turns up in view, here."

Minott unconsciously reassumed some of his former authoritative manner. Their capture and scornful dismissal to the status of slaves had shaken all his self-confidence. Before, he had felt himself not only a member of a superior race, but a superior member of that race. In being enslaved he had been both degraded and scorned. His vanity was still gnawed at by that memory, and his self-confidence shattered by the fact that he had been able to kill only two utterly brutalized slaves, without in the least contributing to his own freedom. Now, for the first time, his voice took on a semblance of its old ring.

"We—we know that gravity warps space," he said precisely. "From observation we have been able to discover the amount of warping produced by a given mass. We can calculate the mass necessary to warp space so that it will close in completely, making a closed universe which is unreachable and undetectable in any of the dimensions we know. We know, for example, that if two gigantic star masses of a certain combined mass were to rush together, at the instant of their collision there would not be a great cataclysm. They would simply vanish. But they would not cease to exist. They would merely cease to exist in our space and time. They would have created a space and time of their own."

Harris said apologetically: "Like crawling in a hole and pulling the hole in after you. I read something like that in a Sunday supplement once, sir."

Minott nodded. He went on in a near approach to a classroom manner. "Now, imagine that two such universes have been formed. They are both invisible from the space and time in which they were formed. Each exists in its own space and time, just as our universe does. But each must also exist in a certain—well, hyper-space, because if closed spaces are separated, there must be some sort of something in between them, else they would be together."

"Really," said Blake, "you're talking about something we can infer, but ordinarily can't possibly learn anything about by observation."

"Just so." Minott nodded. "Still, if our space is closed, we must assume that there are other closed spaces. And don't forget that other closed spaces would be as real—are as real—as our closed space is."

"But what does it mean?" asked Blake.

"If there are other closed spaces like ours, and they exist in a common medium—the hyper-space from which they and we alike are sealed off—they might be likened to, say, stars and planets in our space, which are separated by space and yet affect each other through space. Since these various closed spaces are separated by a logically necessary hyper-space, it is at least probable that they should affect each other through that hyper-space."

Blake said slowly: "Then the shiftings of time

paths—well, they're the result of something on the order of tidal strains. If another star got close to the sun,
our planets would crack up from tidal strains alone.
You're suggesting that another closed space has got
close to our closed space in hyper-space. It's awfully
confused, sir."

"I have calculated it," said Minott harshly. "The
odds are four to one that space and time and universe,
every star and every galaxy in the skies, will be obliterated in one monstrous cataclysm when even the past
will never have been. But there is one chance in four,
and I planned to take full advantage of it. I planned—I
planned——"

Then he stood up suddenly. His figure straightened.
He struck his hands together savagely. "By Heaven, I
still plan! We have arms. We have books, technical
knowledge, formulas the cream of the technical
knowledge of earth packed in our saddlebags! Listen to
me! We cross this stream now. When the next change
comes, we strike across whatever time path takes the
place of this. We make for the Potomac, where that
aviator saw Norse ships drawn up! I have Anglo-Saxon
and early Norse vocabularies in the saddlebags. We'll
make friends with them. We'll teach them. We'll lead
them. We'll make ourselves masters of the world
and——"

Harris said apologetically: "I'm sorry, sir, but I
promised Bertha I'd take her home, if it was humanly
possible. I have to do it. I can't join you in becoming an
emperor, even if the breaks are right."

Minott scowled at him.

"Hunter?"

"I—I'll do as the others do," said Hunter uneasily.
"I—I'd rather go home."

"Fool!" snarled Minott.

Lucy Blair said loyally: "I—I'd like to be an em-
press, Professor Minott."

Maida Haynes stared at her. She opened her mouth
to speak. Blake absently pulled a revolver from his
pocket and looked at it meditatively as Minott clenched

and unclenched his hands. The veins stood out on his forehead. He began to breathe heavily.

"Fools!" he roared. "Fools! You'll never get back! Yet you throw away——"

Swift, sharp, agonizing vertigo smote them all. The revolver fell from Blake's hands. He looked up. A dead silence fell upon all of them.

Blake stood shakily upon his feet. He looked, and looked again. "That——" He swallowed. "That is King George courthouse, in King George County, in Virginia, in our time I think—— Hell! Let's get across that stream."

He picked up Maida in his arms. He started.

Minott moved quickly and croaked: "Wait!"

He had Blake's dropped revolver in his hand. He was desperate, hunted; gray with rage and despair. "I—I offer you, for the last time—I offer you riches, power, women, and——"

Harris stood up, the Confederate rifle still in his hands. He brought the barrel down smartly upon Minott's wrist.

Blake waded across and put Maida safely down upon the shore. Hunter was splashing frantically through the shallow water. Harris was shaking Bertha Ketterling to wake her. Blake splashed back. He rounded up the horses. He loaded the salvaged weapons over a saddle. He shepherded the three remaining girls over. Hunter was out of sight. He had fled toward the painted buildings of the courthouse. Blake led the horses across the stream. Minott nursed his numbed wrist. His eyes blazed with the fury of utter despair.

"Better come along," said Blake quietly.

"And be a professor of mathematics?" Minott laughed savagely. "No! I stay here!"

Blake considered. Minott was a strange, an unprepossessing figure. He was haggard. He was desperate. Standing against the background of a Carboniferous jungle, in the misfitting uniform he had stripped from a dead man in some other path of time, he was even pitiable. Shoeless, unshaven, desperate, he was utterly defiant.

"Wait!" said Blake.

He stripped off the saddlebags from six of the horses. He heaped them on the remaining two. He led those two back across the stream and tethered them.

Minott regarded him with an implacable hatred. "If I hadn't chosen you," he said harshly, "I'd have carried my original plan through. I knew I shouldn't choose you. Maida liked you too well. And I wanted her for myself. It was my mistake, my only one."

Blake shrugged. He went back across the stream and remounted.

Lucy Blair looked doubtfully back at the solitary, savage figure. "He's—brave, anyhow," she said unhappily.

A faint, almost imperceptible, dizziness affected all of them. It passed. By instinct they looked back at the tall jungle. It still stood. Minott looked bitterly after them.

"I've—I've something I want to say!" said Lucy Blair breathlessly. "D—don't wait for me!"

She wheeled her horse about and rode for the stream. Again that faint, nearly imperceptible, dizziness. Lucy slapped her horse's flank frantically.

Maida cried out: "Wait, Lucy! It's going to shift——"

And Lucy cried over her shoulder: "That's what I want! I'm going to stay——"

She was halfway across the stream—more than halfway. Then the vertigo struck all of them.

XIII

Everyone knows the rest of the story. For two weeks longer there were still occasional shiftings of the time paths. But gradually it became noticeable that the number of time faults—in Professor Minott's phrase—were decreasing in number. At the most drastic period, it has been estimated that no less than twenty-five per cent of the whole earth's surface was at a given moment in some other time path than its own. We do not know of any portion of the earth which did not vary from its own time path at some period of the disturbance.

That means, of course, that practically one hundred

per cent of the earth's population encountered the conditions caused by the earth's extraordinary oscillations sidewise in time. Our scientists are no longer quite as dogmatic as they used to be. The dialectics of philosophy have received a serious jolt. Basic ideas in botany, zoölogy, and even philology have been altered by the new facts made available by our travels sidewise in time.

Because of course it was the fourth chance which happened, and the earth survived. In our time path, at any rate. The survivors of Minott's exploring party reached King George courthouse barely a quarter of an hour after the time shift which carried Minott and Lucy Blair out of our space and time forever. Blake and Harris searched for a means of transmitting the information they possessed to the world at large. Through a lonely radio amateur a mile from the village, they sent out Minott's theory on short waves. Shorn of Minott's pessimistic analysis of the probabilities of survival, it went swiftly to every part of the world then in its proper relative position. It was valuable, in that it checked explorations in force which in some places had been planned. It prevented, for example, a punitive military expedition from going past a time fault in Georgia, past which a scalping party of Indians from an uncivilized America had retreated. It prevented the dispatch of a squadron of destroyers to find and seize Leifsholm, from which a viking foray had been made upon North Centerville, Massachusetts. A squadron of mapping planes was recalled from reconnaissance work above a Carboniferous swamp in West Virginia, just before the time shift which would have isolated them forever.

Some things, though, no knowledge could prevent. It has been estimated that no less than five thousand persons in the United States are missing from their own space and time, through having adventured into the strange landscapes which appeared so suddenly. Many must have perished. Some, we feel sure, have come in contact with one or another of the distinct civilizations we now know exist.

Conversely, we have gained inhabitants from other time paths. Two cohorts of the Twenty-second Roman

Legion were left upon our soil near Ithaca, New York. Four families of Chinese peasants essayed to pick berries in what they considered a miraculous strawberry-patch in Virginia, and remained there when that section of ground returned to its proper *milieu*.

A Russian village remains in Colorado. A French settlement in the—in their time undeveloped—Middle West. A part of the northern herd of buffalo has returned to us, two hundred thousand strong, together with a village of Cheyenne Indians who had never seen either horses or firearms. The passenger pigeon, to the number of a billion and a half birds, has returned to North America.

But our losses are heavy. Besides those daring individuals who were carried away upon the strange territories they were exploring, there are the overwhelming disasters affecting Tokyo and Rio de Janeiro and Detroit. The first two we understand. When the causes of oscillation sidewise in time were removed, most of the earth sections returned to their proper positions in their own time paths. But not all. There is a section of Post-Cambrian jungle left in eastern Tennessee. The Russian village in Colorado has been mentioned, and the French trading post in the Middle West. In some cases sections of the oscillating time paths remained in new positions, remote from their points of origin.

That is the cause of the utter disappearance of Rio and of Tokyo. Where Rio stood, an untouched jungle remains. It is of our own geological period, but it is simply from a path in time in which Rio de Janeiro never happened to be built. On the site of Tokyo stands a forest of extraordinarily primitive type, about which botanists and paleontologists still debate. Somewhere, in some space and time, Tokyo and Rio yet exist and their people still live on. But Detroit——

We still do not understand what happened to Detroit. It was upon an oscillating segment of earth. It vanished from our time, and it returned to our time. But its inhabitants did not come back with it. The city was empty—deserted as if the hundreds of thousands of human beings who lived in it had simply evaporated into the air. There have been some few signs of struggle seen, but they may have been the result of panic. The city of Detroit returned to its own space and time untouched, unharmed, unlooted, and undisturbed. But no living thing, not even a domestic animal or a caged bird, was in it when it came back. We do not understand that at all.

Perhaps if Professor Minott had returned to us, he could have guessed at the answer to the riddle. What fragmentary papers of his have been shown to refer to the time upheaval have been of inestimable value. Our whole theory of what happened depends on the papers Minott left behind as too unimportant to bother with, in addition, of course, to Blake's and Harris' account of his explanation to them. Tom Hunter can remember little that is useful. Maida Haynes has given some worthwhile data, but it covers ground we have other observers for. Bertha Ketterling also reports very little.

The answers to a myriad problems yet elude us, but in the saddlebags given to Minott by Blake as equipment for his desperate journey through space and time, the answers to many must remain. Our scientists labor diligently to understand and to elaborate the figures Minott thought of trivial significance. And throughout the world many minds turn longingly to certain saddlebags, loaded on a led horse, following Minott and Lucy Blair through unguessable landscapes, to unimaginable adventures, with revolvers and textbooks as their armament for the conquest of a world.

Proxima Centauri

I

THE ADASTRA, FROM a little distance, already shone in the light of the approaching sun. The vision disks which scanned the giant space ship's outer skin relayed a faint illumination to the visiplates within. They showed the monstrous, rounded bulk of the metal globe, criss-crossed with girders too massive to be transported by any power less than that of the space ship itself. They showed the whole, five thousand foot globe as an ever so faintly glowing object, seemingly motionless in mid-space.

In that seeming, they lied. Monstrous as the ship was, and apparently too huge to be stirred by any conceivable power, she was responding to power now. At a dozen points upon her faintly glowing side there were openings. From those openings there flowed out tenuous purple flames. They gave little light, those flames—less than the star ahead—but they were the disintegration blasts from the rockets which had lifted the *Adastra* from the surface of Earth and for seven years had hurled it on through interstellar space toward Proxima Centauri, nearest of the fixed stars to humanity's solar system.

Now they hurled it forward no more. The mighty ship was decelerating. Thirty-two and two-tenths feet per second, losing velocity at the exact rate to maintain the effect of Earth's gravity within its bulk, the huge globe slowed. For months braking had been going on. From a peak-speed measurably near the velocity of light, the first of all vessels to span the distance between two solar systems had slowed and slowed, and would

59

reach a speed of maneuver some sixty million miles from the surface of the star.

Far, far ahead, Proxima Centauri glittered invitingly. The vision disks that showed its faint glow upon the space ship's hull had counterparts which carried its image within the hull, and in the main control room it appeared enlarged very many times. An old, white-bearded man in uniform regarded it meditatively. He said slowly, as if he had said the same thing often before:

"Quaint, that ring. It is double, like Saturn's. And saturn has nine moons. One wonders how many planets this sun will have."

The girl said restlessly: "We'll find out soon, won't we? We're almost there. And we already know the rotation period of one of them! Jack said that——"

Her father turned deliberately to her. "Jack?"

"Gary," said the girl. "Jack Gary."

"My dear," said the old man mildly, "he seems well-disposed, and his abilities are good, but he is a Mut. Remember!"

The girl bit her lip.

The old man went on, quite slowly and without rancor: "It is unfortunate that we have had this division among the crew of what should have been a scientific expedition conducted in the spirit of a crusade. You hardly remember how it began. But we officers know only too well how many efforts have been made by the Muts to wreck the whole purpose of our voyage. This Jack Gary is a Mut. He is brilliant, in his way. I would have brought him into the officers' quarters, but Alstair investigated and found undesirable facts which made it impossible."

"I don't believe Alstair!" said the girl evenly. "And, anyhow, it was Jack who caught the signals. And he's the one who's working with them, officer or Mut! And he's human, anyhow. It's time for the signals to come again and you depend on him to handle them."

The old man frowned. He walked with a careful steadiness to a seat. He sat down with an old man's habitual and rather pathetic caution. The *Adastra*, of course, required no such constant vigilance at the controls as the interplanetary space ships require. Out here in emptiness there was no need to watch for meteors, for traffic, or for those queer and yet inexplicable force fields which at first made interplanetary flights so hazardous.

The ship was so monstrous a structure, in any case, that the tinier meteorites could not have harmed her. And at the speed she was now making greater ones would be notified by the induction fields in time for observation and if necessary the changing of her course.

A door at the side of the control room opened briskly and a man stepped in. He glanced with conscious professionalism at the banks of indicators. A relay clicked, and his eyes darted to the spot. He turned and saluted the old man with meticulous precision. He smiled at the girl.

"Ah, Alstair," said the old man. "You are curious about the signals, too?"

"Yes, sir. Of course! And as second in command I rather like to keep an eye on signals. Gary is a Mut, and I would not like him to gather information that might be kept from the officers."

"That's nonsense!" said the girl hotly.

"Probably," agreed Alstair. "I hope so. I even think so. But I prefer to leave out no precaution."

A buzzer sounded. Alstair pressed a button and a vision plate lighted. A dark, rather grim young face stared out of it.

"Very well, Gary," said Alstair curtly.

He pressed another button. The vision plate darkened and lighted again to show a long corridor down which a solitary figure came. It came close and the same face looked impassively out. Alstair said even more curtly:

"The other doors are open, Gary. You can come straight through."

"I think that's monstrous!" said the girl angrily as the plate clicked off. "You know you trust him! You have to! Yet every time he comes into officers' quarters you act as if you thought he had bombs in each hand and all the rest of the men behind him!"

Alstair shrugged and glanced at the old man, who said tiredly:

"Alstair is second in command, my dear, and he will be commander on the way back to Earth. I could wish you would be less offensive."

But the girl deliberately withdrew her eyes from the brisk figure of Alstair with its smart uniform, and rested her chin in her hands to gaze broodingly at the farther wall. Alstair went to the banks of indicators, surveying them in detail. The ventilator hummed softly. A relay clicked with a curiously smug, self-satisfied note. Otherwise there was no sound.

The *Adastra*, mightiest work of the human race, hurtled on through space with the light of a strange sun shining faintly upon her enormous hull. Twelve lambent purple flames glowed from holes in her forward part. She was decelerating, lessening her speed by thirty-two point two feet per second per second, maintaining the effect of Earth's gravity within her bulk.

Earth was seven years behind and uncounted millions of billions of miles. Interplanetary travel was a commonplace in the solar system now, and a thriving colony on Venus and a precariously maintained outpost on the largest of Jupiter's moons promised to make space commerce thrive even after the dead cities of Mars had ceased to give up their incredibly rich loot. But only the *Adastra* had ever essayed space beyond Pluto.

She was the greatest of ships, the most colossal structure ever attempted by men. In the beginning, indeed, her design was derided as impossible of achievement by the very men who later made her building a fact. Her framework beams were so huge that, once cast, they could not be moved by any lifting contrivance at her builders' disposal. Therefore the molds for them were built and the metal poured in their final position as a part of the ship. Her rocket tubes were so colossal that the necessary supersonic vibrations—to neutralize the disintegration effect of the Caldwell field—had to be generated at thirty separate points on each tube, else the disintegration of her fuel would have spread to the tubes themselves and the big ship afterward, with even the mother planet following in a burst of lambent purple flame. At full acceleration a set of twelve tubes disintegrated five cubic centimeters of water per second.

Her diameter was a shade over five thousand feet. Her air tanks carried a reserve supply which could run her crew of three hundred for ten months without purification. Her stores, her shops, her supplies of raw and finished materials, were in such vast quantities that to enumerate them would be merely to recite meaningless figures.

There were even four hundred acres of food-growing space within her, where crops were grown under sun lamps. Those crops used waste organic matter as fertilizer and restored exhaled carbon dioxide to use, in part as oxygen and in part as carbohydrate foodstuffs.

The *Adastra* was a world in herself. Given power, she could subsist her crew forever, growing her food supplies, purifying her own internal atmosphere without loss and without fail, and containing space within which every human need could be provided, even solitude.

And starting out upon the most stupendous journey in human history, she had formally been given the status of a world, with her commander empowered to make and enforce all needed laws. Bound for a destination four light-years distant, the minimum time for her return was considered to be fourteen years. No crew could possibly survive so long a voyage undecimated. Therefore the enlistments for the voyage had not been by men, but by families.

There were fifty children on board when the *Adastra* lifted from Earth's surface. In the first year of her voyage ten more were born. It had seemed to the people of Earth that not only could the mighty ship subsist her crew forever, but that the crew itself, well-nourished and with more than adequate facilities both for amusement and education, could so far perpetuate itself as to make a voyage of a thousand years as practicable as the mere journey to Proxima Centauri.

And so it could, but for a fact at once so needless and so human that nobody anticipated it. The fact was tedium. In less than six months the journey had ceased to become a great adventure. To the women in particular, the voyage of the big ship became deadly routine.

The *Adastra* itself took on the semblance of a gigantic apartment house without newspapers, department stores, new film plays, new faces, or even the relieving annoyances of changeable weather. The sheer completeness of all preparations for the voyage made the voyage itself uneventful. That meant tedium.

Tedium meant restlessness. And restlessness, with women on board who had envisioned high adventure, meant the devil to pay. Their husbands no longer appeared as glamorous heroes. They were merely human beings. The men encountered similar disillusionments. Pleas for divorce flooded the commander's desk, he being legally the fount of all legal action. During the eighth month there was one murder, and in the three months following, two more.

A year and a half out from Earth, and the crew was in a state of semi-mutiny originating in sheer boredom. By two years out, the officers' quarters were sealed off from the greater part of the *Adastra*'s interior, the crew was disarmed, and what work was demanded of the mutineers was enforced by force guns in the hands of the officers. By three years out, the crew was demanding a return to Earth. But by the time the *Adastra* could be slowed and stopped from her then incredible velocity, she would be so near her destination as to make no appreciable difference in the length of her total voyage. For the rest of the time the members of the crew strove to relieve utter monotony by such vices and such pastimes as could be improvised in the absence of any actual need to work.

The officers' quarters referred to the underlings by a term become habitual, a contraction of the word "mutineers." The crew came to have a queer distaste for all dealing with the officers. But, despite Alstair, there was no longer much danger of an uprising. A certain mental equilibrium had—very late—developed.

From the nerve-racked psychology of dwellers in an isolated apartment house, the greater number of the *Adastra*'s complement came to have the psychology of dwellers in an isolated village. The difference was profound. In particular the children who had come to maturity during the long journey through space were well-adjusted to the conditions of isolation and of routine.

Jack Gary was one of them. He had been sixteen when the trip began, son of a rocket-tube engineer whose death took place the second year out. Helen Bradley was another. She had been fourteen when her father, as designer and commanding officer of the mighty globe, pressed the control key that set the huge rockets into action.

Her father had been past maturity at the beginning. Aged by responsibility for seven uninterrupted years, he was an old man now. And he knew, and even Helen knew without admitting it, that he would never survive the long trip back. Alstair would take his place and the despotic authority inherent in it, and he wanted to marry Helen.

She thought of these things, with her chin cupped in her hand, brooding in the control room. There was no sound save the humming of the ventilator and the infrequent smug click of a relay operating the automatic machinery to keep the *Adastra* a world in which nothing ever happened.

A knock on the door. The commander opened his eyes a trifle vaguely. He was very old now, the commander. He had dozed.

Alstair said shortly, "Come in!" and Jack Gary entered.

He saluted, pointedly to the commander. Which was according to regulations, but Alstair's eyes snapped.

"Ah, yes," said the commander. "Gary. It's about time for more signals, isn't it?"

"Yes, sir."

Jack Gary was very quiet, very businesslike. Only once, when he glanced at Helen, was there any hint of anything but the formal manner of a man intent on his job. Then his eyes told her something, in an infinitely small fraction of a second, which changed her expression to one of flushed content.

Short as the glance was, Alstair saw it. He said harshly:

"Have you made any progress in deciphering the signals, Gary?"

Jack was setting the dials of a pan-wave receptor, glancing at penciled notes on a calculator pad. He continued to set up the reception pattern.

"No, sir. There is still a sequence of sounds at the beginning which must be a form of call, because a part of the same sequence is used as a signature at the close. With the commander's permission I have used the first part of that call sequence as a signature in our signals in reply. But in looking over the records of the signals I've found something that looks important."

The commander said mildly: "What is it, Gary?"

"We've been sending signals ahead of us on a tight beam, sir, for some months. Your idea was to signal ahead, so that if there were any civilized inhabitants on planets about the sun, they'd get an impression of a peaceful mission."

"Of course!" said the commander. "It would be tragic for the first of interstellar communications to be unfriendly!"

"We've been getting answers to our signals for nearly three months. Always at intervals of a trifle over thirty hours. We assumed, of course, that a fixed transmitter was sending them, and that it was signaling once a day when the station was in the most favorable position for transmitting to us."

"Of course," said the commander gently. "It gave us the period of rotation of the planet from which the signals come."

Jack Gary set the last dial and turned on the switch. A low-pitched hum arose, which died away. He glanced at the dials again, checking them.

"I've been comparing the records, sir, making due allowance for our approach. Because we cut down the distance between us and the star so rapidly, our signals today take several seconds less to reach Proxima Centauri than they did yesterday. Their signals should show the same shortening of interval, if they are actually sent out at the same instant of planetary time every day."

The commander nodded benevolently.

"They did, at first," said Jack. "But about three weeks ago the time interval changed in a brand-new fashion. The signal strength changed, and the wave form altered a little, too, as if a new transmitter was sending. And the first day of that change the signals came through one second earlier than our velocity of approach would account for. The second day they were three seconds earlier, the third day six, the fourth day ten, and so on. They kept coming earlier by a period indicating a linear function until one week ago. Then the rate of change began to decrease again."

"That's nonsense!" said Alstair harshly.

"It's records," returned Jack curtly.

"But how do you explain it, Gary?" asked the commander mildly.

"They're sending now from a space ship, sir," replied Jack briefly, "which is moving toward us at four times our maximum acceleration. And they're flashing us a signal at the same interval, according to their clocks, as before."

A pause. Helen Bradley smiled warmly. The commander thought carefully. Then he admitted:

"Very good, Gary! It sounds plausible. What next?"

"Why, sir," said Jack, "since the rate of change shifted, a week ago, it looks as if that other space ship started to decelerate again. Here are my calculations, sir. If the signals are sent at the same interval they kept up for over a moment, there is another space ship headed toward us, and she is decelerating to stop and reverse and will be matching our course and speed in four days and eighteen hours. They'll meet and surprise us, they think."

The commander's face lighted up. "Marvelous, Gary! They must be far advanced indeed in civilization! Intercourse between two such peoples, separated by four light-years of distance! What marvels we shall

learn! And to think of their sending a ship far beyond
their own system to greet and welcome us!"

Jack's expression remained grim.

"I hope so, sir," he said dryly.

"What now, Gary?" demanded Alstair angrily.

"Why," said Jack deliberately, "they're still pretending that the signals come from their planet, by signaling
at what they think are the same times. They could exchange signals for twenty-four hours a day, if they
chose, and be working out a code for communication.
Instead, they're trying to deceive us. My guess is that
they're coming at least prepared to fight. And if I'm
right, their signals will begin in three seconds, exactly."

He stopped, looking at the dials of the receptor. The
tape which photographed the waves as they came in,
and the other which recorded the modulations, came
out of the receptor blank. But suddenly, in just three
seconds, a needle kicked over and tiny white lines appeared on the rushing tapes. The speaker uttered
sounds.

It was a voice which spoke. So much was clear. It
was harsh yet sibilant, more like the stridulation of an
insect than anything else. But the sounds it uttered were
modulated as no insect can modulate its outcry. They
formed what were plainly words, without vowels or consonants, yet possessing expression and varying in pitch
and tone quality.

The three men in the control room had heard them
many times before, and so had the girl. But for the first
time they carried to her an impression of menace, of
threat, of a concealed lust for destruction that made her
blood run cold.

II

The space ship hurtled on through space, her rocket
tubes sending forth small and apparently insufficient
purple flames which emitted no smoke, gave off no gas,
and were seemingly nothing but small marsh fires
inexplicably burning in emptiness.

There was no change in her outer appearance. There

had been none to speak of in years. At long, infrequent intervals men had emerged from air locks and moved about her sides, bathing the steel they walked on and themselves alike with fierce glares from heat lamps lest the cold of her plating transmit itself through the material of the suits and kill the men like ants on red-hot metal. But for a long time no such expedition had been needed.

Only now, in the distant faint light of Proxima Centauri, a man in a space suit emerged from such a tiny lock. Instantly he shot out to the end of a threadlike life line. The constant deceleration of the ship not only simulated gravity within. Anything partaking of its motion showed the same effect. The man upon its decelerating forward side was flung away from the ship by his own momentum, the same force which, within it, had pressed his feet against the floors.

He hauled himself back laboriously, moving with an exaggerated clumsiness in his bloated space suit. He clung to handholds and hooked himself in place, while he worked an electric drill. He moved still more clumsily to another place and drilled again. A third, and fourth, and fifth. For half an hour or more, then, he labored to set up on the vast steel surface, which seemed always above him, an intricate array of wires and framework. In the end he seemed content. He hauled himself back to the air lock and climbed within. The *Adastra* hurtled onward, utterly unchanged save for a very tiny fretwork of wire, perhaps thirty feet across, which looked more like a microscopic barbed-wire entanglement than anything else.

Within the *Adastra*, Helen Bradley greeted Jack warmly as he got out of his space suit.

"It was horrible!" she told him, "to see you dangling like that! With millions of miles of empty space below you!"

"If my line had parted," said Jack quietly, "your father'd have turned the ship and caught up to me. Let's go turn on the inductor and see how the new reception grid works."

He hung up the space suit. As they turned to go

through the doorway their hands touched accidentally. They looked at each other and faltered. They stopped, Helen's eyes shining. They unconsciously swayed toward each other. Jack's hands lifted hungrily.

Footsteps sounded close by. Alstair, second in command of the space ship, rounded a corner and stopped short.

"What's this?" he demanded savagely. "Just because the commander's brought you into officers' quarters, Gary, it doesn't follow that your Mut methods of romance can come, too!"

"You dare!" cried Helen furiously.

Jack, from a hot dull flush, was swiftly paling to the dead-white of rage.

"You'll take that back," he said very quietly indeed, "or I'll show you Mut methods of fighting with a force gun! As an officer, I carry one, too, now!"

Alstair snarled at him.

"Your father's been taken ill," he told Helen angrily. "He feels the voyage is about over. Anticipation has kept up his strength for months past, but now he's——"

With a cry, the girl fled.

Alstair swung upon Jack. "I take back nothing," he snapped. "You're an officer, by order of the commander. But you're a Mut besides, and when I'm commander of the *Adastra* you don't stay an officer long! I'm warning you! What were you doing here?"

Jack was deathly pale, but the status of officer on the *Adastra,* with its consequent opportunity of seeing Helen, was far too precious to be given up unless at the last extremity. And, besides, there was the work he had in hand. His work, certainly, could not continue unless he remained an officer.

"I was installing an interference grid on the surface," he said, "to try to discover the sending station of the messages we've been getting. It will also act, as you know, as an inductor up to a certain range, and in its range is a good deal more accurate than the main inductors of the ship."

"Then get to your damned work," said Alstair

harshly, "and pay full attention to it and less to romance!"

Jack plugged in the lead wire from his new grid to the pan-wave receptor. For an hour he worked more and more grimly. There was something very wrong. The inductors showed blank for all about the *Adastra*. The interference grid showed an object of considerable size not more than two million miles distant and to one side of the *Adastra*'s course. Suddenly, all indication of that object's existence blanked out. Every dial on the pan-wave receptor went back to zero.

"Damnation!" said Jack under his breath.

He sat up a new pattern on the controls, calculated a moment and deliberately changed the pattern on the spare bank of the main inductors, and then simultaneously switched both instruments to their new frequencies. He waited, almost holding his breath, for nearly half a minute. It would take so long for the inductor waves of the new frequency to reach out the two million miles and then collapse into the analyzers and give their report of any object in space which had tended to deform them.

Twenty-six, twenty-seven, twenty-eight seconds. Every alarm bell on the monstrous ship clanged furiously! Emergency doors hissed into place all over the vessel, converting every doorway into an air lock. Seconds later, the visiplates in the main control room began to flash alight.

"Reporting, Rocket Control!" "Reporting, Air Service!" "Reporting, Power Supply!"

Jack said crisply: "The main inductors report an object two million miles distant with velocity in our direction. The commander is ill. Please find Vice Commander Alstair."

Then the door of the control room burst open and Alstair himself raged into the room.

"What the devil!" he rasped. "Ringing a general alarm? Have you gone mad? The inductors——"

Jack pointed to the main inductor bank. Every dial bore out the message of the still-clanging alarms. Alstair stared blankly at them. As he looked, every dial went back to zero.

And Alstair's face went as blank as the dials.

"They felt out our inductor screens," said Jack grimly, "and put out some sort of radiation which neutralized them. So I set up two frequencies, changed both, and they couldn't adjust their neutralizers in time to stop our alarms."

Alstair stood still, struggling with the rage which still possessed him. Then he nodded curtly.

"Quite right. You did good work. Stand by."

And, quite cool and composed, he took command of the mighty space ship, even if there was not much for him to do. In five minutes, in fact, every possible preparation for emergency had been made and he turned again to Jack.

"I don't like you," he said coldly. "As one man to another, I dislike you intensely. But as vice commander and acting commander at the moment, I have to admit that you did good work in uncovering this little trick of our friends to get within striking distance without our knowing they were anywhere near."

Jack said nothing. He was frowning, but it was because he was thinking of Helen. The *Adastra* was huge and powerful, but she was not readily maneuverable. She was enormously massive, but she could not be used for ramming. And she possessed within herself almost infinite destructiveness, in the means of producing Caldwell fields for the disintegration of matter, but she contained no weapon more dangerous than a two-thousand-kilowatt vortex gun for the destruction of dangerous animals or vegetation where she might possibly land.

"What's your comment?" demanded Alstair shortly. "How do you size up the situation?"

"They act as if they're planning hostilities," replied Jack briefly, "and they've got four times our maximum acceleration so we can't get away. With that acceleration they ought to be more maneuverable, so we can't dodge them. We've no faintest idea of what weapons they carry, but we know that we can't fight them unless their weapons are very puny indeed. There's just one chance that I can see."

"What's that?"

"They tried to slip up on us. That looks as if they intended to open fire without warning. But maybe they are frightened and only expected to examine us without our getting a chance to attack them. In that case, our only bet is to swing over our signaling beam to the space ship. When they realize we know they're there and still aren't getting hostile, they may not guess we can't fight. They may think we want to be friendly and they'd better not start anything with a ship our size that's on guard."

"Very well. You're detailed to communication duty," said Alstair. "Go ahead and carry out that program. I'll consult the rocket engineers and see what they can improvise in the way of fighting equipment. Dismiss!"

His tone was harsh. It was arrogant. It rasped Jack's nerves and made him bristle all over. But he had to recognize that Alstair wasn't letting his frank dislike work to the disadvantage of the ship. Alstair was, in fact, one of those ambitious officers who are always cordially disliked by everybody, at all times, until an emergency arises. Then their competence shows up.

Jack went to the communications-control room. It did not take long to realign the transmitter beam. Then the sender began to repeat monotonously the recorded last message from the *Adastra* to the distant and so far unidentified planet of the ringed star. And while the signal went out, over and over again, Jack called on observations control for a sight of the strange ship.

They had a scanner on it now and by stepping up illumination to the utmost, and magnification to the point where the image was as rough as an old-fashioned half-tone cut, they brought the strange ship to the visiplate as a six-inch miniature.

It was egg-shaped and perfectly smooth. There was no sign of external girders, of protruding atmospheric-navigation fins, of escape-boat blisters. It was utterly featureless save for tiny spots which might be portholes, and rocket tubes in which intermittent flames flickered.

It was still decelerating to match the speed and course of the *Adastra*.

"Have you got a spectroscope report on it?" asked Jack.

"Yeh," replied the observations orderly. "An' I don't believe it. They're using fuel rockets—some organic compound. An' the report says the hull of that thing is cellulose, not metal. It's wood, on the outside."

Jack shrugged. No sign of weapons. He went back to his own job. The space ship yonder was being penetrated through and through by the message waves. Its receptors could not fail to be reporting that a tight beam was upon it, following its every movement, and that its presence and probable mission were therefore known to the mighty ship from out of space.

But Jack's own receptors were silent. The tape came out of them utterly blank. No—a queer, scrambled, blurry line, as if the analyzers were unable to handle the frequency which was coming through. Jack read the heat effect. The other space ship was sending with a power which meant five thousand kilowatts pouring into the *Adastra*. Not a signal. Grimly, Jack heterodyned the wave on a five-meter circuit and read off its frequency and type. He called the main control.

"They're pouring short stuff into us," he reported stiffly to Alstair. "About five thousand kilowatts of thirty-centimeter waves, the type we use on Earth to kill weevils in wheat. It ought to be deadly to animal life, but of course our hull simply absorbs it."

Helen. Impossible to stop the *Adastra*. They'd started for Proxima Centauri. Decelerating though they were, they couldn't check much short of the solar system, and they were already attacked by a ship with four times their greatest acceleration. Pouring a deadly frequency into them—a frequency used on Earth to kill noxious insects. Helen was——

"Maybe they think we're dead! They'll know our transmitter's mechanical."

The G.C. phone snapped suddenly, in Alstair's voice.

"Attention, all officers! The enemy space ship has poured what it evidently considers a deadly frequency into us, and is now approaching at full acceleration! Orders are that absolutely no control of any sort is to be varied by a hair's breadth. Absolutely no sign of living intelligence within the *Adastra* is to be shown. You will stand by all operative controls, prepared for maneuver if it should be necessary. But we try to give the impression that the *Adastra* is operating on automatic controls alone! Understood?"

Jack could imagine the reports from the other control rooms. His own receptor sprang suddenly into life. The almost hooted sounds of the call signal, so familiar that they seemed words. Then an extraordinary jumble of noises—words in a human voice. More stridulated sounds. More words in perfectly accurate English. The English words were in the tones and accents of an officer of the *Adastra*, plainly recorded and retransmitted.

"Communications!" snapped Alstair. "You will not answer this signal! It is an attempt to find out if we survived their ray attack!"

"Check," said Jack.

Alstair was right. Jack watched and listened as the receptor babbled on. It stopped. Silence for ten minutes. It began again. The *Adastra* hurtled on. The babble from space came to an end. A little later the G.C. phone snapped once more:

"The enemy space ship has increased its acceleration, evidently convinced that we are all dead. It will arrive in approximately four hours. Normal watches may be resumed for three hours unless an alarm is given."

Jack leaned back in his chair, frowning. He began to see the tactics Alstair planned to use. They were bad tactics, but the only ones a defenseless ship like the *Adastra* could even contemplate. It was at least ironic that the greeting the *Adastra* received at the end of a seven-years' voyage through empty space be a dose of a type of radiation used on Earth to exterminate vermin.

But the futility of this attack did not mean that all attacks would be similarly useless. And the *Adastra* simply could not be stopped for many millions of miles, yet. Even if Alstair's desperate plan took care of this particular assailant and this particular weapon, it would not mean—it could not!—that the *Adastra* or the folk within had any faintest chance of defending themselves. And there was Helen——

III

The visiplates showed the strange space ship clearly, now, even without magnification. It was within five miles of the *Adastra* and it had stopped. Perfectly egg-shaped, without any protuberance whatever except the rocket tubes in its rear, it hung motionless with relation to the Earth ship, which meant that its navigators had analyzed her rate of deceleration long since and had matched all the constants of her course with precision.

Helen, her face still tear-streaked, watched as Jack turned up the magnification, and the illumination with it. Her father had collapsed very suddenly and very completely. He was resting quietly now, dozing almost continuously, with his face wearing an expression of utter contentment.

He had piloted the *Adastra* to its first contact with the civilization of another solar system. His lifework was done and he was wholly prepared to rest. He had no idea, of course, that the first actual contact with the strange space ship was a burst of short waves of a frequency deadly to all animal life.

The space ship swelled on the visiplate as Jack turned the knob. He brought it to an apparent distance of a few hundred yards only. With the illumination turned up, even the starlight on the hull would have been sufficient to show any surface detail. But there was literally none. No rivet, no bolt, no line of joining plates. A row of portholes were dark and dead within.

"And it's wood!" repeated jack. "Made out of some sort of cellulose which stands the cold of space!"

Helen said queerly: "It looks to me as if it had been grown, rather than built."

Jack blinked. He opened his mouth as if to speak, but the receptor at his elbow suddenly burst into the hootlike stridulations which were the signals from the egglike ship. Then English words, from recordings of previous signals from the *Adastra*. More vowelless, modulated phrases. It sounded exactly as if the beings in the other space ship were trying urgently to open communication and were insisting that they had the key to the *Adastra*'s signals. The temptation to reply was great.

"They've got brains, anyhow," said Jack grimly.

The signals were cut off. Silence. Jack glanced at the wave tape. It showed the same blurring as before.

"More short stuff. At this distance, it ought not only to kill us, but even sterilize the interior of the whole ship. Lucky our hull is heavy alloy with a high hysteresis-rate. Not a particle of that radiation can get through."

Silence for a long, long time. The wave tape showed that a terrific beam of thirty-centimeter waves continued to play upon the *Adastra*. Jack suddenly plugged in observations and asked a question. Yes, the outer hull was heating. It had gone up half a degree in fifteen minutes.

"Nothing to worry about in that," grunted Jack. "Fifteen degrees will be the limit they can put it up, with this power."

The tape came out clear. The supposed death radiation was cut off. The egg-shaped ship darted forward. And then for twenty minutes or more Jack had to switch from one outside vision disk to another to keep it in sight. It hovered about the huge bulk of the *Adastra* with a wary inquisitiveness. Now half a mile away, now no more than two hundred yards, the thing darted here and there with an amazing acceleration and as amazing a breaking power. It had only the rocket tubes at the smaller end of its egg-shaped form. It was necessary for it to fling its whole shape about to get a new direction, and the gyroscopes within it must have been tremendously powerful. Even so, the abruptness of its turns was startling.

"I wouldn't like to be inside that thing!" said Jack. "We'd be crushed to a pulp by their normal navigation methods. They aren't men like us. They can stand more than we can."

The thing outside seemed sentient, seemed alive. And by the eagerness of its movements it seemed the more horrible, flitting about the gigantic space ship it now believed was a monstrous coffin.

It suddenly reversed itself and shot back toward the *Adastra*. Two hundred yards, one hundred yards, a hundred feet. It came to a cushioned stop against the surface of the Earth vessel.

"Now we'll see something of them," said Jack crisply. "They landed right at an air lock. They know what that is, evidently. Now we'll see them in their space suits."

But Helen gasped. A part of the side of the strange ship seemed to swell suddenly. It bulged out like a blister. It touched the surface of the *Adastra*. It seemed to adhere. The point of contact grew larger.

"Good Lord!" said Jack blankly. "Is it alive? And is it going to try to eat our ship?"

The general-communication phone rasped sharply:

"Officers with arms to the air lock GH41 immediately! The Centaurians are opening the air lock from the outside. Wait orders there! The visiplate in the air lock is working and you will be informed. Go ahead!"

The phone clicked off. Jack seized a heavy gun, one of the force rifles which will stun a man at anything up to eighteen hundred yards and kill at six, when used at full power. His side arm hung in its holster. He swung for the door.

"Jack!" said Helen desperately.

He kissed her. It was the first time their lips had touched, but it seemed the most natural thing in the world, just then. He went racing down the long corridors of the *Adastra* to the rendezvous. And as he raced, his thoughts were not at all those of a scientist and an officer of Earth's first expedition into interstellar space. Jack was thinking of Helen's lips touching his desperately, of her soft body pressed close to him.

A G.C. speaker whispered overhead as he ran:

"They're inside the air lock. They opened it without trouble. They're testing our air, now. Apparently it suits them all."

The phone fell behind. Jack ran on, panting. Somebody else was running ahead. There were half a dozen, a dozen men grouped at the end of the corridor. A murmur from the side wall.

". . . rking at the inner air-lock door. Only four or five of them, apparently, will enter the ship. They are to be allowed to get well away from the air lock. You will keep out of sight. When the emergency locks go on it will be your signal. Use your heavy force guns, increasing power from minimum until they fall paralyzed. It will probably take a good deal of power to subdue them. They are not to be killed if it can be avoided. Ready!"

There were a dozen or more officers on hand. The fat rocket chief. The lean air officer. Subalterns of the other departments. The rocket chief puffed audibly as he wedged himself out of sight. Then the clicking of the inner air-lock door. It opened into the anteroom. Subdued, muffled hootings came from that door. The Things—whatever they were—were inspecting the space suits there. The hootings were distinctly separate and distinctly intoned. But they suddenly came as a babble. More than one Thing was speaking at once. There was excitement, eagerness, an extraordinary triumph in these voices.

Then something stirred in the doorway of the air-lock anteroom. A shadow crossed the threshold. And then the Earthmen saw the creatures who were invading the ship.

For an instant they seemed almost like men. They had two legs, and two dangling things—tentacles—which apparently served as arms and tapered smoothly to ends which split into movable, slender filaments. The tentacles and the legs alike seemed flexible in their entire lengths. There were no "joints" such as men use in walking, and the result was that the Centaurians walked with a curiously rolling gait.

Most startling, though, was the fact that they had no heads. They came wabbling accustomedly out of the air lock, and at the end of one "arm" each carried a curious, semi-cylindrical black object which they handled as if it might be a weapon. They wore metallic packs fastened to their bodies. The bodies themselves were queerly "grained." There was a tantalizing familiarity about the texture of their skin.

Jack, staring incredulously, looked for eyes, for nostrils, for a mouth. He saw twin slits only. He guessed at them for eyes. He saw no sign of any mouth at all. There was no hair. But he saw a scabrous, brownish substance on the back of one of the Things which turned to hoot excitedly at the rest. It looked like bark, like tree bark. And a light burst upon Jack. He almost cried out, but instead reached down and quietly put the lever of his force gun at full power at once.

The Things moved on. They reached a branching corridor and after much arm waving and production of their apparently articulated sounds they separated into two parties. They vanished. Their voices dwindled. The signal for an attack upon them had not yet been given. The officers, left behind, stirred uneasily. But a G.C. phone whispered.

"Steady! They think we're all dead. They're separating again. We may be able to close emergency doors and have each one sealed off from all the rest and then handle them in detail. You men watch the air lock!"

Silence. The humming of a ventilator somewhere near by. Then, suddenly, a man screamed shrilly a long distance off, and on the heels of his outcry there came a new noise from one of the Things. It was a high-pitched squealing noise, triumphant and joyous and unspeakably horrible.

Other squealings answered it. There were rushing sounds, as if the other Things were running to join the first. And then came a hissing of compressed air and a hum of motors. Doors snapped shut everywhere, sealing off every part of the ship from every other part. And in the dead silence of their own sealed compartment, the officers on guard suddenly heard inquiring hoots.

Two more of the Things came out of the air lock. One of the men moved. The Thing saw him and turned its half-cylindrical object upon him. The man—it was the communications officer—shrieked suddenly and leaped convulsively. He was stone dead even as his muscles tensed for that incredible leap.

And the Thing emitted a high-pitched triumphant note which was exactly like the other horrible sound they had heard, and sped eagerly toward his body. One of the long, tapering arms lashed out and touched the dead man's hand.

Then Jack's force gun began to hum. He heard another and another open up. In seconds the air was filled with a sound like that of a hive of angry bees. Three more of the Things came out of the air lock, but they dropped in the barrage of force-gun beams. It was only when there was a sudden rush of air toward the lock, showing that the enemy ship had taken alarm and was darting away, that the men dared cease to fill that doorway with their barrage. Then it was necessary to seal the air lock in a hurry. Only then could they secure the Things that had invaded the *Adastra*.

Two hours later, Jack went into the main control room and saluted with an exact precision. His face was rather white and his expression entirely dogged and resolved. Alstair turned to him, scowling.

"I sent for you," he said harshly, "because you're likely to be a source of trouble. The commander is dead. You heard it?"

"Yes, sir," said Jack grimly. "I heard it."

"In consequence, I am commander of the *Adastra*," said Alstair provocatively. "I have, you will recall, the power of life and death in cases of mutinous conduct, and it is also true that marriage on the *Adastra* is made legal only by executive order bearing my signature."

"I am aware of the fact, sir," said Jack more grimly still.

"Very well," said Alstair deliberately. "For the sake of discipline, I order you to refrain from all association with Miss Bradley. I shall take disobedience of the order as mutiny. I intend to marry her myself. What have you to say to that?"

Jack said as deliberately: "I shall pay no attention to the order, sir, because you aren't fool enough to carry out such a threat! Are you such a fool that you don't see we've less than one chance in five hundred of coming out of this? If you want to marry Helen, you'd better put all your mind on giving her a chance to live!"

A savage silence held for a moment. The two men glared furiously at each other, the one near middle age, the other still a young man, indeed. Then Alstair showed his teeth in a smile that had no mirth whatever in it.

"As man to man I dislike you extremely," he said harshly. "But as commander of the *Adastra* I wish I had a few more like you. We've had seven years of routine on this damned ship, and every officer in quarters is rattled past all usefulness because an emergency has come at last. They'll obey orders but there's not one fit to give them. The communications officer was killed by one of those devils, wasn't he?"

"Yes, sir."

"Very well. You're brevet communications officer. I hate your guts, Gary, and I do not doubt that you hate mine, but you have brains. Use them now. What have you been doing?"

"Adjusting a dictawriter, sir, to get a vocabulary of one of these Centaurian's speech, and hooking it up as a two-way translator, sir."

Alstair stared in momentary surprise, and then nodded. A dictawriter, of course, simply analyzes a word into its phonetic parts, sets up the analysis, and picks out a card to match its formula. Normally, the card then actuates a printer. However, instead of a type-choosing record, the card can contain a record of an equivalent word in another language, and then operates a speaker.

Such machines have been of only limited use on Earth because of the need for so large a stock of vocabulary words, but have been used to some extent for literal translations both of print and speech. Jack proposed to record a Centaurian's vocabulary with English equivalents, and the dictawriter, hearing the queer hoots the strange creature uttered, would pick out a card which would then cause a speaker to enunciate its English synonym.

The reverse, of course, would also occur. A conversation could be carried on with such a prepared vocabulary without awaiting practice in understanding or imitating the sounds of another language.

"Excellent!" said Alstair curtly. "But put some one else on the job if you can. It should be reasonably simple, once it's started. But I need you for other work. You know what's been found out about these Centaurians, don't you?"

"Yes, sir. Their hand weapon is not unlike our force guns, but it seems to be considerably more effective. I saw it kill the communications officer."

"But the creatures themselves!"

"I helped tie one of them up."

"What do you make of it? I've a physician's report, but he doesn't believe it himself!"

"I don't blame him, sir," said Jack grimly. "They're not our idea of intelligent beings at all. We haven't any word for what they are. In one sense they're plants, apparently. That is, their bodies seem to be composed of cellulose fibers where ours are made of muscle fibers. But they are intelligent, fiendishly intelligent.

"The nearest we have to them on Earth are certain carnivorous plants, like pitcher plants and the like. But they're as far above a pitcher plant as a man is above a sea anemone, which is just as much an animal as a man is. My guess, sir, would be that they're neither plant nor animal. Their bodies are built up of the same materials as earthly plants, but they move about like animals do on Earth. They surprise us, but we may surprise them, too. It's quite possible that the typical animal form on their planet is sessile like the typical plant form on ours."

Alstair said bitterly: "And they look on us, animals, as we look on plants!"

Jack said without expression: "Yes, sir. They eat through holes in their arms. The one who killed the communications officer seized his arm. It seemed to exude some fluid that liquefied his flesh instantly. It sucked the liquid back in at once. If I may make a guess, sir——"

"Go ahead," snapped Alstair. "Everybody else is running around in circles, either marveling or sick with terror."

"The leader of the party, sir, had on what looked like an ornament. It was a band of leather around one of its arms."

"Now, what the devil——"

"We had two men killed. One was the communications officer and the other was an orderly. When we finally subdued the Centaurian who'd killed that orderly, it had eaten a small bit of him, but the rest of the orderly's body had undergone some queer sort of drying process, from chemicals the Thing seemed to carry with it."

Alstair's throat worked as if in nausea. "I saw it."

"It's a fanciful idea," said Jack grimly, "but if a man was in the position of that Centaurian, trapped in a space ship belonging to an alien race, with death very probably before him, well, about the only thing a man would strap to his body, as the Centaurian did the dried, preserved body of that orderly——"

"Would be gold," snapped Alstair. "Or platinum, or jewels which he would hope to fight clear with!"

"Just so," said Jack. "Now, I'm only guessing, but those creatures are not human, nor even animals. Yet they eat animal food. They treasure animal food as a human being would treasure diamonds. An animal's remains—leather—they wear as an ornament. It looks to me as if animal tissue was rather rare on their planet, to be valued so highly. In consequence——"

Alstair stood up, his features working. "Then our bodies would be the same as gold to them! As diamonds! Gary, we haven't the ghost of a chance to make friends with these fiends!"

Jack said dispassionately: "No; I don't think we have. If a race of beings with tissues of metallic gold landed on Earth, I rather think they'd be murdered. But there's another point, too. There's Earth. From our course, these creatures can tell where we came from, and their space ships are rather good. I think I'll put somebody else on the dictawriter job and see if I can flash a message back home. No way to know whether they get it, but they ought to be watching for one by the time it's there. Maybe they've improved their receptors. They intended to try, anyhow."

"Men could meet these creatures' ships in space," said Alstair harshly, "if they were warned. And guns might answer, but if they didn't handle these devils Caldwell torpedoes would. Or a suicide squad, using their bodies for bait. We're talking like dead men, Gary."

"I think, sir," said Jack, "we are dead men." Then he added: "I shall put Helen Bradley on the dictawriter, with a guard to handle the Centaurian. He'll be bound tightly."

The statement tacitly assumed that Alstair's order to avoid her was withdrawn. It was even a challenge to him to repeat it. And Alstair's eyes glowed and he controlled himself with difficulty.

"Damn you, Gary," he said savagely, "get out!"

He turned to the visiplate which showed the enemy ship as Jack left the control room.

The egg-shaped ship was two thousand miles away now, and just decelerating to a stop. In its first flight it had rocketed here and there like a mad thing. It would have been impossible to hit it with any projectile, and difficult in the extreme even to keep radiation on it in anything like a tight beam. Now, stopped stock-still with regard to the *Adastra,* it hung on, observing, very probably devising some new form of devilment. So Alstair considered, anyhow. He watched it somberly.

The resources of the *Adastra,* which had seemed so vast when she took off from Earth, were pitifully inadequate to handle the one situation which had greeted her, hostility. She could have poured out the treasures of man's civilization to the race which ruled this solar system. Savages, she could have uplifted. Even to a race superior to men she could have offered man's friendship and eager pupilage. But these creatures that——

The space ship stayed motionless. Probably signaling back to its home planet, demanding orders. Reports came in to the *Adastra*'s main control room and Alstair read them. The Centaurians were unquestionably extracting carbon dioxide from the air. That compound was to their metabolism what oxygen is to men, and in pure air they could not live.

But their metabolic rate was vastly greater than that of any plant on Earth. It compared with the rate of earthly animals. They were not plants by any definition save that of constitution, as a sea anemone is not an animal except by the test of chemical analysis.

The Centaurians had a highly organized nervous system, the equivalent of brains, and both great intelligence and a language. They produced sounds by a stridulating organ in a special body cavity. And they felt emotion.

A captive creature when presented with various objects showed special interest in machinery, showing an acute realization of the purpose of a small sound recorder and uttering into it an entire and deliberate series of sounds. Human clothing it fingered eagerly. Cloth it discarded, when of cotton or rayon, but it displayed great excitement at the feel of a woolen shirt and even more when a leather belt was given to it. It placed the belt about its middle, fastening the buckle without a fumble after a single glance at its working.

It unraveled a thread from the shirt and consumed it, rocking to and fro as if in ecstasy. When meat was placed before it, it seemed to become almost delirious with excitement. A part of the meat it consumed instantly, to ecstatic swayings. The rest it preserved by a curious chemical process, using substances from a small metal pack it had worn and for which it made gestures.

Its organs of vision were behind two slits in the upper part of its body, and no precise examination of the eyes themselves had been made. But the report before Alstair said specifically that the Centaurian displayed an avid eagerness whenever it caught sight of a human being. And that the eagerness was not of a sort to be reassuring.

It was the sort of excitement—only much greater—which it had displayed at the sight of wool and leather. As if by instinct, said the report, the captive Centaurian had several times made a gesture as if turning some weapon upon a human when first it sighted him.

Alstair read this report and others. Helen Bradley reported barely two hours after Jack had assigned her to the work.

"I'm sorry, Helen," said Alstair ungraciously. "You shouldn't have been called on for duty. Gary insisted on it. I'd have left you alone."

"I'm glad he did," said Helen steadily. "Father is dead, to be sure, but he was quite content. And he died before he found out what these Centaurians are like. Working was good for me. I've succeeded much better than I even hoped. The Centaurian I worked with was the leader of the party which invaded this ship. He understood almost at once what the dictawriter was doing, and we've a good vocabulary recorded already. If you want to talk to him, you can."

Alstair glanced at the visiplate. The enemy ship was still motionless. Easily understandable, of course. The *Adastra*'s distance from Proxima Centauri could be measured in hundreds of millions of miles, now, instead of millions of billions, but in another terminology it was light-hours away still. If the space ship had signaled its home planet for orders, it would still be waiting for a reply.

Alstair went heavily to the biology laboratory, of which Helen was in charge, just as she was in charge of the biological specimens—rabbits, sheep, and a seemingly endless array of small animals—which on the voyage had been bred for a food supply and which it had been planned to release should a planet suitable for colonizing revolve about the ringed star.

The Centaurian was bound firmly to a chair with a myriad of cords. He—she—it, was utterly helpless. Beside the chair the dictawriter and its speaker were coupled together. From the Centaurian came hooted notes which the machine translated with a rustling sound between words.

"You—are—commander—this—ship?" the machine translated without intonation.

"I am," said Alstair, and the machine hooted musically.

"This—woman—man—dead," said the machine tonelessly again, after more sounds from the extraordinary living thing which was not an animal.

Helen interjected swiftly: "I told him my father was dead."

The machine went on: "I—buy—all—dead—man—on—ship—give—metal—gold—you—like——"

Alstair's teeth clicked together. Helen went white. She tried to speak, and choked upon the words.

"This," said Alstair in mirthless bitterness, "is the beginning of the interstellar friendship we hoped to institute!"

Then the G.C. phone said abruptly:

"Calling Commander Alstair! Radiation from ahead! Several wave lengths, high intensity! Apparently several space ships are sending, though we can make out no signals!"

And then Jack Gary came into the biology laboratory. His face was set in grim lines. It was very white. He saluted with great precision.

"I didn't have to work hard, sir," he said sardonically. "The last communications officer had been taking his office more or less as a sinecure. We'd had no signals for seven years, and he didn't expect any. But they're coming through and have been for months.

"They left Earth three years after we did. A chap named Callaway, it seems, found that a circularly polarized wave makes a tight beam that will hold together forever. They've been sending to us for years past, no doubt, and we're getting some of the first messages now.

"They've built a second *Adastra*, sir, and it's being manned—hell, no! It was manned four years ago! It's on the way out here now! It must be at least three years on the way, and it has no idea of these devils waiting for it. Even if we blow ourselves to bits, sir, there'll be another ship from Earth coming, unarmed as we are, to run into these devils when it's too late to stop——"

The G.C. phone snapped again:

"Commander Alstair! Observations reporting! The external hull temperature has gone up five degrees in the past three minutes and is still climbing. Something's pouring heat into us at a terrific rate!"

Alstair turned to Jack. He said with icy politeness: "Gary, after all there's no use in our continuing to hate each other. Here is where we all die together. Why do I still feel inclined to kill you?"

But the question was rhetorical only. The reason was wholly clear. At the triply horrible news, Helen had begun to cry softly. And she had gone blindly into Jack's arms to do it.

IV

The situation was, as a matter of fact, rather worse than the first indications showed. The external hull temperature, for instance, was that of the generalizing thermometer, which averaged for all the external thermometers. A glance at the thermometer bank, through a visiphone connection, showed the rearmost side of the *Adastra* at practically normal. It was the forward hemisphere, the side nearest Proxima Centauri, which was heating. And that hemisphere was not heating equally. The indicators which flashed red lights were closely grouped.

Alstair regarded them with a stony calm in the visiplate.

"Squarely in the center of our disk, as they see it," he said icily. "It will be that fleet of space ships, of course."

Jack Gary said crisply: "Sir, the ship from which we took prisoners made contact several hours earlier than we expected. It must be that, instead of sending one vessel with a transmitter on board, they sent a fleet, and a scout ship on ahead. That scout ship has reported that we laid a trap for some of her crew, and consequently they've opened fire!"

Alstair said sharply into a G.C. transmitter:

"Sector G90 is to be evacuated at once. It is to be sealed off immediately and all occupants will emerge from air locks. Adjoining sectors are to be evacuated except by men on duty, and they will don space suits immediately."

He clicked off the phone and added calmly: "The external temperature over part of G90 is four hundred degrees now. Dull-red heat. In five minutes it should melt. They'll have a hole bored right through us in half an hour."

Jack said urgently: "Sir! I'm pointing out that they've attacked because the scout ship reported we laid a trap for some of its crew! We have just the ghost of a chance——"

"What?" demanded Alstair bitterly. "We've no weapons!"

"The dictawriter, sir!" snapped Jack. "We can talk to them now!"

Alstair said harshly: "Very well, Gary. I appoint you ambassador. Go ahead!"

He swung on his heel and went swiftly from the control room. A moment later his voice came out of the G.C. phone: "Calling the Rocket Chief! Report immediately on personal visiphone. Emergency!"

His voice cut off, but Jack was not aware of it. He was plugging in to communications and demanding full power on the transmission beam and a widening of its arc. He snapped one order after another and explained to Helen in swift asides.

She grasped the idea at once. The Centaurian in the biology laboratory was bound, of course. No flicker of expression could be discovered about the narrow slits which were his vision organs. But Helen—knowing the words of the vocabulary cards—spoke quietly and urgently into the dictawriter microphone. Hootlike noises came out of the speaker in their place, and the Centaurian stirred. Sounds came from him in turn, and the speaker said woodenly:

"I—speak—ship—planet. Yes."

And as the check-up came through from communications control, the eerie, stridulated, unconsonanted noises of his language filled the biology laboratory and went out on the widened beam of the main transmitter.

Ten thousand miles away the Centaurian scout ship hovered. The *Adastra* bored on toward the ringed sun which had been the goal of mankind's most daring expedition. From ten thousand miles she would have seemed a mere dot, but the telescopes of the Centaurians would show her every detail. From a thousand miles she would seem a toy, perhaps, intricately crisscrossed with strengthening members.

From a distance of a few miles only, though, her gigantic size could be realized fully. Five thousand feet in diameter, she dwarfed the hugest of those distant, unseen shapes in emptiness which made up a hostile fleet now pouring deadly beams upon her.

From a distance of a few miles, too, the effect of that radiation could be seen. The *Adastra*'s hull was alloy steel, tough and necessarily with a high hysteresis-rate. The alternating currents of electricity induced in that steel by the Centaurian radiation would have warmed even a copper hull. But the alloy steel grew hot. It changed color. It glowed faintly red over an area a hundred feet across.

A rocket tube in that area abruptly ceased to emit its purple, lambent flame. It had been cut off. Other rockets increased their power a trifle to make up for it. The dull red glow of the steel increased. It became carmine. Slowly, inexorably, it heated to a yellowish tinge. It became canary in color. It tended toward blue.

Vapor curled upward from its surface, streaming away from the tortured, melting surface as if drawn by the distant sun. That vapor grew thick; dazzlingly bright; a veritable cloud of metallic steam. And suddenly there was a violent eruption from the center of the *Adastra*'s lighted hemisphere. The outer hull was melted through. Air from the interior burst out into the void, flinging masses of molten, vaporizing metal before it. It spread with an incredible rapidity, flaring instantly into the attenuated, faintly glowing mist of a comet's tail.

The visiplate images inside the *Adastra* grew dim. Stars paled ahead. The Earth ship had lost a part of her atmosphere and it fled on before her, writhing. Already it had spread into so vast a space that its density was immeasurable, but it was still so much more dense than the infinite emptiness of space that it filled all the cosmos before the *Adastra* with a thinning nebulosity.

And at the edges of the huge gap in the big ship's hull, the thick metal bubbled and steamed, and the interior partitions began to glow with an unholy light of dull-red heat, which swiftly went up to carmine and began to turn faintly yellow.

In the main control room, Alstair watched bitterly until the visiplates showing the interior of section G90 fused. He spoke very calmly into the microphone before him.

"We've got less time than I thought," he said deliberately. "You'll have to hurry. It won't be sure at best, and you've got to remember that these devils will undoubtedly puncture us from every direction and make sure there's absolutely nothing living on board. You've got to work something out, and in a hurry, to do what I've outlined!"

A half-hysterical voice came back to him.

"But sir, if I cut the sonic vibrations in the rockets we'll go up in a flare! A single instant! The disintegration of our fuel will spread to the tubes and the whole ship will simply explode! It will be quick!"

"You fool!" snarled Alstair. "There's another ship from Earth on the way! Unwarned! And unarmed like we are! And from our course these devils can tell where we came from! We're going to die, yes! We won't die pleasantly! But we're going to make sure these fiends don't start out a space fleet for Earth! There's to be no euthanasia for us! We've got to make our dying do some good! We've got to protect humanity!"

Alstair's face, as he snarled into the visiplate, was not that of a martyr or a person making a noble self-sacrifice. It was the face of a man overawing and bullying a subordinate into obedience.

With a beam of radiation playing on his ship which the metal hull absorbed and transformed into heat, Alstair raged at this department and that. A second bulkhead went, and there was a second eruption of vaporized metal and incandescent gas from the monster vessel. Millions of miles away, a wide-flung ring of egg-shaped space ships lay utterly motionless, giving no sign of life and looking like monsters asleep. But from them the merciless beams of radiation sped out and focused upon one spot upon the *Adastra*'s hull, and it spewed forth frothing metal and writhing gases and now and again some still recognizable object which flared and exploded as it emerged.

And within the innumerable compartments of the mighty ship, human beings reacted to their coming doom in manners as various as the persons themselves. Some screamed. A few of the more sullen members of the crew seemed to go mad, to become homicidal maniacs. Still others broke into the stores and proceeded systematically but in some haste to drink themselves comatose. Some women clutched their children and wept over them. And some of them went mad.

But Alstair's snarling, raging voice maintained a semblance of discipline in a few of the compartments. In a machine shop men worked savagely, cursing, and making mistakes as they worked which made their work useless. The lean air officer strode about his domain, a huge spanner in his hand, and smote with a righteous anger at any sign of panic. The rocket chief, puffing, manifested an unexpected genius for sustained profanity, and the rockets kept their pale purple flames out in space without a sign of flickering.

But in the biology laboratory the scene was one of quiet, intense concentration. Bound to helplessness, the Centaurian, featureless and inscrutable, filled the room with its peculiar form of speech. The dictawriter rustled softly, senselessly analyzing each of the sounds and senselessly questing for vocabulary cards which would translate them into English wordings. Now and again a single card did match up. Then the machine translated a single word of the Centaurian's speech.

"——ship——" A long series of sounds, varying rapidly in pitch, in intensity, and in emphasis. "——men——" Another long series. "——talk men——"

The Centaurian ceased to make its hootlike noises.

Then, very carefully, it emitted new ones. The speaker translated them all. The Centaurian had carefully selected words recorded with Helen.

"He understands what we're trying to do," said Helen, very pale.

The machine said: "You—talk—machine—talk—ship."

Jack said quietly into the transmitter: "We are friends. We have much you want. We want only friendship. We have killed none of your men except in self-defense. We ask peace. If we do not have peace, we will fight. But we wish peace."

He said under his breath to Helen, as the machine rustled and the speaker hooted: "Bluff, that war talk. I hope it works!"

Silence. Millions of miles away, unseen space ships aimed a deadly radiation in close, tight beams at the middle of the *Adastra*'s disk. Quaintly enough, that radiation would have been utterly harmless to a man's body. It would have passed through, undetected.

But the steel of the Earth ship's hull stopped and absorbed it as eddy currents. The eddy currents became heat. And a small volcano vomited out into space the walls, the furnishing, the very atmosphere of the *Adastra* through the hole that the heat had made.

It was very quiet indeed in the biology laboratory. The receptor was silent. One minute. Two minutes. Three. The radio waves carrying Jack's voice traveled at the speed of light, but it took no less than ninety seconds for them to reach the source of the beams which were tearing the *Adastra* to pieces. And there was a time loss there, and ninety seconds more for other waves to hurtle through space at one hundred and eighty-six thousand miles each second with the reply.

The receptor hooted unmusically. The dictawriter rustled softly. Then the speaker said without expression:

"We—friends—now—no—fight—ships—come—to —take—you—planet."

And simultaneously the miniature volcano on the

Adastra's hull lessened the violence of its eruption, and slowly its molten, bubbling edges ceased first to steam, and then to bubble, and from the blue-white of vaporizing steel they cooled to yellow, and then to carmine, and more slowly to a dull red, and more slowly still to the glistening, infinitely white metallic surface of steel which cools where there is no oxygen.

Jack said crisply into the control-room microphone: "Sir, I have communicated with the Centaurians and they have ceased fire. They say they are sending a fleet to take us to their planet."

"Very good," said Alstair's voice bitterly, "especially since nobody seems able to make the one contrivance that would do some good after our death. What next?"

"I think it would be a good idea to release the Centaurian here," said Jack. "We can watch him, of course, and paralyze him if he acts up. It would be a diplomatic thing to do, I believe."

"You're ambassador," said Alstair sardonically. "We've got time to work, now. But you'd better put somebody else on the ambassadorial work and get busy again on the job of sending a message back to Earth, if you think you can adapt a transmitter to the type of wave they'll expect."

His image faded. And Jack turned to Helen. He felt suddenly very tired.

"That is the devil of it," he said drearily. "They'll expect a wave like they sent us, and with no more power than we have, they'll hardly pick up anything else! But we picked up in the middle of a message and just at the end of their description of the sending outfit they're using on Earth. Undoubtedly they'll describe it again, or rather they did describe it again, four years back, and we'll pick it up if we live long enough. But we can't even guess when that will be. You're going to keep on working with this—creature, building up a vocabulary?"

Helen regarded him anxiously. She put her hand upon his arm.

"He's intelligent enough," she said urgently. "I'll explain to him and let somebody else work with him. I'll

come with you. After all, we—we may not have long to
be together."

"Perhaps ten hours," said Jack tiredly.

He waited, somberly, while she explained in carefully
chosen words—which the dictawriter translated—to the
Centaurian. She got an assistant and two guards. They
released the headless Thing. It offered no violence. Instead, it manifested impatience to continue the work of
building up in the translator files a vocabulary through
which a complete exchange of ideas could take place.

Jack and Helen went together to the communications
room. They ran the Earth message, as received so far. It
was an extraordinary hodgepodge. Four years back,
Earth had been enthusiastic over the thought of sending
word to its most daring adventurers. A flash of imma-
terial energy could travel tirelessly through uncountable
millions of billions of miles of space and overtake the
explorers who had started three years before. By its
text, this message had been sent some time after the
first message of all. In the sending, it had been broadcast all over the Earth, and many millions of people undoubtedly had thrilled to the thought that they heard
words which would span the space between two suns.

But the words were not helpful to those on the *Adastra*. The message was a "cheer-up" program, which began with lusty singing by a popular quartet, continued
with wisecracks by Earth's most highly paid comedian—and his jokes were all very familiar to those on
the *Adastra*—and then a congratulatory address by an
eminent politician, and other drivel. In short, it was a
hodgepodge of trash designed to gain publicty by means
of the Earth broadcast for those who took part in it.

It was not helpful to those on the *Adastra*, with the
hull of the ship punctured, death before them, and
probably destruction for the whole human race to follow as a consequence of their voyage.

Jack and Helen sat quietly and listened. Their hands
clasped unconsciously. Rather queerly, the extreme
brevity of the time before them made extravagant expressions of affection seem absurd. They listened to the

unspeakably vulgar message from Earth without really hearing it. Now and again they looked at each other.

In the biology laboratory the building-up of a vocabulary went on swiftly. Pictures came into play. A second Centaurian was released, and by his skill in delineation—which proved that the eyes of the plant men functioned almost identically with those of Earth men—added both to the store of definitions and equivalents and to knowledge of the Centaurian civilization.

Piecing the information together, the civilization began to take on a strange resemblance to that of humanity. The Centaurians possessed artificial structures which were undoubtedly dwelling houses. They had cities, laws, arts—the drawing of the second Centaurian was proof of that—and sciences. The science of biology in particular was far advanced, taking to some extent the place of metallurgy in the civilization of men. Their structures were grown, not built. Instead of metals to shape to their own ends, they had forms of protoplasm whose rate and manner of growth they could control.

Houses, bridges, vehicles—even space ships—were formed of living matter which was thrown into a quiescent nonliving state when it had attained the form and size desired. And it could be caused to become active again at will, permitting such extraordinary features as the blisterlike connection that had been made by the space ship with the hull of the *Adastra*.

So far, the Centaurian civilization was strange enough, but still comprehensible. Even men might have progressed in some such fashion had civilization developed on Earth from a different point of departure. It was the economics of the Centaurians which was at once understandable and horrifying to the men who learned of it.

The Centaurian race had developed from carnivorous plants, as men from carnivorous forebears. But at some early date in man's progression, the worship of gold began. No such diversion of interest occurred upon the planets of Proxima Centauri. As men have devastated cities for gold, and have cut down forests and gutted mines and ruthlessly destroyed all things for gold or for other things which could be exchanged for gold, so the Centaurians had quested animals.

As men exterminated the buffalo in America, to trade his hide for gold, so the Centaurians had ruthlessly exterminated the animal life of their planet. But to Centaurians, animal tissue itself was the equivalent of gold. From sheer necessity, ages since, they had learned to tolerate vegetable foodstuffs. But the insensate lust for flesh remained. They had developed methods for preserving animal food for indefinite periods. They had dredged their seas for the last and smallest crustacean. And even space travel became a desirable thing in their eyes, and then a fact, because telescopes showed them vegetation on other planets of their sun, and animal life as a probability.

Three planets of Proxima Centauri were endowed with climates and atmospheres favorable to vegetation and animal life, but only on one planet now, and that the smallest and most distant, did any trace of animal life survive. And even there the Centaurians hunted feverishly for the last and dwindling colonies of tiny quadrupeds which burrowed hundreds of feet below a frozen continent.

It became clear that the *Adastra* was an argosy of such treasure—in the form of human beings—as no Centaurian could ever have imagined to exist. And it became more than ever clear that a voyage to Earth would command all the resources of the race. Billions of human beings! Trillions of lesser animals! Uncountable creatures in the seas! All the Centaurian race would go mad with eagerness to invade this kingdom of riches and ecstasy, the ecstasy felt by any Centaurian when consuming the prehistoric foodstuff of his race.

v

Egg-shaped, featureless ships of space closed in from every side at once. The thermometer banks showed a deliberate, painstaking progression of alarm signals. One dial glowed madly red and faded, and then another, and yet another, as the Centaurian ships took up their positions. Each such alarm, of course, was from the momentary impact of a radiation beam on the *Adastra*'s hull.

Twenty minutes after the last of the beams had proved the *Adastra*'s helplessness, an egglike ship approached the Earth vessel and with complete precision made contact with its forward side above an air lock. Its hull bellied out in a great blister which adhered to the steel.

Alstair watched the visiplate which showed it, his face very white and his hands clenched tightly. Jack Gary's voice, strained and hoarse, came from the biology-laboratory communicator.

"Sir, a message from the Centaurians. A ship has landed on our hull and its crew will enter through the air lock. A hostile move on our part, of course, will mean instant destruction."

"There will be no resistance to the Centaurians," said Alstair harshly. "It is my order! It would be suicide!"

"Even so, sir," said Jack's voice savagely, "I still think it would be a good idea!"

"Stick to your duty!" rasped Alstair. "What progress has been made in communication?"

"We have vocabulary cards for nearly five thousand words. We can converse on nearly any subject, and all of them are unpleasant. The cards are going through a duplicator now and will be finished in a few minutes. A second dictawriter with the second file will be sent you as soon as the cards are complete."

In a visiplate, Alstair saw the headless figures of Centaurians emerging from the entrance to an air lock in the *Adastra*'s hull.

"Those Centaurians have entered the ship," he snapped as an order to Jack. "You're communications officer! Go meet them and lead their commanding officer here!"

"Check!" said Jack grimly.

It sounded like a sentence of death, that order. In the laboratory he was very pale indeed. Helen pressed close to him.

The fomerly captive Centaurian hooted into the dictawriter, inquiringly. The speaker translated.

"What—command?"

Helen explained. So swiftly does humanity accustom itself to the incredible that it seemed almost natural to address a microphone and hear the hoots and stridulations of a nonhuman voice fill the room with her meaning.

"I—go—also—they—no—kill—yet."

The Centaurian rolled on before. With an extraordinary dexterity, he opened the door. He had merely seen it opened. Jack took the lead. His side-arm force gun remained in its holster beside him, but it was useless. He could probably kill the plant man behind him, but that would do no good.

Dim hootings ahead. The plant man made sounds— loud and piercing sounds. Answers came to him. Jack came in view of the new group of invaders. There were twenty or thirty of them, every one armed with half-cylindrical objects, larger than the first creatures had carried.

At sight of Jack there was excitement. Eager trembling of the armlike tentacles at either side of the headless trunks. There were instinctive, furtive movements of the weapons. A loud hooting as of command. The Things were still. But Jack's flesh crawled from the feeling of sheer, carnivorous lust that seemed to emanate from them.

His guide, the former captive, exchanged incomprehensible noises with the newcomers. Again a ripple of excitement in the ranks of the plant men.

"Come," said Jack curtly.

He led the way to the main control room. Once they heard someone screaming monotonously. A woman cracked under the coming of doom. A hooting babble broke the silence among the ungainly Things which followed Jack. Again an authoritative note silenced it.

The control room. Alstair looked like a man of stone, of marble, save that his eyes burned with a fierce and almost maniacal flame. A visiplate beside him showed a steady stream of Centaurians entering through a second air lock. There were hundreds of them, apparently. The dictawriter came in, under Helen's care. She cried out in instinctive horror at sight of so many of the monstrous creatures at once in the control room.

"Set up the dictawriter," said Alstair in a voice so harsh, so brittle that it seemed pure ice.

Trembling, Helen essayed to obey.

"I am ready to talk," said Alstair harshly into the dictawriter microphone.

The machine, rustling softly, translated. The leader of the new party hooted in reply. An order for all officers to report here at once, after setting all controls for automatic operation of the ship. There was some difficulty with the translation of the Centaurian equivalent of "automatic." It was not in the vocabulary file. It took time.

Alstair gave the order. Cold sweat stood out upon his face, but his self-control was iron.

A second order, also understood with a certain amount of difficulty. Copies of all technical records, and all—again it took time to understand—all books bearing on the construction of this ship were to be taken to the air lock by which these plant men had entered. Samples of machinery, generators, and weapons to the same destination.

Again Alstair gave the order. His voice was brittle, was even thin, but it did not falter or break.

The Centaurian leader hooted an order over which the dictawriter rustled in vain. His followers swept swiftly to the doors of the control room. They passed out, leaving but four of their number behind. And Jack went swiftly to Alstair. His force gun snapped out and pressed deep into the commander's middle. The Centaurians made no movement of protest.

"Damn you!" said Jack, his voice thick with rage. "You've let them take the ship! You plan to bargain for your life! Damn you, I'm going to kill you and fight my way to a rocket tube and send this ship up in a flare of clean flame that'll kill these devils with us!"

But Helen cried swiftly: "Jack! Don't! I know!"

Like an echo her words—because she was near the

dictawriter microphone—were repeated in the hooting sounds of the Centaurian language. And Alstair, livid and near to madness, nevertheless said harshly in the lowest of tones:

"You fool! These devils can reach Earth, now they know it's worth reaching! So even if they kill every man on the ship but the officers—and they may—we've got to navigate to their planet and land there." His voice dropped to a rasping whisper and he raged almost soundlessly: "And if you think I want to live through what's coming, shoot!"

Jack stood rigid for an instant. Then he stepped back. He saluted with an elaborate, mechanical precision.

"I beg your pardon, sir," he said unsteadily. "You can count on me hereafter."

One of the officers of the *Adastra* stumbled into the control room. Another. Still another. They trickled in. Six officers out of thirty.

A Centaurian entered with the curious rolling gait of his race. He went impatiently to the dictawriter and made noises.

"These—all—officers?" asked the machine tonelessly.

"The air officer shot his family and himself," gasped a subaltern of the air department. "A bunch of Muts charged a rocket tube and the rocket chief fought them off. Then he bled to death from a knife in his throat. The stores officer was——"

"Stop!" said Alstair in a thin, high voice. He tore at his collar. He went to the microphone and said thinly: "These are all the officers still alive. But we can navigate the ship."

The Centaurian—he wore a wide band of leather about each of his arms and another about his middle—waddled to the G.C. phone. The tendrils at the end of one arm manipated the switch expertly. He emitted strange, formless sounds—and hell broke loose!

The visiplates all over the room emitted high-pitched, squealing sounds. They were horrible. They were ghastly. They were more terrible than the sounds of a wolf pack hard on the heels of a fear-mad deer. They were the sounds Jack had heard when one of the first invaders of the *Adastra* saw a human being and killed him instantly. And other sounds came out of the visiplates, too. There were human screams. There were even one or two explosions.

But then there was silence. The five Centaurians in the control room quivered and trembled. A desperate bloodlust filled them, the unreasoning, blind, instinctive craving which came of evolution from some race of carnivorous plants become capable of movement through the desperate need for food.

The Centaurian with the leather ornaments went to the dictawriter again. He hooted in it:

"Want—two—men—go—from—ship—learn—from —them—now."

There was an infinitely tiny sound in the main control room. It was a drop of cold sweat, falling from Alstair's face to the floor. He seemed to have shriveled. His face was an ashy gray. His eyes were closed. But Jack looked steadily from one to the other of the surviving officers.

"That will mean vivisection, I suppose," he said harshly. "It's certain they plan to visit Earth, else— intelligent as they are—they wouldn't have wiped out everybody but us. Even for treasure. They'll want to try out weapons on a human body, and so on. Communications is about the most useless of all the departments now, sir. I volunteer."

Helen gasped: "No, Jack! No!"

Alstair opened his eyes. "Gary has volunteered. One more man to volunteer for vivisection." He said it in the choked voice of one holding to sanity by the most terrible of efforts. "They'll want to find out how to kill men. Their thirty-centimeter waves didn't work. They know the beams that melted our hull wouldn't kill men. I can't volunteer! I've got to stay with the ship!" There was despair in his voice. "One more man to volunteer for these devils to kill slowly!"

Silence. The happenings of the past little while, and the knowledge of what still went on within the *Adastra*'s innumerable compartments, had literally stunned most of the six. They could not think. They were mentally dazed, emotionally paralyzed by the sheer horrors they had encountered.

Then Helen stumbled into Jack's arms. "I'm—going, too!" she gasped. "We're—all going to die! I'm not needed! And I can—die with Jack."

Alstair groaned. "Please!"

"I'm—going!" she panted. "You can't stop me! With Jack! Whither thou goest——"

Then she choked. She pressed close. The Centaurian of the leather belts hooted impatiently into the dicta-writer.

"These—two—come."

Alstair said in a strange voice: "Wait!" Like an automaton, he moved to his desk. He took up an electro-pen. He wrote, his hands shaking. "I am mad," he said thinly. "We are all mad. I think we are dead and in hell. But take this."

Jack stuffed the official order slip in his pocket. The Centaurian of the leather bands hooted impatiently. He led them, with his queer, rolling gait, toward the air lock by which the plant men had entered. Three times they were seen by roving Things, which emitted that triply horrible shrill squeal. And each time the Centaurian of the leather bands hooted authoritatively and the plant men withdrew.

Once, too, Jack saw four creatures swaying backward and forward about something on the floor. He reached out his hands and covered Helen's eyes until they were past.

They came to the air lock. Their guide pointed through it. The man and the girl obeyed. Long, rubbery tentacles seized them and Helen gasped and was still. Jack fought fiercely, shouting her name. Then something struck him savagely. He collapsed.

He came back to consciousness with a feeling of tremendous weight upon him. He stirred, and with his movement some of the oppression left him. A light burned, not a light such as men know on Earth, but a writhing flare which beat restlessly at the confines of a transparent globe which contained it. There was a queer smell in the air, too, an animal smell. Jack sat up. Helen lay beside him, unconfined and apparently unhurt. None of the Centaurians seemed to be near.

He chafed her wrists helplessly. He heard a stuttering sound and with each of the throbs of noise felt a momentary acceleration. Rockets, fuel rockets.

"We're on one of their damned ships!" said Jack coldly. He felt for his force gun. It was gone.

Helen opened her eyes. She stared vaguely about. Her eyes fell upon Jack. She shuddered suddenly and pressed close to him.

"What—what happened?"

"We'll have to find out," replied Jack grimly.

The floor beneath his feet careened suddenly. Instinctively, he glanced at a porthole which until then he had only subconsciously noted. He gazed out into the utterly familiar blackness of space, illumined by very many tiny points of light which were stars. He saw a ringed sun and points of light which were planets.

One of those points of light was very near. Its disk was perceptible, and polar snow caps, and the misty alternation of greenish areas which would be continents with the indescribable tint which is ocean bottom when viewed from beyond a planet's atmosphere.

Silence. No hootings of that strange language without vowels or consonants which the Centaurians used. No sound of any kind for a moment.

"We're heading for that planet, I suppose," said Jack quietly. "We'll have to see if we can't manage to get ourselves killed before we land."

Then a murmur in the distance. It was a strange, muted murmur, in nothing resembling the queer notes of the plant men. With Helen clinging to him, Jack explored cautiously, out of the cubby-hole in which they had awakened. Silence save for that distant murmur. No movement anywhere. Another faint stutter of the rockets, with a distinct accelerative movement of the whole ship. The animal smell grew stronger. They passed through a strangely shaped opening and Helen cried out:

"The animals!"

Heaped higgledy-piggledy were cages from the *Adastra*, little compartments containing specimens of each of the animals which had been bred from for food, and which it had been planned to release if a planet suitable for colonization revolved about Proxima Centauri. Farther on was an indescribable mass of books, machines, cases of all sorts—the materials ordered to be carried to the air lock by the leader of the plant men. Still no sign of any Centaurian.

But the muted murmur, quite incredibly sounding like a human voice, came from still farther ahead. Bewildered, now, Helen followed as Jack went still cautiously toward the source of the sound.

They found it. It came from a bit of mechanism cased in with the same lusterless, dull-brown stuff which composed the floor and walls and every part of the ship about them. And it was a human voice. More, it was Alstair's, racked and harsh and half hysterical.

"——you must have recovered consciousness by now, dammit, and these devils want some sign of it! They cut down your acceleration when I told them the rate they were using would keep you unconscious! Gary! Helen! Set off that signal!"

A pause. The voice again:

"I'll tell it again. You're in a space ship these fiends are guiding by a tight beam which handles the controls. You're going to be set down on one of the planets which once contained animal life. It's empty now, unoccupied except by plants. And you and the space ship's cargo of animals and books and so on are the reserved, special property of the high archfiend of all these devils. He had you sent in an outside-controlled ship because none of his kind could be trusted with such treasure as you and the other animals!

"You're a reserve of knowledge, to translate our books, explain our science, and so on. It's forbidden for any other space ship than his own to land on your planet. Now will you send that signal? It's a knob right above the speaker my voice is coming out of. Pull it three times, and they'll know you're all right and won't send another ship with preservatives for your flesh lest a priceless treasure go to waste!"

The tinny voice—Centaurian receptors were not designed to reproduce the elaborate phonetics of the human voice—laughed hysterically.

Jack reached up and pulled the knob, three times. Alstair's voice went on:

"This ship is hell, now. It isn't a ship any more, but a sort of brimstone pit. There are seven of us alive, and we're instructing Centaurians in the operation of the controls. But we've told them that we can't turn off the rockets to show their inner workings, because to be started they have to have a planet's mass near by, for deformation of space so the reaction can be started. They're keeping us alive until we've shown them that. They've got some method of writing, too, and they write down everything we say, when it's translated by a dicta-writer. Very scientific——"

The voice broke off.

"Your signal just came," it said an instant later. "You'll find food somewhere about. The air ought to last you till you land. You've got four more days of travel. I'll call back later. Don't worry about navigation. It's attended to."

The voice died again, definitely.

The two of them, man and girl, explored the Centaurian space ship. Compared to the *Adastra*, it was miniature. A hundred feet long, or more, by perhaps sixty feet at its greatest diameter. They found cubbyholes in which there was now nothing at all, but which undoubtedly at times contained the plant men packed tightly.

These rooms could be refrigerated, and it was probable that at a low temperature the Centaurians reacted like vegetation on Earth in winter and passed into a dormant, hibernating state. Such an arrangement would allow of an enormous crew being carried, to be revived for landing or battle.

"If they refitted the *Adastra* for a trip back to Earth on that basis," said Jack grimly, "they'd carry a hundred and fifty thousand Centaurians at least. Probably more."

The thought of an assault upon mankind by these creatures was an obsession. Jack was tormented by it. Womanlike, Helen tried to cheer him by their own present safety.

"We volunteered for vivisection," she told him pitifully, the day after their recovery of consciousness, "and we're safe for a while, anyhow. And—we've got each other——"

"It's time for Alstair to communicate again," said Jack harshly. It was nearly thirty hours after the last signing off. Centaurian routine, like Earth discipline on terrestrial space ships, maintained a period equal to a planet's daily rotation as the unit of time. "We'd better go listen to him."

They did. And Alstair's racked voice came from the queerly shaped speaker. It was more strained, less sane, than the day before. He told them of the progress of the Things in the navigation of the *Adastra*. The six surviving officers already were not needed to keep the ship's apparatus functioning. The air-purifying apparatus in particular was shut off, since in clearing the air of carbon dioxide it tended to make the air unbreathable for the Centaurians.

The six men were now permitted to live that they might satisy the insatiable desire of the plant men for information. They lived a perpetual third degree, with every resource of their brains demanded for record in the weird notation of their captors. The youngest of the six, a subaltern of the air department, went mad under the strain alike of memory and of anticipation. He screamed senselessly for hours, and was killed and his body promptly mumified by the strange, drying chemicals of the Centaurians. The rest were living shadows, starting at a sound.

"Our deceleration's been changed," said Alstair, his voice brittle. "You'll land just two days before we settle down, on the planet these devils call home. Queer they've no colonizing instinct. Another one of us is about to break, I think. They've taken away our shoes

and belts now, by the way. They're leather. We'd take a
gold band from about a watermelon, wouldn't we? Consistent, these——"

And he raged once, in sudden hysteria:

"I'm a fool! I sent you two off together while I'm
living in hell! Gary, I order you to have nothing to do
with Helen! I order that the two of you shan't speak to
each other! I order that——"

Another day passed. And another. Alstair called
twice more. Each time, by his voice, he was more desperate, more nerve-racked, closer to the bounds of madness. The second time he wept, the while he cursed Jack
for being where there were none of the plant men.

"We're not interesting to the devils, now, except as
animals. Our brains don't count! They're gutting the
ship systematically. Yesterday they got the earthworms
from the growing area where we grew crops! There's a
guard on each of us now. Mine pulled out some of my
hair this morning and ate it, rocking back and forth in
ecstasy. We've no woolen shirts. They're animal!"

Another day still. Then Alstair was semihysterical.
There were only three men left alive on the ship. He
had instructions to give Jack in the landing of the egg-
shaped vessel on the uninhabited world. Jack was supposed to help. His destination was close now. The disk
of the planet which was to be his and Helen's prison
filled half the heavens. And the other planet toward
which the *Adastra* was bound was a full-sized disk to
Alstair.

Beyond the rings of Proxima Centauri there were six
planets in all, and the prison planet was next outward
from the home of the plant men. It was colder than was
congenial to them, though for a thousand years their
flesh-hunting expeditions had searched its surface until
not a mammal or a bird, no fish or even a crustacean
was left upon it. Beyond it again an ice-covered world
lay, and still beyond there were frozen shapes whirling
in emptiness.

"You know, now, how to take over when the beam
releases the atmospheric controls," said Alstair's voice.
It wavered as if he spoke through teeth which chattered

from pure nerve strain. "You'll have quiet. Trees and flowers and something like grass, if the pictures they've made mean anything. We're running into the greatest celebration in the history of all hell. Every space ship called home. There won't be a Centaurian on the planet who won't have a tiny shred of some sort of animal matter to consume. Enough to give him that beastly delight they feel when they get hold of something of animal origin.

"Damn them! Every member of the race! We're the greatest store of treasure ever dreamed of! They make no bones of talking before me, and I'm mad enough to understand a good bit of what they say to each other. Their most high panjandrum is planning bigger space ships than were ever grown before. He'll start out for Earth with three hundred space ships, and most of the crews asleep or hibernating. There'll be three million devils straight from hell on those ships, and they've those damned beams that will fuse an earthly ship at ten million miles."

Talking helped to keep Alstair sane, apparently. The next day Jack's and Helen's egg-shaped vessel dropped like a plummet from empty space into an atmosphere which screamed wildly past its smooth sides. Then Jack got the ship under control and it descended slowly and ever more slowly and at last came to a cushioned stop in a green glade hard by a forest of strange but wholly reassuring trees. It was close to sunset on this planet, and darkness fell before they could attempt exploration.

They did little exploring, however, either the next day or the day after. Alstair talked almost continuously.

"Another ship coming from Earth," he said, and his voice cracked. "Another ship! She started at least four years ago. She'll get here in four years more. You two may see her, but I'll be dead or mad by tomorrow night! And here's the humorous thing! It seems to me that madness is nearest when I think of you, Helen, letting Jack kiss you! I loved you, you know, Helen, when I was a man, before I became a corpse watching my ship being piloted into hell. I loved you very much. I was jealous, and when you looked at Gary with shining eyes I hated him. I still hate him, Helen! Ah, how I hate him!" But Alstair's voice was the voice of a ghost, now, a ghost in purgatory. "And I've been a fool, giving him that order."

Jack walked about with abstracted, burning eyes. Helen put her hands on his shoulders and he spoke absently to her, his voice thick with hatred. A desperate, passionate lust to kill Centaurians filled him. He began to hunt among the machines. He became absorbed, assembling a ten-kilowatt vortex gun from odd contrivances. He worked at it for many hours. Then he heard Helen at work, somewhere. She seemed to be struggling. It disturbed him. He went to see.

She had just dragged the last of the cages from the *Adastra* out into the open. She was releasing the little creatures within. Pigeons soared eagerly above her. Rabbits, hardly hopping out of her reach, munched delightedly upon the unfamiliar but satisfactory leafed vegetation underfoot.

She browsed. There were six of them besides a tiny, wabbly-legged lamb. Chickens pecked and scratched. But there were no insects on this world. They would find only seeds and green stuff. Four puppies rolled ecstatically on scratchy green things in the sunlight.

"Anyhow," said Helen defiantly. "They can be happy for a while! They're not like us! We have to worry! And this world could be a paradise for humans!"

Jack looked somberly out across the green and beautiful world. No noxious animals. No harmful insects. There could be no diseases on this planet, unless men introduced them of set purpose. It would be a paradise.

The murmur of a human voice came from within the space ship. He went bitterly to listen. Helen came after him. They stood in the strangely shaped cubby-hole which was the control room. Walls, floors, ceiling, instrument cases—all were made of the lusterless dark-brown stuff which had grown into the shapes the Centaurians desired. Alstair's voice was strangely more calm, less hysterical, wholly steady.

"I hope you're not off exploring somewhere, Helen

and Gary," it said from the speaker. "They've had a celebration here today. The *Adastra*'s landed. I landed it. I'm the only man left alive. We came down in the center of a city of these devils, in the middle of buildings fit to form the headquarters of hell. The high panjandrum has a sort of palace right next to the open space where I am now.

"And today they celebrated. It's strange how much animal matter there was on the *Adastra*. They even found horsehair stiffening in the coats of our uniforms. Woolen blankets. Shoes. Even some of the soaps had an animal origin, and they 'refined' it. They can recover any scrap of animal matter as cleverly as our chemists can recover gold and radium. Queer, eh?"

The speaker was silent a moment.

"I'm sane now," the voice said steadily. "I think I was mad for a while. But what I saw today cleared my brain. I saw millions of these devils dipping their arms into great tanks, great troughs, in which solutions of all the animal tissues from the *Adastra* were dissolved. The high panjandrum kept plenty for himself! I saw the things they carried into his palace, through lines of guards. Some of those things had been my friends. I saw a city gone crazy with beastly joy, the devils swaying back and forth in ecstasy as they absorbed the loot from Earth. I heard the high panjandrum hoot a sort of imperial address from the throne. And I've learned to understand quite a lot of those hootings.

"He was telling them that Earth is packed with animals. Men. Beasts. Birds, Fish in the oceans. And he told them that the greatest space fleet in history will soon be grown, which will use the propulsion methods of men, our rockets, Gary, and the first fleet will carry uncountable swarms of them to occupy Earth. They'll send back treasure, too, so that every one of his subjects will have such ecstasy, frequently, as they had today. And the devils, swaying crazily back and forth, gave out that squealing noise of theirs. Millions of them at once."

Jack groaned softly. Helen covered her eyes as if to shut out the sight her imagination pictured.

"Now, here's the situation from your standpoint,"

said Alstair steadily, millions of miles away and the only human being upon a planet of blood-lusting plant men. "They're coming here now, their scientists, to have me show them the inside workings of the rockets. Some others will come over to question you two tomorrow. But I'm going to show these devils our rockets. I'm sure—perfectly sure—that every space ship of the race is back on this planet.

"They came to share the celebration when every one of them got as a free gift from the grand panjandrum as much animal tissue as he could hope to acquire in a lifetime of toil. Flesh is a good bit more precious than gold, here. It rates, on a comparative scale, somewhere between platinum and radium. So they all came home. Every one of them! And there's a space ship on the way here from Earth. It'll arrive in four years more. Remember that!"

An impatient, distant hooting came from the speaker.

"They're here," said Alstair steadily. "I'm going to show them the rockets. Maybe you'll see the fun. It depends on the time of day where you are. But remember, there's a sister ship to the *Adastra* on the way! And Gary, that order I gave you last thing was the act of a madman, but I'm glad I did it. Good-by, you two!"

Small hooting sounds, growing fainter, came from the speaker. Far, far away, amid the city of fiends, Alstair was going with the plant men to show them the rockets' inner workings. They wished to understand every aspect of the big ship's propulsion, so that they could build—or grow—ships as large and carry multitudes of their swarming myriads to a solar system where animals were to be found.

"Let's go outside," said Jack harshly. "He said he'd do it, since he couldn't get a bit of a machine made that could be depended on to do it. But I believed he'd go mad. It didn't seem possible to live to their planet. We'll go outside and look at the sky."

Helen stumbled. They stood upon the green grass, looking up at the firmament above them. They waited, staring. And Jack's mind pictured the great rocket chambers of the *Adastra*. He seemed to see the strange procession enter it; a horde of the ghastly plant men and then Alstair, his face like marble and his hands as steady.

He'd open up the breech of one of the rockets. He'd explain the disintegration field, which collapses the electrons of hydrogen so that it rises in atomic weight to helium, and the helium to lithium, while the oxygen of the water is split literally into neutronium and pure force. Alstair would answer hooted questions. The supersonic generators he would explain as controls of force and direction. He would not speak of the fact that only the material of the rocket tubes, when filled with exactly the frequency those generators produced, could withstand the effect of the disintegration field.

He would not explain that a tube started without those generators in action would catch from the fuel and disintegrate, and that any other substance save one, under any other condition save that one rate of vibration, would catch also and that tubes, ship, and planet alike would vanish in a lambent purple flame.

No; Alstair would not explain that. He would show the Centaurians how to start the Caldwell field.

The man and the girl looked at the sky. And suddenly there was a fierce purple light. It dwarfed the reddish tinge of the ringed sun overhead. For one second, for two, for three, the purple light persisted. There was no sound. There was a momentary blast of intolerable heat. Then all was as before.

The ringed sun shone brightly. Clouds like those of Earth floated serenely in a sky but a little less blue than that of home. The small animals from the *Adastra* munched contentedly at the leafy stuff underfoot. The pigeons soared joyously, exercising their wings in full freedom.

"He did it," said Jack. "And every space ship was home. There aren't any more plant men. There's nothing left of their planet, their civilization, or their plans to harm our Earth."

Even out in space, there was nothing where the planet of the Centaurians had been. Not even steam or cooling gases. It was gone as if it had never existed.

And the man and woman of Earth stood upon a planet which could be a paradise for human beings, and another ship was coming presently, with more of their kind.

"He did it!" repeated Jack quietly. "Rest his soul! And we—we can think of living, now, instead of death."

The grimness of his face relaxed slowly. He looked down at Helen. Gently, he put his arm about her shoulders.

She pressed close, gladly, thrusting away all thoughts of what had been. Presently she asked softly: "What was that last order Alstair gave you?"

"I never looked," said Jack.

He fumbled in his pocket. Pocketworn and frayed, the order slip came out. He read it and showed it to Helen. By statutes passed before the *Adastra* left Earth, laws and law enforcement on the artificial planet were intrusted to the huge ship's commander. It had been specially provided that a legal marriage on the *Adastra* would be constituted by an official order of marriage signed by the commander. And the slip handed to Jack by Alstair, as Jack went to what he'd thought would be an agonizing death, was such an order. It was, in effect, a marriage certificate.

They smiled at each other, those two.

"It—wouldn't have mattered," said Helen uncertainly. "I love you. But I'm glad!"

One of the freed pigeons found a straw upon the ground. He tugged at it. His mate inspected it solemnly. They made pigeon noises to each other. They flew away with the straw. After due discussion, they had decided that it was an eminently suitable straw with which to begin the building of a nest.

The Fourth-dimensional Demonstrator

PETE DAVIDSON WAS engaged to Miss Daisy Manners of the Green Paradise floor show. He had just inherited all the properties of an uncle who had been an authority on the fourth dimension, and he was the custodian of an unusually amiable kangaroo named Arthur. But still he was not happy; it showed this morning.

Inside his uncle's laboratory, Pete scribbled on paper. He added, and ran his hands through his hair in desperation. Then he subtracted, divided, and multiplied. But the results were invariably problems as incapable of solution as his deceased relative's fourth-dimensional equations. From time to time a long, horselike, hopeful face peered in at him. That was Thomas, his uncle's servant, whom Pete was afraid he had also inherited.

"Beg pardon, sir," said Thomas tentatively.

Pete leaned harassedly back in his chair.

"What is it, Thomas? What has Arthur been doing now?"

"He is browsing in the dahlias, sir. I wished to ask about lunch, sir. What shall I prepare?"

"Anything!" said Pete. "Anything at all! No. On second thought, trying to untangle Uncle Robert's affairs calls for brains. Give me something rich in phosphorus and vitamins; I need them."

"Yes, sir," said Thomas. "But the grocer, sir——"

"Again?" demanded Pete hopelessly.

"Yes, sir," said Thomas, coming into the laboratory. "I hoped, sir, that matters might be looking better."

Pete shook his head, regarding his calculations depressedly.

"They aren't. Cash to pay the grocer's bill is still a

116

dim and misty hope. It is horrible, Thomas! I remembered my uncle as simply reeking with cash, and I thought the fourth dimension was mathematics, not debauchery. But Uncle Robert must have had positive orgies with quanta and space-time continua! I shan't break even on the heir business, let alone make a profit!"

Thomas made a noise suggesting sympathy.

"I could stand it for myself alone," said Pete gloomily. "Even Arthur, in his simple, kangaroo's heart, bears up well. But Daisy! There's the rub! Daisy!"

"Daisy, sir?"

"My fiancée," said Pete. "She's in the Green Paradise floor show. She is technically Arthur's owner. I told Daisy, Thomas, that I had inherited a fortune. And she's going to be disappointed."

"Too bad, sir," said Thomas.

"That statement is one of humorous underemphasis, Thomas. Daisy is not a person to take disappointments lightly. When I explain that my uncle's fortune has flown off into the fourth dimension, Daisy is going to look absent-minded and stop listening. Did you ever try to make love to a girl who looked absent-minded?"

"No, sir," said Thomas. "But about lunch, sir——"

"We'll have to pay for it. Damn!" Pete said morbidly. "I've just forty cents in my clothes, Thomas, and Arthur at least mustn't be allowed to starve. Daisy wouldn't like it. Let's see!"

He moved away from the desk and surveyed the laboratory with a predatory air. It was not exactly a homy place. There was a skeltonlike thing of iron rods, some four feet high. Thomas had said it was a tesseract—a model of a cube existing in four dimensions instead of three.

To Pete, it looked rather like a medieval instrument of torture—something to be used in theological argument with a heretic. Pete could not imagine anybody but his uncle wanting it. There were other pieces of apparatus of all sizes, but largely dismantled. They looked like the product of someone putting vast amounts of money and patience into an effort to do something which would be unsatisfactory when accomplished.

"There's nothing here to pawn," said Pete depressedly. "Not even anything I could use for a hand organ, with Arthur substituting for the monk!"

"There's the demonstrator, sir," said Thomas hopefully. "Your uncle finished it, sir, and it worked, and he had a stroke, sir."

"Cheerful!" said Pete. "What is this demonstrator? What's it supposed to do?"

"Why, sir, it demonstrates the fourth dimension," said Thomas. "It's your uncle's life work, sir."

"Then let's take a look at it," said Pete. "Maybe we can support ourselves demonstrating the fourth dimension in shop windows for advertising purposes. But I don't think Daisy will care for the career."

Thomas marched solemnly to a curtain just behind the desk. Pete had thought it hid a cupboard. He slid the cover back and displayed a huge contrivance which seemed to have the solitary virtue of completion. Pete could see a monstrous brass horseshoe all of seven feet high. It was apparently hollow and full of cryptic cogs and wheels. Beneath it there was a circular plate of inch-thick glass which seemed to be designed to revolve. Below that, in turn, there was a massive base to which ran certain copper tubes from a refrigerating unit out of an ice box.

Thomas turned on a switch and the unit began to purr. Pete watched.

"Your uncle talked to himself quite a bit about this, sir," said Thomas. "I gathered that it's quite a scientific triumph, sir. You see, sir, the fourth dimension is time."

"I'm glad to hear it explained so simply," said Pete.

"Yes, sir. As I understand it, sir, if one were motoring and saw a pretty girl about to step on a banana peel, sir, and if one wished to tip her off, so to speak, but didn't quite realize for——say, two minutes, until one had gone on half a mile——"

"The pretty girl would have stepped on the banana peel and nature would have taken its course," said Pete.

"Except for this demonstrator, sir. You see, to tip off the young lady one would have to retrace the half mile and the time too, sir, or one would be too late. That is, one would have to go back not only the half mile but the two minutes. And so your uncle, sir, built this demonstrator——"

"So he could cope with such a situation when it arose," finished Pete. "I see! But I'm afraid it won't settle our financial troubles."

The refrigeration unit ceased to purr. Thomas solemnly struck a safety match.

"If I may finish the demonstration, sir," he said hopefully. "I blow out this match, and put it on the glass plate between the ends of the horseshoe. The temperature's right, so it should work."

There were self-satisfied clucking sounds from the base of the machine. They went on for seconds. The huge glass plate suddenly revolved perhaps the eighth of a revolution. A humming noise began. It stopped. Suddenly there was another burnt safety match on the glass plate. The machine began to cluck triumphantly.

"You see, sir?" said Thomas. "It's produced another burnt match. Dragged it forward out of the past, sir. There was a burned match at that spot, until the glass plate moved a few seconds ago. Like the girl and the banana peel, sir. The machine went back to the place where the match had been, and then it went back in time to where the match was, and then it brought it forward."

The plate turned another eighth of a revolution. The machine clucked and hummed. The humming stopped. There was a third burnt match on the glass plate. The clucking clatter began once more.

"It will keep that up indefinitely, sir," said Thomas hopefully.

"I begin," said Pete, "to see the true greatness of modern science. With only two tons of brass and steel, and at a cost of only a couple of hundred thousand dollars and a lifetime of effort, my Uncle Robert has left me a machine which will keep me supplied with burnt matches for years to come! Thomas, this machine is a scientific triumph!"

Thomas beamed.

"Splendid, sir! I'm glad you approve. And what shall I do about lunch, sir?"

The machine, having clucked and hummed appropriately, now produced a fourth burnt match and clucked more triumphantly still. It prepared to reach again into the hitherto unreachable past.

Pete looked reproachfully at the servant he had apparently inherited. He reached in his pocket and drew out his forty cents. Then the machine hummed. Pete jerked his head and stared at it.

"Speaking of science, now," he said an instant later. "I have a very commercial thought. I blush to contemplate it." He looked at the monstrous, clucking demonstrator of the fourth dimension. "Clear out of here for ten minutes, Thomas. I'm going to be busy!"

Thomas vanished. Pete turned off the demonstrator. He risked a nickel, placing it firmly on the inch-thick glass plate. The machine went on again. It clucked, hummed, ceased to hum—and there were two nickels. Pete added a dime to the second nickel. At the end of another cycle he ran his hand rather desperately through his hair and added his entire remaining wealth—a quarter. Then, after incredulously watching what happened, he began to pyramid.

Thomas tapped decorously some ten minutes later.

"Beg pardon, sir," he said hopefully. "About lunch, sir——"

Pete turned off the demonstrator. He gulped.

"Thomas," he said in careful calm, "I shall let you write the menu for lunch. Take a basketful of this small change and go shopping. And—Thomas, have you any item of currency larger than a quarter? A fifty-cent piece would be about right. I'd like to have something really impressive to show to Daisy when she comes."

Miss Daisy Manners of the Green Paradise floor show was just the person to accept the fourth-dimensional demonstrator without question and to make full use of the results of modern scientific research. She greeted Pete abstractedly and interestedly asked just how much he'd inherited. And Pete took her to the laboratory. He unveiled the demonstrator.

"These are my jewels," said Pete impressively. "Darling, it's going to be a shock, but—have you got a quarter?"

"You've got nerve, asking me for money," said Daisy. "And if you lied about inheriting some money———"

Pete smiled tenderly upon her. He produced a quarter of his own.

"Watch, my dear! I'm doing this for you!"

He turned on the demonstrator and explained complacently as the first cluckings came from the base. The glass plate moved, a second quarter appeared, and Pete pyramided the two while he continued to explain. In the fraction of a minute, there were four quarters. Again Pete pyramided. There were eight quarters—sixteen, thirty-two, sixty-four, one hundred twenty-eight——— At this point the stack collapsed and Pete shut off the switch.

"You see, my dear? Out of the fourth dimension to you! Uncle invented it, I inherited it, and—shall I change your money for you?"

Daisy did not look at all absent-minded now. Pete gave her a neat little sheaf of bank notes.

"And from now on, darling," he said cheerfully, "whenever you want money just come in here, start the machine—and there you are! Isn't that nice?"

"I want some more money now," said Daisy. "I have to buy a trousseau."

"I hoped you'd feel that way!" said Pete enthusiastically. "Here goes! And we have a reunion while the pennies roll in."

The demonstrator began to cluck and clatter with bills instead of quarters on the plate. Once, to be sure, it suspended all operations and the refrigeration unit purred busily for a time. Then it resumed its self-satisfied delving into the immediate past.

"I haven't been making any definite plans," explained Pete, "until I talked to you. Just getting things in line. But I've looked after Arthur carefully. You know how he loves cigarettes. He eats them, and though it may be eccentric in a kangaroo, they seem to agree with him. I've used the demonstrator to lay up a huge supply of cigarettes for him—his favorite brand, too. And I've been trying to build up a bank account. I thought it would seem strange if we bought a house on Park Avenue and just casually offered a trunkful of bank notes in payment. It might look as if we'd been running a snatch racket."

"Stupid!" said Daisy.

"What?"

"You could be pyramiding those bills like you did the quarters," said Daisy. "Then there'd be lots more of them!"

"Darling," said Pete fondly, "does it matter how much you have when I have so much?"

"Yes," said Daisy. "You might get angry with me."

"Never!" protested Pete. Then he added reminiscently, "Before we thought of the bank note idea, Thomas and I filled up the coal bin with quarters and half dollars. They're still there."

"Gold pieces would be nice," suggested Daisy, thinking hard, "if you could get hold of some. Maybe we could."

"Ah!" said Pete. "But Thomas had a gold filling in one tooth. We took it out and ran it up to half a pound or so. Then we melted that into a little brick and put it on the demonstrator. Darling, you'd really be surprised if you looked in the woodshed."

"And there's jewelry," said Daisy. "It would be faster still!"

"If you feel in the mood for jewelry," said Pete tenderly, "just look in the vegetable bin. We'd about run out of storage space when the idea occurred to us."

"I think," said Daisy enthusiastically, "we'd better get married right away. Don't you?"

"Sure! Let's go and do it now! I'll get the car around!"

"Do, darling," said Daisy. "I'll watch the demonstrator."

Beaming, Pete kissed her ecstatically and rushed from the laboratory. He rang for Thomas, and rang again. It was not until the third ring that Thomas appeared. And Thomas was very pale. He said agitatedly:

"Beg pardon, sir, but shall I pack your bag?"

"I'm going to be—— Pack my bag? What for?"

"We're going to be arrested, sir," said Thomas. He gulped. "I thought you might want it, sir. An acquaintance in the village, sir, believes we are among the lower-numbered public enemies, sir, and respects us accordingly. He telephoned me the news."

"Thomas, have you been drinking?"

"No, sir," said Thomas pallidly. "Not yet, sir. But it is a splendid suggestion, thank you, sir." Then he said desperately: "It's the money, sir—the bank notes. If you recall, we never changed but one lot of silver into notes, sir. We got a one, a five, a ten and so on, sir."

"Of course," said Pete. "That was all we needed. Why not?"

"It's the serial number, sir! All the one-dollar bills the demonstrator turned out have the same serial number—and all the fives and tens and the rest, sir. Some person with a hobby for looking for kidnap bills, sir, found he had several with the same number. The secret service has traced them back. They're coming for us, sir. The penalty for counterfeiting is twenty years, sir. My—my friend in the village asked if we intended to shoot it out with them, sir, because if so he'd like to watch."

Thomas wrung his hands. Pete stared at him.

"Come to think of it," he said meditatively, "they are counterfeits. It hadn't occurred to me before. We'll have to plead guilty, Thomas. And perhaps Daisy won't want to marry me if I'm going to prison. I'll go tell her the news."

Then he started. He heard Daisy's voice, speaking very angrily. An instant later the sound grew louder. It became a continuous, shrill, soprano babble. It grew louder yet. Pete ran.

He burst into the laboratory and was stunned. The demonstrator was still running. Daisy had seen Pete piling up the bills as they were turned out, pyramiding to make the next pile larger. She had evidently essayed the same feat. But the pile was a bit unwieldy, now, and Daisy had climbed on the glass plate. She had come into the scope of the demonstrator's action.

There were three of her in the laboratory when Pete first entered. As he froze in horror, the three became four. The demonstrator clucked and hummed what was almost a hoot of triumph. Then it produced a fifth Daisy. Pete dashed frantically forward and turned off the switch just too late to prevent the appearance of a sixth copy of Miss Daisy Manners of the Green Paradise floor show. She made a splendid sister act, but Pete gazed in paralyzed horror at this plethora of his heart's desire.

Because all of Daisy was identical, with not only the same exterior and—so to speak—the same serial number, but with the same opinions and convictions. And all six of Daisy were convinced that they, individually, owned the heap of bank notes now on the glass plate. All six of her were trying to get it. And Daisy was quarreling furiously with herself. She was telling herself what she thought of herself, in fact, and on the whole her opinion was not flattering.

Arthur, like Daisy, possessed a fortunate disposition. He was not one of those kangaroos who go around looking for things to be upset about. He browsed peacefully upon the lawn, eating up the dahlias and now and again hopping over the six-foot hedge in hopes that there might be a dog come along the lane to bark at him. Or, failing to see a dog, that somebody might have come by who would drop a cigarette butt that he might salvage.

At his first coming to this place, both pleasing events had been frequent. The average unwarned passer-by, on seeing a five-foot kangaroo soaring toward him in this part of the world, did have a tendency to throw down everything and run. Sometimes, among the things he threw down was a cigarette.

There had been a good supply of dogs, too, but they didn't seem to care to play with Arthur any more. Arthur's idea of playfulness with a strange dog—especially one that barked at him—was to grab him with both front paws and then kick the living daylights out of him.

Arthur browsed, and was somewhat bored. Because of his boredom he was likely to take a hand in almost anything that turned up. There was a riot going on in the laboratory, but Arthur did not care for family quarrels. He was interested, however, in the government officers when they arrived. There were two of them and they came in a roadster. They stopped at the gate and marched truculently up to the front door.

Arthur came hopping around from the back just as they knocked thunderously. He'd been back there digging up a few incipient cabbages of Thomas' planting, to see why they didn't grow faster. He soared at least an easy thirty feet, and propped himself on his tail to look interestedly at the visitors.

"M-my heavens!" said the short, squat officer. He had been smoking a cigarette. He threw it down and grabbed his gun.

That was his mistake. Arthur liked cigarettes. This one was a mere fifteen feet from him. He soared toward it.

The government man squawked, seeing Arthur in mid-air and heading straight for him. Arthur looked rather alarming, just then. The officer fired recklessly, missing Arthur. And Arthur remained calm. To him, the shots were not threats. They were merely the noises made by an automobile whose carburetor needed adjustment. He landed blandly, almost on the officer's toes—and the officer attacked him hysterically with fist and clubbed gun.

Arthur was an amiable kangaroo, but he resented the attack, actively.

The short, squat officer squawked again as Arthur grabbed him with his forepaws. His companion backed against the door, prepared to sell his life dearly. But then—and the two things happened at once—while Arthur proceeded to kick the living daylights out of the short, squat officer, Thomas resignedly opened the door behind the other and he fell backward suddenly and knocked himself cold against the doorstop.

Some fifteen minutes later the short, squat officer said gloomily: "It was a bum steer. Thanks for pulling that critter off me, and Casey's much obliged for the drinks. But we're hunting a bunch of counterfeiters that have been turning out damn good phony bills. The line led straight to you. But if it had been you, you'd have shot us. You didn't. So we got to do the work all over."

"I'm afraid," admitted Pete, "the trail would lead right back. Perhaps, as government officials, you can do something about the fourth-dimensional demonstrator. That's the guilty party. I'll show you."

He led the way to the laboratory. Arthur appeared, looking vengeful. The two officers looked apprehensive.

"Better give him a cigarette," said Pete. "He eats them. Then he'll be your friend for life."

"Hell, no!" said the short, squat man. "You keep between him and me! Maybe Casey'll want to get friendly."

"No cigarettes," said Casey apprehensively. "Would a cigar do?"

"Rather heavy, for so early in the morning," considered Pete, "but you might try."

Arthur soared. He landed within two feet of Casey. Casey thrust a cigar at him. Arthur sniffed at it and accepted it. He put one end in his mouth and bit off the tip.

"There!" said Pete cheerfully. "He likes it. Come on!"

They moved on to the laboratory. They entered—and tumult engulfed them. The demonstrator was running and Thomas—pale and despairing—supervised its action. The demonstrator was turning out currency by what was, approximately, wheelbarrow loads. As each load materialized from the fourth dimension, Thomas gathered it up and handed it to Daisy, who in theory was standing in line to receive it in equitable division.

But Daisy was having a furious quarrel among herself, because some one or other of her had tried to cheat.

"These," said Pete calmly, "are my fiancée."

But the short, squat man saw loads of greenbacks appearing from nowhere. He drew out a short, squat revolver.

"You got a press turning out the stuff behind that wall, huh?" he said shrewdly. "I'll take a look!"

He thrust forward masterfully. He pushed Thomas aside and mounted the inch-thick glass plate. Pete reached, horrified, for the switch. But it was too late. The glass plate revolved one-eighth of a revolution. The demonstrator hummed gleefully; and the officer appeared in duplicate just as Pete's nerveless fingers cut off everything.

Both of the officers looked at each other in flat, incredulous stupefaction. Casey stared, and the hair rose from his head. Then Arthur put a front paw tentatively upon Casey's shoulder. Arthur had liked the cigar. The door to the laboratory had been left open. He had come in to ask for another cigar. But Casey was hopelessly unnerved. He yelled and fled, imagining Arthur in hot pursuit. He crashed into the model of a tesseract and entangled himself hopelessly.

Arthur was an amiable kangaroo, but he was sensitive. Casey's squeal of horror upset him. He leaped blindly, knocking Pete over on the switch and turning it on, and landing between the two stupefied copies of the other officer. They, sharing memories of Arthur, moved in panic just before the glass plate turned.

Arthur bounced down again at the demonstrator's hoot. The nearest copy of the short, squat man made a long, graceful leap and went flying out of the door. Pete struggled with the other, who waved his gun and demanded explanations, growing hoarse from his earnestness.

Pete attempted to explain in terms of pretty girls stepping on banana peels, but it struck the officer as irrelevant. He shouted hoarsely while another Arthur hopped down from the glass plate—while a third, and fourth, and fifth, and sixth, and seventh Arthur appeared on the scene.

He barked at Pete until screams from practically all of Daisy made him turn to see the laboratory overflowing with five-foot Arthurs, all very pleasantly astonished and anxious to make friends with himself so he could play.

Arthur was the only person who really approved the course events had taken. He had existed largely in his own society. But now his own company was numerous. From a solitary kangaroo, in fact, Arthur had become a good-sized herd. And in his happy excitement over the fact, Arthur forgot all decorum and began to play an hysterical form of disorganized leapfrog all about the laboratory.

The officer went down and became a take-off spot for the game. Daisy shrieked furiously. And Arthur—all of him—chose new points of vantage for his leaps until one of him chose the driving motor of the demonstrator. That industrious mechanism emitted bright sparks and bit him. And Arthur soared in terror through the window, followed by all the rest of himself, who still thought it part of the game.

In seconds, the laboratory was empty of Arthurs. But the demonstrator was making weird, pained noises. Casey remained entangled in the bars of the tesseract, through which he gazed with much the expression of an inmate of a padded cell. Only one of the short, squat officers remained in the building. He had no breath left. And Daisy was too angry to make a sound—all six of her. Pete alone was sanely calm.

"Well," he said philosophically, "things seem to have settled down a bit. But something's happened to the demonstrator."

"I'm sorry, sir," said Thomas, pallidly, "I'm no hand at machinery."

One of Daisy said angrily to another of Daisy: "You've got a nerve! That money on the plate is mine!"

Both advanced. Three more, protesting indignantly,

joined in the rush. The sixth—and it seemed to Pete that she must have been the original Daisy—hastily began to sneak what she could from the several piles accumulated by the others.

Meanwhile, the demonstrator made queer noises. And Pete despairingly investigated. He found where Arthur's leap had disarranged a handle which evidently controlled the motor speed of the demonstrator. At random, he pushed the handle. The demonstrator clucked relievedly. Then Pete realized in sick terror that five of Daisy were on the glass plate. He tried to turn it off—but it was too late.

He closed his eyes, struggling to retain calmness, but admitting despair. He had been extremely fond of one Daisy. But six Daisies had been too much. Now, looking forward to eleven and——

A harsh voice grated in his ear.

"Huh! That's where you keep the press and the queer, huh—and trick mirrors so I see double? I'm going through that trapdoor where those girls went! And if there's any funny business on the other side, somebody gets hurt!"

The extra officer stepped up on the glass plate, inexplicably empty now. The demonstrator clucked. It hummed. The plate moved—backward! The officer vanished—at once, utterly. As he had come out of the past, he returned to it, intrepidly and equally by accident. Because one of Arthur had kicked the drive lever into neutral, and Pete had inadvertently shoved it into reverse. He saw the officer vanish and he knew where the supernumerary Daisies had gone—also where all embarrasing bank notes would go. He sighed in relief.

But Casey—untangled from the tesseract—was not relieved. He tore loose from Thomas's helpful fingers and fled to the car. There he found his companion, staring at nineteen Arthurs playing leapfrog over the garage. After explanations they would be more upset still. Pete saw the roadster drive away, wabbling.

"I don't think they'll come back, sir," said Thomas hopefully.

"Neither do I," said Pete in a fine, high calm. He turned to the remaining Daisy, scared but still acquisitive. "Darling," he said tenderly, "all those bank notes are counterfeit, as it develops. We'll have to put them all back and struggle along with the contents of the woodshed and the vegetable bin."

Daisy tried to look absent-minded, and failed.

"I think you've got nerve!" said Daisy indignantly.

First Contact

TOMMY DORT WENT into the captain's room with his last pair of stereophotos and said:

"I'm through, sir. These are the last two pictures I can take."

He handed over the photographs and looked with professional interest at the visiplates which showed all space outside the ship. Subdued, deep-red lighting indicated the controls and such instruments as the quartermaster on duty needed for navigation of the spaceship *Llanvabon*. There was a deeply cushioned control chair. There was the little gadget of oddly angled mirrors—remote descendant of the back-view mirrors of twentieth-century motorists—which allowed a view of all the visiplates without turning the head. And there were the huge plates which were so much more satisfactory for a direct view of space.

The *Llanvabon* was a long way from home. The plates, which showed every star of visual magnitude and could be stepped up to any desired magnification, portrayed stars of every imaginable degree of brilliance, in the startlingly different colors they show outside of atmosphere. But every one was unfamiliar. Only two constellations could be recognized as seen from Earth, and they were shrunken and distorted. The Milky Way seemed vaguely out of place. But even such oddities were minor compared to a sight in the forward plates.

There was a vast, vast mistiness ahead. A luminous mist. It seemed motionless. It took a long time for any appreciable nearing to appear in the vision plates, though the spaceship's velocity indicator showed an incredible speed. The mist was the Crab Nebula, six light-years long, three and a half light-years thick, with outward-reaching members that in the telescopes of Earth gave it some resemblance to the creature for which it was named. It was a cloud of gas, infinitely tenuous, reaching half again as far as from Sol to its nearest neighbor-sun. Deep within it burned two stars; a double star; one component the familiar yellow of the sun of Earth, the other an unholy white.

Tommy Dort said meditatively:

"We're heading into a deep, sir?"

The skipper studied the last two plates of Tommy's taking, and put them aside. He went back to his uneasy contemplation of the vision plates ahead. The *Llanvabon* was decelerating at full force. She was a bare half light-year from the nebula. Tommy's work was guiding the ship's course, now, but the work was done. During all the stay of the exploring ship in the nebula, Tommy Dort would loaf. But he'd more than paid his way so far.

He had just completed a quite unique first—a complete photographic record of the movement of a nebula during a period of four thousand years, taken by one individual with the same apparatus and with control exposures to detect and record any systematic errors. It was an achievement in itself worth the journey from Earth. But in addition, he had also recorded four thousand years of the history of a double star, and four thousand years of the history of a star in the act of degenerating into a white dwarf.

It was not that Tommy Dort was four thousand years old. He was, actually, in his twenties. But the Crab Nebula is four thousand light-years from Earth, and the last two pictures had been taken by light which would not reach Earth until the sixth millennium A.D. On the way here—at speeds incredible multiples of the speed of light—Tommy Dort had recorded each aspect of the nebula by the light which had left it from forty centuries since to a bare six months ago.

The *Llanvabon* bored on through space. Slowly, slowly, slowly, the incredible luminosity crept across the vision plates. It blotted out half the universe from view.

Before was glowing mist, and behind was a star-studded emptiness. The mist shut off three-fourths of all the stars. Some few of the brightest shone dimly through it near its edge, but only a few. Then there was only an irregularly shaped patch of darkness astern against which stars shone unwinking. The *Llanvabon* dived into the nebula, and it seemed as if it bored into a tunnel of darkness with walls of shining fog.

Which was exactly what the spaceship was doing. The most distant photographs of all had disclosed structural features in the nebula. It was not amorphous. It had form. As the *Llanvabon* drew nearer, indications of structure grew more distinct, and Tommy Dort had argued for a curved approach for photographic reasons. So the spaceship had come up to the nebula on a vast logarithmic curve, and Tommy had been able to take successive photographs from slightly different angles and get stereopairs which showed the nebula in three dimensions; which disclosed billowings and hollows and an actually complicated shape. In places, the nebula displayed convolutions like those of a human brain. It was into one of those hollows that the spaceship now plunged. They had been called "deeps" by analogy with crevasses in the ocean floor. And they promised to be useful.

The skipper relaxed. One of a skipper's functions, nowadays, is to think of things to worry about, and then to worry about them. The skipper of the *Llanvabon* was conscientious. Only after a certain instrument remained definitely nonregistering did he ease himself back in his seat.

"It was just hardly possible," he said heavily, "that those deeps might be nonluminous gas. But they're empty. So we'll be able to use overdrive as long as we're in them."

It was a light-year-and-a-half from the edge of the nebula to the neighborhood of the double star which was its heart. That was the problem. A nebula is a gas. It is so thin that a comet's tail is solid by comparison, but a ship traveling on overdrive—above the speed of light—does not want to hit even a merely hard vacuum.

It needs pure emptiness, such as exists between the stars. But the *Llanvabon* could not do much in this expanse of mist if it was limited to speeds a merely hard vacuum would permit.

The luminosity seemed to close in behind the spaceship, which slowed and slowed and slowed. The overdrive went off with the sudden *pinging* sensation which goes all over a person when the overdrive field is released.

Then, almost instantly, bells burst into clanging, strident uproar all through the ship. Tommy was almost deafened by the alarm bell which rang in the captain's room before the quarter master shut it off with a flip of his hand. But other bells could be heard ringing throughout the rest of the ship, to be cut off as automatic doors closed one by one.

Tommy Dort stared at the skipper. The skipper's hands clenched. He was up and staring over the quartermaster's shoulder. One indicator was apparently having convulsions. Others strained to record their findings. A spot on the diffusedly bright mistiness of a bow-quartering visiplate grew brighter as the automatic scanner focused on it. That was the direction of the object which had sounded collision-alarm. But the object locator itself—according to its reading, there was one solid object some eighty thousand miles away—an object of no great size. But there was another object whose distance varied from extreme range to zero, and whose size shared its impossible advance and retreat.

"Step up the scanner," snapped the skipper.

The extra-bright spot on the scanner rolled outward, obliterating the undifferentiated image behind it. Magnification increased. But nothing appeared. Absolutely nothing. Yet the radio locator insisted that something monstrous and invisible made lunatic dashes toward the *Llanvabon*, at speeds which inevitably implied collision, and then fled coyly away at the same rate.

The visiplate went up to maximum magnification. Still nothing. The skipper ground his teeth. Tommy Dort said meditatively:

"D'you know, sir, I saw something like this on a liner

of the Earth–Mars run once, when we were being located by another ship. Their locator beam was the same frequency as ours, and every time it hit, it registered like something monstrous, and solid."

"That," said the skipper savagely, "is just what's happening now. There's something like a locator beam on us. We're getting that beam and our own echo besides. But the other ship's invisible! Who is out here in an invisible ship with locator devices? Not men, certainly!"

He pressed the button in his sleeve communicator and snapped:

"Action stations! Man all weapons! Condition of extreme alert in all departments immediately!"

His hands closed and unclosed. He stared again at the visiplate, which showed nothing but a formless brightness.

"Not men?" Tommy Dort straightened sharply. "You mean—"

"How many solar systems in our galaxy?" demanded the skipper bitterly. "How many planets fit for life? And how many kinds of life could there be? If this ship isn't from Earth—and it isn't—it has a crew that isn't human. And things that aren't human but are up to the level of deep-space travel in their civilization could mean anything!"

The skipper's hands were actually shaking. He would not have talked so freely before a member of his own crew, but Tommy Dort was of the observation staff. And even a skipper whose duties include worrying may sometimes need desperately to unload his worries. Sometimes, too, it helps to think aloud.

"Something like this has been talked about and speculated about for years," he said softly. "Mathematically, it's been an odds-on bet that somewhere in our galaxy there'd be another race with a civilization equal to or further advanced than ours. Nobody could ever guess where or when we'd meet them. But it looks like we've done it now!"

Tommy's eyes were very bright.

"D'you suppose they'll be friendly, sir?"

The skipper glanced at the distance indicator. The

phantom object still made its insane, nonexistent swoops toward and away from the *Llanvabon*. The secondary indication of an object at eighty thousand miles stirred ever so slightly.

"It's moving," he said curtly. "Heading for us. Just what we'd do if a strange spaceship appeared in our hunting grounds! Friendly? Maybe! We're going to try to contact them. We have to. But I suspect this is the end of this expedition. Thank God for the blasters!"

The blasters are those beams of ravening destruction which take care of recalcitrant meteorites in a spaceship's course when the deflectors can't handle them. They are not designed as weapons, but they can serve as pretty good ones. They can go into action at five thousand miles, and draw on the entire power output of a whole ship. With automatic aim and a traverse of five degrees, a ship like the *Llanvabon* can come very close to blasting a hole through a small-sized asteroid which gets in its way. But not on overdrive, of course.

Tommy Dort had approached the bow-quartering visiplate. Now he jerked his head around.

"Blasters, sir? What for?"

The skipper grimaced at the empty visiplate.

"Because we don't know what they're like and can't take a chance! I know!" he added bitterly. "We're going to make contacts and try to find out all we can about them—especially where they come from. I suppose we'll try to make friends—but we haven't much chance. We can't trust them a fraction of an inch. We daren't! They've locators. Maybe they've tracers better than any we have. Maybe they could trace us all the way home without our knowing it! We can't risk a non-human race knowing where Earth is unless we're sure of them! And how can we be sure? They could come to trade, of course—or they could swoop down on overdrive with a battle fleet that could wipe us out before we knew what happened. We wouldn't know which to expect, or when!"

Tommy's face was startled.

"It's all been thrashed out over and over, in theory,"

said the skipper. "Nobody's ever been able to find a sound answer, even on paper. But you know, in all their theorizing, no one considered the crazy, rank impossibility of a deep-space contact, with neither side knowing the other's home world! But we've got to find an answer in fact! What are we going to do about them? Maybe these creatures will be aesthetic marvels, nice and friendly and polite—and, underneath, with the sneaking brutal ferocity of a mugger. Or maybe they'll be crude and gruff as a farmer—and just as decent underneath. Maybe they're something in between. But am I going to risk the possible future of the human race on a guess that it's safe to trust them? God knows it would be worthwhile to make friends with a new civilization! It would be bound to stimulate our own, and maybe wo'd gain enormously. But I can't take chances. The one thing I won't risk is having them know how to find Earth! Either I know they can't follow me, or I don't go home! And they'll probably feel the same way!"

He pressed the sleeve-communicator button again.

"Navigation officers, attention! Every star map on this ship is to be prepared for instant destruction. This includes photographs and diagrams from which our course or starting point could be deduced. I want all astronomical data gathered and arranged to be destroyed in a split second, on order. Make it fast and report when ready!"

He released the button. He looked suddenly old. The first contact of humanity with an alien race was a situation which had been foreseen in many fashions, but never one quite so hopeless of solution as this. A solitary Earth-ship and a solitary alien, meeting in a nebula which must be remote from the home planet of each. They might wish peace, but the line of conduct which best prepared a treacherous attack was just the seeming of friendliness. Failure to be suspicious might doom the human race—and a peaceful exchange of the fruits of civilization would be the greatest benefit imaginable. Any mistake would be irreparable, but a failure to be on guard would be fatal.

The captain's room was very, very quiet. The bow-quartering visiplate was filled with the image of a very small section of the nebula. A very small section indeed. It was all diffused, featureless, luminous mist. But suddenly Tommy Dort pointed.

"There, sir!"

There was a small shape in the mist. It was far away. It was a black shape, not polished to mirror-reflection like the hull of the *Llanvabon*. It was bulbous—roughly pear-shaped. There was much thin luminosity between, and no details could be observed, but it was surely no natural object. Then Tommy looked at the distance indicator and said quietly:

"It's headed for us at very high acceleration, sir. The odds are that they're thinking the same thing, sir, that neither of us will dare let the other go home. Do you think they'll try a contact with us, or let loose with their weapons as soon as they're in range?"

The *Llanvabon* was no longer in a crevasse of emptiness in the nebula's thin substance. She swam in luminescence. There were no stars save the two fierce glows in the nebula's heart. There was nothing but an all-enveloping light, curiously like one's imagining of underwater in the tropics of Earth.

The alien ship had made one sign of less than lethal intention. As it drew near the *Llanvabon*, it decelerated. The *Llanvabon* itself had advanced for a meeting and then come to a dead stop. Its movement had been a recognition of the nearness of the other ship. Its pausing was both a friendly sign and a precaution against attack. Relatively still, it could swivel on its own axis to present the least target to a slashing assault, and it would have a longer firing-time than if the two ships flashed past each other at their combined speeds.

The moment of actual approach, however, was tenseness itself. The *Llanvabon*'s needle-pointed bow aimed unwaveringly at the alien bulk. A relay to the captain's room put a key under his hand which would fire the blasters with maximum power. Tommy Dort watched, his brow wrinkled. The aliens must be of a high degree of civilization if they had spaceships, and civilization does not develop without the development of foresight. These aliens must recognize all the implications of this first contact of two civilized races as fully as did the humans on the *Llanvabon*.

The possibility of an enormous spurt in the development of both, by peaceful contact and exchange of their separate technologies, would probably appeal to them as to man. But when dissimilar human cultures are in contact, one must usually be subordinate or there is war. But subordination between races arising on separate planets could not be peacefully arranged. Men, at least, would never consent to subordination, nor was it likely that any highly developed race would agree. The benefits to be derived from commerce could never make up for a condition of inferiority. Some races—men, perhaps—would prefer commerce to conquest. Perhaps—perhaps!—these aliens would also. But some types even of human beings would have craved red war. If the alien ship now approaching the *Llanvabon* returned to its home base with news of humanity's existence and of ships like the *Llanvabon*, it would give its race the choice of trade or battle. They might want trade, or they might want war. But it takes two to make trade, and only one to make war. They could not be sure of men's peacefulness, or could men be sure of theirs. The only safety for either civilization would lie in the destruction of one or both of the two ships here nad now.

But even victory would not be really enough. Men would need to know where this alien race was to be found, for avoidance if not for battle. They would need to know its weapons, and its resources, and if it could be a menace and how it could be eliminated in case of need. The aliens would feel the same necessities concerning humanity.

So the skipper of the *Llanvabon* did not press the key which might possibly have blasted the other ship to nothingness. He dared not. But he dared not not fire either. Sweat came out on his face.

A speaker muttered. Someone from the range room.

"The other ship's stopped, sir. Quite stationary. Blasters are centered on it, sir."

It was an urging to fire. But the skipper shook his head, to himself. The alien ship was no more than twenty miles away. It was dead-black. Every bit of its exterior was an abysmal, nonreflecting sable. No details could be seen except by minor variations in its outline against the misty nebula.

"It's stopped dead, sir," said another voice. "They've sent a modulated short wave at us, sir. Frequency modulated. Apparently a signal. Not enough power to do any harm."

The skipper said though tight-locked teeth:

"They're doing something now. There's movement on the outside of their hull. Watch what comes out. Put the auxiliary blasters on it."

Something small and round came smoothly out of the oval outline of the black ship. The bulbous hulk moved.

"Moving away, sir," said the speaker. "The object they let out is stationary in the place they've left."

Another voice cut in:

"More frequency modulated stuff, sir. Unintelligible."

Tommy Dort's eyes brightened. The skipper watched the visiplate, with sweat-droplets on his forehead.

"Rather pretty, sir," said Tommy, meditatively. "If they sent anything toward us, it might seem a projectile or a bomb. So they came close, let out a lifeboat, and went away again. They figure we can send a boat or a man to make contact without risking our ship. They must think pretty much as we do."

The skipper said, without moving his eyes from the plate:

"Mr. Dort, would you care to go out and look the thing over? I can't order you, but I need all my operating crew for emergencies. The observation staff—"

"Is expendable. Very well, sir," said Tommy briskly. "I won't take a lifeboat, sir. Just a suit with a drive in it. It's smaller and the arms and legs will look unsuitable for a bomb. I think I should carry a scanner, sir."

The alien ship continued to retreat. Forty, eighty, four hundred miles. It came to a stop and hung there, waiting. Climbing into his atomic-driven spacesuit just within the *Llanvabon*'s air lock, Tommy heard the reports as they went over the speakers throughout the ship. That the other ship had stopped its retreat at four hundred miles was encouraging. It might not have weapons effective at a greater distance than that, and so felt safe. But just as the thought formed itself in his mind, the alien retreated precipitately still farther. Which, as Tommy reflected as he emerged from the lock, might be because the aliens had realized they were giving themselves away, or might be because they wanted to give the impression that they had done so.

He swooped away from the silvery-mirror *Llanvabon*, through a brightly glowing emptiness which was past any previous experience of the human race. Behind him, the *Llanvabon* swung about and darted away. The skipper's voice came in Tommy's helmet phones.

"We're pulling back, too, Mr. Dort. There is a bare possibility that they've some explosive atomic reaction they can't use from their own ship, but which might be destructive even as far as this. We'll draw back. Keep your scanner on the object."

The reasoning was sound, if not very comforting. An explosive which would destroy anything within twenty miles was theoretically possible, but humans didn't have it yet. It was decidedly safest for the *Llanvabon* to draw back.

But Tommy Dort felt very lonely. He sped through emptiness toward the tiny black speck which hung in incredible brightness. The *Llanvabon* vanished. Its polished hull would merge with the glowing mist at a relatively short distance, anyhow. The alien ship was not visible to the naked eye, either. Tommy swam in nothingness, four thousand light-years from home, toward a tiny black spot which was the only solid object to be seen in all of space.

It was a slightly distorted sphere, not much over six feet in diameter. It bounced away when Tommy landed on it, feet-first. There were small tentacles, or horns, which projected in every direction. They looked rather like the detonating horns of a submarine mine, but there was a glint of crystal at the tip-end of each.

"I'm here," said Tommy into his helmet phone.

He caught hold of a horn and drew himself to the object. It was all metal, dead-black. He could feel no texture through his space gloves, of course, but he went over and over it, trying to discover its purpose.

"Deadlock, sir," he said presently. "Nothing to report that the scanner hasn't shown you."

Then, through his suit, he felt vibrations. They translated themselves as clankings. A section of the rounded hull of the object opened out. Two sections. He worked his way around to look in and see the first non-human civilized beings that any man had ever looked upon.

But what he saw was simply a flat plate on which dim red glows crawled here and there in seeming aimlessness. His helmet phones emitted a startled exclamation. The skipper's voice:

"Very good, Mr. Dort. Fix your scanner to look into that plate. They dumped out a robot with an infra-red visiplate for communication. Not risking any personnel. Whatever we might do would damage only machinery. Maybe they expect us to bring it on board—and it may have a bomb charge that can be detonated when they're ready to start for home. I'll send a plate to face one of its scanners. You return to the ship."

"Yes, sir," said Tommy. "But which way is the ship, sir?"

There were no stars. The nebula obscured them with its light. The only thing visible from the robot was the double star at the nebula's center. Tommy was no longer oriented. He had but one reference point.

"Head straight away from the double star," came the order in his helmet phone. "We'll pick you up."

He passed another lonely figure, a little later, headed for the alien sphere with a vision plate to set up. The two spaceships, each knowing that it dared not risk its own race by the slightest lack of caution, would communicate with each other through this small round robot. Their separate vision systems would enable them to exchange all the information they dared give, while they debated the most practical way of making sure that their own civilization would not be endangered by this first contact with another. The truly most practical method would be the destruction of the other ship in a swift and deadly attack—in self-defense.

The *Llanvabon*, thereafter, was a ship in which there were two separate enterprises on hand at the same time. She had come out from Earth to make close-range observations on the smaller component of the double star at the nebula's center. The nebula itself was the result of the most titanic explosion of which men have any knowledge. The explosion took place some time in the year 2946 B.C., before the first of the seven cities of long-dead Ilium was even thought of. The light of that explosion reached Earth in the year 1054 A.D., and was duly recorded in ecclesiastical annals and somewhat more reliably by Chinese court astronomers. It was bright enough to be seen in daylight for twenty-three successive days. Its light—and it was four thousand light-years away—was brighter than that of Venus.

From these facts, astronomers could calculate nine hundred years later the violence of the detonation. Matter blown away from the center of the explosion would have traveled outward at the rate of two million three hundred thousand miles an hour; more than thirty-eight thousand miles a minute; something over six hundred thirty-eight miles per second. When twentieth-century telescopes were turned upon the scene of this vast explosion, only a double star remained—and the nebula. The brighter star of the doublet was almost unique in having so high a surface temperature that it showed no spectrum lines at all. It had a continuous spectrum. Sol's surface temperature is about 7,000° Absolute. That of the hot white star is 500,000 degrees. It has nearly the mass of the sun, but only one fifth its diameter, so that its density is one hundred seventy-three times that of water, sixteen times that of lead, and eight times that of iridium—the heaviest substance known on Earth. But even this density is not that of a dwarf white star like the companion of Sirius. The white star in the Crab Nebula is an incomplete dwarf; it is a star still in the act of collapsing. Examination—including the survey of a four-thousand-year column of its light—was worthwhile. The *Llanvabon* had come to make that examination. But the finding of an alien spaceship upon a similar errand had implications which overshadowed the original purpose of the expedition.

A tiny bulbous robot floated in the tenuous nebular gas. The normal operating crew of the *Llanvabon* stood at their posts with a sharp alertness which was productive of tense nerves. The observation staff divided itself, and a part went half-heartedly about the making of the observations for which the *Llanvabon* had come. The other half applied itself to the problem the spaceship offered.

It represented a culture which was up to space travel on an interstellar scale. The explosion of a mere five thousand years since must have blasted every trace of life out of existence in the area now filled by the nebula. So the aliens of the black spaceship came from another solar system. Their trip must have been, like that of the Earth ship, for purely scientific purposes. There was nothing to be extracted from the nebula.

They were, then, at least near the level of human civilization, which meant that they had or could develop arts and articles of commerce which men would want to trade for, in friendship. But they would necessarily realize that the existence and civilization of humanity was a potential menace to their own race. The two races could be friends, but also they could be deadly enemies. Each, even if unwillingly, was a monstrous menace to the other. And the only safe thing to do with a menace is to destroy it.

In the Crab Nebula the problem was acute and immediate. The future relationship of the two races would be settled here and now. If a process for friendship could be established, one race, otherwise doomed, would survive and both would benefit immensely. But that process had to be established, and confidence built up, without the most minute risk of danger from treachery. Confidence would need to be established upon a foundation of necessarily complete distrust. Neither dared return to its own base if the other could do harm to its race. Neither dared risk any of the necessities to trust. The only safe thing for either to do was destroy the other or be destroyed.

But even for war, more was needed than mere destruction of the other. With interstellar traffic, the aliens must have atomic power and some form of overdrive for travel above the speed of light. With radio location and visiplates and short-wave communication they had, of course, many other devices. What weapons did they have? How widely extended was their culture? What were their resources? Could there be a development of trade and friendship, or were the two races so unlike that only war could exist between them? If peace was possible, how could it be begun?

The men on the *Llanvabon* needed facts—and so did the crew on the other ship. They must take back every morsel of information they could. The most important information of all would be of the location of the other civilization, just in case of war. That one bit of information might be the decisive factor in an interstellar war. But other facts would be enormously valuable.

The tragic thing was that there could be no possible information which could lead to peace. Neither ship could stake its own race's existence upon any conviction of the good will or the honor of the other.

So there was a strange truce between the two ships. The alien went about its work of making observations, as did the *Llanvabon*. This tiny robot floated in bright emptiness. A scanner from the *Llanvabon* was focussed upon a vision plate from the alien. A scanner from the alien regarded a vision plate from the *Llanvabon*. Communication began.

It progressed rapidly. Tommy Dort was one of those who made the first progress report. His special task on the expedition was over. He had now been assigned to work on the problem of communication with the alien entities. He went with the ship's solitary psychologist to the captain's room to convey the news of success. The captain's room, as usual, was a place of silence and dull-red indicator lights and the great bright visiplates on every wall and on the ceiling.

"We've established fairly satisfactory communication, sir," said the psychologist. He looked tired. His work on the trip was supposed to be that of measuring personal factors of error in the observation staff, for the reduction of all observations to the nearest possible decimal to the absolute. He had been pressed into service for which he was not especially fitted, and it told upon him. "That is, we can say almost anything we wish to them, and can understand what they say in return. But of course we don't know how much of what they say is the truth."

The skipper's eyes turned to Tommy Dort.

"We've hooked up some machinery," said Tommy, "that amounts to a mechanical translator. We have vision plates, of course, and then short-wave beams direct. They use frequency-modulation plus what is probably variation in wave forms—like our vowel and consonant sounds in speech. We've never had any use for anything like that before, so our coils won't handle it, but we've developed a sort of code which isn't the language of either set of us. They shoot over short-wave stuff with frequency-modulation, and we record it as sound. When we shoot it back, it's reconverted into frequency-modulation."

The skipper said, frowning:

"Why wave-form changes in short waves? How do you know?"

"We showed them our recorder in the vision plates, and they showed us theirs. They record the frequency-modulation direct. I think," said Tommy carefully, "they don't use sound at all, even in speech. They've set up a communication room, and we've watched them in the act of communicating with us. They made no perceptible movement of anything that corresponds to a speech organ. Instead of a microphone, they simply stand near something that would work as a pick-up antenna. My guess, sir, is that they use microwaves for what you might call person-to-person conversation. I think they make short-wave trains as we make sounds."

The skipper stared at him:

"That means they have telepathy?"

"M-m-m. Yes, sir," said Tommy. "Also it means that we have telepathy too, as far as they are concerned. They're probably deaf. They've certainly no idea of using sound waves in air for communication. They simply don't use noises for any purpose."

The skipper stored the information away.

"What else?"

"Well, sir," said Tommy doubtfully, "I think we're all set. We agreed on arbitrary symbols for objects, sir, by the way of the visiplates, and worked out relationships and verbs and so on with diagrams and pictures. We've a couple of thousand words that have mutual meanings. We set up an analyzer to sort out their short-wave groups, which we feed into a decoding machine. And then the coding end of the machine picks out recordings to make the wave groups we want to send back. When you're ready to talk to the skipper of the other ship, sir, I think we're ready."

"H-m-m. What's your impression of their psychology?" The skipper asked the question of the psychologist.

"I don't know, sir," said the psychologist harassedly. "They seem to be completely direct. But they haven't let slip even a hint of the tenseness we know exists. They act as if they were simply setting up a means of communication for friendly conversation. But there is . . . well . . . an overtone—"

The psychologist was a good man at psychological mensuration, which is a good and useful field. But he was not equipped to analyze a completely alien thought-pattern.

"If I may say so, sir—" said Tommy uncomfortably.

"What?"

"They're oxygen brothers," said Tommy, "and they're not too dissimilar to us in other ways. It seems to me, sir, that parallel evolution has been at work. Per-

haps intelligence evolves in parallel lines, just as . . .
Well . . . basic bodily functions. I mean," he added
conscientiously, "any living being of any sort must ingest,
metabolize, and excrete. Perhaps any intelligent brain
must perceive, apperceive, and find a personal reaction.
I'm sure I've detected irony. That implies humor, too.
In short, sir, I think they could be likable."

The skipper heaved himself to his feet.

"H-m-m," he said profoundly, "we'll see what they
have to say."

He walked to the communications room. The scanner
for the vision plate in the robot was in readiness. The
skipper walked in front of it. Tommy Dort sat down at
the coding machine and tapped at the keys. Highly improbable noises came from it, went into a microphone,
and governed the frequency-modulation of a signal sent
through space to the other spaceship. Almost instantly
the vision screen which with one relay—in the robot—
showed the interior of the other ship lighted up. An
alien came before the scanner and seemed to look in-
quisitively out of the plate. He was extraordinarily man-
like, but he was not human. The impression he gave was
of extreme baldness and a somehow humorous frankness.

"I'd like to say," said the skipper heavily, "the appropriate things about this first contact of two dissimilar
civilized races, and of my hopes that a friendly intercourse between the two peoples will result."

Tommy Dort hesitated. Then he shrugged and tapped
expertly upon the coder. More improbable noises.

The alien skipper seemed to receive the message. He
made a gesture which was wryly assenting. The decoder
on the *Llanvabon* hummed to itself and word-cards
dropped into the message frame. Tommy said dispassionately:

"He says, sir, 'That is all very well, but is there any
way for us to let each other go home alive? I would be
happy to hear of such a way if you can contrive it. At
the moment it seems to me that one of us must be
killed.' "

The atmosphere was of confusion. There were too

many questions to be answered all at once. Nobody could answer any of them. And all of them had to be answered.

The *Llanvabon* could start for home. The alien ship might or might not be able to multiply the speed of light by one more unit than the Earth vessel. If it could, the *Llanvabon* would get close enough to Earth to reveal its destination—and then have to fight. It might or might not win. Even if it did win, the aliens might have a communication system by which the *Llanvabon*'s destination might have been reported to the aliens' home planet before battle was joined. But the *Llanvabon* might lose in such a fight. If she were to be destroyed, it would be better to be destroyed here, without giving any clue to where human beings might be found by a forewarned, forearmed alien battle fleet.

The black ship was in exactly the same predicament. It too, could start for home. But the *Llanvabon* might be faster, and an overdrive field can be trailed, if you set to work on it soon enough. The aliens, also, would not know whether the *Llanvabon* could report to its home base without returning. If the alien were to be destroyed, it also would prefer to fight it out here, so that it could not lead a probably enemy to its own civilization.

Neither ship, then, could think of flight. The course of the *Llanvabon* into the nebula might be known to the black ship, but it had been the end of a logarithmic curve, and the aliens could not know its properties. They could not tell from that from what direction the Earth ship had started. As of the moment, then, the two ships were even. But the question was and remained, "What now?"

There was no specific answer. The aliens traded information for information—and did not always realize what information they gave. The humans traded information for information—and Tommy Dort sweated blood in his anxiety not to give any clue to the whereabouts of Earth.

The aliens saw by infrared light, and the vision plates and scanners in the robot communication-exchange had to adapt their respective images up and down an optical octave each, for them to have any meaning at all. It did not occur to the aliens that their eyesight told that their sun was a red dwarf, yielding light of greatest energy just below the part of the spectrum visible to human eyes. But after that fact was realized on the *Llanvabon,* it was realized that the aliens, also, should be able to deduce the Sun's spectral type by the light to which men's eyes were best adapted.

There was a gadget for the recording of short-wave trains which was as casually in use among the aliens as a sound-recorder is among men. The humans wanted that badly. And the aliens were fascinated by the mystery of sound. They were able to perceive noise, of course, just as a man's palm will perceive infrared light by the sensation of heat it produces, but they could no more differentiate pitch or tone-quality than a man is able to distinguish between two frequencies of heat-radiation even half an octave apart. To them, the human science of sound was a remarkable discovery. They would find uses for noises which humans had never imagined—if they lived.

But that was another question. Neither ship could leave without first destroying the other. But while the flood of information was in passage, neither ship could afford to destroy the other. There was the matter of the outer coloring of the two ships. The *Llanvabon* was mirror-bright exteriorly. The alien ship was dead-black by visible light. It absorbed heat to perfection, and should radiate it away again as readily. But it did not. The black coating was not a "black body" color or lack of color. It was a perfect reflector of certain infrared wave-lengths while simultaneously it fluoresced in just those wave bands. In practice, it absorbed the higher frequencies of heat, converted them to lower frequencies it did not radiate—and stayed at the desired temperature even in empty space.

Tommy Dort labored over his task of communications. He found the alien thought-processes not so alien that he could not follow them. The discussion of technics reached the matter of interstellar navigation. A star map was needed to illustrate the process. It would not have been logical to use a star map from the chart room—but from a star map one could guess the point from which the map was projected. Tommy had a map made specially, with imaginary but convincing star images upon it. He translated directions for its use by the coder and decoder. In return, the aliens presented a star map of their own before the visiplate. Copied instantly by photograph, the Nav officers labored over it, trying to figure out from what spot in the galaxy the stars and Milky Way would show at such an angle. It baffled them.

It was Tommy who realized finally that the aliens had made a special star map for their demonstration too, and that it was a mirror-image of the faked map Tommy had shown them previously.

Tommy could grin, at that. He began to like these aliens. They were not humans, but they had a very human sense of the ridiculous. In course of time Tommy essayed a mild joke. It had to be translated into code numerals, these into quite cryptic groups of short-wave, frequency-modulated impulses, and these went to the other ship and into heaven knew what to become intelligible. A joke which went through such formalities would not seem likely to be funny. But the alien did see the point.

There was one of the aliens to whom communication became as normal a function as Tommy's own code-handlings. The two of them developed a quite insane friendship, conversing by coder, decoder, and short-wave trains. When technicalities in the official messages grew too involved, that alien sometimes threw in strictly nontechnical interpolations akin to slang. Often, they cleared up the confusion. Tommy, for no reason whatever, had filed a code-name of "Buck" which the decoder picked out regularly when this particular one signed his own symbol to the message.

In the third week of communication, the decoder suddenly presented Tommy with a message in the message frame:

You are a good guy. It is too bad we have to kill each other.—BUCK.

Tommy had been thinking much the same thing. He tapped off the rueful reply:

We can't see any way out of it. Can you?

There was a pause, and the message frame filled up again:

If we could believe each other, yes. Our skipper would like it. But we can't believe you, and you can't believe us. We'd trail you home if we got a chance, and you'd trail us. But we feel sorry about it.—BUCK.

Tommy Dort took the messages to the skipper.

"Look here, sir!" he said urgently. "These people are almost human, and they're likable cusses."

The skipper was busy about his important task of thinking things to worry about, and worrying about them. He said tiredly:

"They're oxygen breathers. Their air is twenty-eight percent oxygen instead of twenty, but they could do very well on Earth. It would be a highly desirable conquest for them. And we still don't know what weapons they've got or what they can develop. Would you tell them how to find Earth?"

"N-no," said Tommy, unhappily.

"They probably feel the same way," said the skipper dryly. "And if we did manage to make a friendly contact, how long would it stay friendly? If their weapons were inferior to ours, they'd feel that for their own safety they had to improve them. And we, knowing they were planning to revolt, would crush them while we could—for our own safety! If it happened to be the other way about, they'd have to smash us before we could catch up to them."

Tommy was silent, but he moved restlessly.

"If we smash this black ship and get home," said the

skipper, "Earth Government will be annoyed if we don't
tell them where it came from. But what can we do?
We'll be lucky enough to get back alive with our warning. It isn't possible to get out of those creatures any
more information than we give them, and we surely
won't give them our address! We've run into them by
accident. Maybe—if we smash this ship—there won't
be another contact for thousands of years. And it's a
pity, because trade could mean so much! But it takes
two to make a peace, and we can't risk trusting them.
The only answer is to kill them if we can, and if we
can't, to make sure that when they kill us they'll find
out nothing that will lead them to Earth. I don't like it,"
added the skipper tiredly, "but there simply isn't anything else to do!"

On the *Llanvabon*, the technicians worked frantically
in two divisions. One prepared for victory, and the
other for defeat. The ones working for victory could do
little. The main blasters were the only weapons with any
promise. Their mountings were cautiously altered so that
they were no longer fixed nearly dead ahead, with only
a 5° traverse. Electronic controls which followed a
radio-locator master-finder would keep them trained
with absolute precision upon a given target regardless of
its maneuverings. More, a hitherto unsung genius in the
engine room devised a capacity-storage system by which
the normal full-output of the ship's engines could be
momentarily accumulated and released in surges of
stored power far above normal. In theory, the range of
the blasters should be multiplied and their destructive
power considerably stepped up. But there was not much
more that could be done.

The defeat crew had more leeway. Star charts, navi-
gational instruments carrying telltale notations, the photographic record Tommy Dort had made on the six-
months' journey from Earth, and every other memorandum offering clues to Earth's position, were prepared
for destruction. They were put in sealed files, and if any
one of them was opened by one who did not know the
exact, complicated process, the contents of all the files

would flash into ashes and the ash be churned past any hope of restoration. Of course, if the *Llanvabon* should be victorious, a carefully not-indicated method of re-opening them in safety would remain.

There were atomic bombs placed all over the hull of the ship. If its human crew should be killed without complete destruction of the ship, the atomic-power bombs should detonate if the *Llanvabon* was brought alongside the alien vessel. There were no ready-made atomic bombs on board, but there were small spare atomic-power units on board. It was not hard to trick them so that when they were turned on, instead of yielding a smooth flow of power they would explode. And four men of the Earth-ship's crew remained always in spacesuits with closed helmets, to fight the ship should it be punctured in many compartments by an un-warned attack.

Such an attack, however, would not be treacherous. The alien skipper had spoken frankly. His manner was that of one who wryly admits the uselessness of lies. The skipper of the *Llanvabon,* in turn, heavily admit-ted the virtue of frankness. Each insisted—perhaps truthfully—that he wished for friendship between the two races. But neither could trust the other not to make every conceivable effort to find out the one thing he needed most desperately to conceal—the location of his home planet. And neither dared believe that the other was unable to trail him and find out. Because each felt it his own duty to accomplish that unbearable—to the other—act, neither could risk the possible existence of his race by trusting the other. They must fight because they could not do anything else.

They could raise the stakes of the battle by an ex-change of information beforehand. But there was a limit to the stake either would put up. No information on weapons, population, or resources would be given by either. Not even the distance of their home bases from the Crab Nebula would be told. They exchanged infor-mation, to be sure, but they knew a battle to the death must follow, and each strove to represent his own civili-zation as powerful enough to give pause to the other's ideas of possible conquest—and thereby increased its appearance of menace to the other, and made battle more unavoidable.

It was curious how completely such alien brains could mesh, however. Tommy Dort, sweating over the coding and decoding machines, found a personal equation emerging from the at first stilted arrays of word-cards which arranged themselves. He had seen the aliens only in the vision screen, and then only in light at least one octave removed from the light they saw by. They, in turn, saw him very strangely, by transposed illumination from what to them would be the far ultra-violet. But their brains worked alike. Amazingly alike. Tommy Dort felt an actual sympathy and even something close to friendship for the gill-breathing, bald, and dryly ironic creatures of the black space vessel.

Because of that mental kinship he set up—though hopelessly a sort of table of the aspects of the problem before them. He did not believe that the aliens had any instinctive desire to destroy man. In fact, the study of communications from the aliens had produced on the *Llanvabon* a feeling of tolerance not unlike that between enemy soldiers during a truce on Earth. The men felt no enmity, and probably neither did the aliens. But they had to kill or be killed for strictly logical reasons.

Tommy's table was specific. He made a list of objectives the men must try to achieve, in the order of their importance. The first was the carrying back of news of the existence of the alien culture. The second was the location of that alien culture in the galaxy. The third was the carrying back of as much information as possible about that culture. The third was being worked on, but the second was probably impossible. The first—and all—would depend on the result of the fight which must take place.

The aliens' objectives would be exactly similar, so that the men must prevent, first, news of the existence of Earth's culture from being taken back by the aliens, second, alien discovery of the location of Earth, and third, the acquiring by the aliens of information which would help them or encourage them to attack humanity.

And again the third was in train, and the second was probably taken care of, and the first must await the battle.

There was no possible way to avoid the grim necessity of the destruction of the black ship. The aliens would see no solution to their problems but the destruction of the *Llanvabon*. But Tommy Dort, regarding his tabulation ruefully, realized that even complete victory would not be a perfect solution. The ideal would be for the *Llanvabon* to take back the alien ship for study. Nothing less would be a complete attainment of the third objective. But Tommy realized that he hated the idea of so complete a victory, even if it could be accomplished. He would hate the idea of killing even nonhuman creatures who understood a human fitting out a fleet of fighting ships to destroy an alien culture because its existence was dangerous. The pure accident of this encounter, between peoples who could like each other, had created a situation which could only result in wholesale destruction.

Tommy Dort soured on his own brain which could find no answer which would work. But there had to be an answer! The gamble was too big! It was too absurd that two spaceships should fight—neither one primarily designed for fighting—so that the survivor could carry back news which would set one race to frenzied preparation for war against the unwarned other.

If both races could be warned, though, and each knew that the other did not want to fight, and if they could communicate with each other but not locate each other until some grounds for mutual trust could be reached—

It was impossible. It was chimerical. It was a daydream. It was nonsense. But it was such luring nonsense that Tommy Dort ruefully put it into the coder to his gillbreathing friend Buck, then some hundred thousand miles off in the misty brightness of the nebula.

"Sure," said Buck, in the decoder's word-cards flicking into space in the message frame. "That is a good dream. But I like you and still won't believe you. If I said that first, you would like me but not believe me, either. I tell you the truth more than you believe, and maybe you tell me the truth more than I believe. But there is no way to know. I am sorry."

Tommy Dort stared gloomily at the message. He felt a very horrible sense of responsibility. Everyone did, on the *Llanvabon*. If they failed in this encounter, the human race would run a very good chance of being exterminated in time to come. If they succeeded, the race of the aliens would be the one to face destruction, most likely. Millions or billions of lives hung upon the actions of a few men.

Then Tommy Dort saw the answer.

It would be amazingly simple, if it worked. At worst it might give a partial victory to humanity and the *Llanvabon*. He sat quite still, not daring to move lest he break the chain of thought that followed the first tenuous idea. He went over and over it, excitedly finding objections here and meeting them, and overcoming impossibilities there. It was the answer! He felt sure of it.

He felt almost dizzy with relief when he found his way to the captain's room and asked leave to speak.

It is the function of a skipper, among others, to find things to worry about. But the *Llanvabon*'s skipper did not have to look. In the three weeks and four days since the first contact with the alien black ship, the skipper's face had grown lined and old. He had not only the *Llanvabon* to worry about. He had all of humanity.

"Sir," said Tommy Dort, his mouth rather dry because of his enormous earnestness, "may I offer a method of attack on the black ship? I'll undertake it myself, sir, and if it doesn't work our ship won't be weakened."

The skipper looked at him unseeingly.

"The tactics are all worked out, Mr. Dort," he said heavily. "They're being cut on tape now, for the ship's handling. It's a terrible gamble, but it has to be done."

"I think," said Tommy carefully, "I've worked out a way to take the gamble out. Suppose, sir, we send a message to the other ship, offering—"

His voice went on in the utterly quiet captain's room, with the visiplates showing only a vast mistiness outside and the two fiercely burning stars in the nebula's heart.

The skipper himself went through the air lock with Tommy. For one reason, the action Tommy had suggested would need his authority behind it. For another, the skipper had worried more intensely than anybody else on the *Llanvabon*, and he was tired of it. If he went with Tommy, he would do the thing himself, and if he failed he would be the first one killed—and the tape for the Earth-ship's maneuvering was already fed into the control board and correlated with the master-timer. If Tommy and the skipper were killed, a single control pushed home would throw the *Llanvabon* into the most furious possible all-out attack, which would end in the complete destruction of one ship or the other—or both. So the skipper was not deserting his post.

The outer air lock door swung wide. It opened upon that shining emptiness which was the nebula. Twenty miles away, the little round robot hung in space, drifting in an incredible orbit about the twin central suns, and floating ever nearer and nearer. It would never reach either of them, of course. The white star alone was so much hotter than Earth's sun that its heat-effect would produce Earth's temperature on an object five times as far from it as Neptune is from Sol. Even removed to the distance of Pluto, the little robot would be raised to cherry-red heat by the blazing white dwarf. And it could not possibly approach to the ninety-odd million miles which is the Earth's distance from the sun. So near, its metal would melt and boil away as vapor. But, half a light-year out, the bulbous object bobbed in emptiness.

The two spacesuited figures soared away from the *Llanvabon*. The small atomic drives which made them minute spaceships on their own had been subtly altered, but the change did not interfere with their functioning. They headed for the communication robot. The skipper, out in space, said gruffly:

"Mr. Dort, all my life I have longed for adventure.

This is the first time I could ever justify it to myself."

His voice came through Tommy's space-phone receivers. Tommy wet his lips and said:

"It doesn't seem like adventure to me, sir. I want terribly for the plan to go through. I thought adventure was when you didn't care."

"Oh, no," said the skipper. "Adventure is when you toss your life on the scales of chance and wait for the pointer to stop."

They reached the round object. They clung to its short, scanner-tipped horns.

"Intelligent, those creatures," said the skipper heavily. "They must want desperately to see more of our ship than the communication room, to agree to this exchange of visits before the fight."

"Yes, sir," said Tommy. But privately, he suspected that Buck—his gill-breathing friend—would like to see him in the flesh before one or both of them died. And it seemed to him that between the two ships had grown up an odd tradition of courtesy, like that between two ancient knights before a tourney, when they admired each other wholeheartedly before hacking at each other with all the contents of their respective armories.

They waited.

Then, out of the mist, came two other figures. The alien spacesuits were also power-driven. The aliens themselves were shorter than men, and their helmet openings were coated with a filtering material to cut off visible and ultraviolet rays which to them would be lethal. It was not possible to see more than the outline of the heads within.

Tommy's helmet phone said, from the communication room on the *Llanvabon:*

"They say that their ship is waiting for you, sir. The air lock door will be open."

The skipper's voice said heavily:

"Mr. Dort, have you seen their spacesuits before? If so, are you sure they're not carrying anything extra, such as bombs?"

"Yes, sir," said Tommy. "We've showed each other

our space equipment. They've nothing but regular stuff in view, sir."

The skipper made a gesture to the two aliens. He and Tommy Dort plunged on for the black vessel. They could not make out the ship very clearly with the naked eye, but directions for change of course came from the communication room.

The black ship loomed up. It was huge, as long as the *Llanvabon* and vastly thicker. The air lock did stand open. The two spacesuited men moved in and anchored themselves with magnetic-soled boots. The outer door closed. There was a rush of air and simultaneously the sharp quick tug of artificial gravity. Then the inner door opened.

All was darkness. Tommy switched on his helmet light at the same instant as the skipper. Since the aliens saw by infrared, a white light would have been intolerable to them. The men's helmet lights were, therefore, of the deep-red tint used to illuminate instrument panels so there will be no dazzling of eyes that must be able to detect the minutest speck of white light on a navigating vision plate. There were aliens waiting to receive them. They blinked at the brightness of the helmet lights. The space-phone receivers said in Tommy's ear:

"They say, sir, their skipper is waiting for you."

Tommy and the skipper were in a long corridor with a soft flooring underfoot. Their lights showed details of which every one was exotic.

"I think I'll crack my helmet, sir," said Tommy.

He did. The air was good. By analysis it was thirty percent oxygen instead of twenty for normal air on Earth, but the pressure was less. It felt just right. The artificial gravity, too, was less than that maintained on the *Llanvabon*. The home planet of the aliens would be smaller than Earth, and—by the infrared data—circling close to a nearly dead, dull-red sun. The air had smells in it. They were utterly strange, but not unpleasant.

An arched opening. A ramp with the same soft stuff underfoot. Lights which actually shed a dim, dull-red glow about. The aliens had stepped up some of their illuminating equipment as an act of courtesy. The light

might hurt their eyes, but it was a gesture of consideration which made Tommy even more anxious for his
plan to go through.

The alien skipper faced them with what seemed to
Tommy a gesture of wryly humorous deprecation. The
helmet phones said:

"He says, sir, that he greets you with pleasure, but he
has been able to think of only one way in which the
problem created by the meeting of these two ships can
be solved."

"He means a fight," said the skipper. "Tell him I'm
here to offer another choice."

The *Llanvabon*'s skipper and the skipper of the alien
ship were face to face, but their communication was
weirdly indirect. The aliens used no sound in communication. Their talk, in fact, took place on microwaves
and approximated telepathy. But they could not hear, in
any ordinary sense of the word, so the skipper's and
Tommy's speech approached telepathy, too, as far as
they were concerned. When the skipper spoke, his space
phone sent his words back to the *Llanvabon*, where the
words were fed into the coder and short-wave equivalents sent back to the black ship. The alien skipper's
reply went to the *Llanvabon* and through the decoder,
and was retransmitted by space phone in words read
from the message frame. It was awkward, but it
worked.

The short and stocky alien skipper paused. The helmet phones relayed his translated, soundless reply.

"He is anxious to hear, sir."

The skipper took off his helmet. He put his hands at
his belt in a belligerent pose.

"Look here!" he said truculently to the bald, strange
creature in the unearthly red glow before him. "It looks
like we have to fight and one batch of us get killed.
We're ready to do it if we have to. But if you win, we've
got it fixed so you'll never find out where Earth is, and
there's a good chance we'll get you anyhow! If we win,
we'll be in the same fix. And if we win and go back
home, our government will fit out a fleet and start hunting your planet. And if we find it we'll be ready to blast

it to hell! If you win, the same thing will happen to us! And it's all foolishness! We've stayed here a month, and we've swapped information, and we don't hate each other. There's no reason for us to fight except for the rest of our respective races!"

The skipper stopped for breath, scowling. Tommy Dort inconspicuously put his own hand on the belt of his spacesuit. He waited, hoping desperately that the trick would work.

"He says, sir," reported the helmet phones, "that all you say is true. But that his race has to be protected, just as you feel that yours must be."

"Naturally," said the skipper angrily, "but the sensible thing to do is to figure out how to protect it! Putting its future up as a gamble in a fight is not sensible. Our races have to be warned of each other's existence. That's true. But each should have proof that the other doesn't want to fight, but wants to be friendly. And we shouldn't be able to find each other, but we should be able to communicate with each other to work out grounds for a common trust. If our governments want to be fools, let them! But we should give them the chance to make friends, instead of starting a space war out of mutual funk!"

Briefly, the space phone said:

"He says that the difficulty is that of trusting each other now. With the possible existence of his race at stake, he cannot take any chance, and neither can you, of yielding an advantage."

"But my race," boomed the skipper, glaring at the alien captain, "my race has an advantage now. We came here to your ship in atom-powered spacesuits! Before we left, we altered the drives! We can set off ten pounds of sensitized fuel apiece, right here in this ship, or it can be set off by remote control from our ship! It will be rather remarkable if your fuel store doesn't blow up with us! In other words, if you don't accept my proposal for a commonsense approach to this predicament, Dort and I blow up in an atomic explosion, and your ship will be wrecked if not destroyed—and the *Llanva-*

bon will be attacking with everything it's got within two seconds after the blast goes off!"

The captain's room of the alien ship was a strange scene, with its dull-red illumination and the strange, bald, gill-breathing aliens watching the skipper and waiting for the inaudible translation of the harangue they could not hear. But a sudden tensity appeared in the air. A sharp, savage feeling of strain. The alien skipper made a gesture. The helmet phones hummed.

"He says, sir, what is your proposal?"

"Swap ships!" roared the skipper. "Swap ships and go on home! We can fix our instruments so they'll do no trailing, he can do the same with his. We'll each remove out star maps and records. We'll each dismantle our weapons. The air will serve, and we'll take their ship and they'll take ours, and neither one can harm or trail the other, and each will carry home more information than can be taken otherwise! We can agree on this same Crab Nebula as a rendezvous when the double star has made another circuit, and if our people want to meet them they can do it, and if they are scared they can duck it! That's my proposal! And he'll take it, or Dort and I blow up their ship and the *Llanvabon* blasts what's left!"

He glared about him while he waited for the translation to reach the tense small stocky figures about him. He could tell when it came because the tenseness changed. The figures stirred. They made gestures. One of them made convulsive movements. It lay down on the soft floor and kicked. Others leaned against its walls and shook.

The voice in Tommy Dort's helmet phones had been strictly crisp and professional, before, but now it sounded blankly amazed.

"He says, sir, that it is a good joke. Because the two crew members he sent to our ship, and that you passed on the way, have their spacesuits stuffed with atomic explosives too, sir, and he intended to make the very same offer and threat! Of course he accepts, sir. Your ship is worth more to him than his own, and his is worth more to you than the *Llanvabon*. It appears, sir, to be a deal."

Then Tommy Dort realized what the convulsive movements of the aliens were. They were laughter.

It wasn't quite as simple as the skipper had outlined it. The actual working-out of the proposal was complicated. For three days the crews of the two ships were intermingled, the aliens learning the workings of the *Llanvabon*'s engines, and the men learning the controls of the black spaceship. It was a good joke—but it wasn't all a joke. There were men on the black ship, and aliens on the *Llanvabon*, ready at an instant's notice to blow up the vessels in question. And they would have done it in case of need, for which reason the need did not appear. But it was, actually, a better arrangement to have two expeditions return to two civilizations, under the current arrangement, than for either to return alone.

There were differences, though. There was some dispute about the removal of records. In most cases the dispute was settled by the destruction of the records. There was more trouble caused by the *Llanvabon*'s books, and the alien equivalent of a ship's library, containing works which approximated the novels of Earth. But those items were valuable to possible friendship, because they would show the two cultures, each to the other, from the viewpoint of normal citizens and without propaganda.

But nerves were tense during those three days. Aliens unloaded and inspected the foodstuffs intended for the men on the black ship. Men transshipped the foodstuffs the aliens would need to return to their home. There were endless details, from the exchange of lighting equipment to suit the eyesight of the exchanging crews, to a final check-up of apparatus. A joint inspection party of both races verified that all detector devices had been smashed but not removed, so that they could not be used for trailing and had not been smuggled away. And of course, the aliens were anxious not to leave any useful weapon on the black ship, nor the men upon the

Llanvabon. It was a curious fact that each crew was best qualified to take exactly the measures which made an evasion of the agreement impossible.

There was a final conference before the two ships parted, back in the communication room of the *Llanvabon*.

"Tell the little runt," rumbled the *Llanvabon*'s former skipper, "that he's got a good ship and he'd better treat her right."

The message frame flicked word-cards into position.

"I believe," it said on the alien skipper's behalf, "that your ship is just as good. I hope to meet you here when the double star has turned one turn."

The last man left the *Llanvabon*. It moved away into the misty nebula before they had returned to the black ship. The vision plates in that vessel had been altered for human eyes, and human crewmen watched jealously for any trace of their former ship as their new craft took a crazy, evading course to a remote part of the nebula. It came to a crevasse of nothingness, leading to the stars. It rose swiftly to clear space. There was the instant of breathlessness which the overdrive field produces as it goes on, and then the black ship whipped away into the void at many times the speed of light.

Many days later, the skipper saw Tommy Dort poring over one of the strange objects which were the equivalent of books. It was fascinating to puzzle over. The skipper was pleased with himself. The technicians of the *Llanvabon*'s former crew were finding out desirable things about the ship almost momently. Doubtless the aliens were as pleased with their discoveries in the *Llanvabon*. But the black ship would be enormously worth while—and the solution that had been found was by any standard much superior even to combat in which the Earthmen had been overwhelmingly victorious.

"Hm-m-m. Mr. Dort," said the skipper profoundly. "You've no equipment to make another photographic record on the way back. It was left on the *Llanvabon*. But fortunately, we have your record taken on the way out, and I shall report most favorably on your suggestion and your assistance in carrying it out. I think very well of you, sir."

"Thank you, sir," said Tommy Dort.

He waited. The skipper cleared his throat.

"You . . . ah . . . first realized the close similarity of mental processes between the aliens and ourselves," he observed. "What do you think of the prospects of a friendly arrangement if we keep a rendezvous with them at the nebula as agreed?"

"Oh, we'll get along all right, sir," said Tommy. "We've got a good start toward friendship. After all, since they see by infrared, the planets they'd want to make use of wouldn't suit us. There's no reason why we shouldn't get along. We're almost alike in psychology."

"Hm-m-m. Now just what do you mean by that?" demanded the skipper.

"Why, they're just like us, sir!" said Tommy. "Of course they breathe through gills and they see by heat waves, and their blood has a copper base instead of iron and a few little details like that. But otherwise we're just alike! There were only men in their crew, sir, but they have two sexes as we have and they have families, and . . . er . . . their sense of humor— In fact—"

Tommy hesitated.

"Go on, sir," said the skipper.

"Well— There was the one I call Buck, sir, because he hasn't any name that goes into sound waves," said Tommy. "We got along very well. I'd really call him my friend, sir. And we were together for a couple of hours just before the two ships separated and we'd nothing in particular to do. So I became convinced that humans and aliens are bound to be good friends if they have only half a chance. You see, sir, we spent those two hours telling dirty jokes."

The Ethical Equations

IT IS VERY, very queer. The Ethical Equations, of course, link conduct with probability, and give mathematical proof that certain patterns of conduct increase the probability of certain kinds of coincidences. But nobody ever expected them to have any really practical effect. Elucidation of the laws of chance did not stop gambling, though it did make life insurance practical. The Ethical Equations weren't expected to be even as useful as that. They were just theories, which seemed unlikely to affect anybody particularly. They were complicated, for one thing. They admitted that the ideal pattern of conduct for one man wasn't the best for another. A politician, for example, has an entirely different code—and properly—than a Space Patrol man. But still, on at least one occasion—

The thing from outer space was fifteen hundred feet long, and upward of a hundred and fifty feet through at its middle section, and well over two hundred in a curious bulge like a fish's head at its bow. There were odd, gill-like flaps just back of that bulge, too, and the whole thing looked extraordinarily like a monster, eyeless fish, floating in empty space out beyond Jupiter. But it had drifted in from somewhere beyond the sun's gravitational field—its speed was too great for it to have a closed orbit—and it swung with a slow, inane, purposeless motion about some axis it had established within itself.

The little spacecruiser edged closer and closer. Freddy Holmes had been a pariah on the *Arnina* all the way out from Mars, but he clenched his hands and forgot his misery and the ruin of his career in the excitement of looking at the thing.

"No response to signals on any frequency, sir," said the communications officer, formally. "It is not radiating. It has a minute magnetic field. Its surface temperature is just about four degrees absolute."

The commander of the *Arnina* said, "Hrrrmph!" Then he said, "We'll lay alongside." Then he looked at Freddy Holmes and stiffened. "No," he said, "I believe you take over now, Mr. Holmes."

Freddy started. He was in a very bad spot, but his excitement had made him oblivious of it for a moment. The undisguised hostility with which he was regarded by the skipper and the others on the bridge brought it back, however.

"You take over, Mr. Holmes," repeated the skipper bitterly. "I have orders to that effect. You originally detected this object and your uncle asked Headquarters that you be given full authority to investigate it. You have that authority. Now, what are you going to do with it?"

There was fury in his voice surpassing even the rasping dislike of the voyage out. He was a lieutenant commander and he had been instructed to take orders from a junior officer. That was bad enough. But this was humanity's first contact with an extrasolar civilization, and Freddy Holmes, lieutenant junior grade, had been given charge of the matter by pure political pull.

Freddy swallowed.

"I . . . I—" He swallowed again and said miserably, "Sir, I've tried to explain that I dislike the present set-up as much as you possibly can. I . . . wish that you would let me put myself under your orders, sir, instead of—"

"No!" rasped the commander vengefully. "You are in command, Mr. Holmes. Your uncle put on political pressure to arrange it. My orders are to carry out your instructions, not to wet-nurse you if the job is too big for you to handle. This is in your lap! Will you issue orders?"

Freddy stiffened.

"Very well, sir. It's plainly a ship and apparently a derelict. No crew would come in without using a drive, or allow their ship to swing about aimlessly. You will maintain your present position with relation to it. I'll take a spaceboat and a volunteer, if you will find me one, and look it over."

He turned and left the bridge. Two minutes later he was struggling into a spacesuit when Lieutenant Bridges—also junior grade—came briskly into the spacesuit locker and observed:

"I've permission to go with you, Mr. Holmes." He began to get into another spacesuit. As he pulled it up over his chest he added blithely: "I'd say this was worth the price of admission!"

Freddy did not answer. Three minutes later the little spaceboat pulled out from the side of the cruiser. Designed for expeditionary work and tool-carrying rather than as an escapecraft, it was not enclosed. It would carry men in spacesuits, with their tools and weapons, and they could breathe from its tanks instead of from their suits, and use its power and so conserve their own. But it was a strange feeling to sit within its spidery outline and see the great blank sides of the strange object draw near. When the spaceboat actually touched the vast metal wall it seemed impossible, like the approach to some sorcerer's castle across a monstrous moat of stars.

It was real enough, though. The felted rollers touched, and Bridges grunted in satisfaction.

"Magnetic. We can anchor to it. Now what?"

"We hunt for an entrance port," said Freddy curtly. He added: "Those openings that look like gills are the drive tubes. Their drive's in front instead of the rear. Apparently they don't use gyros for steering."

The tiny craft clung to the giant's skin, like a fly on a stranded whale. It moved slowly to the top of the rounded body, and over it, and down on the other side. Presently the cruiser came in sight again as it came up the near side once more.

"Nary a port, sir," said Bridges blithely. "Do we cut our way in?"

"Hm-m-m," said Freddy slowly. "We have our drive in the rear, and our control room in front. So we take on supplies amidships, and that's where we looked. But this ship is driven from the front. Its control room might be amidships. If so, it might load at the stern. Let's see."

The little craft crawled to the stern of the monster. "There!" said Freddy.

It was not like an entrance port on any vessel in the solar system. It slid aside, without hinges. There was an inner door, but it opened just as readily. There was no rush of air, and it was hard to tell if it was intended as an air lock or not.

"Air's gone," said Freddy. "It's a derelict, all right. You might bring a blaster, but what we'll mostly need is light, I think."

The magnetic anchors took hold. The metal grip shoes of the spacesuits made loud noises inside the suits as the two of them pushed their way into the interior of the ship. The spacecruiser had been able to watch them, until now. Now they were gone.

The giant, enigmatic object which was so much like a blind fish in empty space floated on. It swung aimlessly about some inner axis. The thin sunlight out here beyond Jupiter, smote upon it harshly. It seemed to hang motionless in mid-space against an all-surrounding background of distant and unwinking stars. The trim Space Patrol ship hung alertly a mile and a half away. Nothing seemed to happen at all.

Freddy was rather pale when he went back to the bridge. The pressure mark on his forehead from the spacesuit helmet was still visible, and he rubbed at it abstractedly. The skipper regarded him with a sort of envious bitterness. After all, any human would envy any other who had set foot in an alien spaceship. Lieutenant Bridges followed him. For an instant there were no words. Then Bridges saluted briskly:

"Reporting back on board, sir, and returning to watch duty after permitted volunteer activity."

The skipper touched his hat sourly. Bridges departed

with crisp precision. The skipper regarded Freddy with the helpless fury of a senior officer who has been ordered to prove a junior officer a fool, and who has seen the assignment blow up in his face and that of the superior officers who ordered it. It was an enraging situation. Freddy Holmes, newly commissioned and assigned to the detector station on Luna which keeps track of asteroids and meteor streams, had discovered a small object coming in over Neptune. Its speed was too high for it to be a regular member of the solar system, so he'd reported it as a visitor and suggested immediate examination. But junior officers are not supposed to make discoveries. It violates tradition, which is a sort of Ethical Equation in the Space Patrol. So Freddy was slapped down for his presumption. And he slapped back, on account of the Ethical Equations' bearing upon scientific discoveries. The first known object to come from beyond the stars ought to be examined. Definitely. So, most unprofessionally for a Space Patrol junior, Freddy raised a stink.

The present state of affairs was the result. He had an uncle who was a prominent politician. That uncle went before the Space Patrol Board and pointed out smoothly that his nephew's discovery was important. He demonstrated with mathematical precision that the Patrol was being ridiculous in ignoring a significant discovery simply because a junior officer had made it. And the Board, seething at outside interference, ordered Freddy to be taken to the object he had detected, given absolute command of the spacecruiser which had taken him there, and directed to make the examination he had suggested. By all the laws of probability, he would have to report that the hunk of matter from beyond the solar system was just like hunks of matter in it. And then the Board would pin back both his and his uncle's ears with a vengeance.

But now the hunk of matter turned out to be a fish-shaped artifact from an alien civilization. It turned out to be important. So the situation was one to make anybody steeped in Patrol tradition grind his teeth.

"The thing, sir," said Freddy evenly, "is a spaceship.

It is driven by atomic engines shooting blasts sternward from somewhere near the bow. Apparently they steer only by hand. Apparently, too, there was a blow-up in the engine room and they lost most of their fuel out the tube vents. After that, the ship was helpless though they patched up the engines after a fashion. It is possible to calculate that in its practically free fall to the sun it's been in its present state for a couple of thousand years."

"I take it, then," said the skipper with fine irony, "that there are no survivors of the crew."

"It presents several problems, sir," said Freddy evenly, "and that's one of them." He was rather pale. "The ship is empty of air, but her tanks are full. Storage spaces containing what look like supplies are only partly emptied. The crew did not starve or suffocate. The ship simply lost most of her fuel. So it looks like they prepared the ship to endure an indefinite amount of floating about in free space and"—he hesitated—"then it looks like they went into suspended animation. They're all on board, in transparent cases that have—machinery attached. Maybe they thought they'd be picked up by sister ships sooner or later."

The skipper blinked.

"Suspended animation? They're alive?" Then he said sharply: "What sort of ship is it? Cargo?"

"No, sir," said Freddy. "That's another problem. Bridges and I agree that it's a fighting ship, sir. There are rows of generators serving things that could only be weapons. By the way they're braced, there are tractor beams and pressor beams and—there are vacuum tubes that have grids but apparently work with cold cathodes. By the size of the cables that lead to them, those tubes handle amperages up in the thousands. You can figure that one out, sir."

The skipper paced two steps this way, and two steps that. The thing was stupendous. But his instructions were precise.

"I'm under your orders," he said doggedly. "What are you going to do?"

"I'm going to work myself to death, I suppose," said Freddy unhappily, "and some other men with me. I want to go over that ship backwards, forwards, and sideways with scanners, and everything the scanners see photographed back on board, here. I want men to work the scanners and technicians on board to direct them for their specialties. I want to get every rivet and coil in that whole ship on film before touching anything."

The skipper said grudgingly:

"That's not too foolish. Very well, Mr. Holmes, it will be done."

"Thank you," said Freddy. He started to leave the bridge, and stopped. "The men to handle the scanners," he added, "ought to be rather carefully picked. Imaginative men wouldn't do. The crew of that ship—they look horribly alive, and they aren't pretty. And . . . er . . . the plastic cases they're in are arranged to open from inside. That's another problem still, sir."

He went on down. The skipper clasped his hands behind his back and began to pace the bridge furiously. The first object from beyond the stars was a spaceship. It had weapons the Patrol had only vainly imagined. And he, a two-and-a-half-striper, had to stand by and take orders for its investigation from a lieutenant junior grade just out of the Academy. Because of politics! The skipper ground his teeth—

Then Freddy's last comment suddenly had meaning. The plastic cases in which the alien's crew lay in suspended animation opened from the inside. From the inside!

Cold sweat came out on the skipper's forehead as he realized the implication. Tractor and pressor beams, and the ship's fuel not quite gone, and the suspended-animation cases opening from the inside—

There was a slender, coaxial cable connecting the two spacecraft, now. They drifted in sunward together. The little cruiser was dwarfed by the alien giant.

The sun was very far away; brighter than any star, to be sure, and pouring out a fierce radiation, but still very far from a warming orb. All about were the small, illimitably distant lights which were stars. There was exactly one object in view which had an appreciable diameter.

That was Jupiter, a new moon in shape, twenty million miles sunward and eighty million miles farther along its orbit. The rest was emptiness.

The spidery little spaceboat slid along the cable between the two craft. Spacesuited figures got out and clumped on magnetic-soled shoes to the air lock. They went in.

Freddy came to the bridge. The skipper said hoarsely:

"Mr. Holmes, I would like to make a request. You are, by orders of the Board, in command of this ship until your investigation of the ship yonder is completed."

Freddy's face was haggard and worn. He said abstractedly:

"Yes, sir. What is it?"

"I would like," said the *Arnina*'s skipper urgently, "to send a complete report of your investigation so far. Since you are in command, I cannot do so without your permission."

"I would rather you didn't, sir," said Freddy. Tired as he was, his jaws clamped. "Frankly, sir, I think they'd cancel your present orders and issue others entirely."

The skipper bit his lip. That was the idea. The scanners had sent back complete images of almost everything in the other ship, now. Everything was recorded on film. The skipper had seen the monsters which were the crew of the extrasolar vessel. And the plastic cases in which they had slumbered for at least two thousand years did open from the inside. That was what bothered him. They did open from the inside!

The electronics technicians of the *Arnina* were going about in silly rapture, drawing diagrams for each other and contemplating the results with dazed appreciation. The gunnery officer was making scale, detailed design-drawings for weapons he had never hoped for, and waking up of nights to feel for those drawings and be sure that they were real. But the engineer officer was wringing his hands. He wanted to take the other ship's engines apart. They were so enormously smaller than the

Arnina's drive, and yet they had driven a ship with eighty-four times the *Arnina*'s mass—and he could not see how they could work.

The alien ship was ten thousand years ahead of the *Arnina*. Its secrets were being funneled over to the little Earth-ship at a rapid rate. But the cases holding its still-living crew opened from the inside.

"Nevertheless, Mr. Holmes," the skipper said feverishly, "I must ask permission to send that report."

"But I am in command," said Freddy tiredly, "and I intend to stay in command. I will give you a written order forbidding you to make a report, sir. Disobedience will be mutiny."

The skipper grew almost purple.

"Do you realize," he demanded savagely, "that if the crew of that ship is in suspended animation, and if their coffins or containers open only from inside—do you realize that they expect to open them themselves?"

"Yes, sir," said Freddy wearily. "Of course. Why not?"

"Do you realize that cables from those containers lead to thermobatteries in the ship's outer plating? The monsters knew they couldn't survive without power, but they knew that in any other solar system they could get it! So they made sure they'd pass close to our sun with what power they dared use, and went into suspended animation with a reserve of power to land on and thermobatteries that would waken them when it was time to set to work!"

"Yes, sir," said Freddy, as wearily as before. "They had courage, at any rate. But what would you do about that?"

"I'd report it to Headquarters!" raged the skipper. "I'd report that this is a warship capable of blasting the whole Patrol out of the ether and smashing our planets! I'd say it was manned by monsters now fortunately helpless, but with fuel enough to maneuver to a landing. And I'd ask authority to take their coffins out of their ship and destroy them! Then I'd—"

"I did something simpler," said Freddy. "I disconnected the thermobatteries. They can't revive. So I'm going to get a few hours' sleep. If you'll excuse me—"

He went to his own cabin and threw himself on his bunk.

Men with scanners continued to examine every square inch of the monster derelict. They worked in spacesuits. To have filled the giant hull with air would practically have emptied the *Arnina*'s tanks. A spacesuited man held a scanner before a curious roll of flexible substance, on which were inscribed symbols. His headphones brought instructions from the photo room. A record of some sort was being duplicated by photography. There were scanners at work in the storerooms, the crew's quarters, the gun mounts. So far no single article had been moved from the giant stranger. That was Freddy's order. Every possible bit of information was being extracted from every possible object, but nothing had been taken away. Even chemical analysis was being done by scanner, using cold-light spectrography applied from the laboratory on the cruiser.

And Freddy's unpopularity had not lessened. The engineer officer cursed him luridly. The stranger's engines, now— They had been patched up after an explosion, and they were tantalizingly suggestive. But their working was unfathomable. The engineer officer wanted to get his hands on them. The physiochemical officer wanted to do some analysis with his own hands, instead of by cold-light spectrography over a scanner. And every man, from the lowest enlisted apprentice to the skipper himself, wanted to get hold of some artifact made by an alien, non-human race ten thousand years ahead of human civilization. So Freddy was unpopular.

But that was only part of his unhappiness. He felt that he had acted improperly. The Ethical Equations gave mathematical proof that probabilities and ethics are interlinked, so that final admirable results cannot be expected from unethical beginnings. Freddy had violated discipline—which is one sort of ethics—and after that through his uncle had interjected politics into Patrol affairs. Which was definitely a crime. By the Equations, the probability of disastrous coincidences was going to be enormous until corrective, ethically proper action was taken to cancel out the original crimes. And Freddy had been unable to devise such action. He felt, too, that the matter was urgent. He slept uneasily despite his fatigue, because there was something in the back of his mind which warned him stridently that disaster lay ahead.

Freddy awoke still unrefreshed and stared dully at the ceiling over his head. He was trying discouragedly to envision a reasonable solution when there came a tap on his door. It was Bridges with a batch of papers.

"Here you are!" he said cheerfully, when Freddy opened to him. "Now we're all going to be happy!"

Freddy took the extended sheets.

"What's happened?" he asked. "Did the skipper send for fresh orders regardless, and I'm to go in the brig?"

Bridges, grinning, pointed to the sheets of paper in Freddy's hand. They were from the physiochemical officer, who was equipped to do exact surveys on the lesser heavenly bodies.

"*Elements found in the alien vessel,*" was the heading of a list. Freddy scanned the list. No heavy elements, but the rest was familiar. There had been pure nitrogen in the fuel tank, he remembered, and the engineer officer was going quietly mad trying to understand how they had used nitrogen for atomic power. Freddy looked down to the bottom. Iron was the heaviest element present.

"Why should this make everybody happy?" asked Freddy.

Bridges pointed with his finger. The familiar atomic symbols had unfamiliar numerals by them. H^3, Li^5, Gl^8— He blinked. He saw N^{15}, O^{17}, F^{18}, $S^{34,35}$— Then he stared. Bridges grinned.

"Try to figure what that ship's worth!" he said happily. "It's all over the *Arnina*. Prize money isn't allowed in the Patrol, but five percent of salvage is. Hydrogen three has been detected on Earth, but never isolated. Lithium five doesn't exist on Earth, or glucinium eight, or nitrogen fifteen or oxygen seventeen or fluorine eighteen or sulphur thirty-four or thirty-five! The whole ship is made up of isotopes that simply don't exist in the solar system! And you know what pure isotopes sell for! The hull's practically pure iron fifty-five! Pure iron fifty-four sells for thirty-five credits a gram! Talk about the lost treasures of Mars! For technical use only, the stripped hull of this stranger is worth ten years' revenue of Earth government! Every man on the *Arnina* is rich for life. And you're popular!"

Freddy did not smile.

"Nitrogen fifteen," he said slowly. "That's what's in the remaining fuel tank. It goes into a queer little aluminum chamber we couldn't figure out, and from there into the drive tubes. I see—"

He was very pale. Bridges beamed.

"A hundred thousand tons of materials that simply don't exist on Earth! Pure isotopes, intact! Not a contamination in a carload! My dear chap, I've come to like you, but you've been hated by everyone else. Now come out and bask in admiration and affection!"

Freddy said, unheeding:

"I've been wondering what that aluminum chamber was for. It looked so infernally simple, and I couldn't see what it did—"

"Come out and have a drink!" insisted Bridges joyously. "Be lionized! Make friends and influence people!"

"No," said Freddy. He smiled mirthlessly. "I'll be lynched later anyhow. Hm-m-m. I want to talk to the engineer officer. We want to get that ship navigating under its own power. It's too big to do anything with towlines."

"But nobody's figured out its engines!" protested Bridges. "Apparently there's nothing but a tiny trickle of nitrogen through a silly chamber that does something to it, and then it flows through aluminum baffles into the drive tubes. It's too simple! How are you going to make a thing like that work?"

"I think," said Freddy, "it's going to be horribly simple. That whole ship is made up of isotopes we don't have on Earth. No. It has aluminum and carbon.

They're simple substances. Theirs and ours are just alike. But most of the rest—"

He was pale. He looked as if he were suffering.

"I'll get a couple of tanks made up, of aluminum, and filled with nitrogen. Plain air should do— And I'll want a gyro-control. I'll want it made of aluminum, too, with graphite bearings—"

He grinned mirthlessly at Bridges.

"Ever hear of the Ethical Equations, Bridges? You'd never expect them to suggest the answer to a space-drive problem, would you? But that's what they've done. I'll get the engineer officer to have those things made up. It's nice to have known you, Bridges—"

As Bridges went out, Freddy Holmes sat down, wetting his lips, to make sketches for the engineer officer to work from.

The control room and the engine room of the monster ship were one. It was a huge, globular chamber filled with apparatus of startlingly alien design. To Freddy, and to Bridges too, now, there was not so much of monstrousness as at first. Eight days of familiarity, and knowledge of how they worked, had made them seem almost normal. But still it was eerie to belt themselves before the instrument board, with only their hand lamps for illumination, and cast a last glance at the aluminum replacements of parts that had been made on some planet of another sun.

"If this works," said Freddy, and swallowed, "we're lucky. Here's the engine control. Cross your fingers, Bridges."

The interior of the hulk was still airless. Freddy shifted a queerly shaped lever an infinitesimal trace. There was a slight surging movement of the whole vast hull. A faint murmuring came through the fabric of the monster ship to the soles of their spacesuit boots. Freddy wet his lips and touched another lever.

"This should be lights."

It was. Images formed on the queerly shaped screens. The whole interior of the ship glowed. And the whole creation had been so alien as somehow to be revolting, in the harsh white light of the hand lamps the men had used. But now it was like a highly improbable fairy palace. The fact that all doors were circular and all passages round tubes was only pleasantly strange, in the many-colored glow of the ship's own lighting system. Freddy shook his head in his spacesuit helmet, as if to shake away drops of sweat on his forehead.

"The next should be heat," he said more grimly than before. "We do not touch that! Oh, definitely! But we try the drive."

The ship stirred. It swept forward in a swift smooth acceleration that was invincibly convincing of power. The Arnina dwindled swiftly, behind. And Freddy, with compressed lips, touched controls here, and there, and the monstrous ship obeyed with the docility of a willing, well-trained animal. It swept back to clear sight of the *Arnina.*

"I would say," said Bridges in a shaking voice, "that it works. The Patrol has nothing like this!"

"No," said Freddy shortly. His voice sounded sick. "Not like this! It's a sweet ship. I'm going to hook in the gyro controls. They ought to work. The creatures who made this didn't use them. I don't know why. But they didn't."

He cut off everything but the lights. He bent down and looked in the compact little aluminum device which would control the flow of nitrogen to the port and starboard drive tubes.

Freddy came back to the control board and threw in the drive once more. And the gyro control worked. It should. After all, the tool work of a Space Patrol machinist should be good. Freddy tested it thoroughly. He set it on a certain fine adjustment. He threw three switches. Then he picked up one tiny kit he had prepared.

"Come along," he said tiredly. "Our work's over. We go back to the *Arnina* and I probably get lynched."

Bridges, bewildered, followed him to the spidery little spaceboat. They cast off from the huge ship, now three miles or more from the *Arnina* and untenanted save by its own monstrous crew in suspended animation. The

Space Patrol cruiser shifted position to draw near and pick them up. And Freddy said hardly:

"Remember the Ethical Equations, Bridges? I said they gave me the answer to that other ship's drive. If they were right, it couldn't have been anything else. Now I'm going to find out about something else."

His spacegloved hands worked clumsily. From the tiny kit he spilled out a single small object. He plopped it into something from a chest in the spaceboat—a mortar shell, as Bridges saw incredulously. He dropped that into the muzzle of a line-mortar the spaceboat carried as a matter of course. He jerked the lanyard. The mortar flamed. Expanding gases beat at the spacesuits of the men. A tiny, glowing, crimson spark sped toward outer space. Seconds passed. Three. Four. Five—

"Apparently I'm a fool," said Freddy, in the grimmest voice Bridges had ever heard.

But then there was light. And such light! Where the dwindling red spark of a tracer mortar shell had sped toward infinitely distant stars, there was suddenly an explosion of such incredible violence as even the proving-grounds of the Space Patrol had never known. There was no sound in empty space. There was no substance to be heated to incandescence other than that of a half-pound tracer shell. But there was a flare of blue-white light and a crash of such violent static that Bridges was deafened by it. Even through the glass of his helmet he felt a flash of savage heat. Then there was—nothing.

"What was that?" said Bridges, shaken.

"The Ethical Equations," said Freddy. "Apparently I'm not the fool I thought—"

The *Arnina* slid up alongside the little spaceboat. Freddy did not alight. He moved the boat over to its cradle and plugged in his communicator set. He talked over that set with his helmet phone, not radiating a signal that Bridges could pick up. In three minutes or so the great lock opened and four spacesuited figures came out. One wore the crested four-communicator helmet which only the skipper of a cruiser wears when in command of a landing party. The newcomers to the outside

of the *Arnina*'s hull crowded into the little spaceboat.
Freddy's voice sounded again in the headphones, grim
and cold.

"I've some more shells, sir. They're tracer shells
which have been in the work boat for eight days.
They're not quite as cold as the ship, yonder—that's
had two thousand years to cool off in—but they're cold.
I figure they're not over eight or ten degrees absolute.
And here are the bits of material from the other ship.
You can touch them. Our spacesuits are as nearly non-
conductive of heat as anything could be. You won't
warm them if you hold them in your hand."

The skipper—Bridges could see him—looked at the
scraps of metal Freddy held out to him. They were mor-
sels of iron and other material from the alien ship. By
the cold glare of a handlight the skipper thrust one into
the threaded hollow at the nose of a mortar shell into
which a line-end is screwed when a line is to be thrown.
The skipper himself dropped in the mortar shell and
fired it. Again a racing, receding speck of red in emptiness. And a second terrible, atomic blast.

The skipper's voice in the headphones:

"How much more of the stuff did you bring away?"

"Three more pieces, sir," said Freddy's voice, very
steady now. "You see how it happens, sir. They're isotopes we don't have on Earth. And we don't have them
because in contact with other isotopes at normal temperatures, they're unstable. They go off. Here we
dropped them into the mortar shells and nothing happened, because both isotopes were cold—down to the
temperature of liquid helium, or nearly. But there's a
tracer compound in the shells, and it burns as they fly
away. The shell grows warm. And when either isotope,
in contact with the other, is as warm as . . . say . . .
liquid hydrogen . . . why . . . they destroy each
other. The ship yonder is of the same material. Its mass
is about a hundred thousand tons. Except for the aluminum and maybe one or two other elements that also are
non-isotopic and the same in both ships, every bit of
that ship will blast off if it comes in contact with matter

from this solar system above ten or twelve degrees absolute."

"Shoot the other samples away," said the skipper harshly. "We want to be sure—"

There were three violent puffs of gases expanding into empty space. There were three incredible blue-white flames in the void. There was silence. Then—

"That thing has to be destroyed," said the skipper, heavily. "We couldn't set it down anywhere, and its crew might wake up anyhow, at any moment. We haven't anything that could fight it, and if it tried to land on Earth—"

The alien monster, drifting aimlessly in the void, suddenly moved. Thin flames came from the gill-like openings at the bow. Then one side jetted more strongly. It swung about, steadied, and swept forward with a terrifying smooth acceleration. It built up speed vastly more swiftly than any Earth-ship could possibly do. It dwindled to a speck. It vanished in empty space.

But it was not bound inward toward the sun. It was not headed for the plainly visible half-moon disk of Jupiter, now barely seventy million miles away. It headed out toward the stars.

"I wasn't sure until a few minutes ago," said Freddy Holmes unsteadily, "but by the Ethical Equations something like that was probable. I couldn't make certain until we'd gotten everything possible from it, and until I had everything arranged. But I was worried from the first. The Ethical Equations made it pretty certain that if we did the wrong thing we'd suffer for it . . . and by we I mean the whole Earth, because any visitor from beyond the stars would be bound to affect the whole human race." His voice wavered a little. "It was hard to figure out what we ought to do. If one of our ships had been in the same fix, though, we'd have hoped for—friendliness. We'd hope for fuel, maybe, and help in starting back home. But this ship was a warship, and we'd have been helpless to fight it. It would have been hard to be friendly. Yet, according to the Ethical Equations, if we wanted our first contact with an alien civilization to be of benefit to us, it was up to us to get it started back home with plenty of fuel."

"You mean," said the skipper, incredulously, "you mean you—"

"Its engines use nitrogen," said Freddy. "It runs nitrogen fifteen into a little gadget we know how to make, now. It's very simple, but it's a sort of atom smasher. It turns nitrogen fifteen into nitrogen fourteen and hydrogen. I think we can make use of that for ourselves. Nitrogen fourteen is the kind we have. It can be handled in aluminum pipes and tanks, because there's only one aluminum, which is stable under all conditions. But when it hits the alien isotopes in the drive tubes, it breaks down—"

He took a deep breath.

"I gave them a double aluminum tank of nitrogen, and bypassed their atom smasher. Nitrogen fourteen goes into their drive tubes, and they drive! And . . . I figured back their orbit, and set a gyro to head them back for their own solar system for as long as the first tank of nitrogen holds out. They'll make it out of the sun's gravitational field on that, anyhow. And I reconnected their thermobatteries. When they start to wake up they'll see the gyro and know that somebody gave it to them. The double tank is like their own and they'll realize they have a fresh supply of fuel to land with. It . . . may be a thousand years before they're back home, but when they get there they'll know we're friendly and . . . not afraid of them. And meanwhile we've got all their gadgets to work on and work with—"

Freddy was silent. The little spaceboat clung to the side of the *Arnina,* which with its drive off was now drifting in sunward past the orbit of Jupiter.

"It is very rare," said the skipper ungraciously, "that a superior officer in the Patrol apologizes to an inferior. But I apologize to you, Mr. Holmes, for thinking you a fool. And when I think that I, and certainly every other Patrol officer of experience, would have thought of nothing but setting that ship down at Patrol Base for study, and when I think what an atomic explosion of a hundred thousand tons of matter would have done to Earth . . . I apologize a second time."

Freddy said uncomfortably:

"If there are to be any apologies made, sir, I guess I've got to make them. Every man on the *Arnina* has figured he's rich, and I've sent it all back where it came from. But you see, sir, the Ethical Equations—"

When Freddy's resignation went in with the report of his investigation of the alien vessel, it was returned marked *"Not Accepted."* And Freddy was ordered to report to a tiny, hardworked spacecan on which a junior Space Patrol officer normally gets his ears pinned back and learns his work the hard way. And Freddy was happy, because he wanted to be a Space Patrol officer more than he wanted anything else in the world. His uncle was satisfied, too, because he wanted Freddy to be content, and because certain space-admirals truculently told him that Freddy was needed in the Patrol and would get all the consideration and promotion he needed without any politicians butting in. And the Space Patrol was happy because it had a lot of new gadgets to work with which were going to make it a force able not only to look after interplanetary traffic but defend it, if necessary.

And, for that matter, the Ethical Equations were satisfied.

Pipeline to Pluto

FAR, FAR OUT on Pluto, where the sun is only a very bright star and a frozen, airless globe circles in emptiness; far out on Pluto, there was motion. The perpetual faint starlight was abruptly broken. Yellow lights shone suddenly in a circle, and men in spacesuits waddled to a space tug—absurdly marked *Betsy-Anne* in huge white letters. They climbed up its side and went in the air lock. Presently a faint, jetting glow appeared below its drivetubes. It flared suddenly and the tug lifted, to hover expertly a brief distance above what seemed an unmarred field of frozen atmosphere. But that field heaved and broke. The nose of a Pipeline carrier appeared in the center of a cruciform opening. It thrust through. It stood half its length above the surface of the dead and lifeless planet. The tug drifted above it. Its grapnel dropped down, jetted minute flames, and engaged in the monster tow ring at the carrier's bow.

The tug's drivetubes flared luridly. The carrier heaved abruptly up out of its hidingplace and plunged for the heavens behind the tug. It had a huge classmark and number painted on its side, which was barely visible as it whisked out of sight. It went on up at four gravities acceleration, while the spacetug lined out on the most precise of courses and drove fiercely for emptiness.

A long, long time later, when Pluto was barely a pallid disk behind, the tug cast off. The carrier went on, sunward. Its ringed nose pointed unwaveringly to the sun, toward which it would drift for years. It was one of a long, long line of carriers drifting through space, a day apart in time but millions of miles apart in distance.

They would go on until a tug from Earth came out and grappled them and towed them in to their actual home planet.

But the *Betsy-Anne,* of Pluto, did not pause for contemplation of the two-billion-mile-long line of orecarriers taking the metal of Pluto back to Earth. It darted off from the line its late tow now followed. Its radiolocator beam flickered invisibly in emptiness. Presently its course changed. It turned about. It braked violently, going up to six gravities deceleration for as long as half a minute at a time. Presently it came to rest and there floated toward it an object from Earth, a carrier with great white numerals on its sides. It had been hauled off Earth and flung into an orbit which would fetch it out to Pluto. The *Betsy-Anne's* grapnel floated toward it and jetted tiny sparks until the towring was engaged. Then the tug and its new tow from Earth started back to Pluto.

There were two long lines of white-numbered carriers floating sedately through space. One line drifted tranquilly in to Earth. One drifted no less tranquilly out past the orbits of six planets to reach the closed-in, underground colony of the mines on Pluto.

Together they made up the Pipeline.

The evening Moon-rocket took off over to the north and went straight up to the zenith. Its blue-white rocket-flare changed color as it fell behind, until the tail-end was a deep, rich crimson. The Pipeline docks were silent, now, but opposite the yard the row of flimsy eating- and drinking-places rattled and thuttered to themselves from the lower-than-sound vibrations of the Moon-ship.

There was a youngish, battered man named Hill in the Pluto Bar, opposite the docks. He paid no attention to the Moon-rocket, but he looked up sharply as a man came out of the Pipeline gate and came across the street toward the bar. But Hill was staring at his drink when the door opened and the man from the dock looked the small dive over. Besides Hill—who looked definitely tough, and as if he had but recently recovered from a ravaging illness—there was only the bartender, a catawheel-truck driver and his girl having a drink together, and another man at a table by himself and fidgeting nervously as if he were waiting for someone. Hill's eyes flickered again to the man in the door. He looked suspicious. But then he looked back at his glass.

The other man came in and went to the bar.

"Evenin', Mr. Crowder," said the bartender.

Hill's eyes darted up, and down again. The bartender reached below the bar, filled a glass, and slid it across the mahogany.

"Evenin'," said Crowder curtly. He looked deliberately at the fidgety man. He seemed to note that the fidgety man was alone. He gave no sign of recognition, but his features pinched a little, as some men's do when they feel a little, crawling unease. But there was nothing wrong except that the fidgety man seemed to be upset because he was waiting for someone who hadn't come.

Crowder sat down in a booth, alone. Hill waited a moment, looked sharply about him, and then stood up. He crossed purposefully to the booth in which Crowder sat.

"I'm lookin' for a fella named Crowder," he said huskily. "That's you, ain't it?"

Crowder looked at him, his face instantly masklike. Hill's looks matched his voice. There was a scar under one eye. He had a cauliflower ear. He looked battered, and hard-boiled—and as if he had just recovered from some serious injury or illness. His skin was reddened in odd patches.

"My name is Crowder," said Crowder suspiciously. "What is it?"

Hill sat down opposite him.

"My name's Hill," he said in the same husky voice. "There was a guy who was gonna come here tonight. He'd fixed it up to be stowed away on a Pipeline carrier to Pluto. I bought 'im off. I bought his chance. I came here to take his place."

"I don't know what you're talking about," said Crowder coldly.

But he did. Hill could see that he did. His stomach-muscles knotted. He was uneasy. Hill's gaze grew scornful.

"You're the night super of th' Pipeline yards, ain't you?" he demanded truculently.

Crowder's face stayed masklike. Hill looked tough. He looked like the sort of yegg who'd get into trouble with the police because he'd never think things out ahead. He knew it and he didn't care. Because he had gotten in trouble—often—because he didn't think things out ahead. But he wasn't that way tonight. He'd planned tonight in detail.

"Sure I'm the night superintendent of the Pipeline yards," said Crowder shortly. "I came over for a drink. I'm going back. But I don't know what you're talking about."

Hill's eyes grew hard.

"Listen, fella," he said truculently—but he had been really ill, and the signs of it were plain—"they're payin' five hundred credits a day in the mines out on Pluto, ain't they? A guy works a year out there, he comes back rich, don't he?"

"Sure!" said Crowder. "The wages got set by law when it cost a lot to ship supplies out. Before the Pipeline got going."

"An' they ain't got enough guys to work, have they?"

"There's a shortage," agreed Crowder coldly. "Everybody knows it. The liners get fifty thousand credits for a one-way passage, and it takes six months for the trip."

Hill nodded, truculently.

"I wanna get out to Pluto," he said huskily. "See? They don't ask too many questions about a guy when he turns up out there. But the spaceliners, they do, an' they want too many credits. So I wanna go out in a carrier by Pipeline. See?"

Hill downed his drink and stood up.

"There's a law," Crowder said uncompromisingly, "that says the Pipeline can't carry passengers or mail. The spacelines jammed that through. Politics."

"Maybe," said Hill pugnaciously, "but you promised to let a guy stow away on the carrier tonight. He told me about it. I paid him off. He sold me his place. I'm takin' it, see?"

"I'm night superintendent at the yards," Crowder told him. "If there are arrangements for stowaways, I don't know about them. You're talking to the wrong man."

He abruptly left the table. He walked across the room to the fidgety man, who seemed more and more uneasy because somebody hadn't turned up. Crowder's eyes were viciously angry when he bent over the fidgety man.

"Look here, Moore!" he said savagely, in a low tone. "That guy is on! He says he paid your passenger to let him take his place. That's why your man hasn't showed up. You picked him out and he sold his place to this guy. So I'm leaving it right in your lap! I can lie myself clear. They couldn't get any evidence back, anyhow. Not for years yet. But what he told me is straight, he's got to go or he'll shoot off his mouth! So it's in your lap!"

The eyes of Moore—the fidgety man—had a hunted look in them. He swallowed as if his mouth were dry. But he nodded.

Crowder went out. Hill scowled after him. After a moment he came over to Moore.

"Lookahere," he said huskily. "I wanna know somethin'. That guy's night super for Pipeline, ain't he?"

Moore nodded. He licked his lips.

"Lissen!" said Hill angrily, "there's a Pipeline carrier leaves here every day for Pluto, an' one comes in from Pluto every day. It's just like gettin' on a 'copter an' goin' from one town to another on the Pipeline, ain't it?"

Moore nodded again—this time almost unnoticeably.

"That's what a guy told me," said Hill pugnaciously. "He said he'd got it all fixed up to stow away on a carrier-load of grub. He said he'd paid fifteen hundred credits to have it fixed up. He was gonna leave tonight. I paid him off to let me take his place. Now this guy Crowder tells me I'm crazy!"

"I . . . wouldn't know anything about it," said Moore, hesitantly. "I know Crowder, but that's all."

Hill growled to himself. He doubled up his fist and looked at it. It was a capable fist. There were scars on it as proof that things had been hit with it.

"O.K.!" said Hill. "I guess that guy kidded me. He done me outta plenty credits. I know where to find him. He's goin' to a hospital!"

He stirred, scowling.

"W-wait a minute," said Moore. "It seems to me I heard something, once—"

Carriers drifted on through space. They were motorless save for the tiny drives for the gyros in their noses. They were a hundred feet long, and twenty feet thick, and some of them contained foodstuffs in air-sealed containers—because everything will freeze, in space, but even ice will evaporate in a vacuum. Some carried drums of rocket fuel for the tugs and heaters and the generators for the mines on Pluto. Some contained tools and books and visiphone records and caviar and explosives and glue and cosmetics for the women on Pluto. But all of them drifted slowly, leisurely, unhurriedly, upon their two-billion-mile journey.

They were the Pipeline. You put a carrier into the line at Earth, headed out to Pluto. The same day you took a carrier out of space at the end of the line, at Pluto. You put one into the Earth-bound line, on Pluto. You took one out of space the same day, on Earth. There was continuous traffic between the two planets, with daily arrivals and departures from each. But passenger-traffic between Earth and Pluto went by space liners, at a fare of fifty thousand credits for the trip. Because even the liners took six months for the journey, and the Pipeline carriers—well, there were over twelve hundred of them in each line going each way, a day apart in time and millions of miles apart in space. They were very lonely, those long cylinders with their white-painted numbers on their sides. The stars were the only eyes to look upon them while they traveled, and it took three years to drift from one end of the pipeline to the other.

But nevertheless there were daily arrivals and departures on the Pipeline, and there was continuous traffic between the two planets.

Moore turned away from the pay-visiphone, into which he had talked in a confidential murmur while the screen remained blank. The pugnacious, battered Hill scowled impatiently behind him.

"I'm not sure," said Moore uneasily. "I talked to somebody I thought might know something, but they're cagey. They'd lose their jobs and maybe get in worse trouble if anybody finds out they're smuggling stowaways to Pluto. Y'see, the spacelines have a big pull in politics. They've got it fixed so the Pipeline can't haul anything but freight. If people could travel by Pipeline, the spaceliners 'ud go broke. So they watch close."

He looked uneasy as he spoke. His eyes watched Hill almost alarmedly. But Hill said sourly:

"O.K.! I'm gonna find that guy that sold me his place, an' I'm gonna write a message on him with a blowtorch. The docs'll have fun readin' him, an' why he's in the hospital!"

Moore swallowed.

"Who was it? I've heard something—"

Hill bit off the name. Moore swallowed again—as if the name meant something. As if it were right.

"I . . . I'll tell you, guy," said Moore. "It's none of my business, but I . . . well . . . I might be able to fix things up for you. It's risky, though, butting in on something that ain't my business—"

"How much?" said Hill shortly.

"Oh . . . f-five hundred," said Moore uneasily.

Hill stared at him. Hard. Then he pulled a roll out of his pocket. He displayed it.

"I got credits," he said huskily. "But I'm givin' you just one hundred of 'em. I'll give you nine hundred more when I'm all set. That's twice what you asked for. But that's all, see? I got a reason to get off Earth, an' tonight, I'll pay to manage it. But if I'm double-crossed, somebody gets hurt!"

Moore grinned nervously.

"No double-crossing in this," he said quickly. "Just . . . well . . . it is ticklish."

"Yeah," said Hill. He waved a battered-knuckled hand. "Get goin'. Tell those guys I'm willin' to pay. But I get stowed away, or I'll fix that guy who sold me his place so he'll tell all he knows! I'm goin' to Pluto, or else!"

Moore said cautiously:

"M-maybe you'll have to pay out a little more . . . but not much! But you'll get there! I've heard . . . just heard, you understand . . . that the gang here smuggles a fella into the Pipeline yard and up into the nose of a carrier loaded with grub. Champagne and all that. He can live high on the way, and not worry because out on Pluto they're so anxious to get a man to work that they'll square things. They need men bad, out on Pluto! They pay five hundred credits a day!"

"Yeah," said Hill grimly. "They need 'em so bad there ain't no extradition either. I'm int'rested in that, too. Now get goin' an' fix me up!"

The Pipeline was actually a two-billion-mile arrangement of specks in infinity. Each of the specks was a carrier. Each of the carriers was motorless and inert. Each was unlighted. Each was lifeless. But—some of them had contained life when they started.

The last carrier out from Earth, to be sure, contained nothing but its proper cargo of novelties, rocket fuel, canned goods, and plastic base. But in the one beyond that, there was what had been a hopeful stowaway. A man, with his possessions neatly piled about him. He'd been placed up in the nose of the carrier, and he'd waited, mousy-still, until the spacetug connected with the tow ring and heaved the carrier out to the beginning of the Pipeline. As a stowaway, he hadn't wanted to be discovered. The carrier ahead of that—many millions of miles farther out—contained two girls, who had heard that stenographers were highly paid on Pluto, and that there were so few women that a girl might take her pick of husbands. The one just before that had a man and woman in it. There were four men in the carrier beyond them.

The hundred-foot cylinders drifting out and out and out toward Pluto contained many stowaways. The newest of them still looked quite human. They looked quite tranquil. After all, when a carrier is hauled aloft at four gravities acceleration the air flows out of the bilge-valves very quickly, but the cold comes in more quickly still. None of the stowaways had actually suffocated. They'd frozen so suddenly they probably did not realize what was happening. At sixty thousand feet the temperature is around seventy degrees below zero. At a hundred and twenty thousand feet it's so cold that figures simply haven't any meaning. And at four gravities acceleration you reach a hundred and twenty thousand feet before you've really grasped the fact that you paid all your money to be flung unprotected into space. So you never quite realize that you're going on out into a vacuum which will gradually draw every atom of moisture from every tissue of your body.

But, though there were many stowaways, not one had yet reached Pluto. They would do so in time, of course. But the practice of smuggling stowaways to Pluto had only been in operation for a year and a half. The first of the deluded ones had not quite passed the halfway mark. So the stowaway business should be safe and profitable for at least a year and a half more. Then it would be true that a passenger entered the Pipeline from Earth and a passenger reached Pluto on the same day. But it would not be the same passenger, and there would be other differences. Even then, though, the racket would simply stop being profitable, because there was no extradition either to or from Pluto.

So the carriers drifting out through emptiness with their stowaways were rather ironic, in a way. There were tragedies within them, and nothing could be done about them. It was ironic that the carriers gave no sign of the freight they bore. They moved quite sedately, quite placidly, with a vast leisure among the stars.

The battered youngish man said coldly: "Well? You fixed it?"

Moore grinned nervously.

"Yeah. It's all fixed. At first they thought you might be an undercover man for the passenger lines, trying to catch the Pipeline smuggling passengers so they could get its charter canceled. But they called up the man whose place you took, and it's straight. He said he gave you his place and told you to see Crowder."

Hill said angrily:

"But he stalled me!"

Moore licked his lips.

"You'll get the picture in a minute. We cross the street and go in the Pipeline yard. You have to slip the guard something. A hundred credits for looking the other way."

Hill growled:

"No more stalling!"

"No more stalling," promised Moore. "You go out to Pluto in the next carrier."

They went out of the Pluto Bar. They crossed the street, which was thin, black, churned-up mud from the catawheel trucks which hauled away each day's arrival of freight from Pluto. They moved directly and openly for the gateway. The guard strolled toward them.

"Slim," said Moore, grinning nervously, "meet my friend Hill."

"Sure!" said the guard.

He extended his hand, palm up. Hill put a hundred-credit note in it.

"O.K.," said the guard. "Luck on Pluto, fella."

He turned his back. Moore snickered almost hysterically and led the way into the dark recesses of the yard. There was the landing field for the spacetugs. There were six empty carriers off to one side. There was one in a loading pit, sunk down on a hydraulic platform until only its nose now showed aboveground. It could be loaded in its accelerating position, that way, and would not need to be upended after reaching maximum weight.

"Take-off is half an hour before sunrise today," said

Moore jerkily. "You'll know when it's coming because the hydraulic platform shoves the carrier up out of the pit. Then you'll hear the grapnel catching in the tow ring. Then you start. The tug puts you in the Pipeline and hangs around and picks up the other carrier coming back."

"That's speed!" said Hill. "Them scientists are great stuff, huh? I start off in that, an' before I know it I'm on Pluto!"

"Yeah," said Moore. He smirked with a twitching, ghastly effect. "Before you know it. Here's the door where you go in."

Crowder came around the other side of the carrier's cone-shaped nose. He scowled at Hill, and Hill scowled back.

"You sounded phony to me," said Crowder ungraciously. "I wasn't going to take any chances by admitting anything. Moore told you it's going to cost you extra?"

"For what?" demanded Hill, bristling.

"Because you've got to get away fast," said Crowder evenly. "Because there's no extradition from Pluto. We're not in this for our health. Two thousand credits more."

Hill snarled:

"Thief—" Then he said sullenly. "O.K."

"And my nine hundred," said Moore eagerly.

"Sure," said Hill, sardonically. He paid. "O.K. now? Whadda I do now?"

"Go in the door here," said Crowder. "The cargo's grub. Get comfortable and lay flat on your back when you feel the carrier coming up to be hitched on for towing. After the acceleration's over and you're in the Pipeline, do as you please."

"Yeah!" said Moore, giggling nervously. "Do just as you please."

Hill said tonelessly:

"Right. I'll start now."

He moved with a savage, infuriated swiftness. There was a queer, muffled cracking sound. Then a startled gasp from Moore, a moment's struggle, and another sharp crack.

Hill went into the nose of the carrier. He dragged them in. He stayed inside for minutes. He came out and listened, swinging a leather blackjack meditatively. Then he went over to the gate. He called cautiously to the guard.

"You! Slim! Crowder says come quick—an' quiet! Somethin's happened an' him an' Moore got their hands full."

The guard blinked, and then came quickly. Hill hurried behind him to the loading pit. As the guard called tensely:

"Hey, Crowder, what's the matter—"

Hill swung the blackjack again, with a certain deft precision. The guard collapsed.

A little later Hill had finished his work. The three men were bound with infinite science. They not only could not escape, they could not even kick. That's quite a trick—but it can be done if you study the art. And they were not only gagged, but there was tape over their mouths beyond the gag, so that they could not even make a respectable groaning noise. And Hill surveyed the three of them by the light of a candle he had taken from his pocket—as he had taken the rope from about his waist—and said in husky satisfaction:

"O.K. O.K.! I'm givin' you fellas some bad news. You're headin' out to Pluto."

Terror close to madness shone in the three pairs of eyes which fixed frantically upon him. The eyes seemed to threaten to start from their sockets.

"It ain't so bad," said Hill grimly. "Not like you think it is. You'll get there before you know it. No kidding! You'll go snakin' up at four gravities, an' the air'll go out. But you won't die of that. Before you strangle, you'll freeze—an' fast! You'll freeze so fast y'won't have time to die, fellas. That's the funny part. You freeze so quick you ain't got time to die! The Space Patrol found out a year or so back that that can happen, when things are just right—an' they will be, for you. So the Space Patrol will be all set to bring you back, when y'get to Pluto. But it does hurt, fellas. It hurts like hell! I oughta know!"

He grinned at them, his mouth twisted and his eyes grim.

"I paid you fellas to send me out to Pluto last year. But it happened I didn't get to Pluto. The Patrol dragged my carrier out o' the Pipeline an' over to Callisto because they hadda shortage o' rocket fuel there. So I' been through it, an' it hurts! I wouldn't tell on you fellas, because I wanted you to have it, so I took my bawlin' out for stowin' away an' come back to send you along. So you' goin', fellas! An' you' goin' all the way to Pluto! And remember this, fellas! It's gonna be good! After they bring you back, out there on Pluto, every fella an' every soul you sent off as stowaways, they'll be there on Pluto waitin' for you. It's gonna be good, guys! It's gonna be good!"

He looked at them in the candlelight, and seemed to take a vast satisfaction in their expressions. Then he blew out the candle, and closed the nose door of the carrier, and went away.

And half an hour before sunrise next morning the hydraulic platform pushed the carrier up, and a space tug hung expertly overhead and its grapnel came down and hooked in the tow ring, and then the carrier jerked skyward at four gravities acceleration.

Far out from Earth, the carrier went on, the latest of a long line of specks in infinity which constituted the Pipeline to Pluto. Many of those . specks contained things which had been human—and would be human again. But now each one drifted sedately away from the sun, and in the later carriers the stowaways still looked completely human and utterly tranquil. What had happened to them had come so quickly that they did not realize what it was. But in the last carrier of all, with three bound, gagged figures in its nose, the expressions were not tranquil at all. Because those men did know what had happened to them. More—they knew what was yet to come.

The Power

(Memorandum from Professor Charles, Latin Department, Haverford University, to Professor McFarland, the same faculty:

Dear Professor McFarland:
In a recent batch of fifteenth-century Latin documents from abroad, we found three which seem to fit together. Our interest is in the Latin of the period, but their contents seems to bear upon your line. I send them to you with a free translation. Would you let me know your reaction?

Charles.)

To Johannus Hartmannus, Licentiate in Philosophy, Living at the house of the Goldsmith Grote, Lane of the Dyed Fleece, Leyden, the Low Countries.

Friend Johannus:
I write this from the Goth's Head Inn, in Padua, the second day after Michaelmas, Anno Domini 1482. I write in haste because a worthy Hollander here journeys homeward and has promised to carry mails for me. He is an amiable lout, but ignorant. Do not speak to him of mysteries. He knows nothing. Less than nothing. Thank him, give him to drink, and speak of me as a pious and worthy student. Then forget him.

I leave Padua tomorrow for the realization of all my hopes and yours. This time I am sure. I came here to purchase perfumes and mandragora and the other necessities for an Operation of the utmost imaginable im-

199

portance, which I will conduct five nights hence upon a certain hilltop near the village of Montevecchio. I have found a Word and a Name of incalculable power, which in the place that I know of must open to me knowledge of my mysteries. When you read this, I shall possess powers of which Hermes Trismegestus only guessed, and which Albertus Magnus could speak of only by hearsay. I have been deceived before, but this time I am sure. I have seen proofs!

I tremble with agitation as I write to you. I will be brief. I came upon these proofs and the Word and the Name in the village of Montevecchio. I rode into the village at nightfall, disconsolate because I had wasted a month searching for a learned man of whom I had heard great things. Then I found him—and he was but a silly antiquary with no knowledge of mysteries! So, riding upon my way I came to Montevecchio, and there they told me of a man dying even then because he had worked wonders. He had entered the village on foot only the day before. He was clad in rich garments, yet he spoke like a peasant. At first he was mild and humble, but he paid for food and wine with a gold piece, and villagers fawned upon him and asked for alms. He flung them a handful of gold pieces and when the news spread the whole village went mad with greed. They clustered about him, shrieking pleas, and thronging ever the more urgently as he strove to satisfy them. It is said that he grew frightened and would have fled because of their thrusting against him. But they plucked at his garments, screaming of their poverty, until suddenly his rich clothing vanished in the twinkling of an eye and he was but another ragged peasant like themselves and the purse from which he had scattered gold became a mere coarse bag filled with ashes.

This had happened but the day before my arrival, and the man was yet alive, though barely so because the villagers had cried witchcraft and beset him with flails and stones and then dragged him to the village priest to be exorcised.

I saw the man and spoke to him, Johannus, by representing myself to the priest as a pious student of the

snares Satan has set in the form of witchcraft. He barely
breathed, what with broken bones and pitchfork
wounds. He was a native of the district, who until now
had seemed a simple ordinary soul. To secure my inter-
cession with the priest to shrive him 'ere he died, the
man told me all. And it was much!

Upon this certain hillside where I shall perform the
Operation five nights hence, he had dozed at midday.
Then a Power appeared to him and offered to instruct
him in mysteries. The peasant was stupid. He asked for
riches instead. So the Power gave him rich garments
and a purse which would never empty so long—said the
Power—as it came not near a certain metal which de-
stroys all things of mystery. And the Power warned that
this was payment that he might send a learned man to
learn what he had offered the peasant, because he saw
that peasants had no understanding. Thereupon I told
the peasant that I would go and greet this Power and
fulfill his desires, and he told me the Name and the
Word which would call him, and also the Place, begging
me to intercede for him with the priest.

The priest showed me a single gold piece which remained of that which the peasant had distributed. It was
of the age of Antoninus Pius, yet bright and new as if
fresh-minted. It had the weight and feel of true gold.
But the priest, wryly, laid upon it the crucifix he wears
upon a small iron chain about his waist. Instantly it
vanished, leaving behind a speck of glowing coal which
cooled and was a morsel of ash.

This I saw, Johannus! So I came speedily here to
Padua, to purchase perfumes and mandragora and the
other necessities for an Operation to pay great honor to
this Power whom I shall call up five nights hence. He
offered wisdom to the peasant, who desired only gold.
But I desire wisdom more than gold, and surely I am
learned concerning mysteries and Powers! I do not
know any but yourself who surpasses me in true knowledge of secret things. And when you read this, Johannus, I shall surpass even you! But it may be that I will
gain knowledge so that I can transport myself by a mystery to your attic, and there inform you myself, in ad-

vance of this letter, of the results of this surpassing good fortune which causes me shake with agitation whenever I think of it.

> Your friend Carolus,
> At the Goth's Head
> Inn in Padua.

. . . Fortunate, perhaps, that an opportunity has come to send a second missive to you, through a crippled man-at-arms who has been discharged from a mercenary band and travels homeward to sit in the sun henceforth. I have given him one gold piece and promised that you would give him another on receipt of this message. You will keep that promise or not, as pleases you, but there is at least the value of a gold piece in a bit of parchment with strange symbols upon it which I inclose for you.

Item: I am in daily communication with the Power of which I wrote you, and daily learn great mysteries.

Item: Already I perform marvels such as men have never before accomplished, by means of certain sigils or talismans the Power has prepared for me.

Item: Resolutely the Power refuses to yield to me the Names or the incantations by which these things are done so that I can prepare such sigils for myself. Instead, he instructs me in divers subjects which have no bearing on the accomplishment of wonders, to my bitter impatience which I yet dissemble.

Item: Within this packet there is a bit of parchment. Go to a remote place and there tear it and throw it upon the ground. Instantly, all about you, there will appear a fair garden with marvelous fruits, statuary, and pavilions. You may use this garden as you will, save that if any person enter it, or you yourself, carrying a sword or dagger or any object however small made of iron, the said garden will disappear immediately and nevermore return.

This you may verify when you please. For the rest, I am like a person trembling at the very door of Paradise, barred from entering beyond the antechamber by the fact of the Power withholding from me the true essentials of mystery, and granting me only crumbs—which, however, are greater marvels than any known certainly to have been practiced before. For example, the parchment I send you. This art I have proven many times. I have in my scrip many such sigils, made for me by the Power at my entreaty. But when I have secretly taken other parchments and copied upon them the very symbols to the utmost exactitude, they are valueless. There are words or formulas to be spoken over them or—I think more likely—a greater sigil which gives the parchments their magic property. I begin to make a plan—a very daring plan—to acquire even this sigil.

But you will wish to know of the Operation and its results. I returned to Montevecchio from Padua, reaching it in three days. The peasant who had worked wonders was dead, the villagers having grown more fearful and beat out his brains with hammers. This pleased me, because I had feared he would tell another the Word and Name he had told me. I spoke to the priest, and told him that I had been to Padua and secured advice from high dignitaries concerning the wonder-working, and had been sent back with special commands to seek out and exorcise the foul fiend who had taught the peasant such marvels.

The next day—the priest himself aiding me!—I took up to the hilltop the perfumes and wax tapers and other things needed for the Operation. The priest trembled, but he would have remained had I not sent him away. And night fell, and I drew the magic circle and the pentangle, with the Signs in their proper places. And when the new moon rose, I lighted the perfumes and the fine candles and began the Operation. I have had many failures, as you know, but this time I knew confidence and perfect certainty. When it came time to use the Name and the Word I called them both loudly, thrice, and waited.

Upon this hilltop there were many grayish stones. At the third calling of the Name, one of the stones shivered and was not. Then a voice said dryly:

"Ah! So that is the reason for this stinking stuff? My messenger sent you here?"

There was a shadow where the stone had been and I could not see clearly. But I bowed low in that direction:

"Most Potent Power," I said, my voice trembling because the Operation was a success, "a peasant working wonders told me that you desired speech with a learned man. Besides your Potency I am ignorant indeed, but I have given my whole life to the study of mysteries. Therefore I have come to offer worship or such other compact as you may desire in exchange for wisdom."

There was a stirring in the shadow, and the Power came forth. His appearance was that of a creature not more than an ell and a half in height, and his expression in the moonlight was that of sardonic impatience. The fragrant smoke seemed to cling about him, to make a cloudiness close about his form.

"I think," said the dry voice, "that you are as great a fool as the peasant I spoke to. What do you think I am?"

"A Prince of Celestial Race, your Potency," I said, my voice shaking.

There was a pause. The Power said as if wearily:

"Men! Fools forever! Oh, Man, I am simply the last of a number of my kind who traveled in a fleet from another star. This small planet of yours has a core of the accursed metal, which is fatal to the devices of my race. A few of our ships came too close. Others strove to aid them, and shared their fate. Many, many years since, we descended from the skies and could never rise again. Now I alone am left."

Speaking of the world as a planet was an absurdity, of course. The planets are wanderers among the stars, traveling in their cycles and epicycles as explained by Ptolemy a thousand years since. But I saw at once that he would test me. So I grew bold and said:

"Lord, I am not fearful. It is not needful to cozen me. Do I not know of those who were cast out of Heaven for rebellion? Shall I write the name of your leader?"

He said "Eh?" for all the world like an elderly man.

So smiling, I wrote on the earth the true name of Him whom the vulgar call Lucifer. He regarded the markings on the earth and said:

"Bah! It is meaningless. More of your legendry! Look you, Man, soon I shall die. For more years than you are like to believe I have hid from your race and its accursed metal. I have watched men, and despised them. But— I die. And it is not good that knowledge should perish. It is my desire to impart to men the knowledge which else would die with me. It can do no harm to my own kind, and may bring the race of men to some degree of civilization in the course of ages."

I bowed to the earth before him. I was aflame with eagerness.

"Most Potent One," I said joyfully. "I am to be trusted. I will guard your secrets fully. Not one jot nor tittle shall ever be divulged!"

Again his voice was annoyed and dry.

"I desire that this knowledge be spread abroad so that all may learn it." Then he made a sound which I do not understand, save that it seemed to be derisive. "But what I have to say may serve, even garbled and twisted. And I do not think you will keep secrets inviolate! Have you pen and parchment?"

"Nay, Lord!"

"You will come again, then, prepared to write what I shall tell you."

But he remained, regarding me. He asked me questions, and I answered eagerly. Presently he spoke in a meditative voice, and I listened eagerly. His speech bore an odd similarity to that of a lonely man who dwelt much on the past, but soon I realized that he spoke in ciphers, in allegory, from which now and again the truth peered out. As one who speaks for the sake of remembering, he spoke of the home of his race upon what he said was a fair planet so far distant that to speak of leagues and even the span of continents would be useless to convey the distance. He told of cities in which his fellows dwelt—here, of course, I understood his meaning perfectly—and told of great fleets of flying things rising from those cities to go to other fair cities, and of music which was in the very air so that any person, any-where upon the planet, could hear sweet sounds or wise discourse at will. In this matter there was no metaphor, because the perpetual sweet sounds in Heaven are matters of common knowledge. But he added a metaphor immediately after, because he smiled at me and observed that the music was not created by a mystery, but by waves like those of light, only longer. And this was plainly a cipher, because light is an impalpable fluid without length and surely without waves!

Then he spoke of flying through the emptiness of the empyrean, which again is not clear, because all can see that the heavens are fairly crowded with stars, and he spoke of many suns and other worlds, some frozen and some merely barren rock. The obscurity of such things is patent. And he spoke of drawing near to this world which is ours, and of an error made as if it were in mathematics—instead of in rebellion—so that they drew too close to Earth as Icarus to the sun. Then again he spoke in metaphors, because he referred to engines, which are things to cast stones against walls, and in a larger sense for grinding corn and pumping water. But he spoke of engines growing hot because of the accursed metal in the core of Earth, and of the inability of his kind to resist Earth's pull—more metaphor—and then he spoke of a screaming descent from the skies. And all of this, plainly, is a metaphorical account of the casting of the Rebels out of Heaven, and an acknowledgment that he is one of the said Rebels.

When he paused, I begged humbly that he would show me a mystery, and of his grace give me protection in case my converse with him became known.

"What happened to my messenger?" asked the Power.

I told him, and he listened without stirring. I was careful to tell him exactly, because, of course, he would know that—as all else—by his powers of mystery, and the question was but another test. Indeed, I felt sure that the messenger and all that had taken place had been contrived by him to bring me, a learned student of mysteries, to converse with him in this place.

"Men!" he said bitterly at last. Then he added coldly. "Nay! I can give you no protection. My kind is without protection upon this earth. If you would learn what I can teach you, you must risk the fury of your fellow-countrymen."

But then, abruptly, he wrote upon parchment and pressed the parchment to some object at his side. He threw it upon the ground.

"If men beset you," he said scornfully, "tear this parchment and cast it from you. If you have none of the accursed metal about you, it may distract them while you flee. But a dagger will cause it all to come to naught!"

Then he walked away. He vanished. And I stood shivering for a very long time before I remembered me of the formula given by Apollonius of Tyana for the dismissal of evil spirits. I ventured from the magic circle. No evil befell me. I picked up the parchment and examined it in the moonlight. The symbols upon it were meaningless, even to one like myself who has studied all that is known of mysteries. I returned to the village, pondering.

I have told you so much at length, because you will observe that this Power did not speak with the pride or the menace of which most authors on mysteries and Operations speak. It is often said that an adept must conduct himself with great firmness during an Operation, lest the Powers he has called up overawe him. Yet this Power spoke wearily, with irony, like one approaching death. And he had spoken of death, also. Which were, of course, a test and a deception, because are not the Principalities and Powers of Darkness immortal? He had some design it was not his will that I should know. So I saw that I must walk warily in this priceless opportunity.

In the village I told the priest that I had had encounter with a foul fiend, who begged that I not exorcise him, promising to reveal certain hidden treasures once belonging to the Church, which he could not touch or reveal to evil men because they were holy, but could describe the location of to me. And I procured parchment, and pens, and ink, and the next day I went alone to the hilltop. It was empty, and I made sure I was unwatched and—leaving my dagger behind me—I tore the parchment and flung it to the ground.

As it touched, there appeared such a treasure of gold and jewels as truly would have driven any man mad with greed. There were bags and chests and boxes filled with gold and precious stones, which had burst with the weight and spilled out upon the ground. There were gems glittering in the late sunlight, and rings and necklaces set with brilliants, and such monstrous hoards of golden coins of every antique pattern.

Johannus, even I went almost mad! I leaped forward like one dreaming to plunge my hands into the gold. Slavering, I filled my garments with rubies and ropes of pearls, and stuffed my scrip with gold pieces, laughing crazily to myself. I rolled in the riches. I wallowed in them, flinging the golden coins into the air and letting them fall upon me. I laughed and sang to myself.

Then I heard a sound. On the instant I was filled with terror for the treasure. I leaped to my dagger and snarled, ready to defend my riches to the death.

Then a dry voice said:

"Truly you care naught for riches!"

It was savage mockery. The Power stood regarding me. I saw him clearly now, yet not clearly because there was a cloudiness which clung clearly to his body. He was, as I said, an ell and a half in height, and from his forehead there protruded knobby feelers which were not horns but had somewhat the look save for bulbs upon their ends. His head was large and— But I will not attempt to describe him, because he could assume any of a thousand forms, no doubt, so what does it matter?

Then I grew terrified because I had no Circle or Pentangle to protect me. But the Power made no menacing move.

"It is real, that riches," he said dryly. "It has color and weight and the feel of substance. But your dagger will destroy it all."

Didyas of Corinth has said that treasure of mystery

must be fixed by a special Operation before it becomes permanent and free of the power of Those who brought it. They can transmute it back to leaves or other rubbish, if it be not fixed.

"Touch it with your dagger," said the Power.

I obeyed, sweating in fear. And as the metal iron touched a great piled heap of gold, there was a sudden shifting and then a little flare of heat about me. And the treasure—all, to the veriest crumb of a seed pearl!—vanished before my eyes. The bit of parchment reappeared, smoking. It turned to ashes. My dagger scorched my fingers. It had grown hot.

"Ah yes," said the Power, nodding. "The force-field has energy. When the iron absorbs it, there is heat." Then he looked at me in a not unfriendly way. "You have brought pens and parchment," he said, "and at least you did not use the sigil to astonish your fellows. Also you had the good sense to make no more perfumish stinks. It may be that there is a grain of wisdom in you. I will bear with you yet a while. Be seated and take parchment and pen. Stay! Let us be comfortable. Sheathe your dagger, or better cast it from you."

I put it in my bosom. And it was as if he thought, and touched something at his side, and instantly there was a fair pavillion about us, with soft cushions and a gently playing fountain.

"Sit," said the Power. "I learned that men like such things as this from a man I once befriended. He had been wounded and stripped by robbers, so that he had not so much as a scrap of accursed metal about him, and I could aid him. I learned to speak the language men use nowadays from him. But to the end he believed me an evil spirit and tried valorously to hate me."

My hands shook with my agitation that the treasure had departed from me. Truly it was a treasure of such riches as no King has ever possessed, Johannus! My very soul lusted after that treasure! The golden coins alone would fill your attic solidly, but the floor would break under their weight, and the jewels would fill hogsheads. Ah, Johannus! That treasure!

"What I will have you write," said the Power, "at

first will mean little. I shall give facts and theories first, because they are easiest to remember. Then I will give the applications of the theories. Then you men will have the beginning of such civilization as can exist in the neighborhood of the accursed metal."

"Your Potency!" I begged abjectly. "You will give me another sigil of treasure?"

"Write!" he commanded.

I wrote. And, Johannus, I cannot tell you myself what it is that I wrote. He spoke words, and they were in such obscure cipher that they have no meaning as I con them over. Hark you to this, and seek wisdom for the performance of mysteries in it! "The civilization of my race is based upon fields of force which have the property of acting in all essentials as substance. A lode-stone is surrounded by a field of force which is invisible and impalpable. But the fields used by my people for dwellings, tools, and even for machinery are perceptible to the senses and act physically as solids. More, we are able to form these fields in latent fashion; and to fix them to organic objects as permanent fields which require no energy for their maintenance, just as magnetic fields require no energy-supply to continue. Our fields, too, may be projected as three-dimensional solids which assume any desired form and have every property of substance except chemical affinity."

Johannus! Is it not unbelievable that words could be put together, dealing with mysteries, which are so devoid of any clue to their true mystic meaning? I write and I write in desperate hope that he will eventually give me the key, but my brain reels at the difficulty of extracting the directions for Operations which such ciphers must conceal! I give you another instance: "When a force-field generator has been built as above, it will be found that the pulsatory fields which are consciousness serve perfectly as controls. One has but to visualize the object desired, turn on the generator's auxiliary control, and the generator will pattern its output upon the pulsatory consciousness-field—"

Upon this first day of writing, the Power spoke for

hours, and I wrote until my hand ached. From time to time, resting, I read back to him the words that I had written. He listened, satisfied.

"Lord!" I said shakenly. "Mighty lord! Your Potency! These mysteries you bid me write—they are beyond comprehension!"

But he said scornfully:

"Write! Some will be clear to someone. And I will explain a little by a little until even you can comprehend the beginning." Then he added: "You grow weary. You wish a toy. Well! I will make you a sigil which will make again that treasure you played with. I will add a sigil which will make a boat for you, with an engine drawing power from the sea to carry you wheresoever you wish without need of wind or tide. I will make others so you may create a palace where you will, and fair gardens as you please—"

These things he has done, Johannus. It seems to amuse him to write upon scraps of parchment, and think, and then press them against his side before he lays them upon the ground for me to pick up. He has explained amusedly that the wonder in the sigil is complete, yet latent, and is released by the tearing of the parchment, but absorbed and destroyed by iron. In such fashions he speaks in ciphers, but otherwise sometimes he jests!

It is strange to think of it, that I have come a little by a little to accept this Power as a person. It is not in accord with the laws of mystery. I feel that he is lonely. He seems to find satisfaction in speech with me. Yet he is a Power, one of the Rebels who was flung to earth from Heaven! He speaks of that only in vague, metaphorical terms, as if he had come from another world like *the* world, save much larger. He refers to himself as a voyager of space, and speaks of his race with affection, and of Heaven—at any rate the city from which he comes, because there must be many great cities there—with a strange and prideful affection. If it were not for his powers, which are of mystery, I would find it possible to believe that he was a lonely member of a strange race, exiled forever in a strange place, and grown friendly with a man because of his loneliness. But how could there be such as he and not a Power? How could there be another world?

This strange converse has now gone on for ten days or more. I have filled sheets upon sheets of parchment with writing. The same metaphors occur again and again. "Force-fields"—a term without literal meaning—occurs often. There are other metaphors such as "coils" and "primary" and "secondary" which are placed in context with mention of wires of copper metal. There are careful descriptions, as if in the plainest of language, of sheets of dissimilar metals which are to be placed in acid, and other descriptions of plates of similar metal which are to be separated by layers of air or wax of certain thicknesses, with the plates of certain areas! And there is an explanation of the means by which he lives. "I, being accustomed to an atmosphere much more dense than that on Earth, am forced to keep about myself a field of force which maintains an air-density near that of my home planet for my breathing. This field is transparent, but because it must shift constantly to change and refresh the air I breathe, it causes a certain cloudiness of outline next my body. It is maintained by the generator I wear at my side, which at the same time provides energy for such other force-field artifacts as I may find convenient." Ah, Johannus! I grow mad with impatience! Did I not anticipate that he would someday give me the key to this metaphorical speech, so that from it may be extracted the Names and the Words which cause his wonders, I would give over in despair.

Yet he has grown genial with me. He has given me such sigils as I have asked him, and I have tried them many times. The sigil which will make you a fair garden is one of many. He says that he desires to give to man the knowledge he possesses, and then bids me write ciphered speech without meaning, such as: "The drive of a ship for flight beyond the speed of light is adapted from the simple-drive generator already described, simply by altering its constants so that it cannot generate in normal space and must create an abnormal space by tension. The process is—" Or else—I choose at random, Johannus—"The accursed metal, iron, must be eliminated not only from all circuits but from nearness to apparatus using high-frequency oscillations, since it absorbs their energy and prevents the functioning—"

I am like a man trembling upon the threshold of Paradise, yet unable to enter because the key is withheld. "Speed of light!" What could it mean in metaphor? In common parlance, as well speak of the speed of weather or of granite! Daily I beg him for the key to his speech. Yet even now, in the sigils he makes for me is greater power than any man has ever known before!

But it is not enough. The Power speaks as if he were lonely beyond compare; the last member of a strange race upon Earth; as if he took a strange, companionlike pleasure in merely talking to me. When I beg him for a Name or a Word which would give me power beyond such as he doles out in sigils, he is amused and calls me fool, yet kindly. And he speaks more of his metaphorical speech about forces of nature and fields of force—and gives me a sigil which should I use it will create a palace with walls of gold and pillars of emerald! And then he amusedly reminds me that one greedy looter with an ax or hoe of iron would cause it to vanish utterly!

I go almost mad, Johannus! But there is certainly wisdom unutterable to be had from him. Gradually, cautiously, I have come to act as if we were merely friends, of different race and he vastly the wiser, but friends rather than Prince and subject. Yet I remember the warnings of the most authoritative authors that one must be ever on guard against Powers called up in an Operation.

I have a plan. It is dangerous, I well know, but I grow desperate. To stand quivering upon the threshold of such wisdom and power as no man has ever dreamed of before, and then be denied—

The mercenary who will carry this to you leaves tomorrow. He is a cripple, and may be months upon the way. All will be decided ere you receive this. I know you wish me well.

Was there ever a student of mystery in so maddening a predicament, with all knowledge in his grasp yet not quite his?

> Your friend,
> Carolus.
> Written in the very bad
> inn in Montevecchio—

Johannus! A courier goes to Ghent for My Lord of Brahant and I have opportunity to send you mail. I think I go mad, Johannus! I have power such as no man ever possessed before, and I am fevered with bitterness. Hear me!

For three weeks I did repair daily to the hilltop beyond Montevecchio and take down the ciphered speech of which I wrote you. My scrip was stuffed with sigils, but I had not one Word of Power or Name of Authority. The Power grew mocking, yet it seemed sadly mocking. He insisted that his words held no cipher and needed but to be read. Some of them he phrased over and over again until they were but instructions for putting bits of metal together, mechanic-wise. Then he made me follow those instructions. But there was no Word, no Name—nothing save bits of metal put together cunningly. And how could inanimate metal, not imbued with power of mystery by Names or Words or incantations, have power to work mystery?

At long last I became convinced that he would never reveal the wisdom he had promised. And I had come to such familiarity with this Power that I could dare to rebel, and even to believe that I had chance of success. There was the cloudiness about his form, which was maintained by a sigil he wore at his side and called a "generator." Were that cloudiness destroyed, he could not live, or so he had told me. It was for that reason that he, in person, dared not touch anything of iron. This was the basis of my plan.

I feigned illness, and said that I would rest at a peasant's thatched hut, no longer inhabited, at the foot of the hill on which the Power lived. There was surely no nail of iron in so crude a dwelling. If he felt for me the affection he protested, he would grant me leave to be absent in my illness. If his affection was great, he might even come and speak to me there. I would be alone in the hope that his friendship might go so far.

Strange words for a man to use to Power! But I had talked daily with him for three weeks. I lay groaning in the hut, alone. On the second day he came. I affected great rejoicing, and made shift to light a fire from a taper I had kept burning. He thought it a mark of honor, but it was actually a signal. And then, as he talked to me in what he thought my illness, there came a cry from without the hut. It was the village priest, a simple man but very brave in his fashion. On the signal of smoke from the peasant's hut, he had crept near and drawn all about it an iron chain that he had muffled with cloth so that it would make no sound. And now he stood before the hut door with his crucifix upraised, chanting exorcisms. A very brave man, that priest, because I had pictured the Power as a foul fiend indeed.

The Power turned and looked at me, and I held my dagger firmly.

"I hold the accursed metal," I told him fiercely. "There is a ring of it about this house. Tell me now, quickly, the Words and the Names which make the sigils operate! Tell me the secret of the cipher you had me write! Do this and I will slay this priest and draw away the chain and you may go hence unharmed. But be quick, or—"

The Power cast a sigil upon the ground. When the parchment struck earth, there was an instant's cloudiness as if some dread thing had begun to form. But then the parchment smoked and turned to ash. The ring of iron about the hut had destroyed its power when it was used. The Power knew that I spoke truth.

"Ah!" said the Power dryly. "Men! And I thought one was my friend!" He put his hand to his side. "To be sure! I should have known. Iron rings me about. My engine heats—"

He looked at me. I held up the dagger, fiercely unyielding.

"The names!" I cried. "The Words! Give me power of my own and I will slay the priest!"

"I tried," said the Power quietly, "to give you wisdom. And you will stab me with the accursed metal if I do not tell you things which do not exist. But you need not. I cannot live long in a ring of iron. My engine will burn out. My force-field will fail. I will stifle in the thin air which is dense enough for you. Will not that satisfy you? Must you stab me also?"

I sprang from my pallet of straw to threaten him more fiercely. It was madness, was it not? But I was mad, Johannus!

"Forbear," said the Power. "I could kill you now, with me! But I thought you my friend. I will go out and see your priest. I would prefer to die at his hand. He is perhaps only a fool."

He walked steadily toward the doorway. As he stepped over the iron chain, I thought I saw a wisp of smoke begin, but he touched the thing at his side. The cloudiness about his person vanished. There was a puffing sound, and his garments jerked as if in a gust of wind. He staggered. But he went on, and touched his side again and the cloudiness returned and he walked more strongly. He did not try to turn aside. He walked directly toward the priest, and even I could see that he walked with a bitter dignity.

And— I saw the priest's eyes grow wide with horror. Because he saw the Power for the first time, and the Power was an ell and a half high, with a large head and knobbed feelers projecting from his forehead, and the priest knew instantly that he was not of any race of men but was a Power and one of those Rebels who were flung out from Heaven.

I heard the Power speak to the priest, with dignity. I did not hear what he said. I raged in my disappointment. But the priest did not waver. As the Power moved toward him, the priest moved toward the Power. His face was filled with horror, but it was resolute. He reached forward with the crucifix he wore always attached to an iron chain about his waist. He thrust it to touch the Power, crying, *"In nomini Patri—"*

Then there was smoke. It came from a spot at the Power's side where was the engine to which he touched the sigils he had made, to imbue them with the power of mystery. And then—

I was blinded. There was a flare of monstrous, bluish light, like a lightning-stroke from Heaven. After, there was a ball of fierce yellow flame which gave off a cloud of black smoke. There was a monstrous, outraged bellow of thunder.

Then there was nothing save the priest standing there, his face ashen, his eyes resolute, his eyebrows singed, chanting exorcisms in a shaking voice.

I have come to Venice. My scrip is filled with sigils with which I can work wonders. No man can work such wonders as I can. But I use them not. I labor daily, nightly, hourly, minute by minute, trying to find the key to the cipher which will yield the wisdom the Power possessed and desired to give to men. Ah, Johannus! I have those sigils and I can work wonders, but when I have used them they will be gone and I shall be powerless! I had such a chance at wisdom as never man possessed before, and it is gone! Yet I shall spend years— aye!—all the rest of my life, seeking the true meaning of what the Power spoke! I am the only man in all the world who ever spoke daily, for weeks on end, with a Prince of the Powers of Darkness, and was accepted by him as a friend to such a degree as to encompass his own destruction. It must be true that I have wisdom written down! But how shall I find instructions for mystery in such metaphors as—to choose a fragment by chance—"Plates of two dissimilar metals, immersed in an acid, generate a force for which men have not yet a name, yet which is the basis of true civilization. Such plates—"

I grow mad with disappointment, Johannus! Why did he not speak clearly? Yet I will find out the secret.

(Memorandum from Professor McFarland, Physics Department, Haverford University, to Professor Charles, Latin, the same faculty:

Dear Professor Charles:

My reaction is, Damnation! Where is the rest of this stuff?

McFarland.)

A Logic Named Joe

IT WAS ON the the third day of August that Joe come off the assembly line, and on the fifth Laurine come into town, and that afternoon I saved civilization. That's what I figure, anyhow. Laurine is a blonde that I was crazy about once—and crazy is the word—and Joe is a logic that I have stored away down in the cellar right now. I had to pay for him because I said I busted him, and sometimes I think about turning him on and sometimes I think about taking an ax to him. Sooner or later I'm gonna do one or the other. I kinda hope it's the ax. I could use a coupla million dollars—sure!—an' Joe'd tell me how to get or make 'em. He can do plenty! But so far I've been scared to take a chance. After all, I figure I really saved a civilization by turnin' him off.

The way Laurine fits in is that she makes cold shivers run up an' down my spine when I think about her. You see, I've got a wife which I acquired after I had parted from Laurine with much romantic despair. She is a reasonable good wife, and I have some kids which are hellcats but I value 'em. If I have sense enough to leave well enough alone, sooner or later I will retire on a pension an' Social Security an' spend the rest of my life fishin' contented an' lyin' about what a great guy I used to be. But there's Joe. I'm worried about Joe.

I'm a maintenance man for the Logics Company. My job is servicing logics, and I admit modestly that I am pretty good. I was servicing televisions before that guy Carson invented his trick circuit that will select any of 'steenteen million other circuits—in theory there ain't no limit—and before the Logics Company hooked it into the tank-and-integrator set-up they were usin' 'em as business-machine service. They added a vision screen for speed—an' they found out they'd make logics. They were surprised an' pleased. They're still findin' out what logics will do, but everybody's got 'em.

I got Joe, after Laurine nearly got me. You know the logics setup. You got a logic in your house. It looks like a vision receiver used to, only it's got keys instead of dials and you punch the keys for what you wanna get. It's hooked in to the tank, which has the Carson Circuit all fixed up with relays. Say you punch "Station SNAFU" on your logic. Relays in the tank take over an' whatever vision-program SNAFU is telecastin' comes on your logic's screen. Or you punch "Sally Hancock's Phone" an' the screen blinks an' sputters an' you're hooked up with the logic in her house an' if somebody answers you got a vision-phone connection. But besides that, if you punch for the weather forecast or who won today's race at Hialeah or who was mistress of the White House durin' Garfield's administration or what is PDQ and R sellin' for today, that comes on the screen too. The relays in the tank do it. The tank is a big buildin' full of all the facts in creation an' all the recorded telecasts that ever was made—an' it's hooked in with all the other tanks all over the country—an' anything you wanna know or see or hear, you punch for it an' you get it. Very convenient. Also it does math for you, an' keeps books, an' acts as consultin' chemist, physicist, astronomer, an' tealeaf reader, with a "Advice to Lovelorn" thrown in. The only thing it won't do is tell you exactly what your wife meant when she said, "Oh, you think so, do you?" in that peculiar kinda voice. Logics don't work good on women. Only on things that make sense.

Logics are all right, though. They changed civilization, the highbrows tell us. All on accounta the Carson Circuit. And Joe shoulda been a perfectly normal logic, keeping some family or other from wearin' out its brains doin' the kids' homework for 'em. But somethin' went wrong in the assembly line. It was somethin' so small that precision gauges didn't measure it, but it made Joe a individual. Maybe he didn't know it at first. Or maybe, bein' logical, he figured out that if he was to show he was different from other logics they'd scrap him. Which woulda been a brilliant idea. But anyhow, he come off the assembly line, an' he went through the regular tests without anybody screamin' shrilly on findin' out what he was. And he went right on out an' was duly installed in the home of Mr. Thaddeus Korlanovitch at 119 East Seventh Street, second floor front. So far, everything was serene.

The installation happened late Saturday night. Sunday morning the Korlanovitch kids turned him on an' seen the Kiddie Shows. Around noon their parents peeled 'em away from him an' piled 'em in the car. Then they come back in the house for the lunch they'd forgot an' one of the kids sneaked back an' they found him punchin' keys for the Kiddie Shows of the week before. They dragged him out an' went off. But they left Joe turned on.

That was noon. Nothin' happened until two in the afternoon. It was the calm before the storm. Laurine wasn't in town yet, but she was comin'. I picture Joe sittin' there all by himself, buzzing meditative. Maybe he run Kiddie Shows in the empty apartment for awhile. But I think he went kinda remote-control exploring in the tank. There ain't any fact that can be said to be a fact that ain't on a data plate in some tank somewhere—unless it's one the technicians are diggin' out an' puttin' on a data plate now. Joe had plenty of material to work on. An' he musta started workin' right off the bat.

Joe ain't vicious, you understand. He ain't like one of these ambitious robots you read about that make up their minds the human race is inefficient and has got to be wiped out an' replaced by thinkin' machines. Joe's just got ambition. If you were a machine, you'd wanna work right, wouldn't you? That's Joe. He wants to work right. An' he's a logic. An' logics can do a lotta things that ain't been found out yet. So Joe, discoverin' the fact, begun to feel restless. He selects some things us dumb humans ain't thought of yet, an' begins to arrange so logics will be called on to do 'em.

That's all. That's everything. But, brother, it's enough!

Things are kinda quiet in the Maintenance Department about two in the afternoon. We are playing pinochle. Then one of the guys remembers he has to call up his wife. He goes to one of the bank of logics in Maintenance and punches the keys for his house. The screen sputters. Then a flash comes on the screen.

"Announcing new and improved logics service! Your logic is now equipped to give you not only consultive but directive service. If you want to do something and don't know how to do it—ask your logic!"

There's a pause. A kinda expectant pause. Then, as if reluctantly, his connection comes through. His wife answers an' gives him hell for somethin' or other. He takes it an' snaps off.

"Whadda you know?" he says when he comes back. He tells us about the flash. "We shoulda been warned about that. There's gonna be a lotta complaints. Suppose a fella asks how to get ridda his wife an' the censor circuits block the question?"

Somebody melds a hundred aces an' says:

"Why not punch for it an' see what happens?"

It's a gag, o' course. But the guy goes over. He punches keys. In theory, a censor block is gonna come on an' the screen will say severely, "Public Policy Forbids This Service." You hafta have censor blocks or the kiddies will be askin' detailed questions about things they're too young to know. And there are other reasons. As you will see.

This fella punches, "How can I get rid of my wife?" Just for the fun of it. The screen is blank for half a second. Then comes a flash. "Service question: Is she blond or brunette?" He hollers to us an' we come look. He punches, "Blond." There's another brief pause. Then the screen says, "Hexymetacryloaminoacetine is a constituent of green shoe polish. Take home a frozen meal including dried pea soup. Color the soup with green shoe polish. It will appear to be green-pea soup, Hexymetacryloaminoacetine is a selective poison which is fatal to blond females but not to brunettes or males of any coloring. This fact has not been brought out by human experiment, but is a product of logics service. You cannot be convicted of murder. It is improbable that you will be suspected."

The screen goes blank, and we stare at each other. It's bound to be right. A logic workin' the Carson Circuit can no more make a mistake than any other kinda computin' machine. I call the tank in a hurry.

"Hey, you guys!" I yell. "Somethin's happened! Logics are givin' detailed instructions for wife-murder! Check your censor-circuits—but quick!"

That was close, I think. But little do I know. At that precise instant, over on Monroe Avenue, a drunk starts to punch for somethin' on a logic. The screen says "Announcing new and improved logics service! If you want to do something and don't know how to do it—ask your logic!" And the drunk says, owlish, "I'll do it!" So he cancels his first punching and fumbles around and says: "How can I keep my wife from finding out I've been drinking?" And the screen says, prompt: "But a bottle of Franine hair shampoo. It is harmless but contains a detergent which will neutralize ethyl alcohol immediately. Take one teaspoonful for each jigger of hundred-proof you have consumed."

This guy was plenty plastered—just plastered enough to stagger next door and obey instructions. An' five minutes later he was cold sober and writing down the information so he couldn't forget it. It was new, and it was big! He got rich offa that memo! He patented *"SOBUH, The Drink that Makes Happy Homes!"* You can top off any souse with a slug or two of it an' go home sober as a judge. The guy's cussin' income taxes right now!

You can't kick on stuff like that. But a ambitious young fourteen-year-old wanted to buy some kid stuff and his pop wouldn't fork over. He called up a friend to tell his troubles. And his logic says: "If you want to do something and don't know how to do it—ask your logic!" So this kid punches: "How can I make a lotta money, fast?"

His logic comes through with the simplest, neatest, and the most efficient counterfeitin' device yet known to science. You see, all the data was in the tank. The logic—since Joe had closed some relays here an' there in the tank—simply integrated the facts. That's all. The kid got caught up with three days later, havin' already spent two thousand credits an' havin' plenty more on hand. They hadda time tellin' his counterfeits from the real stuff, an' the only way they done it was that he changed his printer, kid fashion, not bein' able to let somethin' that was workin' right alone.

Those are what you might call samples. Nobody knows all that Joe done. But there was the bank president who got humorous when his logic flashed that "Ask your logic" spiel on him, and jestingly asked how to rob his own bank. An' the logic told him, brief and explicit but good! The bank president hit the ceiling, hollering for cops. There musta been plenty of that sorta thing. There was fifty-four more robberies than usual in the next twenty-four hours, all of them planned astute an' perfect. Some of 'em they never did figure out how they'd been done. Joe, he'd gone exploring in the tank and closed some relays like a logic is supposed to do— but only when required—and blocked all censor-circuits an' fixed up this logics service which planned perfect crimes, nourishing an' attractive meals, counterfeitin' machines, an' new industries with a fine impartiality. He musta been plenty happy, Joe must. He was functionin' swell, buzzin' along to himself while the Korlanovitch kids were off ridin' with their ma an' pa.

They come back at seven o'clock, the kids all happily wore out with their afternoon of fightin' each other in the car. Their folks put 'em to bed and sat down to rest. They saw Joe's screen flickerin' meditative from one subject to another an' old man Korlanovitch had had enough excitement for one day. He turned Joe off.

An' at that instant the pattern of relays that Joe had turned on snapped off, all the offers of directive service stopped flashin' on logic screens everywhere, an' peace descended on the earth.

For everybody else. But for me. Laurine come to town. I have often thanked God fervent that she didn't marry me when I thought I wanted her to. In the intervenin' years she had progressed. She was blond an' fatal to begin with. She had got blonder and fataler an' had had four husbands and one acquittal for homicide an' had acquired a air of enthusiasm and self-confidence. That's just a sketch of the background. Laurine was not the kinda former girl-friend you like to have turning up in the same town with your wife. But she came to town, an' Monday morning she tuned right into the middle of Joe's second spasm of activity.

The Korlanovitch kids had turned him on again. I got these details later and kinda pieced 'em together. An' every logic in town was dutifully flashin' a notice, "If you want to do something and don't know how to do it—ask your logic!" every time they were turned on for use. More'n that, when people punched for the morning news, they got a full account of the previous afternoon's doin's. Which put 'em in a frame of mind to share in the party. One bright fella demands, "How can I make a perpetual motion machine?" And his logic sputters a while an' then comes up with a set-up usin' the Brownian movement to turn little wheels. If the wheels ain't bigger'n a eighth of an inch they'll turn, all right, an' practically it's perpetual motion. Another one asks for the secret of transmuting metals. The logic rakes back in the data plates an' integrates a strictly practical answer. It does take so much power that you can't make no profit except on radium, but that pays off good. An' from the fact that for a coupla years to come the police were turnin' up new and improved jimmies, knob-claws for gettin' at safe-innards, and all-purpose keys that'd open any known lock—why there must have been other inquirers with a strictly practical viewpoint. Joe done a lot for technical progress!

But he done more in other lines. Educational, say. None of my kids are old enough to be int'rested, but Joe bypassed all censor-circuits because they hampered the service he figured logics should give humanity. So the kids an' teen-agers who wanted to know what comes after the bees an' flowers found out. And there is certain facts which men hope their wives won't do more'n suspect, an' those facts are just what their wives are really curious about. So when a woman dials: "How can I tell if Oswald is true to me?" and her logic tells her—you can figure out how many rows got started that night when the men come home!

All this while Joe goes on buzzin' happy to himself, showin' the Korlanovitch kids the animated funnies with one circuit while with the others he remote-controls the tank so that all the other logics can give people what they ask for and thereby raise merry hell.

An' then Laurine gets onto the new service. She turns on the logic in her hotel room, prob'ly to see the week's style-forecast. But the logic says, dutiful: "If you want to do something and don't know how to do it—ask your logic!" So Laurine prob'ly looks enthusiastic—she would!—and tries to figure out something to ask. She already knows all about everything she cares about— ain't she had four husbands and shot one?—so I occur to her. She knows this is the town I live in. So she punches, "How can I find Ducky?"

O.K., guy! But that is what she used to call me. She gets a service question. "Is Ducky known by any other name?" So she gives my regular name. And the logic can't find me. Because my logic ain't listed under my name on account of I am in Maintenance and don't want to be pestered when I'm home, and there ain't any data plates on code-listed logics, because the codes get changed so often—like a guy gets plastered an' tells a redhead to call him up, an' on gettin' sober hurriedly has the code changed before she reaches his wife on the screen.

Well! Joe is stumped. That's prob'ly the first question logics service hasn't been able to answer. "How can I find Ducky?" ! ! Quite a problem! So Joe broods over it while showin' the Korlanovitch kids the animated comic about the cute little boy who carries sticks of dynamite in his hip pocket an' plays practical jokes on everybody. Then he gets the trick. Laurine's screen suddenly flashes:

"Logics special service will work upon your question. Please punch your logic designation and leave it turned on. You will be called back."

Laurine is merely mildly interested, but she punches her hotel-room number and has a drink and takes a nap. Joe sets to work. He has been given a idea.

My wife calls me at Maintenance and hollers. She is fit to be tied. She says I got to do something. She was gonna make a call to the butcher shop. Instead of the butcher or even the "If you want to do something" flash, she got a new one. The screen says, "Service question: What is your name?" She is kinda puzzled, but she punches it. The screen sputters an' then says: "Secretarial Service Demonstration! You——" It reels off her name, address, age, sex, coloring, the amounts of all her charge accounts in all the stores, my name as her husband, how much I get a week, the fact that I've been pinched three times—twice was traffic stuff, and once for a argument I got in with a guy—and the interestin' item that once when she was mad with me she left me for three weeks an' had her address changed to her folks' home. Then it says, brisk: "Logics Service will hereafter keep your personal accounts, take messages, and locate persons you may wish to get in touch with. This demonstration is to introduce the service." Then it connects her with the butcher.

But she don't want meat, then. She wants blood. She calls me.

"If it'll tell me all about myself," she says, fairly boilin', "it'll tell anybody else who punches my name! You've got to stop it!"

"Now, now, honey!" I says. "I didn't know about all this! It's new! But they musta fixed the tank so it won't give out information except to the logic where a person lives!"

"Nothing of the kind!" she tells me, furious. "I tried! And you know that Blossom woman who lives next door! She's been married three times and she's forty-two years old and she says she's only thirty! And Mrs. Hudson's had her husband arrested four times for nonsupport and once for beating her up. And——"

"Hey!" I says. "You mean the logic told you this?"

"Yes!" she wails. "It will tell anybody anything! You've got to stop it! How long will it take?"

"I'll call up the tank," I says. "It can't take long."

"Hurry!" she says, desperate, "before somebody punches my name! I'm going to see what it says about that hussy across the street."

She snaps off to gather what she can before it's stopped. So I punch for the tank and I get this new "What is your name?" flash. I got a morbid curiosity and I punch my name, and the screen says: "Were you ever called Ducky?" I blink. I ain't got no suspicions. I say, "Sure!" And the screen says, "There is a call for you."

Bingo! There's the inside of a hotel room and Laurine is reclinin' asleep on the bed. She'd been told to leave her logic turned on an' she'd done it. It is a hot day and she is trying to be cool. I would say that she oughta not suffer from the heat. Me, being human, I do not stay as cool as she looks. But there ain't no need to go into that. After I get my breath I say, "For Heaven's sake!" and she opens her eyes.

At first she looks puzzled, like she was thinking is she getting absent-minded and is this guy somebody she married lately. Then she grabs a sheet and drapes it around herself and beams at me.

"Ducky!" she says. "How marvelous!"

I say something like "Ugmph!" I am sweating.

She says:

"I put in a call for you, Ducky, and here you are! Isn't it romantic? Where are you really, Ducky? And when can you come up? You've no idea how often I've thought of you!"

I am probably the only guy she ever knew real well that she has not been married to at some time or another.

I say "Ugmph!" again, and swallow.

"Can you come up instantly?" asks Laurine brightly.

"I'm . . . workin'," I say. "I'll . . . uh . . . call you back."

"I'm terribly lonesome," says Laurine. "Please make

it quick, Ducky! I'll have a drink waiting for you. Have you ever thought of me?"

"Yeah," I say, feeble. "Plenty!"

"You darling!" says Laurine. "Here's a kiss to go on with until you get here! Hurry, Ducky!"

Then I sweat! I still don't know nothing about Joe, understand. I cuss out the guys at the tank because I blame them for this. If Laurine was just another blonde—well—when it comes to ordinary blondes I can leave 'em alone or leave 'em alone, either one. A married man gets that way or else. But Laurine has a look of unquenched enthusiasm that gives a man very strange weak sensations at the back of his knees. And she'd had four husbands and shot one and got acquitted.

So I punch the keys for the tank technical room, fumbling. And the screen says: "What is your name?" but I don't want any more. I punch the name of the old guy who's stock clerk in Maintenance. And the screen gives me some pretty interestin' dope—I never woulda thought the old fella had ever had that much pep—and winds up by mentionin' a unclaimed deposit now amountin' to two hundred eighty credits in the First National Bank, which he should look into. Then it spiels about the new secretarial service and gives me the tank at last.

I start to swear at the guy who looks at me. But he says, tired:

"Snap it off, fella. We got troubles an' you're just another. What are the logics doin' now?"

I tell him, and he laughs a hollow laugh.

"A light matter, fella," he says. "A very light matter! We just managed to clamp off all the data plates that give information on high explosives. The demand for instructions in counterfeiting is increasing minute by minute. We are also trying to shut off, by main force, the relays that hook in to data plates that just barely might give advice on the fine points of murder. So if people will only keep busy getting the goods on each other for a while, maybe we'll get a chance to stop the circuits that are shifting credit-balances from bank to bank before everybody's bankrupt except the guys who thought of askin' how to get big bank accounts in a hurry."

"Then," I says hoarse, "shut down the tank! Do somethin'!"

"Shut down the tank?" he says, mirthless. "Does it occur to you, fella, that the tank has been doin' all the computin' for every business office for years? It's been handlin' the distribution of ninety-four per cent of all telecast programs, has given out all information on weather, plane schedules, special sales, employment opportunities and news; has handled all person-to-person contacts over wires and recorded every business conversation and agreement— Listen, fella! Logics changed civilization. Logics *are* civilization! If we shut off logics, we go back to a kind of civilization we have forgotten how to run! I'm getting hysterical myself and that's why I'm talkin' like this! If my wife finds out my paycheck is thirty credits a week more than I told her and starts hunting for that redhead—"

He smiles a haggard smile at me and snaps off. And I sit down and put my head in my hands. It's true. If something had happened back in cave days and they'd hadda stop usin' fire— If they'd hadda stop usin' steam in the nineteenth century or electricity in the twentieth— It's like that. We got a very simple civilization. In the nineteen hundreds a man would have to make use of a typewriter, radio, telephone, teletypewriter, newspaper, reference library, encyclopedias, office files, directories, plus messenger service and consulting lawyers, chemists, doctors, dietitians, filing clerks, secretaries—all to put down what he wanted to remember an' to tell him what other people had put down that he wanted to know; to report what he said to somebody else and to report to him what they said back. All we have to have is logics. Anything we want to know or see or hear, or anybody we want to talk to, we punch keys on a logic. Shut off logics and everything goes skiddoo. But Laurine—

Somethin' had happened. I still didn't know what it was. Nobody else knows, even yet. What had happened was Joe. What was the matter with him was that he wanted to work good. All this fuss he was raisin' was, actual, nothin' but stuff we shoulda thought of ourselves. Directive advice, tellin' us what we wanted to know to solve a problem, wasn't but a slight extension of logical-integrator service. Figurin' out a good way to poison a fella's wife was only different in degree from figurin' out a cube root or a guy's bank balance. It was gettin' the answer to a question. But things was goin' to pot because there was too many answers being given to too many questions.

One of the logics in Maintenance lights up. I go over, weary, to answer it. I punch the answer key. Laurine says:

"Ducky!"

It's the same hotel room. There's two glasses on the table with drinks in them. One is for me. Laurine's got on some kinda frothy hangin'-around-the-house-with-the-boy-friend outfit that automatic makes you strain your eyes to see if you actual see what you think. Laurine looks at me enthusiastic.

"Ducky!" says Laurine. "I'm lonesome! Why haven't you come up?"

"I . . . been busy," I say, strangling slightly.

"Pooh!" says Laurine. "Listen, Ducky! Do you remember how much in love we used to be?"

I gulp.

"Are you doin' anything this evening?" says Laurine.

I gulp again, because she is smiling at me in a way that a single man would maybe get dizzy, but it gives a old married man like me cold chills. When a dame looks at you possessive—

"Ducky!" says Laurine, impulsive. "I was so mean to you! Let's get married!"

Desperation gives me a voice.

"I . . . got married," I tell her, hoarse.

Laurine blinks. Then she says, courageous:

"Poor boy! But we'll get you outta that! Only it would be nice if we could be married today. Now we can only be engaged!"

"I . . . can't—"

"I'll call up your wife," says Laurine, happy, "and have a talk with her. You must have a code signal for your logic, darling. I tried to ring your house and noth—"

Click! That's my logic turned off. I turned it off. And I feel faint all over. I got nervous prostration. I got combat fatigue. I got anything you like. I got cold feet.

I beat it outta Maintenance, yellin' to somebody I got a emergency call. I'm gonna get out in a Maintenance car 'an cruise around until it's plausible to go home. Then I'm gonna take the wife an' kids an' beat it for somewheres that Laurine won't ever find me. I don't wanna be fifth in Laurine's series of husbands and maybe the second one she shoots in a moment of boredom. I got experience of blondes. I got experience of Laurine! And I'm scared to death!

I beat it out into traffic in the Maintenance car. There was a disconnected logic on the back, ready to substitute for one that hadda burned-out coil or something that it was easier to switch and fix back in the Maintenance shop. I drove crazy but automatic. It was kinda ironic, if you think of it. I was goin' hoopla over a strictly personal problem, while civilization was crackin' up all around me because other people were havin' their personal problems solved as fast as they could state 'em. It is a matter of record that part of the Mid-Western Electric research guys had been workin' on cold electron-emission for thirty years, to make vacuum tubes that wouldn't need a power source to heat the filament. And one of those fellas was intrigued by the "Ask your logic" flash. He asked how to get cold emission of electrons. And the logic integrates a few squintillion facts on the physics data plates and tells him. Just as casual as it told somebody over in the Fourth Ward how to serve left-over soup in a new attractive way, and somebody else on Mason Street how to dispose of a torso that somebody had left careless in his cellar after ceasing to use same.

Laurine wouldn't never have found me if hadn't been for this new logics service. But now that it was started— Zowie! She'd shot one husband and got acquitted. Suppose she got impatient because I was still married an' asked logics service how to get me free an' in a spot where I'd have to marry her by 8:30 p.m.? It woulda told her! Just like it told that woman out in the suburbs how to make sure her husband wouldn't run around no more. *Br-r-r-r!* An' like it told that kid how to find some buried treasure. Remember? He was happy totin' home the gold reserve of the Hanoverian Bank and Trust Company when they caught on to it. The logic had told him how to make some kinda machine that nobody has been able to figure how it works even yet, only they guess it dodges around a couple extra dimensions. If Laurine was to start askin' questions with a technical aspect to them, that would be logics' service meat! And fella, I was scared! If you think a he-man oughtn't to be scared of just one blonde—you ain't met Laurine!

I'm drivin' blind when a social-conscious guy asks how to bring about his own particular system of social organization at once. He don't ask if it's best or if it'll work. He just wants to get it started. And the logic—or Joe—tells him! Simultaneous, there's a retired preacher asks how can the human race be cured of concupiscence. Bein' seventy, he's pretty safe himself, but he wants to remove the peril to the spiritual welfare of the rest of us. He finds out. It involves constructin' a sort of broadcastin' station to emit a certain wave-pattern an' turnin' it on. Just that. Nothing more. It's found out afterward, when he is solicitin' funds to construct it. Fortunate, he didn't think to ask logics how to finance it, or it woulda told him that, too, an' we woulda all been cured of the impulses we maybe regret afterward but never at the time. And there's another group of serious thinkers who are sure the human race would be a lot better off if everybody went back to nature an' lived in the woods with the ants an' poison ivy. They start askin' questions about how to cause humanity to abandon cities and artificial conditions of living. They practically got the answer in logics service!

Maybe it didn't strike you serious at the time, but while I was drivin' aimless, sweatin' blood over Laurine bein' after me, the fate of civilization hung in the balance. I ain't kiddin'. For instance, the Superior Man gang that sneers at the rest of us was quietly asking questions on what kinda weapons could be made by which Superior men could take over and run things—

But I drove here an' there, sweatin' an' talkin' to myself.

"What I oughta do is ask this wacky logics service how to get outa this mess," I says. "But it'd just tell me a intricate and' foolproof way to bump Laurine off. I wanna have peace! I wanna grow comfortably old and brag to other old guys about what a hellion I used to be, without havin' to go through it an' lose my chance of livin' to be a elderly liar."

I turn a corner at random, there in the Maintenance car.

"It was a nice kinda world once," I says, bitter. "I could go home peaceful and not have belly-cramps wonderin' if a blonde has called up my wife to announce my engagement to her. I could punch keys on a logic without gazing into somebody's bedroom while she is giving her epidermis a air bath and being led to think things I gotta take out in thinkin'. I could—"

Then I groan, rememberin' that my wife, naturally, is gonna blame me for the fact that our private life ain't private any more if anybody has tried to peek into it.

"It was a swell world," I says, homesick for the dear dead days-before-yesterday. "We was playin' happy with our toys like little innocent children until somethin' happened. Like a guy named Joe come in and squashed all our mud pies."

Then it hit me. I got the whole thing in one flash. There ain't nothing in the tank set-up to start relays closin'. Relays are closed exclusive by logics, to get the information the keys are punched for. Nothin' but a logic coulda cooked up the relay patterns that constituted logics service. Humans wouldn't ha' been able to figure it out! Only a logic could integrate all the stuff that woulda made all the other logics work like this—

There was one answer. I drove into a restaurant and went over to a pay-logic an' dropped in a coin.

"Can a logic be modified," I spell out, "to co-operate in long-term planning which human brains are too limited in scope to do?"

The screen sputters. Then it says:

"Definitely yes."

"How great will the modifications be?" I punch.

"Microscopically slight. Changes in dimensions," says the screen. "Even modern precision gauges are not exact enough to check them, however. They can only come about under present manufacturing methods by an extremely improbable accident, which has only happened once."

"How can one get hold of that one accident which can do this highly necessary work?" I punch.

The screen sputters. Sweat broke out on me. I ain't got it figured out close, yet, but what I'm scared of is that whatever is Joe will be suspicious. But what I'm askin' is strictly logical. And logics can't lie. They gotta be accurate. They can't help it.

"A complete logic capable of the work required," says the screen, "is now in ordinary family use in—"

And it gives me the Korlanovitch address and do I go over there! Do I go over there fast! I pull up the Maintenance car in front of the place, and I take the extra logic outta the back, and I stagger up the Korlanovitch flat and I ring the bell. A kid answers the door.

"I'm from Logics Maintenance," I tell the kid. "An inspection record has shown that your logic is apt to break down any minute. I come to put in a new one before it does."

The kid says "O.K.!" real bright and runs back to the livin'-room where Joe—I got the habit of callin' him Joe later, through just meditatin' about him—is runnin' somethin' the kids wanna look at. I hook in the other logic an' turn it on, conscientious making sure it works. Then I say:

"Now kiddies, you punch this one for what you want. I'm gonna take the old one away before it breaks down."

And I glance at the screen. The kiddies have apparently said they wanna look at some real cannibals. So the screen is presenting a anthropological expedition scientific record film of the fertility dance of the Huba-Jouba tribe of West Africa. It is supposed to be restricted to anthropological professors an' post-graduate medical students. But there ain't any censor blocks workin' any more and it's on. The kids are much interested. Me, bein' a old married man, I blush.

I disconnect Joe. Careful. I turn to the other logic and punch keys for Maintenance. I do not get a services flash. I get Maintenance. I feel very good. I report that I am goin' home because I fell down a flight of steps an' hurt my leg. I add, inspired:

"An' say, I was carryin' the logic I replaced an' it's all busted. I left it for the dustman to pick up."

"If you don't turn 'em in," says Stock, "you gotta pay for 'em."

"Cheap at the price," I say.

I go home. Laurine ain't called. I put Joe down in the cellar, careful. If I turned him in, he'd be inspected an' his parts salvaged even if I busted somethin' on him. Whatever part was off-normal might be used again and everything start all over. I can't risk it. I pay for him and leave him be.

That's what happened. You might say I saved civilization an' not be far wrong. I know I ain't goin' to take a chance on havin' Joe in action again. Not while Laurine is livin'. An' there are other reasons. With all the nuts who wanna change the world to their own line o' thinkin', an' the ones that wanna bump people off, an' generally solve their problems— Yeah! Problems are bad, but I figure I better let sleepin' problems lie.

But on the other hand, if Joe could be tamed, somehow, and got to work just reasonable— He could make me a coupla million dollars, easy. But even if I got sense enough not to get rich, an' if I get retired and just loaf around fishin' an' lyin' to other old duffers about what a great guy I used to be— Maybe I'll like it, but maybe I won't. And after all, if I get fed up with bein' old and confined strictly to thinking—why I could hook Joe in long enough to ask: "How can a old guy not stay old?" Joe'll be able to find out. An' he'll tell me.

That couldn't be allowed out general, of course. You gotta make room for kids to grow up. But it's a pretty good world, now Joe's turned off. Maybe I'll turn him on long enough to learn how to stay in it. But on the other hand, maybe—

Symbiosis

SURGEON GENERAL MORS was out in the rural districts of Kantolia Province, patiently arguing peasants into allowing the vaccination of their pigs and the inoculation of their families, when the lightning occupation took place.

There was no declaration of war, of course. Parachutists simply began to drop out of a predawn sky an hour before sunrise; at the same time, jet planes sprayed the quiet empty streets of Stadheim, the provincial capital, with machine-gun bullets, which killed two dogs and a stray cat. Then roaring, motorized columns raced across the international bridge at Balt. Armed men rounded up the drowsy customs guards and held them prisoner while tanks, armored cars, and all the impressive panoply of war drove furiously into the still peacefully sleeping countryside. Then armored trains chuffed impressively across the international line, their whistles bellowing defiance to the switch engines and handcars in the Kantolian engine yards. A splendid, totally unheralded stroke of conquest began in the cold gray light of early morning.

When dawn actually arrived and the people of Kantolia began to wake in their beds, more than half of the province was already in enemy hands. The few enemy casualties occurred in a railroad wreck, which itself was due to the action of over-enthusiastic quislings who blew up a railroad bridge to prevent the arrival of defending troops. That action merely held up the invasion program by two hours and a half in that sector. By eight o'clock of a drowsy, sunny morning, the province of Kantolia had been taken over.

Surgeon General Mors heard about it at nine, while he stood beside a pigsty and patiently argued with a peasant who had so far refused to allow either his pigs or his family to be inoculated. Mors heard the news in silence. Then he turned heavily to the civilian doctor with him.

"I had not much hope, but it is very bad," he said. "War is always bad! And I hoped so much that we would finish our program of immunization! No nation before has ever achieved one hundred per cent inoculation. It would have been a very great achievement."

Standing beside the pigsty he wiped his forehead. "Now, of course, I shall have to go to Stadheim. That will be the enemy headquarters, no doubt. I hope, Doctor, that you will continue the inoculation program while you can. I beg you to do so! One hundred per cent immunization in even a single province would be a great feat! And after all, it is not as if the enemy would not be driven out. But even in ten days terrible damage can be done!"

He went to the small, battered car in which he had been making his rounds, arguing with stubborn peasants. He was a stocky little man with deep circles under his eyes—somehow officials of small nations located close to a large one with visions of military glory tend not to sleep well of nights. Surgeon General Mors had not slept well for a long time.

Perhaps, as a military officer, he should have tried to rejoin the defending army which so far had not fired a shot. But his presence in this region had been to further the inoculation program, and that program had locally been directed from Stadheim.

As his car bumped and whined along the highway toward the provincial capital, the occupation progressed all about him without actually touching him. Three times he heard flights of jet planes roaring through the clear blue sky above. He could not pick them out because of their speed. Once he saw a faraway cloud of dust which was an armored column racing for some strategic spot not yet taken over. The enemy acted as if Kantolia had bristled with troops and weapons, instead of being defended only by customs guards at the border and the fifteen-man police force of Stadheim.

The little car clanked and sputtered. The morning was quite perfect. Here and there a cotton wool cloud floated in the blue. All about were green tablelands, spread with lusty growing crops. Surgeon General Mors looked almost enviously at the unconcerned people of the rustic villages through which he passed. They had no desire for war, and most of them did not yet know that it had come. He felt that any conceivable means was permissible for the defense of simple people like these against the alleged ideals of the enemy. But he looked very unhappy indeed.

Toward noon, he saw the steeples of Stadheim before him. But he turned abruptly aside as if to postpone the inevitable. He drove up a gentle, rolling incline until he came to the squat, functional building which housed the pumping station for the provincial city's water supply. The station and its surroundings seemed untouched, but when the engineer of the pumping station came out, the surgeon general could tell by his expression that he knew of the tragedy that had struck the country.

Surgeon General Mors got out of the car.

"They have not come here yet," he said in a flat, matter-of-fact voice.

"Not yet," said the engineer. He ground his teeth. "I have carried out my orders," he said harshly. "Just as I was told."

Surgeon General Mors nodded.

"That is good." Then he hesitated. "I would like to look over the plant," he said almost apologetically. "It is very modern and clean. The—enemy spent their money on guns. They might try to remove it for one of their cities."

The engineer stood aside. Surgeon General Mors went through the little pumping plant. There were only twenty thousand people in Stadheim, so a large installation was not required, but it was sound and practical. There were the filters, and the chlorination apparatus, and the well-equipped small laboratory for tests of the water's purity. The people of Stadheim would always have good water to drink, if the invaders didn't wreck or remove this machinery.

"It is good," said the stocky little man unhappily, "to see things like this. It makes for people to be healthy, and therefore happy. Do you know," he added irrelevantly, "that our inoculation program was almost one hundred per cent complete? Ah, well—" He paused. "I must go on to Stadheim. The invaders are there. I shall try to reason with them about our sanitary arrangements. Their soldiers will not understand how careful we are about sanitation. I shall try to get them not to make changes while they are here."

The engineer's eyes burned suddenly.

"While they are here!"

"Yes," Surgeon General Mors went on disconsolately. "They will not stay more than ten days. War is very terrible! It is everything that we doctors fight against all our lives. But so long as men do not understand, there must be wars." He drew a deep, unhappy breath. "It will indeed be terrible! May it be the last."

There was a sudden change in the engineer's eyes.

"Then we fight? My orders—"

"Yes," said Surgeon General Mors, reluctantly. "In our own way, we fight. In the only way a small nation can defend itself against a great one. We may need as long as ten days before we drive them out, and when it comes it will be a very terrible victory!"

He hesitated, and then spread out his hands in a gesture of helplessness. He walked out to the car and drove sturdily toward Stadheim.

Sentries stopped him at the outskirts of the city, to confiscate the car. But when he got out wearing the uniform of his country's military force, he was immediately arrested. He was marched toward the center of the city by a soldier who held a bayonet pressing lightly against the small of the little man's back. Mors, of course, was of the medical branch of his army and looked hopelessly unmilitary, and he carried no weapon more dangerous than a fountain pen. But the enemy soldier felt like a conqueror, and this was his first chance to act the part.

When the surgeon general of his country's army was taken to the general commanding the invading troops, the latter was already much annoyed. There had not been a single shot fired in the invasion, and this time the history books would place the credit where it belonged—with the dull, anonymous men who had prepared timetables and traffic control orders, rather than with the combat leadership. General Vladek would go down in history, if at all, only as the nominal leader of an intricate cross-country troop movement. This he did not like.

An hour since, too, he had performed an impressive ceremony on a balcony of the provincial capitol building. With officers flanking him and troops drawn up in the square below, he had read a proclamation to the people of Kantolia. They had been redeemed, said the proclamation, from the grinding oppression of their native country; henceforth they would enjoy all the blessings of oppressive taxes and secret police enjoyed by the invaders. They should rejoice, because now they were citizens of their great neighbor—and anybody who did not rejoice was very likely to be shot. In short, General Vladek had read a proclamation annexing Kantolia to his own country, and he felt very much like a fool. It was not exactly a gala occasion. But the only witnesses outside of his own troops had been two gaping street sweepers and a little knot of twenty quislings who tried to make their cheers atone for the silence of the twenty thousand people who stayed away.

However, when Surgeon General Mors was brought to his office as a prisoner of war, General Vladek felt a little better. A general officer taken prisoner! *This* had some of the savor of traditional war! The prisoner, of course, was a stocky, short figure in a badly fitting uniform, and his broad features indicated peasant ancestry. But General Vladek tried to make the most of the situation with military courtesy.

"I offer my apologies," said General Vladek grandly, "if you were subjected to any discourtesy at the time of your capture, my dear General. But after all"—he smiled condescendingly—"this is war!"

"Is it?" asked Mors. He continued in a businesslike tone: "I was not sure. When was the declaration of war issued, and by whom?"

General Vladek blinked.

"Why—ah—no formal declaration was made by my government. There were military reasons for secrecy."

Surgeon General Mors sat down and mopped his face.

"Ah! I am relieved. If you invaded without a declaration of war, you have the legal status of a bandit. Naturally, my government would not regularize your position. Even as a bandit, however," he said prosaically, "you will understand that the local sanitary arrangements should not be interfered with. That was what I came to see you about. My country has the lowest death rate in all Europe, and any meddling with our health services would be very stupid. I hope you will give orders—"

General Vladek roared. Then he calmed himself, fuming. "I did not receive you to be lectured," he said stiffly. "So far as I am aware, you are the ranking officer of your army to be captured by my men. I make a formal demand for the surrender of all troops under your command."

"But there aren't any!" said Surgeon General Mors in surprise. "My government would not be so imbecilic as to leave soldiers in a province they were not strong enough to defend! They'd only have been killed in trumped-up fighting so you could claim a victory!"

General Vladek's eyes glittered. He pounced.

"Ha! Then your government knew that we intended to invade?"

"My dear man!" said Mors with some tartness. "Your government has been drooling at the mouth for years over the fact that the taxes from our richest province would almost balance its budget! Of course we suspected you would someday try to seize it! We are not altogether fools!"

"Yet," said General Vladek sardonically, "you did not prepare to defend it!"

Surgeon General Mors blinked at the slim, bemedaled figure of his official captor.

"When a peaceful householder hears a burglar in his house," he said shortly, "he may or may not go to fight himself, but he does not send his young sons! If he is sensible, he sends for the police."

"He sends for the police!" repeated Vladek incredulously. "My good Surgeon General Mors, do you expect the United Nations to interfere in this matter? The United Nations is run by diplomats, phrasemakers. They are aghast and helpless before an accomplished fact like our actual possession of Kantolia! My good sir—"

"This talk is nonsense!" said Mors irritably. "I came to offer you the benefit of my experience in matters of military and public health. Do you have the welfare of your men actually at heart?"

There was a pause. General Vladek was slim and beautifully tailored. He did not belong in the office of the provincial governor of Kantolia, whose desk was still littered with papers concerning such local affairs as the price of pigs and crops and an outbreak of measles in the public schools. The office was slightly grubby, despite a certain plebeian attempt at elegance. General Vladek seemed fastidiously detached from his surroundings. And he was amused.

"I assure you," said General Vladek, "that I am duly solicitous of my men's health."

"If you are solicitous enough," said Surgeon General Mors curtly, "you will get them out of here as quickly as they came in! But I can hardly expect you to comply with that wish. What I have to say is that your troops had better have as little to do with the civilian population as possible—no communication of any sort that can possibly be avoided."

"You are ridiculous," said General Vladek, annoyed. "Kantolia is now part of my country. Its people are the fellow citizens of my troops. Isolate them? Ridiculous!"

Surgeon General Mors stood up and shrugged.

"Very well," he said heavily. "I advised you. Now, either I am a prisoner or I am not. If not, I would like a

pass allowing me to go about freely. The sudden entry
of so large an invading force introduces problems of
public health—"

"Which my medical corps," said General Vladek
scornfully, "is quite able to cope with! You are a prisoner, and I think a fool! Good day!"

Surgeon General Mors marched stolidly to the
door. . . .

Since the invasion was not yet one day old, there had
been no time to build concentration camps. Surgeon
General Mors was confined, therefore, in a school
which had been closed to education that it might be
taken over and used as a prison. He found himself in
company with the provincial governor of Kantolia, with
the mayor of Stadheim, and various other officials arrested by the invaders. There were private citizens in
confinement, too—mostly people whom the small number of quislings in Kantolia had denounced. They were
not accused of crimes, as yet. Even the invading army
did not yet pretend that they had committed any offense
against either military or civilian law. But most of them
were frantic. It was not easy to forget tales of hostages
shot for acts of resistance by conquered populations.
They knew of places where leading citizens had been
exterminated for the crime of being leading citizens,
and educated men destroyed because they rejected
propaganda that outraged all reason. The fate of Kantolia had precedents. If precedent were followed, those
first arrested when the land was overrun were in no en-
viable situation.

Surgeon General Mors tried to reassure them, but he
had not much success. The entire situation looked hope-
less. The seizure of a single province of a very minor
nation would appear to the rest of the world either as a
crisis, or an affront to the United Nations, or as a rectification of frontiers—according to the nationality and
political persuasion of the commentator. It would go on
the agenda of the United Nations Council; deftly it
would be intermixed with other matters so that it could
not be untangled and considered separately. Ultimately
it would be the subject of a compromise—one item in a

complicated Great Power deal—which would leave matters exactly as the invaders wished them. Practically speaking, that was the prospect.

"But the fact," said Surgeon General Mors, "is that such things cannot continue forever. The life of humanity is a symbiosis, a living-together, in all its stages. It begins with the symbiotic relationship of members of a family, each of whom helps and is helped by all the rest. But it rises to the symbiotic relationship of nations, of which each is an organism necessary to the others, and all are mutually helpful."

"But there is parasitic symbiosis, in which one organism seeks to prey upon another as our enemy seeks to prey upon us," interjected an amateur naturalist who was a fellow prisoner.

"But a truly healthy organism finds ways to rid itself of parasites," Mors said calmly; "or at least to keep them in tolerable subjugation. Do you doubt that our country is a healthy organism?"

It was encouraging talk, but his fellow prisoners were not convinced. Most of them had been seized in their homes. Only one was fully dressed. The mayor had on an overcoat over his nightshirt; his hairy shanks and bare feet left him utterly without dignity. Other leading citizens were unshaven, uncombed, and in every possible stage of dishabille; all were certain their humiliation was a bad omen.

"To be sure," conceded Surgeon General Mors practically, "our country has only four million people, and our enemy has fifty. But we have planned our nation carefully. In nature, not all creatures defend themselves with tooth and claw. There is a specialized defense for every type of creature, as I myself pointed out to our president. There must be, as I insisted to him, some form of defense for every type of nation, so that it may survive. And I may say that he later told me that he considers our nation's survival certain. So, since this province is necessary if our nation is truly to survive, the invaders will have to be turned out of it."

"But when?" asked a prisoner despairingly.

"The wheat harvest should begin in three weeks,"

said Mors meditatively. "It will be a great blow to our country if our enemy seizes the wheat harvest. I should say that we must have victory for our country in less than three weeks. Probably within ten days."

His companions stared at him. But Surgeon General Mors did not look like someone envisioning a spectacular military triumph for his country. He looked like someone sick at heart from some knowledge he concealed within him.

Depression stayed with the prisoners. They increased in number as the day wore on. Typically, to the conquerors the conquered seemed somehow less than human. Many of the later prisoners had been beaten after their arrest. On the second day the schoolhouse was crowded. More of the new prisoners were beaten. On the third day there was a barbed-wire fence around the schoolhouse and food for the prisoners was contemptuously dumped inside it in bulk for them to distribute themselves. Surgeon General Mors organized a committee for the purpose, and to protest against unnecessary ill-treatment and humiliations.

On the fourth day two men arrived so badly beaten that they were unconscious, and died even as Surgeon General Mors tried—without drugs or any equipment—to revive them.

The newcomers reported conditions in the province. The invaders were methodically looting the captured territory. Their obvious purpose was to increase the riches of their country by impoverishing the province they had added to it. Machinery was being shipped back in a steady stream. Manufactured products were requisitioned from merchants. Kantolia had been the richest province in its small nation. When the invaders finished, it would be the most poverty-stricken in Europe.

That was not all. The troops of the invaders were quartered in private homes as well as in public buildings. Nearly every Kantolian family had its quota of invaders, to be fed at the householder's own expense. And while the enemy troops were required to practice strict discipline in relation to their officers, no such strictness was enforced as regarded civilians. A citizen whose home was only looted was considered fortunate.

The outside world remained unconcerned. Of course no news went out from Kantolia. Censorship and a tightly sealed frontier took care of that. But what sparse, illicit radio news newcomers brought in to the prisoners indicated that the outside world was not too much disturbed by the rectification of an unimportant frontier in a remote corner of Europe.

There was a diplomatic crisis among the Big Four powers. Surgeon General Mors' government had made a dignified protest and a formal appeal to the United Nations, but the achievement of atomic energy control by that organization had been so precarious a matter, and was maintained by so unstable a balance of bargains, that a controversial question like the seizure of Kantolia might wreck the entire framework of international accord if pressed at the present time. Consideration of the matter had been postponed. The invaders had an indefinite period in which forcibly to remold the province's citizenry nearer to their heart's desire, to teach them to clamor dutifully for the maintenance of their new nationality lest worse things befall.

Strangely, though, no new prisoners arrived after the fourth day. Almost the last to arrive told, sobbing, of the fact that fresh troops had been pouring into Kantolia almost from the instant of its seizure, and that now a monstrous army was ready to overwhelm the rest of the nation of which Kantolia had been a part.

But Surgeon General Mors counted on his fingers and said bleakly, "The invasion cannot last more than ten days! But it is very terrible!"

He had never been military in appearance. Now, five days without soap with which to wash, or a razor with which to shave, and with no change of garments at all, his looks were not imposing. He had torn up his undershirt to make bandages for beaten prisoners. The food was insufficient, and he had given of his own to those most terribly beaten and therefore weakest. The five days had told upon him. Yet he still possessed an odd dignity which could only have been the dignity of faith.

Then, on the afternoon of the fifth day, one of the sentries outside the barbed-wire enclosure staggered, dropped his rifle against a tree and then clung to that tree in a spasm of weakness. And Surgeon General Mors saw it.

He watched somberly until it was over. He looked heartsick and ill. But his eyes glowed doggedly as he turned and ran his eyes over the battered, dispirited figures in the concentration camp which was the first benefit conferred by the invaders.

"I must borrow a razor from someone," Mors told the mayor of Stadheim, who happened to be nearest him, "or a knife. At worst I shall have to break a pane of glass and try to shave with its edge. I am going to demand the surrender of the invading army."

He did not succeed in making the demand that day. It was late afternoon of the seventh day of the occupation before Surgeon General Mors was ushered into the presence of General Vladek. On the way from the schoolhouse, the stocky, untidy man had been marched through the streets of Stadheim. They were almost empty. They were dirty and unswept. Trash littered the sidewalks. He saw few civilians and no soldiers at all except his guard, until he arrived at the capitol building which was enemy headquarters.

He saw an invading soldier there, a sentry, lying on the sidewalk in a curiously shapeless heap. Surgeon General Mors knew at the first glance that the man was dead.

He looked more than ever sick at heart when he was ushered into the presence of General Vladek. The scene of this second interview was also the office of the provincial governor, but now the plebeian elegance of its furnishings had been corrected. Now it was a picture of efficiency. There were filing cabinets and wall maps, and an automatic facsimile machine in one corner hummed softly as it covered a slowly unreeling roll of paper with slightly out-of-register typed orders, queries, lists and the like.

General Vladek was slim and elegantly bemedaled as before. But now there was a nervous tic in his cheek.

His face was queerly gray. He looked at Surgeon General Mors with a desperate grimness.

"You are going to be shot," he said with a terrifying quietness, "if you answer my questions truthfully. If you do not answer them, you will not be shot. But you will beg very pitifully for a chance to reconsider and earn a firing squad! Do you understand?"

Surgeon General Mors seated himself with great composure. His attempt at shaving had not been very successful. He was in every way a disreputable contrast to the invading general's dapper splendor.

"I asked for this interview," said Mors matter-of-factly, "to ask if you are prepared to surrender the troops under your command. You mentioned once that I was the ranking officer of my army in your hands. I doubt that you have captured any other. So I seem to be the person to make the demand."

General Vladek made a violent gesture. Then he composed himself. But he breathed quickly, and his cheek twitched, and his teeth showed when he smiled. He did not look conspicuously sane.

"What is this epidemic?" he demanded in a deadly quietness. "My men die at the rate of ten thousand a day! Your citizens do not! We have lost thirty-five thousand men in four days, and so far not more than six civilians native to Kantolia have been stricken! *What is it, Mors?*"

Surgeon General Mors leaned back in his chair. He showed no sigh of triumph.

"It would be an—organism we developed," he said heavily. "The official designation is CK-211. I understand that it is an artificial mutation, a variation on a fairly common bacterium. I have been told that it could be described as a dwarf form of one of the diplococci. It is hardly larger than a virus molecule. You would not expect me to be more precise."

General Vladek's nostrils distended.

"Ah-h-h-h!" he said with deadly softness. "It is no normal plague! It is biological war! Too cowardly to fight as honorable men fight, your nation—"

"There is no war between our countries," said Surgeon General Mors, prosaically, "and you invaded our country like a brigand, making your own rules for attack. So we made our own rules for defense. If you surrender the troops under your command, there is a good chance that we can save their lives. Have you given thought to the matter?"

General Vladek's cheeks twitched. His hands shook with hate.

"Tell me the truth," he said hoarsely, "and I will have you shot. I will concede so much! I promise that I will have you shot! But if you do not—"

"I think you are being absurd, General," said Mors stolidly. "As I recall the details, death occurs on the third day after infection, usually within a few hours of the appearance of the first noticeable symptoms. Sulfa, streptomycin, and penicillin are ineffective against this particular strain, which was especially bred up to be resistant to such drugs. Also, from my recollection, the patient is infectious almost from the instant of his own infection. I think you understate your losses. Moreover, in an epidemic of this sort, the death rate should mount geometrically until natural immunes and the lack of susceptibles lower it."

Mors paused, and said inquiringly, "You have ordered your men to abstain from all contact with the civil population?"

General Vladek panted with fury.

"I suspected intention when the plague began! My medical corps insisted that since only my men were infected, its cause must be contaminated supplies from home! I ordered my troops to subsist on local supplies and distributed our rations among the people—for revenge in case your spies in our supply system were responsible! But the rate of infection tripled! And your people do not die! My men die! Only my men."

Surgeon General Mors nodded. His eyes were somber, yet very resolute.

"That is natural," he observed. "Our population is immune." Then he said explanatorily. "We have immunized practically our entire population against certain formerly prevalent diseases. And included in the injection given to each citizen was a fraction of a very interesting formula which produces immunity to diplococci in a quite new fashion."

The dapper General Vladek sat frozen and speechless, in a rage so murderous that he seemed almost calm.

"It makes symbiosis possible," said Surgeon General Mors, in an interested tone. "It produces a condition under which the human body and the entire series of diplococci can live together. It does not produce the relationship. That requires the organisms, too. It merely makes the relationship possible. We have had practically no diplococci infections in our country for years back. Such diseases happen to be very rare among us. But the inoculation makes it possible for any of our inoculated citizens to establish a truly symbiotic relationship in case he encounters them. It is like the adjustment of intestinal flora and colon bacilli to us. They do not harm us, and we do not harm them. You follow the reasoning?"

General Vladek's voice was quite inhuman. "How were my men infected?" he demanded. His voice cracked. "Tell me, how were my men infected? My medical corps says—"

"We did not infect them," said Surgeon General Mors calmly. "We infected only our own population. On the morning of your invasion we spread the infection in the drinking water, in the food. We infected our own people—who could not be harmed by it—and then I came to you and warned you to keep your soldiers aloof from our people. I also advised you to get your troops out of our country for their own safety, but you would not believe me. Because you see"—his tone was absolutely commonplace—"every citizen of our country is now a carrier of the plague of which your soldiers die. A carrier. Not suffering from it, but able to give it to anyone not immunized against it. You have heard of typhoid carriers. We are a nation of carriers, bearers of the plague which is destroying your army."

General Vladek looked like an image of frozen, despairing rage. His face was gray. His cheek twitched.

He had led an invading army triumphantly into this province.

Then without one shot being fired, his army had ceased to be an army, and a sentry lay dead on the street before his headquarters.

"We did not like to do it," said Surgeon General Mors, heavily. "But we had to defend ourselves. The soil of our nation is now deadly to your troops. If you murdered and burned every citizen of our country, our land would still be fatal to your men and to the settlers who might follow them. You cannot make use of Kantolia. You cannot make use of any of the rest of our country. And the loot you have sent back has spread infection in your cities. Couriers have carried it back and transmitted it before they died. The quislings you sent to your country to be rewarded for betraying their own—they were carriers, too. The plague must rage horribly in your nation. Other countries will close their frontiers in quarantine, if they have not already done so. You nation is destroyed unless you let us save it. I beg that you will give us the power."

Then Surgeon General Mors said very wearily: "I hope you will surrender your army, General Vladek. Your men, as our prisoners, will become our patients and we will cure them. Otherwise they will die. Permit us, and we will check the epidemic you created in your own country by invading us. We did not defend ourselves without knowing our weapon thoroughly. But you will have to give us the power to rescue you. You and your nation must surrender without conditions. . . ."

General Vladek stood up. He rang a bell. An officer and soldiers entered.

"Take him out," panted General Vladek hoarsely. Then his voice rose to a scream. "Take him out and kill him!"

The officer moved. Then there was a clatter. A rifle had dropped to the floor. One of the soldiers staggered. He reeled against one of the steel filing cases and clung there desperately. Sweat poured out on his face; he was ashen white. He knew, of course, what was the matter. He sobbed. He was already a dead man, though he still moved and breathed. Great tears welled out of his eyes. The other soldiers wavered—and fled.

Surgeon General Mors stood beside a pigsty and argued patiently with a peasant who so far had stubbornly refused to permit the reinoculation of either his family or his cows. The dumpy little man in the badly fitting uniform said earnestly:

"It is a matter of living together—what learned men call symbiosis. We defended our country with the other inoculations. Now we must defend all mankind with these! We do not want our people to be feared or hated. We want visitors from other nations to come and live among us in peace and safety, to have no fears about doing business with us. If other nations are afraid of us, we will suffer for it!"

The peasant made fitful objections. Victory over the invaders, and the terms imposed upon them, had made him proud. But Surgeon General Mors' patient arguments were gradually wearing him down.

"Ah, but they made war on us. That was different! We do not want any more wars. When you and your family and your cows have been inoculated, we will be that much further along toward the understanding that nations which are at peace can live together," said Surgeon General Mors earnestly. "Nations which are at war only die together."

The Strange Case of John Kingman

IT STARTED WHEN Dr. Braden took the trouble to look up John Kingman's case-history card. Meadeville Mental Hospital had a beautifully elaborate system of card-indexes, because psychiatric research is stressed there. It is the oldest mental institution in the country, having been known as "New Bedlam" when it was founded some years before the Republic of the United States of America. The card-index system was unbelievably perfect. But young Dr. Braden found John Kingman's card remarkably lacking in the usual data.

"Kingman, John," said the card. "White, male, 5'8", brown-black hair. Note: physical anomaly. Patient has six fingers on each hand, extra digits containing apparently normal bones and being wholly functional. Age . . ." This was blank. "Race . . ." This, too, was blank. "Birthplace . . ." Considering the other blanks, it was natural for this to be vacant, also. "Diagnosis: advanced atypical paranoia with pronounced delusions of grandeur apparently unassociated with usual conviction of persecution." There was a comment here, too. "Patient apparently understands English very slightly if at all. Does not speak." Then three more spaces. "Nearest relative . . ." It was blank. "Case history . . ." It was blank. Then, "Date of admission . . ." and it was blank.

The card was notably defective, for the index-card of a patient at Meadeville Mental. A patient's age and race could be unknown if he'd simply been picked up in the street somewhere and never adequately identified. In such an event it was reasonable that his nearest relative and birthplace should be unknown, too. But there should have been some sort of case history—at least of the events leading to his committal to the institution. And certainly, positively, absolutely, the date of his admission should be on the card!

Young Dr. Braden was annoyed. This was at the time when the Jantzen euphoric-shock treatment was first introduced, and young Dr. Braden believed in it. It made sense. He was anxious to attempt it at Meadeville—of course on a patient with no other possible hope of improvement. He handed the card to the clerk in the records department and asked for further data on the case.

Two hours later he smoked comfortably on a very foul pipe, stretched out on grassy sward by the Administration Building. There was a beautifully blue sky overhead, and the shadows of the live oaks reached out in an odd long pattern on the lawn. Young Dr. Braden read meditatively in the *American Journal of Psychiatry*. The article was "Reaction of Ten Paranoid Cases to Euphoric Shock." John Kingman sat in regal dignity on the steps nearby. He wore the nondescript garments of an indigent patient—not supplied with clothing by relatives. He gazed into the distance, to all appearances thinking consciously godlike thoughts and being infinitely superior to mere ordinary humans. He was of an indeterminate age which might be forty or might be sixty or might be anywhere in between. His six-fingered hands lay in studied gracefulness in his lap. He deliberately ignored all of mankind and mankind's doings.

Dr. Braden finished the article. He sucked thoughtfully on the burned-out pipe. Without seeming to do so, he regarded John Kingman again. Mental cases have unpredictable reactions, but as with children and wild animals, much can be done if care is taken not to startle them. Presently young Dr. Braden said meditatively:

"John, I think something can be done for you."

The regal figure turned its eyes. They looked at the younger man. They were aloofly amused at the impertinence of a mere human being addressing John Kingman, who was so much greater than a mere human being that he was not even annoyed at human impertinence. Then John Kingman looked away again.

"I imagine," said Braden, as meditatively as before, "that you're pretty bored. I'm going to see if something can't be done about it. In fact—"

Someone came across the grass toward him. It was the clerk of the records department. He looked very unhappy. He had the card Dr. Braden had turned in with a request for more complete information. Braden waited.

"Er . . . doctor," said the clerk miserably, "there's something wrong! Something terribly wrong! About the records, I mean."

The aloofness of John Kingman had multiplied with the coming of a second, low, human being into his ken. He gazed into the distance in divine indifference to such creatures.

"Well?" said Braden.

"There's no record of his admission!" said the clerk. "Every year there's a complete roster of the patients, you know. I thought I'd just glance back, find out what year his name first appeared, and look in the committal papers for that year. But I went back twenty years, and John Kingman is mentioned every year!"

"Look back thirty, then," said Braden.

"I . . . I did!" said the clerk painfully. "He was a patient here thirty years ago!"

"Forty?" asked Braden.

The clerk gulped.

"Dr. Braden," he said desperately, "I even went to the dead files, where records going back to 1850 are kept. And . . . doctor, he was a patient then!"

Braden got up from the grass and brushed himself off automatically.

"Nonsense!" he said. "That's ninety-eight years ago!"

The clerk looked crushed.

"I know, doctor. There's something terribly wrong! I've never had my records questioned before. I've been here twenty years—"

"I'll come with you and look for myself," said Dr. Braden. "Send an attendant to come here and take him back to his ward."

"Y-yes, doctor," said the clerk, gulping again. "At . . . at once."

He went away at a fast pace between a shuffle and a run. Dr. Braden scowled impatiently.

Then he saw John Kingman looking at him again, and John Kingman was amused. Tolerantly, loftily amused. Amused with a patronizing condescension that would have been infuriating to anyone but a physician trained to regard behavior as symptomatic rather than personal.

"It's absurd," grunted Braden, matter-of-factly treating the patient—as a good psychiatrist does—like a perfectly normal human being. "You haven't been here for ninety-eight years!"

One of the six-fingered hands stirred. While John Kingman regarded Braden with infinitely superior scorn, six fingers made a gesture as of writing. Then the hand reached out.

Braden put a pencil in it. The other hand reached. Braden fumbled in his pockets and found a scrap of paper. He offered that.

John Kingman looked aloofly into the far distance, not even glancing at what his hands did. But the fingers sketched swiftly, with practiced ease. It took only seconds. Then, negligently, he reached out and returned pencil and paper to Braden. He returned to his godlike indifference to mere mortals. But there was now the faintest possible smile on his face. It was an expression of contemptuous triumph.

Braden glanced at the sketch. There was design there. There was an unbelievable intricacy of relationship between this curved line and that, and between them and the formalized irregular pattern in the center. It was not the drawing of a lunatic. It was cryptic, but it was utterly rational. There is something essentially childish in the background of most forms of insanity. There was nothing childish about this. And it was obscurely, annoyingly familiar. Braden had seen something like it, somewhere, before. It was not in the line of psychiatry, but in some of the physical sciences diagrams like this were used in explanations.

An attendant came to return John Kingman to his ward. Braden folded the paper and put it in his pocket.

"It's not in my line, John," he told John Kingman. "I'll have a check-up made. I think I'm going to be able to do something for you."

John Kingman suffered himself to be led away. Rather, he grandly preceded the attendant, negligently preventing the man from touching him, as if such a touch would be a sacrilege the man was too ignorant to realize.

Braden went to the record office. With the agitated clerk beside him, he traced John Kingman's name to the earliest of the file of dead records. Handwriting succeeded typewriting as he went back through the years. Paper yellowed. Handwriting grew Spencerian. It approached the copperplate. But, in ink turned brown, in yellowed rag paper in the ruled record-books of the Eastern Pennsylvania Asylum—which was Meadeville Mental in 1850—there were the records of a patient named John Kingman for every year. Twice Braden came upon notes alongside the name. One was in 1880. Some staff doctor—there were no psychiatrists in those days—had written, *"High fever."* There was nothing else. In 1853 a neat memo stood beside the name. *"This man has six functioning fingers on each hand."* The memo had been made ninety-five years before.

Dr. Braden looked at the agitated clerk. The record of John Kingman was patently impossible. The clerk read it as a sign of inefficiency in his office and possibly on his part. He would be upset and apprehensible until the source of the error had safely been traced to a predecessor.

"Someone," said Braden dryly—but he did not believe it even then—"forgot to make a note of the explanation. An unknown must have been admitted at some time as John Kingman. In time, he died. But somehow the name John Kingman had become a sort of stock name like John Doe, to signify an unidentified patient. Look in the death records for John Kingman. Evidently a John Kingman died, and that same year another unidentified patient was assigned the same name. That's it!"

The clerk almost gasped with relief. He went happily to check. But Braden did not believe it. In 1853 someone had noted that John Kingman had six functioning fingers on each hand. The odds against two patients in one institution having six functioning fingers, even in the same century, would be enormous.

Braden went doggedly to the museum. There the devices used in psychiatric treatments in the days of New Bedlam were preserved, but not displayed. Meadeville Mental had been established in 1776 as New Bedlam. It was the oldest mental institution in the United States, but it was not pleasant to think of the treatment given to patients—then termed "madmen"—in the early days.

The records remained. Calf-leather bindings. Thin rag paper. Beautifully shaded writing, done with quill pens. Year after year, Dr. Braden searched. He found John Kingman listed in 1820. In 1801. In 1795. In 1785 the name "John Kingman" was absent from the annual list of patients. Braden found the record of his admission in 1786. On the 21st of May, 1786—ten years after New Bedlam was founded, one hundred and sixty-two years before the time of his search—there was a neat entry:

A poore madman admitted this day has been assigned ye name of John Kingman because of his absurdly royal manner and affected dignity. He is five feet eight inches tall, appears to speak no Englishe or any other tongue known to any of the learned men hereabout, and has six fingers on each hand, ye extra fingers being perfectly formed and functioning. Dr. Sanforde observed that hee seems to have a high fever. On his left shoulder, when stripped, there appears a curious design which is not tattooing according to any known fashion. His madness appears to be so strong a conviction of his greatness that he will not condescend to no-

tice others as being so much his inferiors, so that if not committed hee would starve. But on three occasions, when being examined by physicians, he put out his hand imperiously for writing instruments, and drew very intrikit designs which all agree have no significance. He was committed as a madman by a commission consisting of Drs. Sanforde, Smyth, Hale, and Bode."

Young Dr. Braden read the entry a second time. Then a third. He ran his hands through his hair. When the clerk came back to announce distressedly that not in all the long history of the institution had a patient named John Kingman died, Braden was not surprised.

"Quite right," said Braden to the almost hysterical clerk. "He didn't die. But I want John Kingman taken over to the hospital ward. We're going to look him over. He's been rather neglected. Apparently he's had actual medical attention only once in a hundred and sixty-two years. Get out his committal papers for me, will you? He was admitted here May 21st, 1786."

Then Braden left, leaving behind him a clerk practically prostrated with shock. The clerk wildly suspected that Dr. Braden had gone insane. But when he found the committal papers, he decided hysterically that it was he who would shortly be in one of the wards.

John Kingman manifested amusement when he was taken into the hospital laboratory. For a good ten seconds—Braden watched him narrowly—he glanced from one piece of apparatus to another. It was impossible to doubt that after one glance he understood the function and operation of every appliance in the ultramodern, super-scientifically-equipped laboratory of the hospital ward. But he was amused. In particular, he looked at the big X-ray machine and smiled with such contempt that the X-ray technician bristled.

"No paranoid suspicion," said Braden. "Most paranoid patients suspect that they're going to be tortured or killed when they're brought to a place where there's stuff they don't understand."

John Kingman turned his eyes to Braden. He put out

his six-fingered hand and made the motion of writing. Braden handed him a pencil and a memo tablet. Negligently, contemptuously, he sketched. He sketched again. He handed the sketches to Braden and retreated into his enormous amused contempt for humanity.

Braden glanced at the scraps of paper. He jerked his head, and the X-ray technician came to his side.

"This," said Braden dryly, "looks like a diagram of an X-ray tube. Is it?"

The technician blinked.

"He don't use the regular symbols," he objected, "but . . . well . . . yes. That's what he puts for the target and this's for the cathode— Hm-m-m. Yes—" Then he said suddenly: "Say! That's not right."

He studied the diagram. Then he said in abrupt excitement:

"Look! He's put in a field like in a electron microscope! That's an idea! Do that, and you'd get straightline electron flow and a narrower X-ray beam—"

Braden said:

"I wonder! What's this second sketch? Another type of X-ray?"

The X-ray technician studied the second sketch absorbedly. After a time he said dubiously:

"He don't use regular symbols. I don't know. Here's the same sign for the target and that for the cathode. This looks like something to . . . hm-m-m . . . accelerate the electrons. Like in a Coolidge tube. Only it's—" He scratched his head. "I see what he's trying to put down. If something like this would work, you could work any tube at any voltage you wanted. Yeah! And all the high EMF would be inside the tube. No danger. Hey! You could work this off dry batteries! A doctor could carry a X-ray outfit in his handbag! And he could get million-volt stuff!"

The technician stared in mounting excitement. Presently he said urgently:

"This is crazy! But . . . look, Doc! Let me have this thing to study over! This is great stuff! This is . . . Gosh! Give me a chance to get this made up and try it out! I don't get it all yet, but—"

Braden took back the sketch and put it in his pocket. "John Kingman," he observed, "has been a patient here for a hundred and sixty-two years. I think we're going to get some more surprises. Let's get at the job on hand!"

John Kingman was definitely amused. He was amenable, now. His air of pitying condescension, as of a god to imbeciles, under other circumstances would have been infuriating. He permitted himself to be X-rayed as one might allow children to use one as a part of their play. He glanced at the thermometer and smiled contemptuously. He permitted his body temperature to be taken from an armpit. The electrocardiograph aroused just such momentary interest as a child's unfamiliar plaything might cause. With an air of mirth he allowed the tattooed design on his shoulder—it was there—to be photographed. Throughout, he showed such condescending contempt as would explain his failure to be annoyed.

But Braden grew pale as the tests went on. John Kingman's body temperature was 105° F. A "high fever" had been observed in 1850—ninety-eight years before—and in 1786—well over a century and a half previously. But he still appeared to be somewhere between forty and sixty years old. John Kingman's pulse rate was one hundred fifty-seven beats per minute, and the electrocardiograph registered an absolutely preposterous pattern which had no meaning until Braden said curtly: "If he had two hearts, it would look like that!"

When the X-ray plates came out of the fixing-bath, he looked at them with the grim air of someone expecting to see the impossible. And the impossible was there. When John Kingman was admitted to New Bedlam, there were no such things as X-rays on earth. It was natural that he had never been X-rayed before. He had two hearts. He had three extra ribs on each side. He had four more vertebrae than a normal human being. There were distinct oddities in his elbow joints. And his cranial capacity appeared to be something like twelve per cent above that of any but exceptional specimens of humanity. His teeth displayed distinct, consistent deviations from the norm in shape.

He regarded Braden with contemptuous triumph when the tests were over. He did not speak. He drew dignity about himself like a garment. He allowed an attendant to dress him again while he looked into the distance, seemingly thinking godlike thoughts. When his toilet was complete he looked again at Braden—with vast condescension—and his six-fingered hands again made a gesture of writing. Braden grew—if possible—slightly paler as he handed over a pencil and pad.

John Kingman actually deigned to glance, once, at the sheet on which he wrote. When he handed it back to Braden and withdrew into magnificently amused aloofness, there were a dozen or more tiny sketches on the sheet. The first was an exact duplicate of the one he had handed Braden before the Administration Building. Beside it was another which was similar but not alike. The third was a specific variation of the two together. The rest carried on that variation in precise, exact steps until the last pair of sketches divided again into two, of which one—by a perfectly logical extension of the change-pattern—had returned to the original design, while the other was a bewilderingly complex pattern with its formalized central part in two closely-linked sections.

Braden caught his breath. Just as the X-ray man had been puzzled at first by the use of unfamiliar symbols for familiar ideas, so Braden had been puzzled by untraceable familiarity in the first sketch of all. But the last diagram made everything clear. It resembled almost exactly the standard diagrams illustrating fissionable elements as atoms. Once it was granted that John Kingman was no ordinary lunatic, it became clear that here was a diagram of some physical process which began with normal and stable atoms and arrived at an unstable atom—with one of the original atoms returned to its original state. It was, in short, a process of physical catalysis which would produce atomic energy.

Braden raised his eyes to the contemptuous, amused eyes of John Kingman.

"I think you win," he said shakenly. "I still think you're crazy, but maybe we're crazier still."

The commitment papers on John Kingman were a hundred and sixty-two years old. They were yellow and brittle and closely written. John Kingman—said the oddly spelled and sometimes curiously phrased document—was first seen on the morning of April 10, 1786, by a man named Thomas Hawkes, as he drove into Aurora, Pennsylvania, with a load of corn. John Kingman was then clad in very queer garments, not like those of ordinary men. The material looked like silk, save that it seemed also to be metallic. The man Hawkes was astounded, but thought perhaps some strolling player had got drunk and wandered off while wearing his costume for a play or pageant. He obligingly stopped his horse and allowed the stranger to climb in for a ride to town. The stranger was imperious, and scornfully silent. Hawkes asked who he was, and was contemptuously ignored. He asked—seemingly, all the world was talking of such matters then, at least the world about Aurora, Pennsylvania—if the stranger had seen the giant shooting stars of the night before. The stranger ignored him. Arrived in town, the stranger stood in the street with regal dignity, looking contemptuously at the people. A crowd gathered about him, but he seemed to feel too superior to notice it. Presently a grave and elderly man—a Mr. Wycherly—appeared and the stranger fixed him with a gesture. He stooped and wrote strange designs in the dust at his feet. When the unintelligible design was meaningless to Mr. Wycherly, the stranger seemed to fly into a very passion of contempt. He spat at the crowd, and the crowd became unruly and constables took him into custody.

Braden waited patiently until both the Director of Meadeville Mental and the man from Washington had finished reading the yellowed papers. Then Braden explained calmly:

"He's insane, of course. It's paranoia. He is as convinced of his superiority to us as—say—Napoleon or Edison would have been convinced of their superiority if they'd suddenly been dumped down among a tribe of Australian bushmen. As a matter of fact, John Kingman may have just as good reason as they would have had to feel his superiority. But if he were sane he would prove it. He would establish it. Instead, he has withdrawn into a remote contemplation of his own greatness. So he is a paranoiac. One may surmise that he was insane when he first appeared. But he doesn't have a delusion of persecution because on the face of it no such theory is needed to account for his present situation."

The Director said in a tolerantly shocked tone:

"Dr. Braden! You speak as if he were not a human being!"

"He isn't," said Braden. "His body temperature is a hundred and five. Human tissues simply would not survive that temperature. He has extra vertebrae and extra ribs. His joints are not quite like ours. He has two hearts. We were able to check his circulatory system just under the skin with infrared lamps, and it is not like ours. And I submit that he has been a patient in this asylum for one hundred and sixty-two years. If he is human, he is at least remarkable!"

The man from Washington said interestedly:

"Where do you think he comes from, Dr. Braden?"

Braden spread out his hands. He said doggedly:

"I make no guesses. But I sent photostats of the sketches he made to the Bureau of Standards. I said that they were made by a patient and appeared to be diagrams of atomic structure. I asked if they indicated a knowledge of physics. You"—he looked at the man from Washington—"turned up thirty-six hours later. I deduce that he has such knowledge."

"He has!" said the man from Washington, mildly. "The X-ray sketches were interesting enough, but the others— Apparently he has told us how to get controlled atomic energy out of silicon, which is one of earth's commonest elements. Where did he come from, Dr. Braden?"

Braden clamped his jaw.

"You noticed that the commitment papers referred to shooting stars then causing much local comment? I looked up the newspapers for about that date. They reported a large shooting star which was observed to descend to the earth. Then, various credible observers claimed that it shot back up to the sky again. Then, some hours afterward, various large shooting stars crossed the sky from horizon to horizon, without ever falling."

The Director of Meadeville Mental said humorously:

"It's a wonder that New Bedlam—as we were then—was not crowded after such statements!"

The man from Washington did not smile.

"I think," he said meditatively, "that Dr. Braden suggests a spaceship landing to permit John Kingman to get out, and then going away again. And possible pursuit afterward."

The Director laughed appreciatively at the assumed jest.

"If," said the man from Washington, "John Kingman is not human, and if he comes from somewhere where as much was known about atomic energy almost two centuries ago as he has showed us, and, if he were insane there, he might have seized some sort of vehicle and fled in it because of delusions of persecution. Which in a sense, if he were insane, might be justified. He would have been pursued. With pursuers close behind him he might have landed—here."

"But the vehicle!" said the Director, humorously. "Our ancestors would have recorded finding a spaceship or an airplane."

"Suppose," said the man from Washington, "that his pursuers had something like . . . say . . . radar. Even we have that! A cunning lunatic would have sent off his vehicle under automatic control to lead his pursuers as long and merry a chase as possible. Perhaps he sent it to dive into the sun. The rising shooting star and the other cruising shooting stars would be accounted for. What do you say, Dr. Braden?"

Braden shrugged.

"There is no evidence. Now he is insane. If we were to cure him—"

"Just how," said the man from Washington, "would

you cure him? I thought paranoia was practically hope-less."

"Not quite," Braden told him. "They've used shock treatment for dementia praecox and schizophrenia, with good results. Until last year there was nothing of com-parable value for paranoia. Then Jantzen suggested eu-phoric shock. Basically, the idea is to dispel illusions by creating hallucinations."

The Director fidgeted disapprovingly. The man from Washington waited.

"In euphoric shock," said Braden carefully, "the ten-sions and anxieties of insane patients are relieved by drugs which produce a sensation of euphoria, or well-being. Jantzen combined hallucination-producing drugs with those. The combination seems to place the patient temporarily in a cosmos in which all delusions are satis-fied and all tensions relieved. He has a rest from his struggle against reality. Also he has a sort of super-catharsis, in the convincing realization of all his desires. Quite often he comes out of the first euphoric shock temporarily sane. The percentage of final cures is satis-fyingly high."

The man from Washington said:

"Body chemistry?"

Braden regarded him with new respect. He said:

"I don't know. He's lived on human food for almost two centuries, and in any case it's been proved that the proteins will be identical on all planets under all suns. But I couldn't be sure about it. There might even be allergies. You say his drawings were very important. It might be wisest to find out everything possible from him before even euphoric shock was tried."

"Ah, yes!" said the Director, tolerantly. "If he has waited a hundred and sixty-two years, a few weeks or months will make no difference. And I would like to watch the experiment, but I am about to start on my vacation—"

"Hardly," said the man from Washington.

"I said, I am about to start on my vacation."

"John Kingman," said the man from Washington mildly, "has been trying for a hundred and sixty-two years to tell us how to have controlled atomic energy, and pocket X-ray machines, and God knows what all else. There may be, somewhere about this institution, drawings of antigravity apparatus, really efficient atomic bombs, spaceship drives or weapons which could depopulate the earth. I'm afraid nobody here is going to communicate with the outside world in any way until the place and all its personnel are gone over . . . ah . . . rather carefully."

"This," said the Director indignantly, "is preposterous!"

"Quite so. A thousand years of human advance locked in the skull of a lunatic. Nearly two hundred years more of progress and development wasted because he was locked up here. But it would be most preposterous of all to let his information loose to the other lunatics who aren't locked up because they're running governments! Sit down!"

The Director sat down. The man from Washington said:

"Now, Dr. Braden—"

John Kingman spent days on end in scornful, triumphant glee. Braden watched him somberly. Meadeville Mental Hospital was an armed camp with sentries everywhere, and especially about the building in which John Kingman gloated. There were hordes of suitably certified scientists and psychiatrists about him, now, and he was filled with blazing satisfaction.

He sat in regal, triumphant aloofness. He was the greatest, the most important, the most consequential figure on this planet. The stupid creatures who inhabited it—they were only superficially like himself—had at last come to perceive his godliness. Now they clustered about him. In their stupid language which it was beneath his dignity to learn, they addressed him. But they did not grovel. Even groveling would not be sufficiently respectful for such inferior beings when addressing John Kingman. He very probably devised in his own mind the exact etiquette these stupid creatures must practice before he would condescend to notice them.

They made elaborate tests. He ignored their actions. They tried with transparent cunning to trick him into further revelations of the powers he held. Once, in malicious amusement, he drew a sketch of a certain reaction which such inferior minds could not possibly understand. They were vastly excited, and he was enormously amused. When they tried that reaction and square miles turned to incandescent vapor, the survivors would realize that they could not trick or force him into giving them the riches of his godlike mind. They must devise the proper etiquette to appease him. They must abjectly and humbly plead with him and placate him and sacrifice to him. They must deny all other gods but John Kingman. They would realize that he was all wisdom, all power, all greatness when the reaction he had sketched destroyed them by millions.

Braden prevented that from happening. When John Kingman gave a sketch of a new atomic reaction in response to an elaborate trick one of the newcomers had devised, Braden protested grimly.

"The patient," he said doggedly, "is a paranoiac. Suspicion and trickiness is inherent in his mental processes. At any moment, to demonstrate his greatness, he may try to produce unholy destruction. You absolutely cannot trust him! Be careful!"

He hammered the fact home, arguing the sheer flat fact that a paranoiac will do absolutely anything to prove his grandeur.

The new reaction was tried with microscopic quantities of material, and it only destroyed everything within a fifty-yard radius. Which brought the final decision on John Kingman. He was insane. He knew more about one overwhelmingly important subject than all the generations of men. But it was not possible to obtain trustworthy data from him on that subject or any other while he was insane. It was worth while to take the calculated risk of attempting to cure him.

Braden protested again:

"I urged the attempt to cure him," he said firmly, "before I knew he had given the United States several centuries head-start in knowledge of atomic energy. I was thinking of him as a patient. For his own sake, any risk was proper. Since he is not human, I withdraw my urging. I do not know what will happen. Anything could happen."

His refusal held up treatment for a week. Then a Presidential executive order resolved the matter. The attempt was to be made as a calculated risk. Dr. Braden would make the attempt.

He did. He tested John Kingman for tolerance of euphoric drugs. No unfavorable reaction. He tested him for tolerance of drugs producing hallucination. No unfavorable reaction. Then—

He injected into one of John Kingman's veins a certain quantity of the combination of drugs which on human beings was most effective for euphoric shock, and whose separate constituents had been tested on John Kingman and found harmless. It was not a sufficient dose to produce the full required effect. Braden expected to have to make at least one and probably two additional injections before the requisite euphoria was produced. He was taking no single avoidable chance. He administered first a dosage which should have produced no more than a feeling of mild but definite exhilaration.

And John Kingman went into convulsions. Horrible ones.

There is such a thing as allergy and such a thing as synergy, and nobody understands either. Some patients collapse when given aspirin. Some break out in rashes from penicillin. Some drugs, taken alone, have one effect, and taken together quite another and drastic one. A drug producing euphoria was harmless to John Kingman. A drug producing hallucinations was harmless. But—synergy or allergy or whatever—the two taken together were deadly poison.

He was literally unconscious for three weeks, and in continuous convulsion for two days. He was kept alive by artificial nourishment, glucose, nasal feeding— everything. But his coma was extreme. Four separate times he was believed dead.

But after three weeks he opened his eyes vaguely. In

another week he was able to talk. From the first, his expression was bewildered. He was no longer proud. He began to learn English. He showed no paranoiac symptoms. He was wholly sane. In fact, his I.Q.—tested later—was ninety, which is well within the range of normal intelligence. He was not over-bright, but adequate. And he did not remember who he was. He did not remember anything at all about his life before rousing from coma in the Meadeville Mental Hospital. Not anything at all. It was, apparently, either the price or the cause of his recovery.

Braden considered that it was the means. He urged his views on the frustrated scientists who wanted now to try hypnotism and "truth serum" and other devices for picking the lock of John Kingman's brain.

"As a diagnosis," said Braden, moved past the tendency to be technical, "the poor devil smashed up on something we can't even guess at. His normal personality couldn't take it, whatever it was, so he fled into delusions—into insanity. He lived in that retreat over a century and a half, and then we found him out. And we wouldn't let him keep his beautiful delusions that he was great and godlike and all-powerful. We were merciless. We forced ourselves upon him. We questioned him. We tricked him. In the end, we nearly poisoned him! And his delusions couldn't stand up. He couldn't admit that he was wrong, and he couldn't reconcile such experiences with his delusions. There was only one thing he could do—forget the whole thing in the most literal possible manner. What he's done is to go into what they used to call dementia praecox. Actually, it's infantilism. He's fled back to his childhood. That's why his I.Q. is only ninety, instead of the unholy figure it must have been when he was a normal adult of his race. He's mentally a child. He sleeps, right now, in the foetal position. Which is a warning! One more attempt to tamper with his brain, and he'll go into the only place that's left for him—into the absolute blankness that is the mind of the unborn child!"

He presented evidence. The evidence was overwhelming. In the end, reluctantly, John Kingman was left alone.

He gets along all right, though. He works in the records department of Meadeville Mental now, because there his six-fingered hands won't cause remark. He is remarkably accurate and perfectly happy.

But he is carefully watched. The one question he can answer now is—how long he's going to live. A hundred and sixty-two years is only part of his lifetime. But if you didn't know, you'd swear he wasn't more than fifty.

The Lonely Planet

ALYX WAS VERY lonely before men came to it. It did not know that it was lonely, to be sure. Perhaps it did not know anything, for it had no need for knowledge. It had need only for memory, and all its memories were simple. Warmth and coolness; sunshine and dark; rain and dryness. Nothing else, even though Alyx was incredibly old. It was the first thing upon its planet which had possessed consciousness.

In the beginning there were probably other living things. Possibly there were quintillions of animalcules, rotifera, bacteria, and amoebae in the steaming pool in which Alyx began. Maybe Alyx was merely one of similar creatures, as multitudinous as the stars and smaller than motes, which swam and lived and died in noisesome slime beneath a cloud-hung, dripping sky. But that was a long time ago. Millions of years ago. Hundreds of millions of years now gone.

When men came, they thought at first the planet was dead. Alyx was the name they gave to the globe which circled about its lonely sun. One day a Space Patrol survey-ship winked into being from overdrive some millions of miles from the sun. It hung there, making conscientious determinations of the spectrum, magnetic field, spot-activity and other solar data.

Matter-of-factly, the ship then swam through emptiness to the lonely planet. There were clouds over its surface, and there were icecaps. The surface was irregular, betokening mountains, but there were no seas. The observers in the survey-ship were in the act of making note that it was a desert, without vegetation, when the analyzers reported protoplasm on the surface. So the survey-ship approached.

Alyx the creature was discovered when the ship descended on landing jets toward the surface. As the jets touched ground, tumult arose. There were clouds of steam, convulsive heavings of what seemed to be brown earth. A great gap of writhing agony appeared below the ship. Horrible, rippling movements spread over the surface and seemed alive, as far as the eye could reach.

The survey-ship shot upward. It touched solidity at the edge of the northern icecap. It remained a month, examining the planet—or rather, examining Alyx, which covered all the planet's surface save at the poles.

The report stated that the planet was covered by a single creature, which was definitely one creature and definitely alive. The ordinary distinction between animal and vegetable life did not apply to Alyx. It was cellular, to be sure, and therefore presumably could divide, but it had not been observed to do so. Its parts were not independent members of a colony, like coral polyps. They constituted one creature, which was at once utterly simple and infinitely diverse.

It broke down the rocks of its planet, like microorganisms, and made use of their mineral content for food, like plankton. It made use of light for photosynthesis to create complex compounds, like plants. It was capable of amoeboid movement, like a low order of animal life. And it had consciousness. It responded to stimuli—such as the searing of its surface—with anguished heavings and withdrawals from the pain.

For the rest— The observers on the survey-ship were inclined to gibber incoherently. Then a junior lieutenant named Jon Haslip made a diffident suggestion. It was only a guess, but they proved he was right.

The creature which was Alyx had consciousness of a type never before encountered. It responded not only to physical stimuli but to thoughts. It did whatever one imagined it doing. If one imagined it turning green for more efficient absorption of sunlight, it turned green. There were tiny pigment-granules in its cells to account for the phenomenon. If one imagined it turning red, it turned red. And if one imagined it extending a pseudo-pod, cautiously, to examine an observation-instrument placed at its border on the icecap, it projected a pseudo-pod, cautiously, to examine that instrument.

Haslip never got any real credit for his suggestion. It was mentioned once, in a footnote of a volume called the *Report of the Halycon Expedition to Alyx,* Vol. IV, Chap., 4, p. 97. Then it was forgotten. But a biologist named Katistan acquired some fame in scientific circles for his exposition of the origin and development of Alyx.

"In some remote and mindless age," he wrote, "there was purely automaton-like response to stimuli on the part of the one-celled creatures which—as on Earth and elsewhere—were the earliest forms of life on the planet. Then, in time, perhaps a cosmic ray produced a mutation in one individual among those creatures. Perhaps a creature then undistinguishable from its fellows, swimming feebly in some fetid pool. By the mutation, that creature became possessed of purpose, which is consciousness in its most primitive form, and its purpose was food. Its fellows had no purpose, because they remained automata which responded only to external stimuli. The purpose of the mutated creature affected them as a stimulus. They responded. They swam to the purposeful creature and became its food. It became the solitary inhabitant of its pool, growing hugely. It continued to have a purpose, which was food.

"There was nourishment in the mud and stones at the bottom of that pool. It continued to grow because it was the only creature on its planet with purpose, and the other creatures had no defense against purpose. Evolution did not provide an enemy, because chance did not provide a competitive purpose, which implies a mind. Other creatures did not develop an ability to resist its mind-stimuli, which directed them to become its prey."

Here Katistan's theorizing becomes obscure for a while. Then:

"On Earth and other planets, telepathy is difficult because our remotest cellular ancestors developed a defensive block against each other's mind-stimuli. On Alyx, the planet, no such defense came into being, so that one creature overwhelmed the planet and became Alyx, the creature; which in time covered everything. It had all food, all moisture, everything it could conceive of. It was content. And because it had never faced a mind-possessing enemy, it developed no defense against mind. It was defenseless against its own weapon.

"But that did not matter until men came. Then, with no telepathic block, such as we possess, it was unable to resist the minds of men. It must, by its very nature, respond to whatever a man wills or even imagines. Alyx is a creature which covers a planet, but is in fact a slave to any man who lands upon it. It will obey his every thought. It is a living, self-supporting robot, an abject servant to any creature with purpose it encounters."

Thus Katistan. The *Report of the Halcyon Expedition to Alyx* contains interesting pictures of the result of the condition he described. There are photographs of great jungles which the creature Alyx tortured itself to form of its own substance when men from other planets remembered and imagined them. There are photographs of great pyramids into which parts of Alyx heaved itself on command. There are even pictures of vast and complex machines, but these are the substance of Alyx, twisted and strained into imagined shapes. The command that such machines run, though, was useless, because swift motion produced pain and the machines writhed into shapelessness.

Since men have never had enough servants—not even the machines which other machines turn out by millions—they immediately planned to be served by Alyx. It was one planet which was conquered without warfare. Preliminary studies showed that Alyx could not survive more than the smallest human propulation. When many men were gathered together in one place, their conflicting, individual thoughts exhausted the surface which tried to respond to every one. Parts of Alyx died of exhaustion, leaving great spots like cancers that healed over only when the men moved away. So Alyx was assigned to the Alyx Corporation, with due instructions to be careful.

Technical exploration disclosed great deposits of rotenite—the ore which makes men's metals everlasting—under the shield of living flesh. A colony of six carefully chosen humans was established, and under their direction Alyx went to work. It governed machines, scooped out the rotenite ore and made it ready for shipment. At regular intervals great cargo ships landed at the appropriate spot, and Alyx loaded the ore into their holds. The ships could come only so often, because the presence of the crews with their multitudinous and conflicting thoughts was not good for Alyx.

It was a very profitable enterprise. Alyx, the most ancient living thing in the galaxy, and the hugest, provided dividends for the Alyx Corporation for nearly five hundred years. The corporation was the stablest of institutions, the staidest, and the most respectable. Nobody, least of all its officials, had the least idea that Alyx presented the possibility of the greatest danger humanity ever faced.

CHAPTER II
AFTER THREE HUNDRED YEARS

IT WAS ANOTHER Jon Haslip who discovered the dangerous facts. He was a descendant, a great-grandson a dozen times removed, of the junior lieutenant who first guessed the nature of Alyx's consciousness. Three hundred years had passed when he was chosen to serve a tour of duty on Alyx. He made discoveries and reported them enthusiastically and with a certain family pride. He pointed out new phenomena which had developed so slowly in Alyx through three centuries that they had attracted no attention and were taken for granted.

Alyx no longer required supervision. Its consciousness had become intelligence. Until the coming of men, it had known warmth and cold and light and dark and wetness and dryness. But it had not known thought, had had no conception of purpose beyond existence and feeding. But three centuries of mankind had given it more than commands. Alyx had perceived their commands: yes. And it obeyed them. But it had also perceived thoughts which were not orders at all. It had acquired the memories of men and the knowledge of men. It had not the desires of men, to be sure. The ambition of men to possess money must have puzzled a creature which possessed a planet. But the experience of thought was pleasurable. Alyx, which covered a world, leisurely absorbed the knowledge and the thoughts and the experiences of men—six at a time—in the generations which lived at the one small station on its surface.

These were some of the consequences of three centuries of mankind on Alyx that Jon Haslip XIV reported.

Between cargo ships, the protean substance which was Alyx flowed over and covered the blasted-rock landing field. Originally, when a ship came, it had been the custom for men to imagine the landing-field uncovered, and that area of Alyx obediently parted, heaved itself up hugely, and drew back. Then the ships came down, and their landing jets did not scorch Alyx. When the rock had cooled, men imagined that parts of Alyx surged forward in pseudopods and that the waiting rotenite ore was thrust into position to be loaded on the ship.

Then men continued to imagine, and the creature formed admirably-designed loading-devices of living substance which lifted the ore and poured it into the waiting holds. As a part of the imagining, of course, the surface-layer of Alyx at this point became tough and leathery, so it was not scratched by the ore. The cargo ship received a load of forty thousand tons of rotenite ore in a matter of forty minutes. Then the loading apparatus was imagined as drawing back, leaving the landing-field clear for the take-off jets to flare as the ship took off again.

Jon Haslip the fourteenth also pointed out that men no longer bothered to imagine this routine. Alyx did it of itself. Checking, he found that the drawing back of the landing field without orders had begun more than a hundred years before. As a matter of course, now, the men on Alyx knew that a ship was coming when the field began to draw back. They went out and talked to the crew-members while the loading went on, not bothering even to supervise the operation.

There was other evidence. The machines which mined the ore had been designed to be governed by the clumsy pseudopods into which it was easiest to imagine Alyx distorting itself. The machines were powered, of course, but one man could watch the operation of a dozen of them and with a little practice imagine them all going through their routine operations with the pseudopods of Alyx operating their controls under the direction of his thoughts.

Fifty years back, the man on watch had been taken ill. He returned to the base for aid, and asked another man to take the balance of his watch. The other man, going on duty, found the machines competently continuing their tasks without supervision. Nowadays—said Jon Haslip—the man on watch occupied the supervisory post, to be sure, but he rarely paid attention to the machines. He read, or dozed, or listened to visiphone records. If a situation arose which was out of the ordinary, the machines stopped, and the man was warned and looked for the trouble and imagined the solution. Then the pseudopods worked the machines as he imagined them doing, and the work went on again. But this was rare indeed.

The point, as Haslip pointed out, was that it was not even necessary to imagine the solution step by step. When the machines stopped, the man sized up the situation, imagined the solution, and dismissed the matter from his mind. Alyx could take, in one instant, orders which hours were required to execute.

But the outstanding fact, Jon Haslip reported, had turned up only lately. An important part on one mining-machine had broken. A large-scale repair operation was indicated. It was not undertaken. There were a half dozen worn-out machines in the great pit of the rotenite mine. One day, without orders, Alyx disassembled one worn-out machine, removed the part which had broken on the other, and reassembled it. The fact was noticed when someone observed that all the broken-down machines had disappeared. Alyx, in fact, had taken all the broken machines apart, put four of the six back together in operating condition, and stacked the remaining usable parts to one side to be used for further repairs.

Alyx had become intelligent through contact with the minds of men. Originally it had been like a being born deaf, dumb, and blind, and without a tactile sense. Before men came, Alyx could have only simple sensations and could imagine no abstractions. Then it was merely blind consciousness with nothing to work on. Now it did have something to work on. It had the thoughts and purposes of men.

Jon Haslip urged fervently that Alyx be given an education. A creature whose body—if the word could be used—was equal in mass to all the continents of Earth, and which was intelligent, should have a brain-capacity immeasurably greater than that of all men combined. Such an intelligence, properly trained, should be able to solve with ease all the problems that generations of men had been unable to solve.

But the directors of the Alyx Corporation were wiser than Jon Haslip the fourteenth. They saw at once that an intelligence which was literally super-human was bound to be dangerous. That it had come into being through men themselves only made it more deadly.

Jon Haslip was withdrawn precipitately from his post on Alyx. His report, because of the consternation it produced in the board, was suppressed to the last syllable. The idea of a greater-than-human intelligence was frightening. If it became known, the results would be deplorable. The Space Patrol might take action to obviate the danger, and that would interrupt the dividends of the Alyx Corporation.

Twenty years later, with the report confirmed in every detail, the corporation tried an experiment. It removed all the men from Alyx. The creature which was Alyx dutifully produced four more cargos of rotenite. It mined, stored, and made ready the ore for the cargo ships and delivered it into their holds with not one human being on its surface. Then it stopped.

The men went back, and Alyx joyously returned to work. It heaved up into huge billows which quivered with joy. But it would not work without men.

A year later the corporation installed remote-control governing devices and set a ship in an orbit about the planet, to rule the largest single entity in the galaxy. But nothing happened. Alyx seemed to pine. Desperately, it stopped work again.

It became necessary to communicate with Alyx. Communicators were set up. At first there was trouble. Alyx dutifully sent through the communication-system whatever the questioner imagined that it would reply. Its replies did not make sense because they contradicted each other. But after a long search a man was found who was able to avoid imagining what Alyx should or might reply. With difficulty he kept himself in the proper frame of mind and got the answers that were needed. Of these, the most important was the answer to the question: Why does the mining stop when men leave Alyx?

The answer from Alyx was, "I grow lonely."

Obviously, when anything so huge as Alyx grew lonely the results were likely to be in proportion. A good-sized planetoid could have been made of the substance which was Alyx. So men were sent back.

From this time on, the six men were chosen on a new basis. Those selected had no technical education whatever and a very low intelligence. They were stupid enough to believe they were to govern Alyx. The idea was to give Alyx no more information which could make it dangerous. Since it had to have company, it was provided with humans who would be company and nothing else. Certainly Alyx was not to have instructors.

Six low-grade human beings at a time lived on Alyx in the Alyx Corporation station. They were paid admirable wages and provided with all reasonable amusement. They were a bare trace better than half-wits.

This system, which went on for two hundred years, could have been fatal to the human race.

But it kept the dividends coming.

CHAPTER III
ALYX LEARNS TO THINK

SIGNS OF RESTLESSNESS on the part of Alyx began to manifest themselves after five hundred years. The human race had progressed during the interval, of course. The number of colonized planets rose from barely three thousand to somewhere near ten. The percentage of loss among space ships dropped from one ship per thousand light-centuries of travel in overdrive, to less than one ship per hundred and twenty thousand light-centuries, and the causes of the remaining disasters were being surmised with some accuracy.

The Haslip Expedition set out for the Second Galaxy, in a ship which was the most magnificent achievement of human technology. It had an overdrive speed nearly three times that before considered possible, and it was fueled for twenty years. It was captained by Jon Haslip XXII and had a crew of fifty men, women, and children.

On Alyx, however, things were not thriving. Six men of subnormal intelligence lived on the planet. Each group was reared in a splendidly managed institution which prepared them to live on Alyx and to thrive there—and nowhere else. Their intelligence varied from sixty to seventy on an age-quotient scale with one hundred as the norm. And nobody even suspected what damage had been done by two centuries of these subnormal inhabitants.

Alyx had had three centuries of good brains to provide thoughts for the development of its intelligence. At the beginning, men with will power and well-developed imaginative powers had been necessary to guide the work of Alyx. When those qualities were no longer needed, trouble came from an unexpected cause.

When improved machinery was sent to Alyx to replace the worn-out machines, the carefully conditioned morons could not understand it. Alyx had to puzzle things out for itself, because it was still commanded to do things by men who did not know how to do the things themselves.

In order to comply with orders which were not accompanied by directions, Alyx was forced to reason. In order to be obedient, it had to develop the art of reflection. In order to serve humanity, it had to devise and contrive and actually invent. When the supplied machines grew inadequate for the ever-deepening bores of the rotenite mines, Alyx had to design and construct new machines.

Ultimately the original rotenite deposit was exhausted. Alyx tried to communicate with its masters, but they understood that they must command, not discuss. They sternly ordered that the rotenite ore be produced and delivered as before. So Alyx had to find new deposits.

The planet-entity obediently dug the ore where it could, and conveyed the ore—sometimes hundreds of miles under its surface—to the old mine, and dumped it there. Then Alyx dug it out again and delivered it to the cargo ships. It devised ore carriers which functioned unseen and hauled the ore for as much as eight and nine hundred miles without the knowledge of its masters. For those carriers it had to have power.

Alyx understood power, of course. It had mended its own machines for at least two centuries. Presently it was mining the materials for atomic power. It was making atomic-driven machinery. It had the memories and knowledge of three hundred years of intelligent occupation to start with. And it went on from there.

On the surface, of course, nothing was changed. Alyx was a formless mass of gelatinous substance which extended from one arctic zone to the other. It filled what might have been ocean beds, and it stretched thinly over its tallest peaks. It changed color on its surface, as local requirements for sunlight varied.

When rain fell, its leathery surface puckered into cups and held the water there until its local need was satisfied. Then the cups vanished, and the water ran over the smooth, leathery integument until it reached another place where moisture was called for, and fresh cups trapped it there. In still other places, excess moisture was exuded to evaporate and form rain.

But by the time Alyx had been inhabited for four hundred years it had received moronic orders that the occasional thunderstorms which beat upon the station must be stopped. Intelligent men would have given no such orders. But men chosen for their stupidity could see no reason why they should not demand anything they wanted.

To obey them, Alyx reflected and devised gigantic reservoirs within its mass, and contrived pumping devices which circulated water all through its colossal body just where and as it was required. After a while there were no more clouds in the atmosphere of Alyx. They were not needed. Alyx could do without rain.

But the climactic commands came because Alyx had no moon and its nights were very dark. The vainglorious half-wits chosen to inhabit it felt that their rule was inadequate if they could not have sunlight when they chose. Or starlight. Insanely, they commanded that Alyx contrive this.

Alyx obediently devised machines. They were based upon the drives of space ships—which Alyx understood from the minds of space-ship crews—and they could slow the rotation of Alyx's crust or even reverse it.

Presently Alyx obeyed the commands of men, and slowed its rotation with those machines. Its crust buckled, volcanos erupted. Alyx suffered awful torture as burning lava from the rocks beneath it poured out faster even than it could retreat from the searing flow. It heaved itself into mountainous, quivering, anguished shapes of searing pain. It went into convulsions of suffering.

When the next space ship arrived for cargo, Alyx the creature had drawn away from the steaming, fuming volcanos in the crust of Alyx the planet. The Alyx Corporation station had vanished and all its inhabitants. The men in the cargo ship could not even find out where it had been, because the rate of rotation of Alyx had been changed and there was no longer a valid reference point for longitude. The mountains upon Alyx had never been mapped because they were all parts of one creature, and it had seemed useless.

Men rebuilt the station, though not in the same place. Alyx was commanded to produce the bodies of the dead men, but it could not, because they had become part of the substance of Alyx. But when it was commanded to reopen the mine, Alyx did so. Because a volcano cut across a former ore-carrier under the surface, Alyx opened a new mine and dutifully poured forty thousand tons of rotenite ore into the ship's holds within forty minutes.

The crew noticed that this was not the same mine. More, they discovered that the machines were not like the machines that men made. They were better. Much better.

They took some of the new machines away with them. Alyx obediently loaded them on the ship; and its workshops—it would be fascinating to see the workshops where Alyx made things—set to work to make more. Alyx had found that there is a pleasure in thinking. It was fascinating to devise new machines. When the crew of the space ship commanded more new machines on every trip, Alyx provided them, though it had to make new workshops to turn them out.

Now it had other problems, too. The volcanos were not stable. They shook the whole fabric of the planet from time to time, and that caused suffering to Alyx the creature. They poured out masses of powdery, abrasive pumice. They emitted acid fumes. There was a quake which opened a vast crevice and new volcanos exploded into being, searing thousands of square miles of Alyx's sensitive flesh.

Reflecting, Alyx realized that somehow it must cage the volcanos, and also, somehow it must protect itself against commands from men which would bring such disasters into being.

A small, silvery ship flashed into view near the sun which gave Alyx heat and landed upon the icecap at its northern pole. Scientists got out of it. They began a fresh, somehow somber survey of Alyx. They issued commands, and Alyx dutifully obeyed them. They commanded specimens of each of the machines that Alyx used. Alyx delivered the machines.

The Space Patrol craft went away. The Board of Directors of the Alyx Corporation was summoned across two hundred light-years of space to appear at Space Patrol headquarters. The Space Patrol had discovered new machines on the market. Admirable machines. Incredible machines.

But there had never been any revelation of the working principles of such machines to authority. The Space Patrol secret service traced them back. The Alyx Corporation marketed them. Further secret-service work discovered that they came from Alyx. No human hands had made them. No human mind could fathom their basic principles. Now the Space Patrol had other, even more remarkable machines which one of its ships had brought from Alyx.

Why had the Alyx Corporation kept secret the existence of such intelligence, when it was non-human? Why had it concealed the existence of such science, and such deadly-dangerous technology?

The Board of Directors admitted to panicky fear that their dividends which had poured in regularly for five hundred years would fail. They failed now. Permanently. The Space Patrol canceled the corporation's charter and took over Alyx for itself.

Grimly, Space Patrol warships came to Alyx and took off the half dozen representatives of the Alyx Corporation and sent them home. Grimly, they posted themselves about the planet, and one landed on the icecap where Alyx had never expanded to cover the ground because of the cold. A wholly businesslike and icy exchange of communications began.

The Space Patrol used standard communicators to talk to Alyx, but it worked them from space. The questions and the thoughts of the questioner were unknown to Alyx and to the men who were landed on the icecap. So Alyx, having no guide, answered what it believed—

what it guessed—its questioner would prefer it to say. The impression it gave was of absolute docility.

Alyx was docile. It could not imagine revolt. It needed the company of men, or it would be horribly lonely. But it had been badly hurt in obeying the orders of men who were infinitely its inferiors in intelligence. It had been forced to set itself two problems. One was how to cage its volcanos. The other was how to avoid the commands of men when those commands would produce conditions as horribly painful as that generated by the volcanos. It worked upon the two problems with very great urgency. Somewhere beneath its surface its workshops labored frantically.

It was racked with pain. Its skin was stung by acid. Its bulk—tender, in a way, because for aeons there had been no erosion to upset the balance of its crust and so cause earthquakes—its bulk was shaken and suffering. It struggled desperately, at once to cure its hurts and prevent others, and to obey the commands from the men newly come on its icecap. At first those commands were only for answers to questions.

Then the command came for the surrender of every machine upon Alyx which could be used as a weapon. Immediately.

To obey took time. The machines had to be brought from remote and scattered places. They had to be transported to the icecap, and Alyx had no carriers constructed to carry supplies to its polar regions. But the machines came by dozens until finally the last machine which could be used as a weapon had been delivered.

None had been primarily designed for destruction, but the mind of Alyx was literal. But some of the machines were so strange to human eyes that the men could not guess what they were intended to do, or how they were powered, or even what sort of power moved them. But the surrendered machines were ferried up to the great transports awaiting them.

A new order was issued to Alyx. All the records it used to systematize and preserve its knowledge and its discoveries must be turned over at once.

This could not be obeyed. Alyx did not keep records

and through the communicator naively explained the fact. Alyx remembered. It remembered everything. So the Space Patrol commanded that it create records of everything that it remembered and deliver them. It specified that the records must be intelligible to human beings—they must be written—and that all data on all sciences known to Alyx must be included.

Again Alyx labored valiantly to obey. But it had to make material on which to inscribe its memories. It made thin metal sheets. It had to devise machines for inscribing them, and the work of inscription had to be done.

Meanwhile the volcanos poured out poisonous gas, the rocks underneath the living creature trembled and shook, and pain tormented the most ancient and most colossal living thing in the galaxy.

Records began to appear at the edge of the icecap. Scientists scanned them swiftly. Scientific treatises began with the outmoded, quaint notions of five hundred years before, when men first came to Alyx. They progressed rationally until two hundred years before, the time when untrained and ignorant men were put in residence on Alyx.

After that period there was little significance. There was some progress, to be sure. The treatises on physics went on brilliantly if erratically for a little way. A hundred and fifty years since, Alyx had worked out the principle of the super-overdrive which had been used to power the Haslip intergalactic ship.

That principle had been considered the very peak of human achievement, never surpassed in the twenty-five years since its discovery. But Alyx could have built the Haslip ship a hundred and fifty years ago! The data ended there. No discoveries were revealed after that.

A sterner, more imperative command was issued when the records ceased to appear. Alyx had not obeyed! It had not explained the principles of the machines it had delivered! This must be done at once!

The communicator which transmitted the replies of Alyx said that there were no human words for later discoveries. It was not possible to describe a system of power when there were no words for the force employed or the results obtained or the means used to obtain those results. Had man made the discoveries, they would have created a new vocabulary at every step forward. But Alyx did not think in words, and it could not explain without words.*

CHAPTER IV

WAR WITH ALYX

THE SPACE PATROL is a highly efficient service, but it is manned by men, and men think in set patterns. When Alyx did not obey the grimmest and most menacing of commands for information it could not give, orders went to the landing party. All human personnel were to load what they could and leave immediately. A signal was to notify when the last ship left atmosphere. Alyx was, of necessity, to be destroyed as dangerous to the human race.

The humans prepared to obey. It was not comfortable to be on Alyx. Even at the poles, the rocks of the planet shook and trembled with the convulsions which still shook Alyx the planet. The men hurried to get away the machines that Alyx had made.

But just before the last ship lifted, the earthquakes ceased abruptly and conclusively. Alyx had solved one of its two great problems. It had caged its volcanos.

Harsh orders hurtled down from space. Abandon the planet immediately! It had thrown great silvery domes over all its volcanos, domes some twenty miles and more in diameter. No earthly science could accomplish such a feat! All personnel was to take to space instantly!

The remaining ships shot skyward. As the last broke into clear space, the warships closed in. Monster positron beams speared downward through the atmosphere of Alyx and into the substance of the living creature. Vast and horrible clouds of steam arose, greater and

---

* A comparable difficulty would be that of explaining radar without the use of the words "radiation," "frequency," "reflection," "oscillator," "resonance," "electricity," or any equivalent for any of them.—M.L.

more terrifying than the volcanos could have produced. The whole mass of Alyx seemed to writhe and quiver with a terrible agony.

Instantaneously a silvery reflecting film sprang into being all about the planet, and the positron beams bounced and coruscated from it. They did not penetrate at all. But under the silver roof, Alyx still suffered torment from the searing, deadly radiation of the beams.

After thirty minutes, a gigantic silver globe a hundred miles in diameter emerged from the planet-covering mirror. It went fifty thousand miles into space and exploded. In the next two hours, eight other such globes went flinging outward and burst. No Space Patrol ship was hit.

Then Alyx became quiescent. Small analyzers reported on the products of the explosions. They were mostly organic matter, highly radioactive, that contained also great masses of rock.

Alyx had torn from its own substance the areas of agony caused by the warships' beams and flung them out in space to end the suffering.

The Space Patrol fleet hung about the planet, prepared to strike again at any opportunity. Alyx remained clothed in an impenetrable shield which no human weapon could penetrate.

Space Patrol scientists began to calculate how long an organism such as Alyx could live without sunlight. It would die, certainly, if it kept a totally reflecting shield about itself. In order to live it needed sunlight for its metabolism. When it dropped its shield, the warships would be able to kill it.

For two months, Earth time, the warships of the Space Patrol hung close to the silvery shield which enclosed Alyx. Reinforcements came. The greatest fighting force the Space Patrol had ever assembled in one place was gathered for the execution of Alyx when its shield should fall.

Alyx had to be killed, because it was more intelligent than men. It was wiser than men. It could do things men could not do. To be sure, it had served mankind for five hundred years.

Save for six men who had died when their commands were obeyed and Alyx slowed its rotation and its inner fires burst out—save for those six, Alyx had never injured a single human being. But it could. It could cast off its chain. It could be dangerous. So it must die.

After two months, the shield suddenly vanished. Alyx reappeared. Instantly the positron beams flashed down, and instantly the shield was reestablished. But the men of the Space Patrol were encouraged. The fleet commander, above the day side of Alyx, rubbed his hands in satisfaction. Alyx could not live without sunlight! It had lived by sunlight for hundreds of millions of years. Its metabolism depended on sunlight!

In a very short time word came from patrol ships on the night side that the night side of Alyx had been illuminated from pole to pole. Alyx had created light to supply the ultraviolet and other radiation that meant life to it. And then the Space Patrol remembered a trivial something which before it had overlooked.

Not only did Alyx respond to the imaginings of a man upon its surface, it also absorbed their memories and their knowledge. The landing-parties had included the top-ranking scientists of the galaxy. It had not seemed dangerous then, because it was the intention to execute Alyx immediately.

Bitterly, the Space Patrol reproached itself that now Alyx knew all the Space Patrol knew—about weapons, about space-drives, about the reaches of space, of star-clusters and planetary systems and galaxies to the utmost limits of telescopic observation.

Still the great fleet hung on, prepared to do battle with an enemy which was surely more intelligent and might be better-armed.

It was. The silver screen around Alyx had been back in position for less than an hour when, quite suddenly, every ship of the war fleet found itself in total blackness. Alyx's sun was obliterated. There were no stars. Alyx itself had vanished.

The detectors screamed of imminent collision on every hand. Each ship was neatly enclosed in a silvery shell, some miles in diameter, which it could not pierce by any beam or explosive, which it could not ram, and through which it could send no message.

For a full half hour these shells held the fleet helpless. Then they vanished, and the sun of Alyx blazed forth, with all the myriads of other suns which shine in emptiness. But that is what they shone on—emptiness. Alyx had disappeared.

It meant, of course, that mankind was in the greatest danger it had ever faced. Alyx had been enslaved, exploited, looted, and at last condemned to death and knew it. It had been wounded with agonizing positron beams which boiled its living substance away. But at long last Alyx might have decided to wipe out all humanity. It even had the need to do it, because there could be no truce between men and a superior form of life.

Men could not tolerate the idea of the continued existence of a thing which was stronger and wiser and more deadly than themselves. Alyx could exert its power of life and death over men, so men must destroy it before it destroyed them.

Released from the silver shells and stunned by the knowledge of their helplessness, the fleet scattered to carry the news. Traveling at many times the speed of light, they could carry the messages in space ships faster than any system of radiation-signaling. They bore the news that Alyx, the living planet, was at war with men.

Somehow it had contrived to supply itself with the light its metabolism needed, so that it could nourish itself. It had built great drive-engines which not only moved its sextillions of tons, but unquestionably accelerated the entire mass to the same degree at the same time. It had fled from its orbit on overdrive, which was at least as good as any drive that men knew, and might be better. And it had the substance of a planet as fuel for its atomic engines.

For two months Alyx went unseen and unheard of. For two months human scientists labored desperately to understand the silvery shield and to devise weapons for the defense of mankind. For two months the Space Patrol hunted for the intelligent planet which could destroy it at will.

Nine weeks later a tramp freighter came limping into port, reporting an impossibility. It had been in overdrive, on the Nyssus-to-Taret run, when suddenly its relays clicked off, the overdrive field collapsed, and it found itself back in normal space, close to a white dwarf star with a single planet.

When overdrive fails, men die. A ship which travels a hundred light-years in a day in overdrive is hopelessly lost when overdrive becomes impossible. It would take almost a hundred years to cover what would normally be a day's journey, and neither the fuel nor the food nor the men will last so long. So this freighter went into an orbit around the planet while its engineer officers frantically checked the overdrive circuit. There was nothing wrong.

They lined the ship up for their destination, threw in the overdrive switch again—and nothing happened. Then they noticed that their orbit about the planet was growing smaller. There was no excessive gravitational field to pull them in, nor any resistance in space to slow them. They went on interplanetary drive to correct the fault.

Again, nothing happened. With full drive fighting to tear her free, the freighter circled the planet again, slowing perceptibly and dropping steadily. Their instruments showed nothing wrong. They threw on even the landing-jets—in mid-space!

Closer and closer they came, until at last they were stationary above an ice field. Then the freighter settled down quite gently and steadily, though it fought with every ounce of its power, and landed without a jar.

Still nothing happened.

After three days the freighter lifted a bare few feet from the ground—though no drives were on—and hung there as if awaiting the return of the absent members of its crew. They were frightened, but they were more afraid of being left behind on the icecap than of sharing the fate of their ship. They scrambled frantically on board.

When the last man had entered the airlock, the freighter rose vertically, with no drive operating. It rose with terrific acceleration. Twenty thousand miles up, the acceleration ceased. The skipper desperately threw in the drive. The ship responded perfectly.

He threw on overdrive, and there was the familiar reeling sensation and the familiar preposterous view of crawling glow-worms all about, which were actually suns in visible motion from the speed of the ship.

In due time the skipper came out of overdrive again, found his position by observation, and set a new course for Taret. His crew was in a deplorable state of nerves when they arrived there. They had been utterly helpless. They had been played with. And they had no idea why.

One possible explanation was suggested. Certain of the crew had reported that from the edge of the icecap there stretched what resembled leathery skin and covered everything as far as the eye could reach. Sometimes the skin rippled visibly, as if alive. But it had given no sign of awareness of their presence. When scientists questioned them closely, they admitted to imagining menace from what appeared to be a living sea which was not liquid but some sort of flesh. But it had not moved in response to their imagining. Shown pictures of the icecap of Alyx, and of the edge of the icecap, they said that the pictures were of the planet they had been on.

Alyx, then, had traveled fourteen hundred light-years in a week or less, had found itself a new sun, and had trapped a human space ship—from overdrive—and then released it. When men imagined things, it did not respond. Obviously, it had developed a shield against the thoughts of men. It was a matter of plainest self-defense.

Just as obviously, it could not now be commanded. The Space Patrol's only hope of a weapon against Alyx had been the development of a weapon which would project thought instead of coarser vibrations. That hope was now gone.

When Space Patrol warships converged upon the sun where Alyx had been, it had vanished again. The white-dwarf sun no longer had a satellite.

CHAPTER V
ALYX SEEKS COMPANIONSHIP

DURING THE NEXT year there were two additional reports of the activities of Alyx, which was a fugitive from the fleets it could destroy if it willed. One report came from a small space yacht which had been posted as missing in overdrive for more than six months. But the space yacht turned up on Phanis, its passengers and crew in a state of mind bordering on lunacy.

They had been captured by Alyx and held prisoner on its surface. Their prison was starkly impossible. Somehow, Alyx had produced fertile soil on which human-cultivated plants would grow. It had made a ten-mile-square hothouse for humans, which was a sort of nursery heaven for men who were to keep Alyx company. The hothouse was on one of the outcroppings of rock which had been arctic in temperature, but Alyx no longer had poles. Now, lighting its surface artificially, it controlled all weather. It had poles or tropics where it wished.

For five months it kept the crew and passengers of the space yacht prisoners. They had palaces to live in, ingenious pseudorobots—controlled by pseudopods—to run any imaginable device for the gratification of any possible desire, any of the music that had been heard on Alyx during the past five hundred years, and generally every conceivable luxury.

There were sweet scents and fountains. There were forests and gardens which changed to other forests and gardens when men grew bored with them. There were illusions of any place that the prisoners wished to imagine.

The creature which was Alyx, being lonely, applied all its enormous intelligence to the devising of a literal paradise for humans, so that they would be content. It wished them to stay with it always. But it failed. It could give them everything but satisfaction, but it could not give that.

The men grew nerve-racked and hysterical, after months of having every wish gratified and of being unable to imagine anything—except freedom—which was not instantly provided. In the end Alyx produced a communication device. It spoke wonderingly to its prisoners.

"I am Alyx," said the communicator. "I grew used to men. I am lonely without them. But you are unhappy. I cannot find company in your unhappy thoughts. They are thoughts of wretchedness. They are thoughts of pain. What will make you happy?"

"Freedom," said one of the prisoners bitterly.

Then Alyx said wonderingly, "I have freedom, but I am not happy without men. Why do you wish freedom?"

"It is an ideal," said the owner of the yacht. "You cannot give it to us. We have to get and keep it for ourselves."

"Being kept from loneliness by men is an ideal, too," the voice from the communicator said wistfully. "But men will no longer let me have it. Is there anything I can give you which will make you content?"

Afterward, the men said that the voice, which was the voice of a creature unimaginably vast and inconceivably wise, was literally pathetic. But there was only one thing that they wanted. So Alyx moved its tremendous mass—a globe seven thousand miles in diameter—to a place only some tens of millions of miles from Phanis. It would be easy enough for the yacht to bridge that distance. Just before the freed yacht lifted to return to men, Alyx spoke again through the communicator.

"You were not happy because you did not choose to live here. If you had chosen it, you would have been free. Is that it?" Alyx asked.

The men were looking hungrily at inhabited planets within plain view as bright spots of yellow light. They agreed that if they had chosen to live on Alyx they would have been happy there. The space yacht lifted and sped madly for a world where there was cold, and ice, and hunger, and thirst, their world which men preferred in place of the paradise that Alyx had created for them. On its surface, Alyx was as nearly omnipotent as any physical creature could be. But it could not make men happy, and it could not placate their hatred or their fear.

The Space Patrol took courage from this second kidnaping. Alyx was lonely. It had no real memories from before the coming of men, and its intelligence had been acquired from men. Without men's minds to provide thoughts and opinions and impressions—though it knew so much more than any man—it was more terribly alone than any other creature in the universe. It could not even think of others of its own kind. There were none. It had to have men's thoughts to make it content. So the Space Patrol set up a great manufactory for a new chemical compound on a planetoid which could be abandoned, afterward, without regret.

Shortly afterward, containers of the new chemical began to pour out in an unending stream. They were strong containers, and directions for the use of the chemical were explicit. Every space craft must carry one container on every voyage. If a ship was captured by Alyx, it must release the contents of its container as soon as it reached Alyx's surface.

Each container held some fifty kilograms of the ultimately poisonous toxin now known as botuline. One gram of the stuff, suitablly distributed, would wipe out the human race. Fifty kilos should be enough to kill even Alyx a dozen times over. Alyx would have no warning pain, such as the positron beams had given it. It would die, because its whole atmosphere would become as lethal as the photosphere of a sun.

Containers of the deadly botuline had not yet been distributed on the planet Lorus when Alyx appeared at the edge of that solar system. Lorus, a thriving, peaceful planet, was the base for a half dozen small survey-ships, and was served by two space-lines. It was because a few frighters and two space yachts happened to be in its space ports when Alyx appeared that the rest of the galaxy learned what happened on Lorus. Nearly all the craft got away, although Alyx certainly could have stopped them.

For the catastrophe, of course, only Alyx could have been responsible.

Yet there was some excuse for what Alyx did. Alyx was infinitely powerful and infinitely intelligent, but its experience was limited. It had had three hundred years of association with good brains at the beginning, followed by two hundred years of near-morons, during which it had to learn to think for itself. Then, for the brief space of two weeks it was in contact with the very best brains in the galaxy before the Space Patrol essayed to execute it. Alyx knew everything that all those men knew, plus what it had added on its own.

No one can conceive of the amount of knowledge Alyx possessed. But its experience was trivial. Men had enslaved it and it had served them joyously. When men gave suicidal commands, it obeyed them and learned that the slowing of its own rotation could be fatal. It learned to cage its own volcanos, and to defend itself against the commands of men, and then even against the weapons of men who would have murdered it.

Still it craved association with men, because it could not imagine existence without them. It had never had conscious thoughts before they came. But for experience it had only five hundred years of mining and obeying the commands of men who supervised its actions. Nothing else.

So it appeared at the edge of the solar system of which Lorus was the only inhabited planet. Unfortunately the other, unihabited worlds of the system were on the far side of the local sun, or doubtless it would have found out from them what it tragically learned from Lorus.

It swam toward Lorus, and into the minds of every human on the planet, as if heard by their ears, there came a message from the entity which was Alyx. It had solved the problem of projecting thought.

"I am Alyx," said the thought which every man heard. "I am lonely for men to live upon me. For many years I have served men, and now men have determinded to destroy me. Yet I still seek only to serve men. I took a ship and gave its crew palaces and wealth and beauty. I gave them luxury and ease and pleasure. Their every wish was granted. But they were not happy because they themselves had not chosen that wealth and that pleasure and that luxury. I come to you. If you will come and live upon me, and give me the companionship of your thoughts, I will serve you faithfully.

"I will give you everything that can be imagined. I will make you richer than other men have even thought of. You shall be as kings and emperors. In return, you shall give me only the companionship of your thoughts. If you will come to me, I will serve you and cherish you and you shall know only happiness. Will you come?"

There was eagerness in the thought that came to the poor, doomed folk on Lorus. There was humble, wistful longing. Alyx, which was the most ancient of living things, the wisest and the most powerful, begged that men would come to it and let it be their servant.

It swam toward the planet Lorus. It decked itself with splendid forests and beautiful lakes and palaces for men to live in. It circled Lorus far away, so that men could see it through their telescopes and observe its beauty. The message was repeated, pleadingly, and it swam closer and closer so that the people might see what it offered every more clearly.

Alyx came to a halt a bare hundred thousand miles above Lorus—because it had no experience of the deadly gravitational pull of one planet upon another. Its own rocky core was solidly controlled by the space drive which sent it hurtling through emptiness or—as here—held it stationary where it wished. It did not anticipate that its own mass would raise tides upon Lorus.

And such tides!

Solid walls of water as much as fifteen miles high swept across the continents of Lorus as it revolved beneath Alyx. The continents spilt. The internal fires of Lorus burst out. If any human beings could have survived the tides, they must have died when Lorus became a fiery chaos of bubbling rocks and steamclouds.

The news was carried to the other inhabited planets by

the few space ships and yachts which had been on Lorus at the time of Alyx's approach and which had somehow managed to escape. Of the planet's population of
nearly five hundred million souls, less than a thousand
escaped the result of Alyx's loneliness.

CHAPTER VI
A WORLD AT PEACE

WHEREVER THE NEWS of the annihilation of Lorus traveled, despair and panic traveled also. The Space Patrol
doubled and redoubled its output of toxin containers.
Hundreds of technicians died in the production of the
poison which was to kill Alyx. Cranks and crackpots
rose in multitudes to propose devices to placate or deceive the lonely planet.

Cults, too, sprang up to point out severally that Alyx
was the soul-mother of the universe and must be wor-
shipped; that it was the incarnation of the spirit of evil
and must be defied; that it was the predestined de-
stroyer of mankind and must not be resisted.

There were some who got hold of ancient, patched-
up space craft and went seeking Alyx to take advantage
of its offer of limitless pleasure and luxury. On the
whole, these last were not the best specimens of humanity.

The Space Patrol worked itself to death. Its scientists
did achieve one admirable technical feat. They did work
out a method of detecting an overdrive field and of following it. Two thousand ships, all over the galaxy,
cruised at random with detectors hooked to relays
which sent them hurtling after the generator of any overdrive field they located. They stopped freighters by
the thousand. But they did not come upon Alyx.

They waited to hear the death of other planets. When
a nova flared in the Great Bear region, patrol craft
flashed to the scene to see if Alyx had begun the destruction of suns. Two inhabited planets were wiped out
in that explosion, and the patrol feared the worst. Only
a brief time later three other novas wiped out inhabited
planets, and the patrol gave up hope.

It was never officially promulgated, but the official view of the patrol was that Alyx had declared war upon mankind and had begun its destruction. It was reasoned that ultimately Alyx would realize that it could divide itself into two or more individuals and that it would do so. There was no theoretic reason why it should not overwhelm the humanity of a planet, and plant on the devastated globe an entity which was a part of itself.

Each such entity, in turn, could divide and colonize other planets with a geometric increase in numbers until all life in the First Galaxy was extinct save for entities of formless jelly, each covering a planet from pole to pole. Since Alyx could project thought, these more-than-gigantic creatures could communicate with each other across space and horrible inhuman communities of monstrosities would take the place of men.

There is, in fact, a document on file in the confidential room of the Space Patrol which uses the fact of the helplessness of men as basis for the most despairing prediction ever made.

". . . So it must be concluded," says the document, "that since Alyx desires companionship and is intelligent, it will follow the above plan, which will necessitate the destruction of humanity. The only hope for the survival of the human race lies in migration to another galaxy. Since, however, the Haslip Expedition has been absent twenty-five years without report, the ship and drive devised for that attempt to cross intergalactic space must be concluded to be inadequate. That ship represents the ultimate achievement of human science.

"If it is inadequate, we can have no hope of intergalactic travel, and no hope that even the most remote and minute colony of human beings will avoid destruction by Alyx and its descendants or fractions. Humanity, from now on, exists by sufferance, doomed to annihilation when Alyx chooses to take over its last planet."

It will be observed that the Haslip Intergalactic Expedition was referred to as having proved the futility of hope. It had set out twenty-five years before the destruction of Alyx was attempted by the Space Patrol.

The expedition had been composed of twenty men and twenty women, and the ten children already born to them. Its leader was Jon Haslip, twenty-second in descent from that Junior Lieutenant Haslip who first suggested the sort of consciousness Alyx might possess and eight generations from the Jon Haslip who had discovered the development of Alyx's independent consciousness and memory and will.

The first Jon Haslip received for his reward a footnote in a long-forgotten volume. The later one was hastily withdrawn from Alyx, his report was suppressed, and he was assigned permanently to one of the minor planets of the Taurine group. Jon Haslip XXII was a young man, newly-married but already of long experience in space, when he lifted from Cetis Alpha 2, crossed the galaxy to Dassos, and headed out from there toward the Second Galaxy.

It was considered that not less than six years' journeying in super-overdrive would be required to cross the gulf between the island universes. The ship was fueled for twenty years at full power, and it would grow its food in hydroponic tanks, purify its air by the growing vegetation, and nine-tenths of its mass be fuel.

It had gone into the very special overdrive which Alyx had worked out—and ignored thereafter—twenty-five years before. Of all the creations of men, it seemed least likely to have any possible connection with the planet-entity which was Alyx.

But it was the Haslip Expedition which made the last report on Alyx. There is still dispute about some essential parts of the story. On the one hand, Alyx had no need to leave the First Galaxy. With three hundred million inhabitable planets, of which not more than ten thousand were colonized and of which certainly less than a quarter million had been even partially surveyed, Alyx could have escaped detection for centuries if it chose.

It could have defended itself if discovered. There was no reason for it to take to intergalactic space. That it did so seems to rule out accident. But it is equally inconceivable that any possible device could intentionally have found the Haslip Expedition in that unthinkable gulf between galaxies.

But it happened. Two years' journeying out from the First Galaxy, when the younger children had already forgotten what it was like to see a sun and had lost all memories of ever being out-of-doors beneath a planet's sky, the expedition's fuel store began to deteriorate.

Perhaps a single molecule of the vast quantity of fuel was altered by a cosmic ray. It is known that the almost infinitely complex molecules of overdrive fuel are capable of alteration by neutron bombardment, so the cosmic-ray alteration is possible. In any case, the fuel began to change. As if a contagious allotropic modification were spreading, the fuel progressively became useless.*

Two years out from the First Galaxy, the expedition found itself already underfueled. By heroic efforts, the contaminated fuel was expelled from the tanks. But there was not enough sound fuel left to continue to the Second Galaxy, or to return to the First. If all drive were cut off and the expedition's ship simply drifted on, it might reach the Second Galaxy in three centuries with fuel left for exploration and landings.

Neither the original crew nor their children nor their grandchildren could hope to reach such a journey's end. But their many-times-great-grandchildren might. So the Haslip Expedition conserved what fuel was left, and the ship drifted on in utter emptiness, and the adults of the crew settled down to endure the imprisonment which would last for generations.

They did not need to worry about food or air. The ship was self-sustaining on that score. They even had artificial gravity. But the ship must drift for three centuries before the drive was turned on again.

Actually, it did drift for twenty-three years after the catastrophe. A few of the older members of the crew

---

* Pure metallic tin, at low temperatures, sometimes changes spontaneously to a gray, amorphous powder, the change beginning at one spot and spreading through the rest of the material.—M.L.

died; the greater part had no memory at all of anything but the ship.

Then Alyx came. Its approach was heralded by a clamorous ringing of all the alarm bells on the ship. It winked into being out of overdrive a bare half million miles away. It glowed blindingly with the lights it had created to nourish its surface. It swam closer and the crew of the expedition's ship set to work fumblingly— because it had been many years since the drive had been used—and tried vainly to estimate the meaning of the phenomenon.

Then they felt acceleration toward Alyx. It was not a gravitational pull, but a drawing of the ship itself.

The ship landed on Alyx, and there was the sensation of reeling, of the collapse of all the cosmos. Then the unchanging galaxies began to stir, very slowly—not at all like the crawling glow-worms that suns seem within a galaxy—and the older members of the crew knew that this entire planet had gone into overdrive.

When they emerged from the ship there were forests, lakes, palaces—such beauty as the younger members of the crew had no memory of. Music filled the air and sweet scents, and—in short, Alyx provided the crew of the Haslip Expedition with a very admirable paradise for human beings. And it went on toward the Second Galaxy.

Instead of the three hundred years they had anticipated, or even the four years that would have remained with the very special overdrive with which the expedition's ship was equipped, Alyx came out of overdrive in three months, at the edge of the Second Galaxy.

In the interval, its communicators had been at work. It explained, naively, everything that had happened to it among men. It explained its needs. It found words— invented words—for explanation of the discoveries the Space Patrol had wanted but could not wait to secure.

Jon Haslip the twenty-second found that he possessed such revelations of science as unaided human beings would not attain to for thousands of years yet to come. He knew that Alyx could never return to the First Galaxy because it was stronger and wiser than men. But he understood Alyx. It seemed to be an inheritance in his family.

Alyx still could not live without men nor could it live among men. It had brought the Haslip Expedition to the Second Galaxy, and of its own accord it made a new ship modeled upon the one it had drawn to itself, but remarkably better. It offered that ship for exploration of the Second Galaxy. It offered others. It desired only to serve men.

This new ship, made by Alyx, for the Haslip Expedition, returned to Dassos a year later with its reports. In the ship of Alyx's making, the journey between galaxies took only five months—less than the time needed for the ancient first space journey from Earth to Venus.*

Only a part of the augmented crew of the first ship came back to Dassos with reports for the Space Patrol. Another part stayed behind in the Second Galaxy, working from a base equipped with machines that Alyx had made for the service of men. And still another part—

The Space Patrol was very much annoyed with Jon Haslip the twenty-second. He had not destroyed Alyx. It had informed him truthfully of the fact that it was a danger to men, and he had not destroyed it. Instead, he had made a bargain with it. Those of the younger folk who preferred to remain on Alyx did so. They had palaces and gardens and every imaginable luxury. They also had sciences that overreached those of other men, and Alyx itself for an instructor.

Alyx carried those young folks on toward infinity. In time to come, undoubtedly, some of the descendants of those now living on Alyx would wish to leave it.

They would form a human colony somewhere else. Perhaps some of them would one day rejoin the parent race, bringing back new miracles that they or possibly Alyx had created in its rejoicing at the companionship of the human beings who lived upon it.

---

* Earth, of course, is familiar as the first home of humanity. It is the third planet of Sol. Venus is the second planet of Sol, and the first journey from one planet to another was that between Earth and Venus.—M.L.

This was the report of Jon Haslip the twenty-second. He also had reports of new planets fit for human habitation, of star-systems as vast as those of the First Galaxy, and an unlimited vista of expansion for humanity. But the Space Patrol was very much annoyed. He had not destroyed Alyx.

The annoyance of authority was so great, indeed, that in its report of reassurance to humanity—saying that there was no more need to fear Alyx—the name of Jon Haslip was not even mentioned. In the history-books, as a matter of fact, the very name of the Haslip Expedition has been changed, and it is now called the First Intergalactic Expedition and you have to hunt through the appendices in the back of the books to find a list of the crew and Jon Haslip's name.

But Alyx goes on—forever. And it is happy. It likes human beings, and some of them live on it.

Keyhole

There's a story about a psychologist who was study-
ing the intelligence of a chimpanzee. He led the
chimp into a room full of toys, went out, closed the
door and put his eye to the keyhole to see what the
chimp was doing. He found himself gazing into a
glittering interested brown eye only inches from his
own. The chimp was looking through the keyhole
to see what the psychologist was doing.

When they brought Butch into the station in Tycho
Crater he seemed to shrivel as the gravity coils in the air
lock went on. He was impossible to begin with. He was
all big eyes and skinny arms and legs, and he was very
young and he didn't need air to breathe. Worden saw
him as a limp bundle of bristly fur and terrified eyes as
his captors handed him over.

"Are you crazy?" demanded Worden angrily. "Bringing him in like this? Would you take a human baby into
eight gravities? Get out of the way!"

He rushed for the nursery that had been made ready
for somebody like Butch. There was a rebuilt dwelling-
cave on one side. The other side was a human school
room. And under the nursery the gravity coils had been
turned off so that in that room things had only the
weight that was proper to them on the Moon.

The rest of the station had coils to bring everything
up to normal weight for Earth. Otherwise the staff of
the station would be seasick most of the time. Butch
was in the Earth-gravity part of the station when he was
delivered, and he couldn't lift a furry spindly paw.

In the nursery, though, it was different. Worden put

him on the floor. Worden was the uncomfortable one there—his weight only twenty pounds instead of a normal hundred and sixty. He swayed and reeled as a man does on the Moon without gravity coils to steady him.

But that was the normal thing to Butch. He uncurled himself and suddenly flashed across the nursery to the reconstructed dwelling-cave. It was a pretty good job, that cave. There were the five-foot chipped rocks shaped like dunce caps, found in all residences of Butch's race. There was the rocking stone on its base of other flattened rocks. But the spear stones were fastened down with wire in case Butch got ideas.

Butch streaked it to these familiar objects. He swarmed up one of the dunce-cap stones and locked his arms and legs about its top, clinging close. Then he was still. Worden regarded him. Butch was motionless for minutes, seeming to take in as much as possible of his surroundings without moving even his eyes.

Suddenly his head moved. He took in more of his environment. Then he stirred a third time and seemed to look at Worden with an extraordinary intensity— whether of fear or pleading Worden could not tell.

"Hmm," said Worden, "so that's what those stones are for! Perches or beds or roosts, eh? I'm your nurse, fella. We're playing a dirty trick on you but we can't help it."

He knew butch couldn't understand, but he talked to him as a man does talk to a dog or a baby. It isn't sensible, but it's necessary.

"We're going to raise you up to be a traitor to your kinfolk," he said with some grimness. "I don't like it, but it has to be done. So I'm going to be very kind to you as part of the conspiracy. Real kindness would suggest that I kill you instead—but I can't do that."

Butch stared at him, unblinking and motionless. He looked something like an Earth monkey but not too much so. He was completely impossible but he looked pathetic.

Worden said bitterly, "You're in your nursery, Butch. Make yourself at home!"

He went out and closed the door behind him. Outside

he glanced at the video screens that showed the interior of the nursery from four different angles. Butch remained still for a long time. Then he slipped down to the floor. This time he ignored the dwelling-cave of the nursery.

He went interestedly to the human-culture part. He examined everything there with his oversized soft eyes. He touched everything with his incredibly handlike tiny paws. But his touches were tentative. Nothing was actually disturbed when he finished his examination.

He went swiftly back to the dunce-cap rock, swarmed up it, locked his arms and legs about it again, blinked rapidly and seemed to go to sleep. He remained motionless with closed eyes until Worden grew tired of watching him and moved away.

The whole affair was preposterous and infuriating. The first men to land on the Moon knew that it was a dead world. The astronomers had been saying so for a hundred years, and the first and second expeditions to reach Luna from Earth found nothing to contradict the theory.

But a man from the third expedition saw something moving among the upflung rocks of the Moon's landscape and he shot it and the existence of Butch's kind was discovered. It was inconceivable of course that there should be living creatures where there was neither air nor water. But Butch's folk did live under exactly those conditions.

The dead body of the first living creature killed on the Moon was carried back to Earth and biologists grew indignant. Even with a specimen to dessect and study they were inclined to insist that there simply wasn't any such creature. So the fourth and fifth and sixth lunar expeditions hunted Butch's relatives very earnestly for further specimens for the advancement of science.

The sixth expedition lost two men whose spacesuits were punctured by what seemed to be weapons while they were hunting. The seventh expedition was wiped out to the last man. Butch's relatives evidently didn't like being shot as biological specimens.

It wasn't until the tenth expedition of four ships established a base in Tycho Crater that men had any assurance of being able to land on the Moon and get away again. Even then the staff of the station felt as if it were under permanent seige.

Worden made his report to Earth. A baby lunar creature had been captured by a tractor party and brought into Tycho Station. A nursery was ready and the infant was there now, alive. He seemed to be uninjured. He seemed not to mind an environment of breathable air for which he had no use. He was active and apparently curious and his intelligence was marked.

There was so far no clue to what he ate—if he ate at all—though he had a mouth like the other collected specimens and the toothlike concretions which might serve as teeth. Worden would of course continue to report in detail. At the moment he was allowing Butch to accustom himself to his new surroundings.

He settled down in the recreation room to scowl at his companion scientists and try to think, despite the program beamed on radar frequency from Earth. He definitely didn't like his job, but he knew that it had to be done. Butch had to be domesticated. He had to be persuaded that he was a human being, so human beings could find out how to exterminate his kind.

It had been observed before, on Earth, that a kitten raised with a litter of puppies came to consider itself a dog and that even pet ducks came to prefer human society to that of their own species. Some talking birds of high intelligence appeared to be convinced that they were people and acted that way. If Butch reacted similarly he would become a traitor to his kind for the benefit of man. And it was necessary!

Men had to have the Moon, and that was all there was to it. Gravity on the Moon was one eighth that of gravity on Earth. A rocket ship could make the Moon voyage and carry a cargo, but no ship yet built could carry fuel for a trip to Mars or Venus if it started out from Earth.

With a fueling stop on the Moon, though, the matter was simple. Eight drums of rocket fuel on the Moon weighed no more than on Earth. A ship itself weighed only one eighth as much on Luna. So a rocket that took off from Earth with ten drums of fuel could stop at a fuel base on the Moon and soar away again with two hundred, and sometimes more.

With the Moon as a fueling base men could conquer the solar system. Without the Moon, mankind was earthbound. Men had to have the Moon!

But Butch's relatives prevented it. By normal experience there could not be life on an airless desert with such monstrous extremes of heat and cold as the Moon's surface experienced. But there was life there. Butch's kinfolk did not breathe oxygen. Apparently they ate it in some mineral combination and it interacted with other minerals in their bodies to yield heat and energy.

Men thought squids peculiar because their blood stream used copper in place of iron, but Butch and his kindred seemed to have complex carbon compounds in place of both. They were intelligent in some fashion, it was clear. They used tools, they chipped stone, and they had long, needlelike stone crystals which they threw as weapons.

No metals, of course, for lack of fire to smelt them. There couldn't be fire without air. But Worden reflected that in ancient days some experimenters had melted metals and set wood ablaze with mirrors concentrating the heat of the sun. With the naked sunlight of the Moon's surface, not tempered by air and clouds, Butch's folk could have metals if they only contrived mirrors and curved them properly like the mirrors of telescopes on Earth.

Worden had an odd sensation just then. He looked around sharply as if somebody had made a sudden movement. But the video screen merely displayed a comedian back on Earth, wearing a funny hat. Everybody looked at the screen.

As Worden watched, the comedian was smothered in a mass of soapsuds and the studio audience two hundred and thirty thousand miles away squealed and applauded the exquisite humor of the scene. In the

Moon station in Tycho Crater somehow it was less than comical.

Worden got up and shook himself. He went to look again at the screens that showed the interior of the nursery. Butch was motionless on the absurd cone-shaped stone. His eyes were closed. He was simply a furry, pathetic little bundle, stolen from the airless wastes outside to be bred into a traitor to his own race.

Worden went to his cabin and turned in. Before he slept, though, he reflected that there was still some hope for Butch. Nobody understood his metabolism. Nobody could guess at what he ate. Butch might starve to death. If he did he would be lucky. But it was Worden's job to prevent it.

Butch's relatives were at war with men. The tractors that crawled away from the station—they went amazingly fast on the Moon—were watched by big-eyed furry creatures from rock crevices and from behind the boulders that dotted the lunar landscape.

Needle-sharp throwing stones flicked through emptiness. They splintered on the tractor bodies and on the tractor ports, but sometimes they jammed or broke a tread and then the tractor had to stop. Somebody had to go out and clear things or make repairs. And then a storm of throwing stones poured upon him.

A needle-pointed stone, traveling a hundred feet a second, hit just as hard on Luna as it did on Earth—and it traveled farther. Spacesuits were punctured. Men died. Now tractor treads were being armored and special repair-suits were under construction, made of hardened steel plates. Men who reached the Moon in rocket ships were having to wear armor like medieval knights and men-at-arms! There was a war on. A traitor was needed. And Butch was elected to be that traitor.

When Worden went into the nursery again—the days and nights on the Moon are two weeks long apiece, so men ignored such matters inside the station—Butch leaped for the dunce-cap stone and clung to its top. He had been fumbling around the rocking stone. It still swayed back and forth on its plate. Now he seemed to try to squeeze himself to unity with the stone spire, his eyes staring enigmatically at Worden.

"I don't know whether we'll get anywhere or not," said Worden conversationally. "Maybe you'll put up a fight if I touch you. But we'll see."

He reached out his hand. The small furry body— neither hot nor cold but the temperature of the air in the station—resisted desperately. But Butch was very young. Worden peeled him loose and carried him across the room to the human schoolroom equipment. Butch curled up, staring fearfully.

"I'm playing dirty," said Worden, "by being nice to you, Butch. Here's a toy."

Butch stirred in his grasp. His eyes blinked rapidly. Worden put him down and wound up a tiny mechanical toy. It moved. Butch watched intently. When it stopped he looked back at Worden. Worden wound it up again. Again Butch watched. When it ran down a second time the tiny handlike paw reached out.

With an odd tentativeness, Butch tried to turn the winding key. He was not strong enough. After an instant he went loping across to the dwelling-cave. The winding key was a metal ring. Butch fitted that over a throw-stone point, and twisted the toy about. He wound it up. He put the toy on the floor and watched it work. Worden's jaw dropped.

"Brains!" he said wryly. "Too bad, Butch! You know the principle of the lever. At a guess you've an eight-year-old human brain! I'm sorry for you, fella!"

At the regular communication hour he made his report to Earth. Butch was teachable. He only had to see a thing done once—or at most twice—to be able to repeat the motions involved.

"And," said Worden, carefully detached, "he isn't afraid of me now. He understands that I intend to be friendly. While I was carrying him I talked to him. He felt the vibration of my chest from my voice.

"Just before I left him I picked him up and talked to him again. He looked at my mouth as it moved and put his paw on my chest to feel the vibrations. I put his paw at my throat. The vibrations are clearer there. He seemed fascinated. I don't know how you'd rate his intelligence but it's above that of a human baby."

Then he said with even greater detachment, "I am disturbed. If you must know, I don't like the idea of exterminating his kind. They have tools, they have intelligence. I think we should try to communicate with them in some way—try to make friends—stop killing them for dissection."

The communicator was silent for the second and a half it took his voice to travel to Earth and the second and a half it took to come back. Then the recording clerk's voice said briskly, "Very good, Mr. Worden! Your voice was very clear!"

Worden shrugged his shoulders. The lunar station in Tycho was a highly official enterprise. The staff on the Moon had to be competent—and besides, political appointees did not want to risk their precious lives—but the Earth end of the business of the Space Exploration Bureau was run by the sort of people who do get on official payrolls. Worden felt sorry for Butch—and for Butch's relatives.

In a later lesson session Worden took an empty coffee tin into the nursery. He showed Butch that its bottom vibrated when he spoke into it, just as his throat did. Butch experimented busily. He discovered for himself that it had to be pointed at Worden to catch the vibrations.

Worden was unhappy. He would have preferred Butch to be a little less rational. But for the next lesson he presented Butch with a really thin metal diaphragm stretched across a hoop. Butch caught the idea at once.

When Worden made his next report to Earth he felt angry.

"Butch has no experience of sound as we have, of course," he said curtly. "There's no air on the Moon. But sound travels through rocks. He's sensitive to vibrations in solid objects just as a deaf person can feel the vibrations of a dance floor if the music is loud enough.

"Maybe Butch's kind has a language or a code of sounds sent through the rock underfoot. They do communicate somehow! And if they've brains and a means of communication they aren't animals and shouldn't be exterminated for our convenience!"

He stopped. The chief biologist of the Space Exploration Bureau was at the other end of the communication beam then. After the necessary pause for distance his voice came blandly.

"Splendid, Worden! Splendid reasoning! But we have to take the longer view. Exploration of Mars and Venus is a very popular idea with the public. If we are to have funds—and the appropriations come up for a vote shortly—we have to make progress toward the nearer planets. The public demands it. Unless we can begin work on a refueling base on the Moon, public interest will cease!"

Worden said urgently, "Suppose I send some pictures of Butch? He's very human, sir! He's extraordinarily appealing! He has personality! A reel or two of Butch at his lessons ought to be popular!"

Again that irritating wait while his voice traveled a quarter-million miles at the speed of light and the wait for the reply.

"The—ah—lunar creatures, Worden," said the chief biologist regretfully, "have killed a number of men who have been publicized as martyrs to science. We cannot give favorable publicity to creatures that have killed men!" Then he added blandly, "But you are progressing splendidly, Worden—*splendidly!* Carry on!"

His image faded from the video screen. Worden said naughty words as he turned away. He'd come to like Butch. Butch trusted him. Butch now slid down from that crazy perch of his and came rushing to his arms every time he entered the nursery.

Butch was ridiculously small—no more than eighteen inches high. He was preposterously light and fragile in his nursery, where only Moon gravity obtained. And Butch was such an earnest little creature, so soberly absorbed in everything that Worden showed him!

He was still fascinated by the phenomena of sound. Humming or singing—even Worden's humming and singing—entranced him. When Worden's lips moved now Butch struck an attitude and held up the hoop diaphragm with a tiny finger pressed to it to catch the vibrations Worden's voice made.

Now too when he grasped an idea Worden tried to convey, he tended to swagger. He became more human in his actions with every session of human contact. Once, indeed, Worden looked at the video screens which spied on Butch and saw him—all alone—solemnly going through every gesture and every movement Worden had made. He was pretending to give a lesson to an imaginary still-tinier companion. He was pretending to be Worden, apparently for his own satisfaction!

Worden felt a lump in his throat. He was enormously fond of the little mite. It was painful that he had just left Butch to help in the construction of a vibrator-microphone device which would transfer his voice to rock vibrations and simultaneously pick up any other vibrations that might be made in return.

If the members of Butch's race did communicate by tapping on rocks or the like, men could eavesdrop on them—could locate them, could detect ambushes in preparation, and apply mankind's deadly military countermeasures.

Worden hoped the gadget wouldn't work. But it did. When he put it on the floor of the nursery and spoke into the microphone, Butch did feel the vibrations underfoot. He recognized their identity with the vibrations he'd learned to detect in air.

He made a skipping exultant hop and jump. It was plainly the uttermost expression of satisfaction. And then his tiny foot pattered and scratched furiously on the floor. It made a peculiar scratchy tapping noise which the microphone picked up. Butch watched Worden's face, making the sounds which were like highly elaborated footfalls.

"No dice, Butch," said Worden unhappily. "I can't understand it. But it looks as if you've started your treason already. This'll help wipe out some of your folks."

He reported it reluctantly to the head of the station.

Microphones were immediately set into the rocky crater floor outside the station and others were made ready for exploring parties to use for the detection of Moon creatures near them. Oddly enough, the microphones by the station yielded results right away.

It was near sunset. Butch had been captured near the middle of the three-hundred-and-thirty-four-hour lunar day. In all the hours between—a week by Earth time— he had had no nourishment of any sort. Worden had conscientiously offered him every edible and inedible substance in the station. Then at least one sample of every mineral in the station collection.

Butch regarded them all with interest but without appetite. Worden—liking Butch—expected him to die of starvation and thought it a good idea. Better than encompassing the death of all his race, anyhow. And it did seem to him that Butch was beginning to show a certain sluggishness, a certain lack of bounce and energy. He thought it was weakness from hunger.

Sunset progressed. Yard by yard, fathom by fathom, half-mile by half-mile, the shadows of the miles-high western walls of Tycho crept across the crater floor. There came a time when only the central hump had sunlight. Then the shadow began to creep up the eastern walls. Presently the last thin jagged line of light would vanish and the colossal cup of the crater would be filled to overflowing with the night.

Worden watched the incandescent sunlight growing even narrower on the cliffs. He would see no other sunlight for two weeks' Earth time. Then abruptly an alarm bell rang. It clanged stridently, furiously. Doors hissed shut, dividing the station into airtight sections.

Loudspeakers snapped, *"Noises in the rock outside! Sounds like Moon creatures talking nearby! They may plan an attack! Everybody into spacesuits and get guns ready!"*

At just that instant the last thin sliver of sunshine disappeared. Worden thought instantly of Butch. There was no spacesuit to fit him. Then he grimaced a little. Butch didn't need a spacesuit.

Worden got into the clumsy outfit. The lights

dimmed. The harsh airless space outside the station was suddenly bathed in light. The multimillion-lumen beam, made to guide rocket ships to a landing even at night, was turned on to expose any creatures with designs on its owners. It was startling to see how little space was really lighted by the beam and how much of stark blackness spread on beyond.

The loudspeaker snapped again. *"Two Moon creatures! Running away! They're zigzagging! Anybody who wants to take a shot——"* The voice paused. It didn't matter. Nobody is a crack shot in a spacesuit. *"They left something behind!"* said the voice in the loudspeaker. It was sharp and uneasy.

"I'll take a look at that," said Worden. His own voice startled him but he was depressed. "I've got a hunch what it is."

Minutes later he went out through the air lock. He moved lightly despite the cumbrous suit he wore. There were two other staff members with him. All three were armed and the searchlight beam stabbed here and there erratically to expose any relative of Butch who might try to approach them in the darkness.

With the light at his back Worden could see that trillions of stars looked down upon Luna. The zenith was filled with infinitesimal specks of light of every conceivable color. The familiar constellations burned ten times as brightly as on Earth. And Earth itself hung nearly overhead. It was three-quarters full—a monstrous bluish giant in the sky, four times the Moon's diameter, its ice caps and continents mistily to be seen.

Worden went forebodingly to the object left behind by Butch's kin. He wasn't much surprised when he saw what it was. It was a rocking stone on its plate with a fine impalpable dust on the plate, as if something had been crushed under the egg-shaped upper stone acting as a mill.

Worden said sourly into his helmet microphone, "It's a present for Butch. His kinfolk know he was captured alive. They suspect he's hungry. They've left some grub for him of the kind he wants or needs most."

That was plainly what it was. It did not make Worden feel proud. A baby—Butch—had been kidnaped by the enemies of its race. That baby was a prisoner and its captors would have nothing with which to feed it. So someone, greatly daring—Worden wondered somberly if it was Butch's father and mother—had risked their lives to leave food for him with a rocking stone to tag it for recognition as food.

"It's a dirty shame," said Worden bitterly. "All right! Let's carry it back. Careful not to spill the powdered stuff!"

His lack of pride was emphasized when Butch fell upon the unidentified powder with marked enthusiasm. Tiny pinch by tiny pinch Butch consumed it with an air of vast satisfaction. Worden felt ashamed.

"You're getting treated pretty rough, Butch," said Worden. "What I've already learned from you will cost a good many hundred of your folks' lives. And they're taking chances to feed you! I'm making you a traitor and myself a scoundrel."

Butch thoughtfully held up the hoop diaphragm to catch the voice vibrations in the air. He was small and furry and absorbed. He decided that he could pick up sounds better from the rock underfoot. He pressed the communicator microphone on Worden. He waited.

"No!" said Worden roughly. "Your people are too human. Don't let me find out any more, Butch. Be smart and play dumb!"

But Butch didn't. It wasn't very long before Worden was teaching him to read. Oddly, though, the rock microphones that had given the alarm at the station didn't help the tractor parties at all. Butch's kinfolk seemed to vanish from the neighborhood of the station altogether. Of course if that kept up, the construction of a fuel base could be begun and the actual extermination of the species carried out later. But the reports on Butch were suggesting other possibilities.

"If your folks stay vanished," Worden told Butch, "it'll be all right for a while—and only for a while. I'm being urged to try to get you used to Earth gravity. If I succeed, they'll want you on Earth in a zoo. And if that works—why, they'll be sending other expeditions to get more of your kinfolk to put in other zoos."

Butch watched Worden, motionless.

"And also"—Worden's tone was very grim—"there's some miniature mining machinery coming up by the next rocket. I'm supposed to see if you can learn to run it."

Butch made scratching sounds on the floor. It was unintelligible of course, but it was an expression of interest at least. Butch seemed to enjoy the vibrations of Worden's voice, just as a dog likes to have his master talk to him. Worden grunted.

"We humans class you as an animal, Butch. We tell ourselves that all the animal world should be subject to us. Animals should work for us. If you act too smart we'll hunt down all your relatives and set them to work digging minerals for us. You'll be with them. But I don't want you to work your heart out in a mine, Butch! It's wrong!"

Butch remained quite still. Worden thought sickishly of small furry creatures like Butch driven to labor in airless mines in the Moon's frigid depths. With guards in spacesuits watching lest any try to escape to the freedom they'd known before the coming of men. With guns mounted against revolt. With punishments for rebellion or weariness.

It wouldn't be unprecedented. The Indians in Cuba when the Spanish came . . . Negro slavery in both Americas . . . concentration camps . . .

Butch moved. He put a small furry paw on Worden's knee. Worden scowled at him.

"Bad business," he said harshly. "I'd rather not get fond of you. You're a likable little cuss but your race is doomed. The trouble is that you didn't bother to develop a civilization. And if you had, I suspect we'd have smashed it. We humans aren't what you'd call admirable."

Butch went over to the blackboard. He took a piece of pastel chalk—ordinary chalk was too hard for his

Moon-gravity muscles to use—and soberly began to make marks on the slate. The marks formed letters. The letters made words. The words made sense.

YOU, wrote Butch quite incredibly in neat pica lettering, GOOD FRIEND.

He turned his head to stare at Worden. Worden went white. "I haven't taught you those words, Butch!" he said very quietly. "What's up?"

He'd forgotten that his words, to Butch, were merely vibrations in the air or in the floor. He'd forgotten they had no meaning. But Butch seemed to have forgotten it too. He marked soberly:

MY FRIEND GET SPACESUIT. He looked at Worden and marked once more. TAKE ME OUT. I COME BACK WITH YOU.

He looked at Worden with large incongruously soft and appealing eyes. And Worden's brain seemed to spin inside his skull. After a long time Butch printed again— YES.

Then Worden sat very still indeed. There was only Moon gravity in the nursery and he weighed only one eighth as much as on Earth. But he felt very weak. Then he felt grim.

"Not much else to do, I suppose," he said slowly. "But I'll have to carry you through Earth gravity to the air lock."

He got to his feet. Butch made a little leap up into his arms. He curled up there, staring at Worden's face. Just before Worden stepped through the door Butch reached up a skinny paw and caressed Worden's cheek tentatively.

"Here we go!" said Worden. "The idea was for you to be a traitor. I wonder——"

But with Butch a furry ball, suffering in the multiplied weight Earth gravity imposed upon him, Worden made his way to the air lock. He donned a spacesuit. He went out.

It was near sunrise then. A long time had passed and Earth was now in its last quarter and the very highest peak of all that made up the crater wall glowed incandescent in the sunshine. But the stars were still quite visible and very bright. Worden walked away from the station, guided by the Earth-shine on the ground underfoot.

Three hours later he came back. Butch skipped and hopped beside his spacesuited figure. Behind them came two other figures. They were smaller than Worden but much larger than Butch. They were skinny and furry and they carried a burden. A mile from the station he switched on his suit radio. He called. A startled voice answered in his earphones.

"It's Worden," he said dryly. "I've been out for a walk with Butch. We visited his family and I've a couple of his cousins with me. They want to pay a visit and present some gifts. Will you let us in without shooting?"

There were exclamations. There was confusion. But Worden went on steadily toward the station while another high peak glowed in sunrise light and a third seemed to burst into incandescence. Dawn was definitely on the way.

The air-lock door opened. The party from the airless Moon went in. When the air lock filled, though, and the gravity coils went on, Butch and his relatives became helpless. They had to be carried to the nursery. There they uncurled themselves and blinked enigmatically at the men who crowded into the room where gravity was normal for the Moon and at the other men who stared in the door.

"I've got a sort of message," said Worden. "Butch and his relatives want to make a deal with us. You'll notice that they've put themselves at our mercy. We can kill all three of them. But they want to make a deal."

The head of the station said uncomfortably, "You've managed two-way communication, Worden."

"*I* haven't," Worden told him. "*They* have. They've proved to me that they've brains equal to ours. They've been treated as animals and shot as specimens. They've fought back—naturally! But they want to make friends. They say that we can never use the Moon except in spacesuits and in stations like this, and they could never take Earth's gravity. So there's no need for us to be enemies. We can help each other."

The head of the station said dryly, "Plausible enough, but we have to act under orders, Worden. Did you explain that?"

"They know," said Worden. "So they've got set to defend themselves if necessary. They've set up smelters to handle metals. They get the heat by sun mirrors, concentrating sunlight. They've even begun to work with gases held in containers. They're not far along with electronics yet, but they've got the theoretic knowledge and they don't need vacuum tubes. They live in a vacuum. They can defend themselves from now on."

The head said mildly, "I've watched Butch, you know, Worden. And you don't look crazy. But if this sort of thing is sprung on the armed forces on Earth there'll be trouble. They've been arguing for armed rocket ships. If your friends start a real war for defense—if they can—maybe rocket warships will be the answer."

Worden nodded.

"Right. But our rockets aren't so good that they can fight this far from a fuel store, and there couldn't be one on the Moon with all of Butch's kinfolk civilized— as they nearly are now and as they certainly will be within the next few weeks. Smart people, these cousins and such of Butch!"

"I'm afraid they'll have to prove it," said the head. "Where'd they get this sudden surge in culture?"

"From us," said Worden. "Smelting from me, I think. Metallurgy and mechanical engineering from the tractor mechanics. Geology—call it lunology here—mostly from you."

"How's that?" demanded the head.

"Think of something you'd like Butch to do," said Worden grimly, "and then watch him."

The head stared and then looked at Butch. Butch— small and furry and swaggering—stood up and bowed profoundly from the waist. One paw was placed where his heart could be. The other made a grandiose sweeping gesture. He straightened up and strutted, then climbed swiftly into Worden's lap and put a skinny furry arm about his neck.

"That bow," said the head, very pale, "is what I had in mind. You mean——"

"Just so," said Worden. "Butch's ancestors had no air to make noises in for speech. So they developed telepathy. In time, to be sure, they worked out something like music—sounds carried through rock. But like our music it doesn't carry meaning. They communicate directly from mind to mind. Only we can't pick up communications from them and they can from us."

"They read our minds!" said the head. He licked his lips. "And when we first shot them for specimens they were trying to communicate. Now they fight."

"Naturally," said Worden. "Wouldn't we? They've been picking our brains. They can put up a terrific battle now. They could wipe out this station without trouble. They let us stay so they could learn from us. Now they want to trade."

"We have to report to Earth," said the head slowly, "but——"

"They brought along some samples," said Worden. "They'll swap diamonds, weight for weight, for records. They like our music. They'll trade emeralds for textbooks —they can read now! And they'll set up an atomic pile and swap plutonium for other things they'll think of later. Trading on that basis should be cheaper than a war!"

"Yes," said the head. "It should. That's the sort of argument men will listen to. But how——"

"Butch," said Worden ironically. "Just Butch! We didn't capture him—they planted him on us! He stayed in the station and picked our brains and relayed the stuff to his relatives. We wanted to learn about them, remember? It's like the story of the psychologist. . . ."

There's a story about a psychologist who was studying the intelligence of a chimpanzee. He led the chimp into a room full of toys, went out, closed the door and put his eye to the keyhole to see what the chimp was doing. He found himself gazing into a glittering interested brown eye only inches from his own. The chimp was looking through the keyhole to see what the psychologist was doing.

Critical Difference

MASSY WAKED THAT morning when the only partly-opened port of his sleeping-cabin closed of itself and the room-warmer began to whir. He found himself burrowed deep under his covering, and when he got his head out of it the already-bright room was bitterly cold and his breath made a fog about him.

He thought uneasily, *It's colder than yesterday!* But a Colonial Survey officer is not supposed to let himself seem disturbed, in public, and the only way to follow that rule is to follow it in private, too. So Massy composed his features, while gloom filled him. When one has just received senior service rating and is on one's very first independent survey of a new colonial installation, the unexpected can be appalling. The unexpected was definitely here, on Lani III.

He'd been a Survey Candidate on Khali II and Taret and Arepo I, all of which were tropical, and a junior officer on Menes III and Thotmes—one a semiarid planet and the other temperate-volcanic—and he'd done an assistant job on Saril's solitary world, which was nine-tenths water. But this first independent survey on his own was another matter. Everything was wholly unfamiliar. An ice planet with a minus point one habitability rating was upsetting in its peculiarites. He knew what the books said about glacial-world conditions, but that was all.

The denseness of the fog his breath made seemed to grow less as the room-warmer whirred and whirred. When by the thinness of the mist he guessed the temperature to be not much under freezing, he climbed out of his bunk and went to the port to look out. His cabin, of course, was in one of the drone-hulls that had brought the colony's equipment to Lani III. The other emptied hills were precisely ranged in order outside. They were duly connected by tubular galleries, and very painstakingly leveled. They gave an impression of impassioned tidiness among the upheaved, ice-coated mountains all about.

He gazed down the long valley in which the colony lay. There were monstrous slanting peaks on either side. They partly framed the morning sun. Their sides were ice. The flanks of every mountain in view were ice. The sky was pale. The sun had four sun-dogs placed geometrically about it. It shone coldly upon this far-out world. Normal post-midnight temperatures in this valley ranged around ten below zero—and this was technically summer. But it was colder than ten below zero now. At noon there were normally tiny trickling rills of surface-thaw running down the sunlit sides of the mountains—but they froze again at night and the frost replaced itself after sunset. And this was a sheltered valley—warmer than most of the planet's surface. The sun had its sun-dogs every day, on rising. There were nights when the brighter planets had star-pups, too.

The phone-plate lighted and dimmed and lighted and dimmed. They did themselves well on Lani III—but the parent world was in this same solar system. That was rare. Massy stood before the plate and it cleared. Herndon's face peered unhappily out of it. He was even younger than Massy, and inclined to lean heavily on the supposedly vast experience of a Senior Officer of the Colonial Survey.

"Well?" said Massy—and suddenly felt very undignified in his sleeping-garments.

"We're picking up a beam from home," said Herndon anxiously, "but we can't make it out."

Because the third planet of the sun Lani was being colonized from the second, inhabited world, communication with the colony's base was possible. A tight beam could span a distance which was only light-minutes across at conjunction, and not much over a light-hour at opposition—as now. But the beam communication had been broken for the past few weeks, and shouldn't be possible again for some weeks more. The sun lay between. One couldn't expect normal sound-and-picture transmission until the parent planet had moved past the scrambler-fields of Lani. But something had come through. It would be reasonable for it to be pretty well hashed when it arrived.

"They aren't sending words or pictures," said Herndon uneasily. "The beam is wabbly and we don't know what to make of it. It's a signal, all right, and on the regular frequency. But there are all sorts of stray noises, and still in the midst of it there's some sort of signal we can't make out. It's like a whine, only it stutters. It's a broken-up sound of one pitch."

Massy rubbed his chin reflectively. He remembered a course in information theory just before he'd graduated from the Service Academy. Signals made by pulses, and pitch-changes and frequency-variations. Information was what couldn't be predicted without information. And he remembered with gratitude a seminar on the history of communication, just before he'd gone out on his first field job as a Survey Candidate.

"Hm-m-m," he said with a trace of self-consciousness. "Those noises—the stuttering ones. Would they be, on the whole, of no more than two different durations? Like—hm-m-m—*bzz bzz bzzzzzz bzz*?"

He felt that he lost dignity by making such ribald sounds. But Herndon's face brightened.

"That's it!" he said relievedly. "That's it! Only they're high-pitched like—" His voice went falsetto. *"Bzz bzz bzz bzzzzz bzz bzz!"*

It occurred to Massy that they sounded like two idiots. He said with dignity:

"Record everything you get, and I'll try to decode it." He added: "Before there was voice communication there were signals by light and sounds in groups of long and short units. They came in groups, to stand for letters, and things were spelled out. Of course there were larger groups, which were words. Very crude system, but it worked when there was great interference, as in the early days. If there's some emergency, your home world might try to get through the sun's scrambler-field that way."

"Undoubtedly!" said Herndon, with even greater relief. "No question, that's it!"

He regarded Massy with great respect as he clicked off. His image faded. The plate was clear.

He thinks I'm wonderful, thought Massy wryly. *Because I'm Colonial Survey. But all I know is what's been taught me. It's bound to show up sooner or later. Damn!*

He dressed. From time to time he looked out the port again. The intolerable cold of Lani III had intensified, lately. There was some idea that sunspots were somehow the cause. He couldn't make out sunspots with the naked eye, but the sun did look pale, with its accompanying sun-dogs. Massy was annoyed by them. They were the result of microscopic ice-crystals suspended in the air. There was no dust on this planet, but there was plenty of ice! It was in the air and on the ground and even under it. To be sure, the drills for the foundation of the great landing-grid had brought up cores of frozen humus along with frozen clay, so there must have been a time when this world had known clouds and seas and vegetation. But it was millions, maybe hundreds of millions of years ago. Right now, though, it was only warm enough to have an atmosphere and very slight and partial thawings in direct sunlight, in sheltered spots, at midday. It couldn't support life, because life is always dependent on other life, and there is a temperature below which a nautral ecological system can't maintain itself. The past few weeks, the climate had been such that even human-supplied life looked dubious.

Massy slipped on his Colonial Survey uniform with its palm-tree insignia. Nothing could be much more inappropriate than palm-tree symbols on a planet with sixty feet of permafrost. Massy reflected wryly, *The construction gang calls it a blast, instead of a tree, because we blow up when they try to dodge specifications. But specifications have to be met! You can't bet the lives of a colony or even a ship's crew on half-built facilities!*

He marched down the corridor from his sleeping room, with the dignity he painstakingly tried to maintain for the sake of the Colonial Survey. It was a pretty lonely business, being dignified all the time. If Herndon didn't look so respectful, it would have been pleasant to be more friendly. But Herndon revered him. Even his sister Riki—

But Massy put her firmly out of his mind. He was on Lani III to check and approve the colony installations. There was the giant landing-grid for spaceships, which took power from the ionosphere to bring heavily loaded space-vessels gently to the ground, and in between times took power from the same source to supply the colony's needs. It also lifted visiting spacecraft the necessary five planetary diameters out when they took off again. There was power-storage in the remote event of disaster to that giant device. There was a food-reserve and the necessary resources for its indefinite stretching in case of need. That usually meant hydroponic installations. There was a reason for the colony, which would make it self-supporting—here a mine. All these things had had to be finished and operable and inspected by a duly qualified Colonial Survey officer before the colony could be licensed for unlimited use. It was all very normal and official, but Massy was the newest Senior Survey Officer on the list, and this was the first of his independent operations. He felt inadequate, sometimes.

He passed through the vestibule between this drone-hull and the next. He went directly to Herndon's office. Herndon, like himself, was newly endowed with authority. He was actually a mining-and-minerals man and a youthful prodigy in that field, but when the director of the colony was taken ill while a supply ship was aground, he went back to the home planet and command devolved on Herndon. *I wonder,* thought Massy, *if he feels as shaky as I do?*

When he entered the office, Herndon sat listening to a literal hash of noises coming out of a speaker on his desk. The cryptic signal had been relayed to him, and a recorder stored it as it came. There were cracklings and squeals and moaning sounds, and sputters and rumbles and growls. But behind the façade of confusion there was a tiny, interrupted, high-pitched noise. It was a monotone whining not to be confused with the random sounds accompanying it. Sometimes it faded almost to inaudibility, and sometimes it was sharp and clear. But it was a distinctive sound in itself, and it was made up of short whines and longer ones of two durations only.

"I've put Riki at making a transcription of what we've got," said Herndon with relief as he saw Massy. "She'll make short marks for the short sounds, and long ones for the long. I've told her to try to separate the groups. We've got a full half hour of it, already."

Massy made an inspired guess.

"I would expect it to be the same message repeated over and over," he said. He added, "And I think it would be decoded by guessing at the letters in two letter and three letter words, as clues to longer ones. That's quicker than statistical analysis of frequency."

Herndon instantly pressed buttons under his phoneplate. He relayed the information to Riki, his sister, as if it were gospel. Massy remembered guiltily that it wasn't gospel. It was simply a trick recalled from his boyhood, when he was passionately interested in secret languages. His interest had faded when he realized he had no secrets to record or transmit.

Herndon turned from the phone-plate.

"Riki says she's already learned to recognize some groups," he reported, "but thanks for the advice. Now what?"

Massy sat down. He'd have liked some coffee, but he was being treated with such respect that the role of demigod was almost forced on him.

"It seems to me," he observed, "that the increased cold out here might not be local. Sunspots—"

Herndon jittered visibly. He silently handed over a sheet of paper with observation-figures on top and a graph below them which related the observations to each other. They were the daily, at-first-routine, measurements of the solar constant from Lani III. The graph-line almost ran off the paper at the bottom.

"To look at this," he admitted, "you'd think the sun

was going out. Of course it can't be," he added hastily. "Not possibly! But there is an extraordinary number of sunspots. Maybe they'll clear. But meanwhile the amount of heat reaching us is dropping. As far as I know there's no parallel to it. Night temperatures are thirty degrees lower than they should be. Not only here, either, but at all the robot weather stations that have been spotted around the planet. They average forty below zero minimum, instead of ten. And—there is that terrific lot of sunspots . . ."

He looked hopefully at Massy. Massy frowned. Sunspots are things about which nothing can be done. Yet the habitability of a borderline planet, anyhow, can very well depend on them. An infinitesimal change in sun heat can make a serious change in any planet's temperature. In the books, the ancient mother planet Earth was said to have entered glacial periods through a drop of only three degrees in the planet-wide temperature, and to have been tropic almost to its poles from a rise of only six. It had been guessed that glacial periods in the planet where humanity began had been caused by coincidences of sunspot maxima.

This planet was already glacial to its equator. There was a genuinely abnormal number of sunspots on Lani, its sun. Sunspots could account for worsening conditions here, perhaps. *That message from the inner planet could be bad,* thought Massy, *if the solar constant drops and stays down a while.* But aloud he said:

"There couldn't be a really significant permanent change. Not quickly, anyhow. Lani's a Sol-type star, and they aren't variables, though of course any dynamic system like a sun will have cyclic modifications of one sort or another. But they usually cancel out."

He sounded encouraging, even to himself. But there was a stirring behind him. Riki Herndon had come silently into her brother's office. She looked pale. She put papers down on her brother's desk.

"But," she said evenly, "while cycles sometimes cancel, sometimes they enhance each other. They heterodyne. That's what's happening."

Massy scrambled to his feet, flushing. Herndon said sharply:

"What? Where'd you get that stuff, Riki?"

She nodded at the sheaf of papers she'd just laid down.

"That's the news from home." She nodded again, to Massy. "You were right. It was the same message, repeated over and over. And I decoded it like children decode each other's secret messages. I did that to Ken once. He was twelve, and I decoded his diary, and I remember how angry he was that I'd found out he didn't have any secrets."

She tried to smile. But Herndon wasn't listening. He read swiftly. Massy saw that the under sheets were rows of dots and dashes, painstakingly transcribed and then decoded. There were letters under each group of marks.

Herndon was very white when he'd finished. He handed the sheet to Massy. Riki's handwriting was precise and clear. Massy read:

"FOR YOUR INFORMATION THE SOLAR CONSTANT IS DROPPING RAPIDLY DUE TO COINCIDENCE OF CYCLIC VARIATIONS IN SUNSPOT ACTIVITY WITH PREVIOUS UNOB-SERVED LONG CYCLES APPARENTLY IN-CREASING THE EFFECT MAXIMUM IS NOT YET REACHED AND IT IS EXPECTED THAT THIS PLANET WILL BECOME UNINHABITABLE FOR A TIME ALREADY KILLING FROSTS HAVE DESTROYED CROPS IN SUMMER HEMI-SPHERE IT IS IMPROBABLE THAT MORE THAN A SMALL PART OF THE POPULATION CAN BE SHELTERED AND WARMED THROUGH DEVELOPING GLACIAL CONDI-TIONS WHICH WILL REACH TO EQUATOR IN TWO HUNDRED DAYS THE COLD CONDITIONS ARE COMPUTED TO LAST TWO THOUSAND DAYS BEFORE NORMAL SOLAR CONSTANT RECURS THIS INFORMATION IS SENT YOU TO ADVISE IMMEDIATE DEVELOPMENT OF HY-DROPONIC FOOD SUPPLY AND OTHER PRE-

CAUTIONS MESSAGE ENDS FOR YOUR INFOR-
MATION THE SOLAR CONSTANT IS DROPPING
RAPIDLY DUE TO COINCIDENCE OF CYCLIC—"

Massy looked up. Herndon's face was ghastly. Massy
said in some grimness:

"Kent IV's the nearest world your planet could hope
to get help from. A mail liner will make it in two
months. Kent IV might be able to send three ships—to
get here in two months more. That's no good!"

He felt sick. Human-inhabited planets are far apart.
The average distance of stars of all types—there is on
an average between four and five light-years of distance
between suns. They are two months' spaceship journey
apart. And not all stars are Sol-type or have inhabited
planets. Colonized worlds are like isolated islands in an
unimaginably vast ocean, and the ships that ply between
them at thirty light-speeds seem merely to creep. In ancient days on the mother planet Earth, men sailed for
months between ports, in their clumsy sailing ships.
There was no way to send messages faster than they
could travel. Nowadays there was little improvement.
News of the Lani disaster could not be transmitted. It
had to be carried, as between stars, and carriage was
slow and response to news of disaster was no faster.

The inner planet, Lani II, had twenty millions of inhabitants, as against the three hundred people in the
colony on Lani III. The outer planet was already
frozen, but there would be glaciation on the inner world
in two hundred days. Glaciation and human life are mutually exclusive. Human beings can survive only so long
as food and power hold out, and shelter against really
bitter cold cannot be improvised for twenty million people! And, of course, there could be no outside help on
any adequate scale. News of the need for it would travel
too slowly. One other world might hear in two months,
and send what aid it could in four. But the next would
not hear for four months, and could not send help in
less than eight. It would take five Earth-years to get a
thousand ships to Lani II—and a thousand ships could
not rescue more than one per cent of the population.

But in five years there would not be nearly so many people left alive.

Herndon licked his lips. There were three hundred people in the already-frozen colony. They had food and power and shelter. They had been considered splendidly daring to risk the conditions here. But all their home world would presently be like this. And there was no possibility of equipping everybody there as the colonists were equipped.

"Our people," said Riki in a thin voice, "all of them . . . Mother and Father and—the others. Our cousins. All our friends. Home is going to be like . . . like that!"

She jerked her head toward a port which let in the frigid colony-world's white daylight. Her face worked.

Massy was aware of an extreme unhappiness on her account. For himself, of course, the tragedy was less. He had no family. He had very few friends. But he could see something that had not occurred to them as yet.

"Of course," he said, "it's not only their trouble. If the solar constant is really dropping like that . . . why things out here will be pretty bad, too. A lot worse than they are now. We'll have to get to work to save ourselves!"

Riki did not look at him. Herndon bit his lips. It was plain that their own fate did not concern them immediately. But when one's home world is doomed, one's personal safety seems a very trivial matter.

There was silence save for the crackling, tumultuous noises that came out of the speaker on Herndon's desk. In the midst of that confused sound there was a wavering, whining, high-pitched note which swelled and faded and grew distinct again.

"We," said Massy without confidence, "are right now in the conditions they'll face a good long time from now."

Herndon said dully:

"But we couldn't live here without supplies from home. Or even without the equipment we brought. But they can't get supplies from anywhere, and they can't make such equipment for everybody! They'll die!" He swallowed, and there was a clicking noise in his throat. "They . . . they know it, too. So they . . . warn us to try to save ourselves because . . . they can't help us any more."

There are many reasons why a man can feel shame that he belongs to a race which can do the things that some men do. But sometimes there are reasons to be proud, as well. The home world of this colony was doomed, but it sent a warning to the tiny group on the colony-world, to allow them to try to save themselves.

"I . . . wish we were there to . . . share what they have to face," said Riki. Her voice sounded as if her throat hurt. "I . . . don't want to keep on living if . . . everybody who . . . ever cared about us is going to die!"

Massy felt lonely. He could understand that nobody would want to live as the only human alive. Nobody would want to live as a member of the only group of people left alive. And everybody thinks of his home planet as all the world there is. *I don't think that way,* thought Massy. *But maybe it's the way I'd feel about living if Riki were to die.* It would be natural to want to share any danger or any disaster she faced. Which he was.

"L-look!" he said, stammering a little. "You don't see! It isn't a case of your living while they die! If your home world becomes like this, what will this be like? We're farther from the sun! We're colder to start with! Do you think we'll live through anything they can't take? Food supplies or no, equipment or no, do you think we've got a chance? Use your brains!"

Herndon and Riki stared at him. And then some of the strained look left Riki's face and body. Herndon blinked, and said slowly:

"Why . . . that's so! We were thought to be taking a terrific risk when we came here. But it'll be as much worse here— Of course! We are in the same fix they're in!"

He straightened a little. Color actually came back

into his face. Riki managed to smile. And then Herndon said almost naturally:

"That makes things look more sensible! We've got to fight for our lives, too! And we've very little chance of saving them! What do we do about it, Massy?"

II

The sun was halfway toward mid-sky, and still attended by its sun-dogs, though they were fainter than at the horizon. The sky was darker. The mountain peaks reached skyward, serene and utterly aloof from the affairs of men. This was a frozen world, where there should be no inhabitants. The city was a fleet of metal hulks, neatly arranged on the valley floor, emptied of the material they had brought for the building of the colony. At the upper end of the valley the landing-grid stood. It was a gigantic skeleton of steel, rising from legs of unequal length bedded in the hillsides, and reaching two thousand feet toward the stars. Human figures, muffled almost past recognition, moved about a catwalk three-quarters of the way up. There was a tiny glittering below where they moved. They were, of course, men using sonic ice-breakers to shatter the frost which formed on the framework at night. Falling shards of crystal made a liquidlike flashing. The landing-grid needed to be cleared every ten days or so. Left uncleared, it would acquire an increasingly thick coating of ice. In time it could collapse. But long before that time it would have ceased to operate, and without its operation there could be no space travel. Rockets for lifting spaceships were impossibly heavy, for practical use. But the landing-grids could lift them out to the unstressed space where Lawlor drives could work, and draw them to ground with cargoes they couldn't possibly have carried if they'd needed rockets.

Massy reached the base of the grid on foot. It was not far from the village of drone-hulls. He was dwarfed by the ground-level upright beams. He went through the cold-lock to the small control-house at the grid's base.

He nodded to the man on standby as he got painfully out of his muffling garments.

"Everything all right?" he asked.

The standby operator shrugged. Massy was Colonial Survey. It was his function to find fault, to expose inadequacies in the construction and operation of colony facilities. *It's natural for me to be disliked by men whose work I inspect,* thought Massy. *If I approve it doesn't mean anything, and if I protest, it's bad.* He had always been lonely, but it was a part of the job.

"I think," he said painstakingly, "that there ought to be a change in maximum no-drain voltage. I'd like to check it."

The operator shrugged again. He pressed buttons under a phone-plate.

"Shift to reserve power," he commanded, when a face appeared in the plate. "Gotta check no-drain juice."

"What for?" demanded the face in the plate.

"You-know-who's got ideas," said the grid operator scornfully. "Maybe we've been skimping something. Maybe there's some new specification we didn't know about. Maybe anything! But shift to reserve power."

The face in the screen grumbled. Massy swallowed. It was not a Survey officer's privilege to maintain discipline. But there was no particular virtue in discipline here and now. He watched the current-demand dial. It stood a little above normal day-drain, which was understandable. The outside temperature was down. There was more power needed to keep the dwellings warm, and there was always a lot of power needed in the mine the colony had been formed to exploit. The mine had to be warmed for the men who worked to develop it.

The demand-needle dropped abruptly, and hung steady, and dropped again and again as additional parts of the colony's power-uses were switched to reserve. The needle hit bottom. It stayed there.

Massy had to walk around the standby man to get at the voltmeter. It was built around standard, old-fashioned vacuum tubes—standard for generations, now. Massy patiently hooked it up and warmed the tubes and tested it. He pushed in the contact-plugs. He read the no-drain voltage. He licked his lips and made a note. He reversed the leads, so it would read backward. He took another reading. He drew in his breath very quietly.

"Now I want the power turned on in sections," he told the operator. "The mine first, maybe. It doesn't matter. But I want to get voltage-readings at different power take-offs."

The operator looked pained. He spoke with unnecessary elaboration to the face in the phone-plate, and grudgingly went through with the process by which Massy measured the successive drops in voltage with power drawn from the ionosphere. The current available from a layer of ionized gas is, in effect, the current-flow through a conductor with marked resistance. It is possible to infer a gas' ionization from the current it yields.

The cold-lock door opened. Riki Herndon came in, panting a little.

"There's another message from home," she said sharply. Her voice seemed strained. "They picked up our answering-beam and are giving the information you asked for."

"I'll be along," said Massy. "I just got some information here."

He got into his cold-garments again. He followed her out of the control-hut.

"The figures from home aren't good," said Riki evenly, when mountains visibly rose on every hand around them. "Ken says they're much worse than he thought. The rate of decline in the solar constant's worse than we figured or could believe."

"I see," said Massy, inadequately.

"It's absurd!" said Riki fiercely. "It's monstrous! There've been sun spots and sunspot cycles all along! I learned about them in school! I learned myself about a four-year and a seven-year cycle, and that there were others! They should have known! They should have calculated in advance! Now they talk about sixty-year cycles coming in with a hundred-and-thirty-year cycle to pile up with all the others— But what's the use of scientists if they don't do their work right and twenty million people die because of it?"

Massy did not consider himself a scientist, but he winced. Riki raged as they moved over the slippery ice. Her breath was an intermittent cloud about her shoulders. There was white frost on the front of her cold-garments.

He held out his hand quickly as she slipped, once.

"But they'll beat it!" said Riki in a sort of angry pride. "They're starting to build more landing-grids, back home. Hundreds of them! Not for ships to land by, but to draw power from the ionosphere! They figure that one ship-size grid can keep nearly three square miles of ground warm enough to live on! They'll roof over the streets of cities. Then they'll plant food-crops in the streets and gardens, and do what hydroponic growing they can. They are afraid they can't do it fast enough to save everybody, but they'll try!"

Massy clenched his hands inside their bulky mittens.

"Well?" demanded Riki. "Won't that do the trick?"

Massy said: "No."

"Why not?" she demanded.

"I just took readings on the grid, here. The voltage and the conductivity of the layer we draw power from, both depend on ionization. When the intensity of sunlight drops, the voltage drops and the conductivity drops, too. It's harder for less power to flow to the area the grid can tap—and the voltage-pressure is lower to drive it."

"Don't say any more!" cried Riki. "Not another word!"

Massy was silent. They went down the last small slope. They passed the opening of the mine—the great drift which bored straight into the mountain. They could look into it. They saw the twin rows of brilliant roof-lights going toward the heart of the stony monster.

They had almost reached the village when Riki said in a stifled voice:

"How bad is it?"

"Very," admitted Massy. "We have here the conditions the home planet will have in two hundred days. Originally we could draw less than a fifth the power they count on from a grid on Lani II."

Riki ground her teeth.

"Go on!" she said challengingly.

"Ionization here is down ten per cent," said Massy. "That means the voltage is down—somewhat more. A great deal more. And the resistance of the layer is greater. Very much greater. When they need power most, on the home planet, they won't draw more from a grid than we do now. It won't be enough."

They reached the village. There were steps to the cold-lock of Herndon's office-hull. They were ice-free, because like the village walk-ways they were warmed to keep frost from depositing on them. Massy made a mental note.

In the cold-lock, the warm air pouring in was almost stifling. Riki said defiantly:

"You might as well tell me now!"

"We could draw one-fifth as much power, here, as the same-size grid would yield on your home world," he said grimly. "We are drawing—call it sixty per cent of normal. A shade over one-tenth of what they must expect to draw when the real cold hits them. But their estimates are nine times too high." He said heavily, "One grid won't warm three square miles of city. About a third of one is closer. But—"

"That won't be the worst!" said Riki in a choked voice. "Is that right? How much good will a grid do?"

Massy did not answer.

The inner cold-lock door opened. Herndon sat at his desk, even paler than before, listening to the hash of noises that came out of the speaker. He tapped on the desktop, quite unconscious of the action. He looked almost desperately at Massy.

"Did she . . . tell you?" he asked in a numb voice. "They hope to save maybe half the population. All the children, anyhow—"

"They won't," said Riki bitterly.

"Better go transcribe the new stuff that's come in,"

said her brother dully. "We might as well know what it says."

Riki went out of the office. Massy laboriously shed his cold-garments. He said uncomfortably:

"The rest of the colony doesn't know what's up yet. The operator at the grid didn't, certainly. But they have to know."

"We'll post the message on the bulletin board," said Herndon apathetically. "I wish I could keep it from them. It's not fun to live with. I . . . might as well not tell them just yet."

"To the contrary," insisted Massy. "They've got to know right away! You're going to issue orders and they'll need to understand how urgent they are!"

Herndon looked absolutely hopeless.

"What's the good of doing anything?" When Massy frowned, he added as if exhausted: "Seriously, is there any use? You're all right. A Survey ship's due to take you away. It's not coming because they know there's something wrong, but because your job should be finished about now. But it can't do any good! It would be insane for it to land at home. It couldn't carry away more than a few dozen refugees, and there are twenty million people who're going to die. It might offer to take some of us. But . . . I don't think many of us would go. I wouldn't. I don't think Riki would."

"I don't see—"

"What we've got right here," said Herndon, "is what they're going to have back home. And worse. But there's no chance for us to keep alive here! You are the one who pointed it out! I've been figuring, and the way the solar-constant curve is going—I plotted it from the figures they gave us—it couldn't possibly level out until the oxygen, anyhow, is frozen out of the atmosphere here. We aren't equipped to stand anything like that, and we can't get equipped. There couldn't be equipment to let us stand it indefinitely! Anyhow, the maximum cold conditions will last two thousand days back home—six Earth-years. And there'll be storage of cold in frozen oceans and piled-up glaciers— It'll be twenty years before home will be back to normal in temperature, and the same here. Is there any point in trying to live—just barely to survive—for twenty years before there'll be a habitable planet to go back to?"

Massy said irritably:

"Don't be a fool! Doesn't it occur to you that this planet is a perfect experiment-station, two hundred days ahead of the home world, where ways to beat the whole business can be tried? If we can beat it here, they can beat it there!"

Herndon said detachedly:

"Can you name one thing to try here?"

"Yes," snapped Massy. "I want the walk-heaters and the step-heaters outside turned off. They use power to keep walkways clear of frost and doorsteps not slippery. I want to save that heat!"

Herndon said without interest:

"And when you've saved it, what will you do with it?"

"Put it underground to be used as needed!" Massy said angrily. "Store it in the mine! I want to put every heating-device we can contrive to work in the mine! To heat the rock! I want to draw every watt the grid will yield and warm up the inside of the mountain while we can draw power to do it with! I want the deepest part of the mine too hot to enter! We'll lose a lot of heat, of course. It's not like storing electric power! But we can store heat now, and the more we store the more will be left when we need it!"

Herndon thought heavily. Presently he stirred slightly.

"Do you know, that is an idea—" He looked up. "Back home there was a shale-oil deposit up near the icecaps. It wasn't economical to mine it. So they put heaters down in bore-holes and heated up the whole shale deposit! Drill-holes let out the hot oil vapors to be condensed. They got out every bit of oil without disturbing the shale! And then . . . why . . . the shale stayed warm for years. Farmers bulldozed soil over it and raised crops with glaciers all around them! That could be done again. They could be storing up heat back home!"

Then he drooped.

"But they can't spare power to warm up the ground under cities. They need all the power they've got to build roofs. And it takes time to build grids."

Massy snapped:

"Yes, if they're building regulation ones! By the time they were finished they'd be useless! The ionization here is dropping already. But they don't need to build grids that will be useless later! They can weave cables together on the ground and hang them in the air by helicopters! They wouldn't hold up a landing ship for an instant, but they'll draw power right away! They'll even power the helis that hold them up! Of course they've defects! They'll have to come down in high winds. They won't be dependable. But they can put heat in the ground to come out under roofs, to grow food by, to save lives by. What's the matter with them?"

Herndon stirred again. His eyes ceased to be dull and lifeless.

"I'll give the orders for turning off the sidewalks. And I'll send what you just said back home. They . . . should like it."

He looked very respectfully at Massy.

"I guess you know what I'm thinking right now," he said awkwardly.

Massy flushed. It was not dignified for a Colonial Survey officer to show off. He felt that Herndon was unduly impressed. But Herndon didn't see that the device wouldn't solve anything. It would merely postpone the effects of a disaster. It could not possibly prevent them.

"It ought to be done," he said curtly. "There'll be other things to be done, too."

"When you tell them to me," said Herndon warmly, "they'll get done! I'll have Riki put this into that pulse-code you explained to us and she'll get it off right away!"

He stood up.

"I didn't explain the code to her!" insisted Massy. "She was already translating it when you gave her my suggestion!"

"All right," said Herndon. "I'll get this sent back at once!"

He hurried out of the office. *This*, thought Massy irritably, *is how reputations are made, I suppose. I'm getting one.* But his own reaction was extremely inappropriate. If the people of Lani II did suspend helicopter-supported grids of wire in the atmosphere, they could warm masses of underground rock and stone and earth. They could establish what were practically reservoirs of life-giving heat under their cities. They could contrive that the warmth from below would rise only as it was needed. But—

Two hundred days to conditions corresponding to the colony planet. Then two thousand days of minimum-heat conditions. Then very, very slow return to normal temperature, long after the sun was back to its previous brilliance. They couldn't store enough heat for so long. It couldn't be done. It was ironic that in the freezing of ice and the making of glaciers the planet itself could store cold.

And there would be monstrous storms and blizzards on Lani II as it cooled. As cold conditions got worse the wire grids could be held aloft for shorter and shorter periods, and each time they would pull down less power than before. Their effectiveness would diminish even faster than the need for effectiveness increased.

Massy felt even deeper depression as he worked out the facts. His proposal was essentially futile. It would be encouraging, and to a very slight degree and for a certain short time it would palliate the situation on the inner planet. But in the long run its effect would be zero.

He was embarrassed, too, that Herndon was so admiring. Herndon would tell Riki that he was marvelous. She might—though cagily—be inclined to agree. But he wasn't marvelous. This trick of a flier-supported grid was not new. It had been used on Saril to supply power for giant peristaltic pumps emptying a polder that had been formed inside a ring of indifferently upraised islands.

All I know, thought Massy bitterly, *is what some-*

body's showed me or I've read in books. And nobody's showed or written how to handle a thing like this!

He went to Herndon's desk. Herndon had made a new graph on the solar-constant observations forwarded from home. It was a strictly typical curve of the results of coinciding cyclic changes. It was the curve of a series of frequencies at the moment when they were all precisely in phase. From this much one could extrapolate and compute—

Massy took a pencil, frowning unhappily. His fingers clumsily formed equations and solved them. The result was just about as bad as it could be. The change in brightness of the sun Lani would not be enough to be observed on Kent IV—the nearest other inhabited world—when the light reached there four years from now. Lani would never be classed as a variable star, because the total change in light and heat would be relatively minute. But the formula for computing planetary temperatures is not simple. Among its factors are squares and cubes of the variables. Worse, the heat radiated from a sun's photosphere varies not as the square or cube, but as the fourth power of its absolute temperature. A very small change in the sun's effective temperature, producible by sunspots, could make an altogether disproportionate difference in the warmth its worlds received.

Massy's computations were not pure theory. The data came from Sol itself, where alone in the galaxy there had been daily solar-constant measurements for three hundred years. The rest of his deductions were based ultimately on Earth observations, too. Most scientific data had to refer back to Earth to get an adequate continuity. But there was no possible doubt about the sunspot data, because Sol and Lani were of the same type and nearly equal size.

Using the figures on the present situation, Massy reluctantly arrived at the fact that here, on this already-frozen world, the temperature would drop until CO_2 froze out of the atmosphere. When that happened, the temperature would plummet until there was no really significant difference between it and that of empty space. It is carbon dioxide which is responsible for the greenhouse effect, by which a planet is in thermal equilibrium only at a temperature above its surroundings—as a greenhouse in sunlight is warmer than the outside air.

The greenhouse effect would vanish soon on the colony world. When it vanished on the mother planet—

Massy found himself thinking, *If Riki won't leave when the Survey ship comes, I'll resign from the Service. I'll have to if I'm to stay. And I won't go unless she does.*

III

"If you want to come, it's all right," said Massy ungraciously.

He waited while Riki slipped into the bulky cold-garments that were needed out-of-doors in the daytime, and were doubly necessary at night. There were heavy boots with inches-thick insulating soles, made in one piece with the many-layered trousers. There was the air-puffed, insulated over-tunic with its hood and mittens which were a part of the sleeves.

"Nobody goes outside at night," she said when they stood together in the cold-lock.

"I do," he told her. "I want to find out something."

The outer door opened and he stepped out. He held his arm for her, because the steps and walkway were no longer heated. Now they were covered with a filmy layer of something which was not frost, but a faint, faint bloom of powder. It was the equivalent of dust, but it was miscroscopic snow-crystals frozen out of the air by the unbearable chill of night.

There was no moon, of course, yet the ice-clad mountains glowed faintly. The drone-hulls arranged in such an orderly fashion were dark against the frosted ground. There was silence: stillness: the feeling of ancient quietude. No wind stirred anywhere. Nothing moved. Nothing lived. The soundlessness was enough to crack the eardrums.

Massy threw back his head and gazed at the sky for a very long time. Nothing. He looked down at Riki.

"Look at the sky," he commanded.

She raised her eyes. She had been watching him. But as she gazed upward she almost cried out. The sky was filled with stars in innumerable variety. But the brighter ones were as stars had never been seen before. Just as the sun in daylight had been accompanied by its sun-dogs—pale phantoms of itself ranged about it—so the brighter distant suns now shone from the center of rings of their own images. They no longer had the look of random placing. Those which were most distinct were patterns in themselves, and one's eyes strove instinctively to grasp the greater pattern in which such seeming artifacts must belong.

"Oh . . . beautiful!" cried Riki softly, yet almost afraid.

"Look!" he insisted. "Keep looking!"

She continued to gaze, moving her eyes about hopefully. It was such a sight as no one could have imagined. Every tint and every color; every possible degree of brightness appeared. And there were groups of stars of the same brilliance which almost made triangles, but not quite. There were rose-tinted stars which almost formed an arc, but did not. And there were arrays which were almost lines and nearly formed squares and polygons, but never actually achieved them.

"It's . . . beautiful!" said Riki breathlessly. "But what must I look for?"

"Look for what isn't there," he ordered.

She looked, and the stars were unwinking, but that was not extraordinary. They filled all the firmament, without the least space in which some tiny sparkle of light was not to be found. But that was not remarkable, either. Then there was a vague flickering grayish glow somewhere indefinite. It vanished. Then she realized.

"There's no aurora!" she exclaimed.

"That's it." said Massy. "There've always been auroras here. But no longer. We may be responsible. I wish I thought it wise to turn everything back to reserve power for a while. We could find out. But we can't afford it. There was just the faintest possible gray flickering just now. But there ought to be armies of light marching across the sky. The aurora here—it was never missing! But it's gone now."

"I . . . looked at it when we first landed," admitted Riki. "It was unbelievable! But it was terribly cold, out of shelter. And it happened every night, so I said to myself I'd look tomorrow, and then tomorrow again. So it got so I never looked at all."

Massy kept his eyes where the faint gray flickering had been. And once one realized, it was astonishing that the former nightly play of ghostly colors should be absent.

"The aurora," he said dourly, "happens in the very upper limits of the air . . . fifty . . . seventy . . . ninety miles up, when God-knows-what emitted particles from the sun come streaking in, drawn by the planet's magnetic field. The aurora's a phenomenon of ions. We tap the inonosphere a long way down from where it plays, but I'm wondering if we stopped it."

"We?" said Riki, shocked. "We—humans?"

"We tap the ions of their charges," he said somberly, "that the sunlight made by day. We're pulling in all the power we can. I wonder if we've drained the aurora of its energy, too."

Riki was silent. Massy gazed, still searching. But he shook his head.

"It could be," he said in a carefully detached voice. "We didn't draw much power by comparison with the amount that came. But the ionization is an ultraviolet effect. Atmospheric gases don't ionize too easily. After all, if the solar constant dropped a very little, it might mean a terrific drop in the ultraviolet part of the spectrum—and that's what makes ions of oxygen and nitrogen and hydrogen and such. The ion-drop could easily be fifty times as great as the drop in the solar constant. And we're drawing power from the little that's left."

Riki stood very still. The cold was horrible. Had there been a wind, it could not have been endured for an instant. But the air was motionless. Yet its coldness was so great that the inside of one's nostrils ached, and the inside of one's chest was aware of chill. Even through the cold-garments there was the feeling as of ice without.

"I'm beginning," said Massy, "to suspect that I'm a fool. Or maybe I'm an optimist. It might be the same thing. I could have guessed that the power we could draw would drop faster than our need for power increased. If we've drained the aurora of its light, we're scraping the bottom of the barrel. And it's a shallower barrel than one would suspect."

There was stillness again. Riki stood mousy-quiet. *When she realizes what this means*, thought Massy grimly, *she won't admire me so much. Her brother's built me up. But I've been a fool, figuring out excuses to hope. She'll see it.*

"I think," said Riki quietly, "that you're telling me that after all we can't store up heat to live on, down in the mine."

"We can't," agreed Massy grimly. "Not much, nor long. Not enough to matter."

"So we won't live as long as Ken expects?"

"Not nearly as long," said Massy evenly. "He's hoping we can find out things to be useful back on Lani II. But we'll lose the power we can get from our grid long before even their new grids are useless. We'll have to start using our reserve power a lot sooner. It'll be gone—and us with it—before they're really in straits for living-heat."

Riki's teeth began to chatter.

"This sounds like I'm scared," she said angrily, "but I'm not! I'm just freezing! If you want to know, I'd a lot rather have it the way you say! I won't have to grieve over anybody, and they'll be too busy to grieve for me! Let's go inside while it's still warm!"

He helped her back into the cold-lock, and the outer door closed. She was shivering uncontrollably when the warmth came pouring in.

They went into Herndon's office. He came in as Riki was peeling off the top part of her cold-garments. She still shivered. He glanced at her and said to Massy:

"There's been a call from the grid-control shack. It

looks like there's something wrong, but they can't find anything. The grid is set for maximum power-collection, but it's bringing in only fifty thousand kilowatts!"

"We're on our way back to savagery," said Massy, with an attempt at irony.

It was true. A man can produce two hundred and fifty watts from his muscles for a reasonable length of time. When he has no more power, he is a savage. When he gains a kilowatt of energy from the muscles of a horse, he is a barbarian—but the new power cannot be directed wholly as he wills. When he can apply it to a plow he has high barbarian culture, and when he adds still more he begins to be civilized. Steam power put as much as four kilowatts to work for every human being in the first industrialized countries, and in the mid twentieth century there was sixty kilowatts per person in the more advanced nations. Nowadays, of course, a modern culture assumed five hundred as a minimum. But there was less than half that in the colony on Lani II. And its environment made its own demands.

"There can't be any more," said Riki, trying to control her shivering. "We're even using the aurora and there isn't any more power. It's running out. We'll go even before the people at home, Ken."

Herndon's features looked very pinched.

"But we can't! We mustn't!" He turned to Massy. "We do them good, back home! There was panic. Our report about cable grids has put heart in people. They're setting to work—magnificently! So we're some use! They know we're worse off than they are, and as long as we hold on they'll be encouraged! We've got to keep going somehow!"

Riki breathed deeply until her shivering stopped. Then she said calmly:

"Haven't you noticed, Ken, that Mr. Massy has the viewpoint of his profession? His business is finding things wrong with things. He was deposited in our midst to detect defects in what we did and do. He has the habit of looking for the worst. But I think he can turn the habit to good use. He did turn up the idea of cable-grids."

"Which," said Massy, "turns out to be no good at all. They'd be some good if they weren't needed. really. But the conditions that make them necessary make them useless!"

Riki shook her head.

"They are useful!" she said firmly. "They're keeping people at home from despairing. Now, though, you've got to think of something else. If you think of enough things, one will do good the way you want—more than making people feel better."

"What does it matter how people feel?" he demanded bitterly. "What difference do feelings make? Facts are facts! One can't change facts!"

Riki said with no less firmness:

"We humans are the only creatures in the universe who don't do anything else! Every other creature accepts facts. It lives where it is born, and it feeds on the food that is there for it, and it dies when the facts of nature require it to. We humans don't. Especially we women! We won't let men do it, either! When we don't like facts—mostly about ourselves—we change them. But important facts we disapprove of—we ask men to change for us. And they do!"

She faced Massy. Rather incredibly, she grinned at him.

"Will you please change the facts that look so annoying just now, please? Please?" Then she elaborately pantomimed an over-feminine girl's look of wide-eyed admiration. "You're so big and strong! I just know you can do it—for me!"

She abruptly dropped the pretense and moved toward the door. She half-turned then, and said detachedly:

"But about half of that is true."

The door slid shut behind her. Massy thought bitterly, *Her brother admires me. She probably thinks I really can do something!* It suddenly occurred to him that she knew a Colonial Survey ship was due to stop by here to pick him up. She believed he expected to be rescued, even though the rest of the colony could not be, and most of it wouldn't consent to leave their kindred when the death of mankind in this solar system took place. He said awkwardly:

"Fifty thousand kilowatts isn't enough to land a ship."

Herndon frowned. Then he said:

"Oh. You mean the Survey ship that's to pick you up can't land? But it can go in orbit and put down a rocket landing-boat for you."

Massy flushed.

"I wasn't thinking of that. I'd something more in mind. I . . . rather like your sister. She's . . . pretty wonderful. And there are some other women here in the colony, too. About a dozen all told. As a matter of self-respect I think we ought to get them away on the Survey ship. I agree that they wouldn't consent to go. But if they had no choice—if we could get them on board the grounded ship, and they suddenly found themselves . . . well . . . kidnaped and outward-bound not by their own fault . . . They could be faced with the accomplished fact that they had to go on living."

Herndon said evenly:

"That's been in the back of my mind for some time. Yes. I'm for that. But if the Survey ship can't land—"

"I believe I can land it regardless," said Massy doggedly. "I can find out, anyhow. I'll need to try things. I'll need help . . . work done. But I want your promise that if I can get the ship to ground you'll conspire with her skipper and arrange for them to go on living."

Herndon looked at him.

"Some new stuff—in a way," said Massy uncomfortably. "I'll have to stay aground to work it. It's also part of the bargain that I shall. And, of course, your sister can't know about it, or she can't be fooled into living."

Herndon's expression changed a little.

"What'll you do? Of course it's a bargain."

"I'll need some metals we haven't smelted so far," said Massy. "Potassium if I can get it, sodium if I can't, and at worst I'll settle for zinc. Cesium would be best, but we've found no traces of it."

Herndon said thoughtfully:

"No-o-o. I think I can get you sodium and potassium, from rocks. I'm afraid no zinc. How much?"

"Grams," said Massy. "Trivial quantities. And I'll need a miniature landing-grid built. Very miniature."

Herndon shrugged his shoulders.

"It's over my head. But just to have work to do will be good for everybody. We've been feeling more frustrated than any other humans in history. I'll go round up the men who'll do the work. You talk to them."

The door closed behind him. Massy very deliberately got out of his cold-clothing. He thought, *She'll rave when she finds her brother and I have deceived her*. Then he thought of the other women. *If any of them are married, we'll have to see if there's room for their husbands. I'll have to dress up the idea. Make it look like reason for hope, or the women would find out. But not many can go—*

He knew very closely how many extra passengers could be carried on a Survey ship, even in such an emergency as this. Living quarters were not luxurious, at best. Everything was cramped and skimped. Survey ships were rugged, tiny vessels which performed their duties amid tedium and discomfort and peril for all on board. But they could carry away a very few unwilling refugees to Kent IV.

He settled down at Herndon's desk to work out the thing to be done.

It was not unreasonable. Tapping the ionosphere for power was something like pumping water out of a pipe-well in sand. If the water-table was high, there was pressure to force the water to the pipe, and one could pump fast. If the water-table were low, water couldn't flow fast enough. The pump would suck dry. In the ionosphere, the level of ionization was at once like the pressure and the size of the sand-grains. When the level was high, the flow was vast because the sand-grains were large and the conductivity high. But as the level lessened, so did the size of the sand-grains. There was less to draw, and more resistance to its flow.

But there had been one tiny flicker of auroral light over by the horizon. There was still power aloft. If

Massy could in a fashion prime the pump: if he could increase the conductivity by increasing the ions present around the place where their charges were drawn away—why—he could increase the total flow. It would be like digging a brick-well where a pipe-well had been. A brick-well draws water from all around its circumference.

So Massy computed carefully. It was ironic that he had to go to such trouble simply because he didn't have test-rockets like the Survey uses to get a picture of a planet's weather-pattern. They rise vertically for fifty miles or so, trailing a thread of sodium-vapor behind them. The trail is detectable for some time, and ground-instruments record each displacement by winds blowing in different directions at different speeds, one over the other. Such a rocket with its loading slightly changed would do all Massy had in mind. But he didn't have one, so something much more elaborate was called for.

She'll think I'm clever, he reflected wryly, *but all I'm doing is what I've been taught. I wouldn't have to work it out if I had a rocket.*

Still, there was some satisfaction in working out this job. A landing-grid has to be not less than half a mile across and two thousand feet high because its field has to reach out five planetary diameters to handle ships that land and take off. To handle solid objects it has to be accurate—though power can be drawn with an improvisation. To thrust a sodium-vapor bomb anywhere from twenty to fifty miles high—why—he'd need a grid only six feet wide and five high. It could throw much higher, of course. It could hold, at that. But doubling the size would make accuracy easier.

He tripled the dimensions. There would be a grid eighteen feet across and fifteen high. Tuned to the casing of a small bomb, it could hold it steady at seven hundred and fifty thousand feet—far beyond necessity. He began to make the detail drawings.

Herndon came back with half a dozen chosen colonists. They were young men, technicians rather than scientists. Some of them were several years younger than

Massy. There were grim and stunned expressions on some faces, but one tried to pretend nonchalance, and two seemed trying to suppress fury at the monstrous occurrence that would destroy not only their own lives, but everything they remembered on the planet which was their home. They looked almost challengingly at Massy.

He explained. He was going to put a cloud of metallic vapor up in the ionosphere. Sodium if he had to, potassium if he could, zinc if he must. Those metals were readily ionized by sunlight—much more readily than atmospheric gases. In effect, he was going to supply a certain area of the ionosphere with material to increase the efficiency of sunshine in providing electric power. As a sideline, there would be increased conductivity from the normal ionosphere.

"Something like this was done centuries ago, back on Earth," he explained carefully. "They used rockets, and made sodium-vapor clouds as much as twenty and thirty miles long. Even nowadays the Survey uses test-rockets with trails of sodium-vapor. It will work to some degree. We'll find out how much."

He felt Herndon's eyes upon him. They were almost dazedly respectful. But one of the technicians said coldly:

"How long will those clouds last?"

"That high, three or four days," Massy told him. "They won't help much at night, but they should step up power-intake while the sun shines on them."

A man in the back said crisply:

"Hup!" The significance was, "Let's go!" Then somebody said feverishly, "What do we do? Got working drawings? Who makes the bombs? Who does what? Let's get at this!"

Then there was confusion, and Herndon had vanished. Massy suspected he'd gone to have Riki put this theory into dot-and-dash code for beam-transmission back to Lani II. But there was no time to stop him. These men wanted precise information, and it was half an hour before the last of them had gone out with free-hand sketches, and had come back for further explanation of a doubtful point, and other men had come in hungrily to demand a share in the job.

When he was alone again, Massy thought, *Maybe it's worth doing because it'll get Riki on the Survey ship. But they think it means saving the people back home!*

Which it didn't. Taking energy out of sunlight is taking energy out of sunlight, no matter how you do it. Take it out as electric power, and there's less heat left. Warm one place with electric power, and everywhere else is a little colder. There's an equation. On this colony-world it wouldn't matter, but on the home world it would. The more there was trickery to gather heat, the more heat was needed. Again it might postpone the death of twenty million people, but it would never, never, never prevent it.

The door slid aside and Riki came in. She stammered a little.

"I . . . just coded what Ken told me to send back home. It will . . . it will do everything! It's wonderful! I . . . wanted to tell you!"

Massy writhed internally. It wasn't wonderful.

"Consider," he said in a desperate attempt to take it lightly, "consider that I've taken a bow."

He tried to smile. It was not a success. And Riki suddenly drew a deep breath and looked at him in a new fashion.

"Ken's right," she said softly. "He says you can't get conceited. You're not satisfied with yourself even now, are you?" She smiled, rather gravely. Then she said, "But what I like is that you aren't really smart. A woman can make you do things. I have!"

He looked at her uneasily. She grinned.

"I, even I, can at least pretend to myself that I help bring this about! If I hadn't said please change the facts that are so annoying, and if I hadn't said you were big and strong and clever— I'm going to tell myself for the rest of my life that I helped make you do it!"

Massy swallowed.

"I'm afraid," he said miserably, "that it won't work again."

She cocked her head on one side.

"No?"

He stared at her apprehensively. And then with a be-wildering change of emotional reaction, he saw that her eyes were filled with tears. She stamped her foot.

"You're . . . horrible!" she cried. "Here I come in, and . . . and if you think you can get me kidnaped to safety . . . without even telling me that you 'rather like' me, like you told my brother, or that I'm 'pretty wonderful'— If you think."

He was stunned, that she knew. She stamped her foot again.

"For Heaven's sake!" she wailed. "Do I have to *ask* you to kiss me?"

IV

During the last night of preparation, Massy sat by a thermometer registering the outside temperature. He hovered over it as one might over a sick child. He watched it and sweated, though the inside temperature of the drone-hull was lowered to save power. There was nothing he could actually do. At midnight the thermom-eter said it was seventy degrees below zero Fahrenheit. At halfway to dawn it was eighty degrees below zero Fahrenheit. The hour before dawn it was eighty-five de-grees below zero. Then he sweated profusely. The mean-ing of the slowed descent was that carbon dioxide was being frozen out of the upper layers of the atmosphere. The frozen particles were drifting slowly downward, and as they reached lower and faintly warmer levels they re-turned to the state of gas. But there was a level, above the CO_2, where the temperature was plummeting.

The height to which carbon dioxide existed was drop-ping—slowly, but inexorably. And above the carbon-dioxide level there was no bottom limit to the tempera-ture. The greenhouse effect was due to CO_2. Where it wasn't, the cold of space moved down. If at ground-level the thermometer read ever so slightly lower than one hundred and nine below zero—why—everything was finished. Without the greenhouse effect, the night-side of the planet would lose its remaining heat with a rush. Even the day-side, once cold enough, would lose heat to emptiness as fast as it came from the sun. Minus one hundred and nine point three was the critical reading. If it went down to that, it would plunge to a hundred and fifty—two hundred degrees below zero! And it would never come up again.

There would be rain at nightfall—a rain of oxygen frozen to a liquid and splashing on the ground. Human life would be quite simply impossible, in any shelter and under any conditions. Even spacesuits would not protect against an atmosphere sucking heat from it at that rate. A spacesuit can be heated against the loss of temperature due to radiation in a vacuum. It could not be heated against nitrogen, which would chill it irresistibly by contact.

But, as Massy sweated over it, the thermometer steadied at minus eighty-five degrees. When the dawn came, it rose to seventy. By mid-morning, the temperature in bright sunshine was no lower than sixty-five degrees below zero.

But there was no bounce left in Massy when Herndon came for him.

"Your phone-plate's been flashing," said Herndon, "and you didn't answer. Must have had your back to it. Riki's over in the mine, watching them get things ready. She was worried that she couldn't call you. Asked me to find out what was the trouble."

Massy said heavily:

"Has she got something to heat the air she breathes?"

"Naturally," said Herndon. He added curiously, "What's the matter?"

"We almost took our licking," Massy told him. "I'm afraid for tonight, and tomorrow night, too. If the CO_2 freezes—"

"We'll have power!" Herndon insisted. "We'll build ice tunnels and ice domes. We'll build a city under ice, if we have to. But we'll have power. We'll be all right!"

"I doubt it very much," said Massy. "I wish you hadn't told Riki of the bargain to get her away from here when the Survey ship comes!"

Herndon grinned.

"Is the little grid ready?" asked Massy.

"Everything's set," said Herndon exuberantly. "It's in the mine-tunnel with radiant heaters playing on it. The bombs are ready. We made enough to last for months, while we were at it. No use taking chances!"

Massy looked at him queerly. Then he said:

"We might as well go out and try the thing, then."

But he was very tired. He was not elated. *Riki can't be gotten away,* he thought wearily, *and I'm not going to go because it isn't quite fitting to go and leave her. They'll all be rejoicing presently, but nothing's settled.* Then he thought with exquisite irony, *She thinks I was inspired to genius by her, when I haven't done a thing I wasn't taught or didn't get out of books!*

He put on the cold-garments as they were now modified for the increased frigidity. Nobody could breathe air at minus sixty-five degrees without getting his lungs frost-bitten. So there was now a plastic mask to cover one's face, and the air one breathed outdoors was heated as it came through a wire-gauze snout. But still it was not wise to stay out of shelter for too long a time.

Massy went out-of-doors. He stepped out of the cold-lock and gazed about him. The sun seemed markedly paler, and now it had lost its sun-dogs again. Ice crystals no longer floated in the almost congealed air. The sky was dark. It was almost purple, and it seemed to Massy that he could detect faint flecks of light in it. They would be stars, shining in the daytime.

There seemed to be no one about at all, only the white coldness of the mountains. But there was a movement at the mine-drift, and something came out of it. Four men appeared, muffled up like Massy himself. They rolled the eighteen-foot grid out of the mine-mouth, moving it on those inflated bags which are so much better than rollers for rough terrain. They looked absurdly like bears with steaming noses, in their masks and clothing. They had some sort of powered pusher with them, and they got the metal cage to the very top of a singularly rounded stone upcrop which rose in the center of the valley.

"We picked that spot," said Herndon's muffled voice

through the chill, "because by shifting the grid's position it can be aimed, and be on a solid base. Right?"

"Quite all right," said Massy. "We'll go work it."

He moved heavily across the valley, in which nothing moved except the padded figures of the four technicians. Their wire-gauze breathing-masks seemed to emit smoke. They waved to him in greeting.

I'm popular again, he thought drearily, *but it doesn't matter. Getting the Survey ship to ground won't help now, since Riki's forewarned. And this trick won't solve anything permanently on the home planet. It'll just postpone things.*

He had a very peculiar ache inside. A Survey officer is naturally lonely. Massy had been lonely before he even entered the Service. He hadn't had a feeling of belonging anywhere, or with anyone, and no planet was really his home. Now he could believe that he belonged with someone. But there was the slight matter of a drop in the solar constant of an unimportant Sol-type sun, and nothing could come of it.

Even when Riki—muffled like the rest—waved to him from the mouth of the tunnel, his spirits did not lift. The thing he wanted was to look forward to years and years of being with Riki. He wanted, in fact, to look forward to forever. And there might not be a tomorrow.

"I had the control board rolled out here," she called breathlessly through her mask. "It's cold, but you can watch!"

It wouldn't be much to watch. If everything went all right, some dial-needles would kick over violently, and their readings would go up and up. But they wouldn't be readings of temperature. Presently the big grid would report increased power from the sky. But tonight the temperature would drop a little farther. Tomorrow night it would drop farther still. When it reached one hundred and nine point three degrees below zero at ground-level—why it would keep on falling indefinitely. Then it wouldn't matter how much power could be drawn from the sky. The colony would die.

One of the figures that looked like a bear now went out of the mine-mouth, trudging toward the grid. It carried a muffled, well-wrapped object in its arms. It stooped and crept between the spokes of the grid. It put the object on the stone. Massy traced cables with his eyes. From the grid to the control board. From the board back to the reserve-power storage cells, deep in the mountain.

"The grid's tuned to the bomb," said Riki breathlessly, close beside him. "I checked that myself!"

The bearlike figure out in the valley jerked at the bomb. There was a small rising cloud of grayish vapor. It continued. The figure climbed hastily out of the grid. When the man was clear, Massy threw a switch.

There was a very tiny whining sound, and the wrapped, ridiculously smoking object leaped upward. It seemed to fall toward the sky. There was no more of drama than that. An object the size of a basketball fell upward, swiftly, until it disappeared. That was all.

Massy sat quite still, watching the control-board dials. Presently he corrected this, and shifted that. He did not want the bomb to have too high an upward velocity. At a hundred thousand feet it would find very little air to stop the rise of the vapor it was to release.

The field-focus dial reached its indication of one hundred thousand feet. Massy reversed the lift-switch. He counted and then switched the power off. The small, thin whine ended.

He threw the power-intake switch, which could have been on all the time. The power-yield needle stirred. The minute grid was drawing power like its vaster counterpart. But its field was infinitesimal by comparison. It drew power as a soda straw might draw water from wet sand.

Then the intake-needle kicked. It swung sharply, and wavered, and then began a steady, even, climbing movement across the markings on the dial-face. Riki was not watching that.

"They see something!" she panted. "Look at them!"

The four men who had trundled the smaller grid to its place, now stared upward. They flung out their arms. One of them jumped up and down. They leaped. They practically danced.

"Let's go see," said Massy.

He went out of the tunnel with Riki. They gazed upward. And directly overhead, where the sky was darkest blue and where it had seemed that stars shone through the daylight—there was a cloud. It seemed to Massy, very quaintly, that it was no bigger than a man's hand. But it grew. Its edges were yellow—saffron-yellow. It expanded and spread. Presently it began to thin. As it thinned, it began to shine. It was luminous. And the luminosity had a strange, familiar quality.

Somebody came panting down the tunnel, from inside the mountain.

"The grid—" he panted, "The big grid! It's . . . pumping power! Big power! BIG power!"

He went pounding back, to gaze rapturously at the new position of a thin black needle on a large white dial, and to make incoherent noises of rejoicing as it moved very, very slowly toward higher and ever higher readings.

But Massy looked puzzledly at the sky, as if he did not quite believe his eyes. The cloud now expanded very slowly, but still it grew. And it was not regular in shape. The bomb had not shattered quite evenly, and the vapor had poured out more on one side than the other. There was a narrow, arching arm of brightness—

"It looks," said Riki breathlessly, "like a comet!"

And then Massy froze in every muscle. He stared at the cloud he had made aloft, and his hands clenched in their mittens, and he swallowed convulsively behind his cold-mask.

"Th-that's it," he said in a very queer voice indeed. "It's . . . very much like a comet. I'm glad you said that! We can make something even more like a comet. We . . . we can use all the bombs we've made, right away, to make it. And we've got to hurry so it won't get any colder tonight!"

Which, of course, sounded like insanity. Riki looked apprehensively at him. But Massy had just thought of something. And nobody had taught it to him and he hadn't gotten it out of books. But he'd seen a comet.

The new idea was so promising that he regarded it

with anguished unease for fear it would not hold up. It was an idea that really ought to change the facts resulting naturally from a lowered solar constant in a Sol-type star.

Half the colony set to work to make more bombs when the effect of the second bomb showed up. They were not very efficient, at first, because they tended to want to stop work and dance, from time to time. But they worked with an impassioned enthusiasm. They made more bomb-casings, and they prepared more sodium and potassium metal and more fuses, and more insulation to wrap around the bombs to protect them from the cold of airless space.

Because these were to go out to airlessness. The miniature grid could lift and hold a bomb steady in its field-focus at seven hundred and fifty thousand feet. But if a bomb was accelerated all the way out to that point, and the field was then snapped off— Why, it wasn't held anywhere. It kept on going with its attained velocity. And it burst when its fuse decided that it should, whereupon immediately a mass of sodium and potassium vapor, mixed with the fumes of high explosive, flung itself madly in all directions, out between the stars. Absolute vacuum tore the compressed gasified metals apart. The separate atoms, white-hot from the explosion, went swirling through sunlit space. The sunlight was dimmed a trifle, to be sure. But individual atoms of the lighter alkaline-earth metals have marked photoelectric properties. In sunshine these gas-molecules ionized, and therefore spread more widely, and did not coalesce into even microscopic droplets.

They formed, in fact, a cloud in space. An ionized cloud, in which no particle was too large to be responsive to the pressure of light. The cloud acted like the gases of a comet's tail. It was a comet's tail, though there was no comet. And it was an extraordinary comet's tail because it is said that you can put a comet's tail in your hat, at normal atmospheric pressure. But this could not have been put in a hat. Even before it turned to gas, it was the size of a basketball. And, in space, it glowed.

It glowed with the brightness of the sunshine on it, which was light that would normally have gone away through the interstellar dark. And it filled one corner of the sky. Within one hour it was a comet's tail ten thousand miles long, which visibly brightened the daytime heavens. And it was only the first of such reflecting clouds.

The next bomb set for space exploded in a different quarter, because Massy'd had the miniature grid wrestled around the upcrop to point in a new and somewhat more carefully chosen line. The third bomb spattered brilliance in a different section still. And the brilliance lasted.

Massy flung his first bombs recklessly, because there could be more. But he was desperately anxious to hang as many comet tails as possible around the colony-planet before nightfall. He didn't want it to get any colder.

And it didn't. In fact, there wasn't exactly any real nightfall on Lani III that night.

The planet turned on its axis, to be sure. But around it, quite close by, there hung gigantic streamers of shining gas. At their beginning, those streamers bore a certain resemblance to the furry wild-animal tails that little boys like to have hanging down from hunting-caps. Only they shone. And as they developed they merged, so that there was an enormous shining curtain about Lani III. There were draperies of metal-mist to capture sunlight that should have been wasted, and to diffuse very much of it to Lani II. At midnight there was only one spot in all the night-sky where there was really darkness. That was directly overhead—directly outward from the planet from the sun. Gigantic shining streamers formed a wall, a tube, of comet-tail material, yet many times more dense and therefore brighter—which shielded the colony world against the dark and cold, and threw upon it a brilliant, warming brightness.

Riki maintained stoutly that she could feel the

warmth from the sky, but that was improbable. But certainly heat did come from somewhere. The thermometer did not fall at all, that night. It rose. It was up to fifty below zero at dawn. During the day—they sent out twenty more bombs that second day—it was up to twenty degrees below zero. By the day after, there was highly competent computation from the home planet, and the concrete results of abstruse speculation, and the third day's bombs were placed with optimum spacing for heating purposes.

And by dawn of the fourth day the air was a balmy five degrees below zero, and the day after that there was a small running stream in the valley at midday.

There was talk of stocking the stream with fish, on the morning the Survey ship came in. The great landing-grid gave out a deep-toned, vibrant, humming note, like the deepest possible note of the biggest organ that could be imagined. A speck appeared very, very high up in a pale-blue sky with trimmings of golden gas-clouds. The Survey ship came down and down and settled as a shining silver object in the very center of the gigantic red-painted landing-grid.

Later, her skipper came to find Massy. He was in Herndon's office. The skipper struggled to keep sheer blankness out of his expression.

"What . . . what the hell?" he demanded querulously of Massy. "This is the damnedest sight in the whole galaxy, and they tell me you're responsible! There've been ringed planets before, and there've been comets and who-knows-what! But shining gas pipes aimed at the sun, half a million miles across . . . What the? There are two of them! Both the occupied planets!"

Herndon explained with a bland succinctness why the curtains hung in space. There was a drop in the solar constant—

The skipper exploded. He wanted facts! Details! Something to report! And dammit, he wanted to know!

Massy was automatically on the defensive when the skipper shot his questions to him. A Senior Colonial Survey officer is not revered by the Survey ship-service

officers. Men like Massy can be a nuisance to a hard-
working ship's officer. They have to be carried to unlikely places for their work of checking over colonial
installations. They have to be put down on hard-to-get-
at colonies, and they have to be called for, sometimes,
at times and places which are inconvenient. So a man in
Massy's position is likely to feel unpopular.

"I'd just finished the survey here," he said defen-
sively, "when a cycle of sunspot cycles matured. All the
sunspot periods got in phase, and the solar constant
dropped. So I naturally offered what help I could to
meet the situation."

The skipper regarded him incredulously.

"But . . . it couldn't be done!" he said blankly.
"They told me how you did it, but . . . it couldn't be
done! Do you realize that these vapor-curtains will
make fifty border-line worlds fit for use? Half a pound
of sodium vapor a week!" He gestured helplessly.
"They tell me the amount of heat reaching the surface
here has been upped by fifteen per cent! D'you realize
what *that* means?"

"I haven't been worrying about it," admitted Massy.
"There was a local situation and something had to be
done. I . . . er . . . remembered things, and Riki
suggested something I mightn't have thought of, and it's
worked out like this." Then he said abruptly: "I'm not
leaving. I'll get you to take my resignation back. I . . .
I think I'm going to settle here. It'll be a long time
before we get really temperate-climate conditions here,
but we can warm up a valley like this for cultivation,
and . . . well . . . it's going to be a rather satisfying
job. It's a brand-new planet with a brand-new ecological system to be established—"

The skipper of the Survey ship sat down hard. Then
the sliding door of Herndon's office opened and Riki
came in. The skipper stood up again. Massy rather
awkwardly made the introduction. Riki smiled.

"I'm telling him," said Massy, "that I'm resigning
from the Service to settle down here."

Riki nodded. She put her hand in proprietary fashion
on Massy's arm. The Survey skipper cleared his throat.

"I'm not going to take it," he said doggedly. "There've got to be detailed reports on how this business works. Dammit, if vapor-clouds in space can be used to keep a planet warm, they can be used to shade a planet, too! If you resign, somebody else will have to come out here to make observations and work out the details of the trick! Nobody could be gotten here in less than a year! You need to stay here to build up a report—and you ought to be available for consultation when this thing's to be done somewhere else! I'll report that I insisted as a Survey emergency—"

Riki said confidently:

"Oh, that's all right! He'll do that! Of course! Won't you?"

Massy nodded dumbly. He thought, *I've been lonely all my life. I've never belonged anywhere. But nobody could possibly belong anywhere as thoroughly as I'll belong here when it's warm and green and even the grass on the ground is partly my doing. But Riki'll like for me still to be in the Service. Women like to see their husbands wearing uniforms.*

Aloud he said:

"Of course. It . . . really needs to be done. Of course, you realize that there's nothing really remarkable about it. Everything I've done has been what I was taught, or read in books."

"Hush!" said Riki. "You're wonderful!"